Dear Reader,

I love doing research about wolves and jaguars, and I visit reserves or zoos whenever I can to observe the animals and learn more about them from their caretakers. When I was visiting the zoo in Waco for Thanksgiving, I witnessed a mating pair getting some loving on! It's exciting to see, and I hope that there will be cubs on a future visit. A boy of about seven said, "Look, Mommy, they're mating." I appreciate that a facility such as this provides opportunities for children to learn about the life processes of wild animals in captivity.

Also, I love it when my fans let me know about wolf news they learn from close to home for them.

Donna Fournier has taken me on trips to two wolf reserves in Minnesota, where she lives, and we visited a bear reserve in northern Minnesota this last trip. She has sent me articles about Isle Royale National Park on an island near her in Lake Superior, where efforts are being made to revive a wolf pack.

Two nonbreeding wolves were all that were left on Isle Royale; at its peak, there had been fifty wolves. Two wolves can't handle the huge population of moose there, so scientists relocated three gray wolves to the island from Minnesota. They hope to introduce about twenty to thirty wolves from the United States and Canada over the next few years to boost the pack size. But one of the three gray wolves, a female, crossed the ice bridge that formed during the polar vortex and returned to her Minnesota home.

It's interesting that if wolves are held in the area where they are released for about a month, they generally get used to their surroundings and make it their home. Wolves are not native to Isle Royale, but scientists believe that they crossed over when ice bridges developed decades earlier, found the prey perfect for raising their pack, and stayed. In this case, the female wanted to return home to Minnesota, and so she did.

Another key factor in relocating wolves is that if they are released at least eighty miles from their home, they are more likely to stay in their new surroundings than to try to return home.

I've read about bears that have been relocated, and the instinct was so strong, they had to return home. My dad's golden retriever traveled across two states to return home to him after military duty required my dad to rehome him with a farmer who lived two states away! He reunited his loving dog with the farmer, and then my dad had to go overseas. That time, the dog stayed with the farmer. But it shows that animals of all kinds have a natural instinct to return to their homes.

Hopefully, the reintroduction of wolves will be a success on Isle Royale, the perfect place for them to raise a family where they are relatively protected from humankind.

Terry Spear

Also by Terry Spear

Wolff Brothers
You Had Me at Wolf

SEAL Wolf
A SEAL in Wolf's Clothing
A SEAL Wolf Christmas
SEAL Wolf Hunting
SEAL Wolf in Too Deep
SEAL Wolf Undercover
SEAL Wolf Surrender

Heart of the Shifter
You Had Me at Jaguar

Billionaire Wolf
Billionaire in Wolf's Clothing
*A Billionaire Wolf for
Christmas*

Silver Town Wolf
Destiny of the Wolf
Wolf Fever
Dreaming of the Wolf
Silence of the Wolf
A Silver Wolf Christmas
Alpha Wolf Need Not Apply
*Between a Wolf and
a Hard Place*
All's Fair in Love and Wolf

*Silver Town Wolf: Home for
the Holidays*

Heart of the Jaguar
Savage Hunter
Jaguar Fever
Jaguar Hunt
Jaguar Pride
A Very Jaguar Christmas

Highland Wolf
Heart of the Highland Wolf
A Howl for a Highlander
*A Highland Werewolf
Wedding*
Hero of a Highland Wolf
A Highland Wolf Christmas

White Wolf
*Dreaming of a White Wolf
Christmas*
Flight of the White Wolf

Heart of the Wolf
Heart of the Wolf
To Tempt the Wolf
Legend of the White Wolf
Seduced by the Wolf

LEGEND
OF THE
WHITE WOLF

TERRY
SPEAR

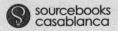
sourcebooks
casablanca

Published by Sourcebooks Casablanca, an imprint of Sourcebooks
P.O. Box 4410, Naperville, Illinois 60567-4410
(630) 961-3900
sourcebooks.com

Originally published as *Legend of the White Wolf* in 2010 in the United States
of America by Sourcebooks Casablanca, an imprint of Sourcebooks.

Printed and bound in the United States of America.
OPM 10 9 8 7 6 5 4 3 2 1

I dedicate Legend of the White Wolf *to my mother, who lost the fight with breast cancer, and to all those who have gone before her or who are facing the same insidious disease. I wish you all my love, Mom, for always being there when I needed you and even to the end listening to my revisions and offering suggestions. You will be in my heart and memories always.*

PROLOGUE

THE BLACK BEAR WAS RUNNING AWAY A HELL OF A LOT faster than Owen Nottingham and his PI partner David Davis thought was possible. Their hunting guide, Trevor Hodges, yelled at them to keep up, but at the rate the bear was going, Owen and David would never last. Already, Owen had shin splints, and his side was aching something fierce. Damn, he'd thought he was in good shape.

They couldn't use dogs to chase down the bear this late in the year in Maine, but the owner of Backcountry Tours, Kintail Silverman, got around that by sending his pet wolves on the hunt. The sleek, white-furred creatures made Owen feel like he was part of a wolf pack, hunting for survival, diving around snow-laden firs, blending in, exhilarated, hunting with the others as a cooperative team.

The experience would have been more pleasurable if his other partners were with them—Cameron MacPherson, who wouldn't hunt for anything other than criminals, and Gavin Summerfield, who'd rather stay in Seattle and work than fly anywhere. But the four of them were like a wolf pack, solving crimes together as a collective unit and socializing as the best of friends throughout the good times and bad.

So Owen wished they could share hunting excursions together too.

He noticed then that he could see only snowy woods in front of them. The wolves and the bear were lost in the forest ahead as the chilly wind howled through the trees. Trevor was still keeping a good pace in the distance. For a white-haired old guy, he was lean and in incredibly great shape.

David had dropped way behind, but Owen was too busy trying to keep up the chase to wait for him to catch up. One last day before their hunt ended. And, hell, they'd tried to bag a bear for the last four years without any luck. The way the bear was outdistancing them in a hurry in the Maine wilderness, Owen was beginning to lose hope they'd make it this time either. But it was the closest they'd come.

When Owen didn't hear David's heavy breathing behind him or his size-ten boots trudging through the deep snow, he turned and looked to see how far behind he was. David was holding his thighs, leaning over, gasping for breath.

"David, you all right?" Owen asked, knowing it was a dumb question when he figured David was trying to catch his second wind and couldn't answer anyway.

David motioned him on, wheezing, his face red and pinched with pain. "Get the bear! I'm fine. Go. I'll catch up."

But it wasn't like David not to keep up on a hunt, so Owen ran back to check on him. "What's wrong?" Owen asked, grabbing his friend's arm to steady him.

"Go. You'll…never…forgive…me…if…we…" David clutched his chest.

The wolves and Trevor circled back and joined them. The old man shook his head. "Chest pains?"

Through clenched teeth, David growled, "From…running… damn it."

David was the oldest of the four partners in their private investigator practice, but at thirty-five, he couldn't be having a heart attack.

With millions of acres of forestland all around them,

they were too deep into the wilderness to get help. Cell phones wouldn't work out here. Owen would have had a satellite phone, but his quit working when they arrived. He knew CPR, but...

He helped David to sit. "What are you feeling?" he asked, trying to disguise the anxiety in his voice, although he couldn't hide a deepening frown, and David noticed.

"Don't be a...worry..." David clutched his chest even harder, his face sweating in the frigid air.

"We can't get any help to him way out here," Trevor said quietly. "If he's having a heart attack, it's not a bad way to go. Quick, no lingering illness."

"No!" Owen snapped. "Do you have any aspirin?" This was his friend from childhood and one of the best partners he'd had while they were still on the police force. How could he just let David die? He couldn't. "I know CPR."

"It won't be enough." Trevor sounded like the voice of reason, but Owen didn't want to hear it.

The image of David lunging in front of him, taking a bullet in the shoulder two years ago, flashed across Owen's mind. He wouldn't let him go. He couldn't.

The wolves watched silently, almost sympathetically, as if one of their pack members was in trouble, their ears perked, their tongues hanging out, panting after the long run.

His hand clutching David's shoulder, Owen clenched his teeth to bite back the overwhelming feeling of hopelessness. "Can't we do something? Anything?"

"Possibly," Trevor said, "but it will change his life and yours forever."

"I'd do anything to save my friend's life," Owen said, figuring Trevor was thinking that he had enough money, they could air-evac David out somewhere, maybe from a clearing where the loggers had been.

Trevor put a hand on Owen's shoulder. "You sure?"

"Anything, damn it. However much it costs, it's worth it."

Trevor looked back at the wolves. The biggest one bowed its head slightly, then bared its teeth and lunged.

Before Owen could fathom what was happening, the wolf bit David in the arm. He cried out in pain.

As Owen swung his rifle to his shoulder to shoot the beast, he caught a blur of white fur in his peripheral vision, right before one of the other wolves pounced on him.

CHAPTER 1

IN THE DARK OF NIGHT, THE ROADS SLUSHY, THE SNOW plowed in dirty heaps beyond the shoulders, Faith O'Malley drove her rented SUV from Maine's Bangor International Airport to Millinocket, a prickle of awareness making her uneasy. She glanced at the rearview mirror, sure the headlights had been tailing her all the way. Which made her wonder again if her father's concern that he'd been followed for some time before her boyfriend stole his research paper was based on reality.

On the other hand, maybe believing someone was stalking her had to do with her work as a forensic scientist, solving crimes and being way too suspicious of everyone and everything. *Normally.* When it came to Hilson Snowdon, she hadn't been suspicious enough.

A mile from the turnoff for the hotel, she heard a tremendous boom. Gunfire?

Her rental swerved toward the shoulder as if a ghostly force had taken control. Adrenaline flooded through her as she twisted the steering wheel to the left, veering away from a speed limit sign. The back end of the vehicle felt like it was listing on the right side. A blowout, not gunfire. A smidgen of relief washed over her. She eased onto the shoulder and pulled the vehicle to a stop but didn't cut the engine. What next?

The truck she thought had been following her pulled up behind her, the lights shining in her rearview mirror. The pickup idled, waiting.

Her heartbeat sped up again. Not about to hang around for the truck driver's help in case he was bad news, she fumbled in her purse for her cell phone, yanked it out, then punched in the number for roadside service.

When the operator asked her location, Faith gave her the exit number off the highway.

"It'll be about an hour, ma'am," the woman said.

"Thanks, I'll be here." *Unfortunately*. Faith hung up when she saw movement near the right back door. She jerked her head around. In the dark of night, looking through tinted windows, Faith couldn't see who had come up behind her vehicle, but she heard the click as the individual yanked on the door handle. *Locked*.

Something pounced against the door. Her heart gave a little start. Large almond-shaped eyes, shining an eerie greenish-orange color, peered in through the window.

Steeling her nerves, she again made sure all the doors were locked and considered driving the mile into town on the bad tire.

What looked like a big, white Samoyed, but not half as fuzzy, raced around the front of the car, her headlights illuminating him as he headed for the driver's side. She wondered if the dog was half Arctic wolf. His long muzzle was not Samoyed in appearance but more wolflike. The person who'd tried the door handle wasn't in sight as the dog jumped against her door. Reflexively, she jerked away from it. The animal peered in at her with its shining eyes, its huge front paws resting on her window.

A key clicked in the front door lock on the passenger's side. Without a second's hesitation, she jammed her foot on the gas pedal and sped off.

Bad tire or no.

Her skin crawling from the experience, Faith slowed up ahead, figuring it would take the dog and his owner a little while to follow her, and she didn't want to make more of a mess of the tire than she had to. She crept toward the off-ramp, hazard lights flashing, then headed for a lighted service station on the corner. The truck's lights had vanished. Either he continued on past the exit, or he was driving without lights.

She parked at the service station where, inside, she found two middle-aged men drinking coffee. They offered to help her change the tire, so she canceled the roadside service. While the men changed the tire, they asked her where she was from and what she was doing here—genuinely friendly, idle talk—while she watched for the pickup that had parked behind her on the road. Either he was afraid she'd tell on him and he was waiting for her to leave the well-lit service station, or she'd somehow missed seeing him drive by when she was getting help to change the tire.

Thanking the men, Faith offered to pay them. They gave her small smiles and declined, the one saying he had a daughter who he hoped someone would help out if she was ever in need. Faith thanked them again, hoping she wouldn't encounter the pickup driver again, left, and a few minutes later arrived at the Woodlands Travel Lodge.

Glancing up at the rearview mirror, she swore the streetlights illuminated the same gray pickup truck that had been following her, but the tinted windows hid the driver as he drove past. *Slowly.* Didn't matter that the speed limit was thirty here or that the road was perfectly drivable, salted or sanded. She still thought he was going much slower than necessary. As if he was checking her out. But maybe it wasn't the same vehicle at all.

Yep, shades of her father. Although after her boyfriend stole her father's research paper, she could see how Dad would be somewhat paranoid.

Faith sighed. She fully intended to get his flash drive back from Hilson, one way or another. Yet as much as her father wanted it returned, he wouldn't tell her what information it held. She'd find out soon enough, just as she had told him. It would be like any other mystery-solving mission she'd tackled. Well, maybe not just like any other. This time, it was personal.

She grabbed her suitcase and was heading inside the blue lodge—her overnight stop before she trekked into the remoter part of Maine and the cabins where she'd stay during her dealing-with-Hilson mission—when her cell phone jingled. She stopped midstream in the lobby, fumbled around in her oversize leather purse, then finally fished the phone out. She kept telling herself she was going to wear it around her neck for easier access, considering how many times her father had called her since she'd left her apartment in Portland, Oregon.

"Yes, I'm finally, finally here, Dad."

"Any sign of Hilson?"

"He's not here. I have to stay at a lodge for the night in Millinocket since it's too late to navigate the wilderness in the dark. At least that's what the owners of the cabins said. Hilson is supposed to be at a cabin resort about two miles or more from mine, only accessible by snowmobile. I'll confront him as soon as I can, return to Millinocket, and call you."

"You don't need to read my research paper, Faith. Just bring it back home safe and sound."

She couldn't understand why he was so secretive about the research he'd done. But now, just as he was going to reveal it at an upcoming conference, voilà! Hilson stole her dad's flash drive as well as his hard drive. "I'll bring it home, Dad. I promise." He should have stored the information in the cloud too. At least she prayed she wouldn't fail him. He hadn't worked on anything else beyond teaching at the local community college in years, and this was so important to him. She kept wondering if Hilson had put the moves on her just so he could get to her father and his research. "Got to check in at the lodge. Call you later."

"Night, Faith. And, Faith?"

"Yes, Dad?"

"I hope you dump the guy."

"Consider him dumped." Although it appeared Hilson had already dumped her. "No way would I trust him again. Love you and good night, Dad."

Everything that had gone on between her and Hilson kept running through Faith's mind like a continuous computer loop. How he'd wined and dined her, bought her gifts, but always held back. As if there was someone else in his life. Maybe someone he was still married to? She'd joked about it, but he'd smiled coolly and made love to her as if to prove no one else existed. And yet, something had been missing.

Then again, maybe it was all her fault. She'd been looking for love but hadn't really felt it for him either. She'd needed the intimacy, but somewhere along the line, it hadn't felt real. Now all she felt toward him was anger, betrayal, hurt, and every other negative emotion in the book—but it all had to do with him stealing her father's research, not the end of her relationship with Hilson. That was what worried her the most. What was wrong with her? He was the last one in a string of failed relationships.

When she reached the front desk, the clerk said to someone on the phone, "Just a minute, honey. Got another customer."

"Faith O'Malley," Faith said, leaning against the counter, ready for a room-service meal, a hot shower, and a good night's sleep after missing one connecting flight due to engine trouble, being delayed three hours because of a snowstorm en route, and having problems getting her assigned rental car. Not to mention the flat tire. What should have taken only a few hours—if everything had gone smoothly—had ended up being an all-day series of disasters.

"Room 318, miss," the clerk said, handing her the card key and nodding as she listened to someone on the phone. She raised her brows at Faith. "Need a wake-up call in the morning?"

"No, thanks." If there was one thing Faith didn't need, it was a wake-up call. Sleeping in was just something she couldn't get her body to agree with. "Do you know where the Backcountry Tours office is?"

"Down the street about a half mile. Can't miss it." The clerk smiled. "Sign out front has a carved white wolf on it. And the owners, Lila Grayson and Kintail Silverman, can be seen around town with a couple of pet wolves in tow when they're not guiding hunting tours in the far backcountry."

"Wolves."

"Yep. Tame, sweetest-natured old things, just like big, beautiful huskies, only pure white."

"Arctic wolves." She thought back to the animal that had pounced on her rental vehicle. It wasn't a Samoyed but a real wolf? Then it had to belong to the people she needed to get in touch with. She'd report the man with the wolf who was following her, whoever he was, to the owner of Backcountry Tours.

"Guess they would be Arctic wolves. The couple is from the Canadian Arctic, up around Yellowknife. Return there in the summers. Real cold-weather folks. Although they like hunting different animals here—black bear, bobcat, moose, rather than caribou and whatever else they go after up there. Pretty neat, huh? Winter home here and summer home there? They don't like the summer heat at all, although it's nothing like living in some hot-weather places like Florida. When I lived there—"

A man jingled his keys behind Faith, and she glanced back. He frowned at her.

"Thanks, I'll be checking out early in the morning," Faith said to the clerk and grabbed her suitcase, then headed for the elevator, looking forward to dinner and a hot shower without any more delays.

Once she reached her room, she slid the key card in. *Green light.* She twisted the handle and pushed. The door didn't budge. She tried again. Same thing. She hated key cards. Why couldn't they just use regular old brass keys?

She tried a third time. This time, she twisted the handle harder and shoved the door more firmly. And was rewarded. Lights were on in the room, and the place was already toasty warm as if the welcoming mat had been set out for her.

Perfect. She walked into the room and glanced at the two queen-size beds, one with the chartreuse covers pulled back from the pillow, a chocolate wrapped in gold foil sitting on the center of it. She smiled and pulled off her parka, peeled off her boots, and was reaching for the phone to call room service when she saw a leather bucket filled with ice. Wow, they sure knew how to coddle their guests.

That was when the bathroom door opened. She whipped around and faced a naked man towel-drying his hair. Or at least until he saw her.

His mouth gaped. Her expression matched his, and he quickly wrapped the towel around his waist. "I didn't think room service would come this soon." He glanced down at her sock-covered feet, her boots lying beside them.

"I'm not… I'm… They gave me a key to your room by accident." Faith tried not to look at the man's physique—too much—but ripped abs, arms muscled just enough to give a woman a good hug, and toned legs that looked like they could run a marathon were just too appealing.

And his eyes—blue like the ocean, dark, hiding a wealth of secrets—held her gaze with way too much interest, as if she were the specialty of the house and just what he'd ordered from the menu. Light-blond stubble covered his square jaw, making him appear a bit roguish and intriguing.

He folded his arms across his broad chest. A light smattering of blond hair trailed down to the towel slung low on his hips. Her gaze dropped lower. He cleared his throat to get her attention, making her skin heat in a flush of awareness, but he wasn't moving out of her path to the door. Just now she wished it were her room, and *he* were part of the amenities.

He inclined his head a little, a hint of a smile on his lips, his eyes sparkling with mischief. "Then I guess I'd better get dressed before—"

A knock rapped on the door.

"Too late." His deeply amused baritone sounded like he was enjoying this a little too much as he turned, took a couple of steps, and opened the door.

Great. Faith was hurrying to pull on her boots when the aroma of steak wafted into the room as a man brought in a tray. Faith's stomach growled. The room-service guy glanced at her, green eyes smiling. She could just imagine what he was thinking, what with the room's occupant wearing a towel and her pulling her boots on.

The toweled guy signed the bill, and the lodge employee grinned, dimples appearing in his ruddy cheeks. "Thanks so much, sir. If you need anything else, just ring." He glanced at Faith, smiled even more as if to say she could visit him next if she had a mind to, then left the room.

"Enough for two of us if you want to split a medium-rare steak, baked potato, and salad," the sandy-haired hunk said.

"Thanks so much for the offer, but I'm returning to the front desk to get the right room key. Have a nice night." She brushed past the mostly naked man, smiled when he smiled, then hurried out of the room.

"The night could have been better," he murmured.

She glanced back at him, wishing he was the kind of man she had been dating, and she could justify staying and splitting his dinner with him, then maybe sharing the chocolate treat resting on his pillow. And more. For the first time ever, she seriously wanted to flirt with a man. Something about him appealed to her, as if he were the real

McCoy—spontaneous and fun-loving—and for an instant, she yearned for that. Wanted to feel that a man who looked like this guy, with a hint of the devil in his expression and actions, found her appealing too.

The man lifted a brow and smiled again, his chiseled features and intensely intriguing gaze nearly irresistible. She faltered but shook her head and hurried for the elevator before she did anything she might regret in the morning. She didn't look back at him, although she wanted to see if he was still watching her. But she felt he was doing just that—observing her, maybe hoping she'd change her mind? Or maybe it was just wishful thinking on her part that someone was truly interested in her after Hilson had ditched her. On further introspection, she hadn't heard the toweled man's door shut.

It wasn't until she returned to the front desk with her suitcase in tow that she realized she'd left her parka on the man's desk chair. She let out her breath in exasperation. Okay, so the day turned night wasn't going to get any better.

A line of five guests was waiting for rooms. The clerk still had the cell phone stuck to her ear as she nodded and chatted it up with the woman first in line.

Faith didn't hesitate to stalk up to the counter, pulling her bag with her. The woman who was being waited on looked at Faith as if she was ready to clobber her for trying to barge in.

"Excuse me," Faith said to the clerk and handed her the key card, "but someone else was already in Room 318."

The girl's eyes widened. Then she smiled. "Oh my, you mean you got the key to Cameron MacPherson's room?" She put her hand to her breast. "If I'd made the mistake, I would have just stayed."

That was saying he wanted the clerk to stay. And jeesh, the clerk had made the mistake. No apology? "Another room, please?"

The clerk held out the new key card. "This one is for Room 317."

"Three seventeen."

"Yep. The numbers were close. It's directly across the hall from Mr. MacPherson's." She winked. "Tell him if he needs anything, just to give me a holler."

Faith shook her head, grabbed the key card, and headed back to the elevator. At least with his room being across from hers, she could ask for her parka without having to traipse across the whole hotel and back.

As soon as she reached her room, she struggled to get the key card to work, then gave the door a shove. The room was dark and cold. She fumbled for the light switch, but when she turned on the lamps, the bedcover wasn't pulled back from the pillow, nor was a gold foil-covered chocolate waiting for her. And of course the ice bucket was perfectly empty. She wondered if Cameron got the special treatment because he was a big tipper or just an incredibly smooth-talking hunk.

She sighed and rolled her bag next to the bed, then headed back for the door. She might as well get this over with before she settled down for the night.

Glancing at her watch, she realized how late it was already. Probably too late to order anything from the kitchen. If she ate at this hour, the food would most likely just sit like a lump in her stomach when she went to bed anyway. She knocked on Cameron MacPherson's door.

While waiting for him, she closed her eyes and yawned. Man, she was ready to skip the shower and just collapse in bed.

The door squeaked opened. Wearing only a pair of stone-washed jeans that looked incredibly soft, shirtless and barefoot, Cameron smiled, but he hadn't brought her parka to the door. He looked every bit as sexy as when he was wearing only a towel.

"Are you sure you don't want to have a bite with me?" He motioned to the tray on the table.

The old werewolf movie with Jack Nicholson was playing on the television, and by the sound of the growling, she envisioned the actor's character had shape-shifted and was fighting the bad wolf if she recalled the movie correctly.

She gave Cameron a tired smile. "Under other circumstances, maybe. I left my parka here."

"You look like you could use a meal, and the kitchen's closed by now." His voice, deep and pleasing, sent little chills of expectation through her.

But she resisted the temptation and held out her hand for her coat. "Thanks, but I'm fine." He retrieved her coat and gave it to her, his hand brushing hers in a sensuous way that made her skin heat again. She thought he looked a little wistful, hopeful that she'd stay and keep him company, but she figured if she did, she would melt under whatever spell he seemed to cast over her. It wasn't like her to be that attracted to a guy she'd just met. She glanced down at his hand, no wedding ring. When her gaze returned to his, he was smiling broadly.

Usually a lot less obvious than that when she was scrutinizing a man's marital status—although he might be married and just not wear a wedding ring—Faith felt her skin heat even more. "Thanks," she said quickly, turned around, and left his room before she made any more of a fool of herself.

But as soon as she reached her door and slipped her hand in her jeans pocket, she realized she didn't have the key.

~~~

Cameron watched the petite blond stand before her room, her parka draped over her arm, her hand shoved into her pocket, but she didn't make a motion to unlock her door.

She'd left the key in the room?

The poor woman. She looked like she was about to pass out from exhaustion. However, he'd seen the way she'd looked at him and checked to see if he was married, which meant only one thing. She'd been intrigued. Might have even stayed for dinner if she had been more impulsive. Probably a good thing she wasn't. At least not the way she looked, wearing a sparkling white sweater that caressed nice-sized breasts and formfitting black jeans that showed off lots of curves, conjuring up the image of *sexy*, soft, and cuddly. Gold curls swept over her shoulders, and she looked like she belonged on a beach in a bikini, soaking up the sun a long way from here.

"Want me to call down and have the hotel staff bring you up another key?"

She hesitated, mulling over her options, he figured, not saying anything for a minute, just staring at the immovable door. Then she turned around and her lush lips, glossed with something shimmering, pink, and sensuous, curved up. Her stunning green eyes sparkled like emeralds in the bright hall lights, mesmerizing him. Hell, he was a sucker for green eyes.

She arched an eyebrow and gave a cute little snort. "Um,

thanks, but I can manage." She straightened her shoulders and trudged down the hall toward the elevator.

She had spunk, he had to admit. And some damned nice curves. He watched her wiggle her tush all the way to the elevator, then waited until she was inside, just in case she changed her mind. She didn't. His loss.

He closed his door and padded back to the bed. But he couldn't put the woman out of his mind. Not that he needed any distractions while he was on his mission, but until tomorrow morning, he couldn't get much done anyway. He slipped out of his jeans and climbed into bed. Bright and early, he was going to check out Backcountry Tours to learn why his friends hadn't arrived home on time without any word of explanation.

Even so, Cameron couldn't help listening for the woman to return to her room, and when he heard the door click open and shut several minutes later, he relaxed a little. Then the door clicked open and shut again. He waited, listening. The ice maker down the hall ground, the ice clunking into the bucket. Then her door opened and shut again.

He tucked his arms behind his head and fantasized how he might have breakfast with the little lady before he took off for his next destination—cabins in the wilderness, no land phones, no cell phone service. He'd have to rely more on his instincts in this investigation. Cameron hoped his friends weren't in any real trouble, hoped they had just been unable to get in touch with him and their PI partner Gavin Summerfield, who was running their business in Seattle in the meantime.

Cameron sighed. Seven days. That was how long the hunting trip was supposed to last. Add a couple of days of travel time. Two weeks, max. They'd even had to turn down some lucrative jobs because they were so short-handed. But it beat the heck out of him how he got stuck leaving Seattle to land in this snow-filled landscape instead of Gavin.

Cameron's cell phone rang. Speak of the devil. *Gavin.* "Hey, no word yet, but I'll be going to the cabins tomorrow after I stop by Backcountry Tours to see if anyone's in the office in the morning. We'll have a phone blackout for a while once I reach the resort. We need to pick up new sat phones. These are worthless."

"I received a garbled message. Sounded like Owen, and he said something about being unable to get word to us. It sounded like he said he and David were all right. And quitting. Quitting the hunt? The static was bad, and I couldn't make out any more before the phone line cut out completely."

"But he really sounded all right? Not under duress? Not in any kind of trouble or anything, were they?"

"I'd like to say no. But the connection was so bad, I couldn't really say."

Cameron was opening his mouth to speak when a woman screamed—from the room across the hall.

CHAPTER 2

THE GRAY-HAIRED MAN APOLOGIZED PROFUSELY AS Faith pushed him out of her room, her towel clutched tightly around her torso, her wet hair wrapped in another. She'd kill the hotel clerk. Couldn't the woman give one customer a room that wasn't already occupied?

If that weren't enough of an embarrassment, here came her knight to the rescue, wearing a pair of vivid-blue silky boxers—and nothing else—none other than Cameron MacPherson.

He raised his brows at her as the man hurried off with his bag, apologizing under his breath.

"Clerk gave him a key to your room?" Cameron asked, a wrinkle creasing his forehead.

Faith began shutting the door to hide her state of undress in case anyone else happened to walk down the hall. "Yes."

"I'll call down and complain to the manager. We haven't been properly introduced though. I'm Cameron MacPherson. And you are?"

"Faith O'Malley." She pressed the door closed a little more.

"Want to have breakfast with me in the morning?"

She was so annoyed with the clerk that she hadn't planned to let the grudge go—until Cameron asked to have breakfast with her. He was just too cute. And persistent. Her stomach grumbled. Although initially she'd thought eating too late could keep her awake, now she reasoned she might sleep better if she had a bite to eat. Besides, Cameron could take her mind off Hilson for a little while. It didn't mean she was going to stay the night or do anything she didn't want to do, she reminded herself.

"Still have some dinner left over?" she asked.

Cameron smiled, the skin beneath his eyes wrinkling, dimples appearing, his blue eyes gleaming with delight, the devilish look saying he'd known he could break her down eventually if he tried long enough. "I'll even dress for dinner."

She wondered just what his definition of *dressed* would be. "Be right over. And thanks...for the rescue." She glanced at his boxers, the same blue as his eyes.

Grinning, he saluted her and stalked back to his room as if his mission was done.

When Faith had said she'd eat with Cameron, she'd surprised and pleased the hell out of him. He really figured he didn't have a chance to convince her he was one of the good guys and just wanted a little company. *Her* kind of company.

He couldn't get the image of her—standing half-naked, wearing only a skimpy towel to cover herself—out of his mind. For certain, the gods had smiled on him tonight.

After hurrying back into his room, he jerked on his jeans and threw the rest of his scattered clothes into his suitcase. Then he moved one of the two pillows he'd been using over to *her* side of the bed. He glanced at the door. He hadn't heard her door opening yet, so he rushed into the bathroom to pick up the wet towel he'd thrown on the floor and hang it up on the towel bar. Afterward, he tossed his toothbrush and toothpaste and shaving gear back into his shaving kit.

Her door opened and closed. He rubbed his bare chest. Shirt? Or no?

He stalked out of the bathroom and grabbed his flannel shirt out of the suitcase, then yanked it on just as she knocked. He returned to the door, opened it, and smiled at Faith. "Dinner's served."

Wearing emerald-green velour running clothes, she looked incredibly soft and touchable, her blond curls caressing her shoulders like he wanted to do.

She smiled a little to see his shirt hanging open. He supposed he should have buttoned it, but she didn't seem to mind.

She raised her brows at the bed where his tray of food was sitting, still covered by the dome to keep it warm, waiting to see if she changed her mind.

He started his salesman's pitch. "I was watching the Jack Nicholson movie in bed. It's about over. Want to see what's coming up after that one?"

She hesitated, then took a deep breath and headed for the bed. "So what's on next?"

"Looks like werewolf movie night. Something called *The Howl of the Wolf.*"

"Ah." She sat on the edge of the bed and slipped off a boot, and already his thoughts were of seeing her take off more. But she yanked off the other boot, dropped it on the carpeted floor to join its mate, then climbed on top of the floral covers. "That's Julie Wildthorn's third book in her werewolf series. I'd heard the book was better, so I never went to see the movie version."

A woman after his own heart. "You like fantasy? Urban fantasy? Paranormal?"

"All of the above." She took the lemon-lime soda he handed her, her legs stretched out on the bed, a whiff of her floral fragrance enticing him to take a deeper breath. "So is this a vacation or business trip for you?" she asked.

"A little of both." Although he hadn't planned on having any fun until she popped into his room and began stripping while he was in the shower. "And you?"

"Strictly business."

He smiled. Yeah, strictly business. That was why she was sitting on his bed, sharing dinner with him. He was glad he hadn't started to eat his dinner, hoping she'd change her mind.

The movie version of *The Howl of the Wolf* began, and he couldn't help but notice the way she smiled at the funny scenes, chuckling under her breath, but her cheeks grew a little flushed when the hero and heroine went beyond kissing, got naked, and ended up in bed together.

She cleared her throat and leaned back against the pillow. He thought she was going to say something. She didn't, and then she sank lower onto the mattress, her eyes half-closed, her long lashes hiding them further, her hand still clasped around the soda can.

When her eyes closed, he reached over and slipped the drink from her hand so she wouldn't spill it, half hoping she'd spend the night. To his regret, her eyes popped open. "Oh…" She stared at the TV, then smiled. "I like the book version better. She ends up with the hunky werewolf, not the wimpy human in the story." A small wrinkle appeared on her forehead, then she turned to Cameron. "If I fall asleep again, wake me and send me home."

He shook his head. "I'm enjoying the company." And he was. The last girl he dated was only into chick flicks. Absolutely no fantasy, no sci-fi, no urban fantasy, no paranormal, historical, westerns, war movies, nothing. He pulled the tray off the bed and settled back against the pillow like Faith had done, only he drew closer this time, enjoying the warmth from her body, her subtle fragrance, the companionship.

Before long, her eyes were shut again, but this time, he slipped his arm under her head. When she smiled at him, her expression quizzical, he said, "I was getting a little chilly. Weren't you?"

She chuckled, the sound low and amused. But she played right along with him and snuggled up nice and close. Too bad she was here strictly on business. He smiled at the notion, but it didn't take long before she closed her eyes again, and he nodded off too.

He hadn't even realized he'd done so until Faith pulled away from him, waking him, and gave him a weary smile. "Guess we missed the end of the movie. Just remember, the werewolf gets the girl in the correct version." Then she climbed off the bed and stretched like a sleek feline wrapped in green velvet-like duds.

He wanted her to stay the night, but he didn't figure she'd agree. Still…he had to make the offer. "Another werewolf tale coming up."

"I've seen *Underworld*." She checked her watch. "It's nearly one, and I've got business to take care of early in the morning. Snowstorm's supposed to be coming."

"Want to have breakfast with me tomorrow?"

She didn't hesitate to respond this time, and he knew

he'd hooked her for a date. "I'm an early riser. Would six be too early for you?"

He frowned, but at the same time, he was glad she'd share another meal with him before he had to traipse off into the wilderness alone. "Uh. Sure. Pick you up at six."

But he could tell from her expression that she was already distancing herself from him.

"Or we could meet down in the restaurant," she said.

That clinched it. But he wasn't letting her go just yet. He shook his head. "I'll knock on your door at six."

When she left his room, he waited at his open doorway while she unlocked her door, but then she just stared into the room. He hoped she was changing her mind about staying with him a little longer and not that something more was wrong.

"Faith?"

"I think the clerk let someone else into my room." Her voice was a little shaky.

Cameron was crossing the floor to check out her room when his door automatically shut behind him. He swore under his breath, realizing at once his room key was lying on the desk.

She raised her brows at him. "Did you leave your key—"

"Yeah."

"You could stay here and watch *Underworld* with me while you're waiting for another room key."

He chuckled and rubbed his hand over her back, but every muscle remained rigid with tension. "You've got a deal. How do you know someone came into your room?" He escorted her inside and shut the door.

"My suitcase was open. My bathroom door was closed.

And my overnight bag is on its side now, not standing upright."

"Check and see if anything's missing." He stalked over to the phone and called the front desk and asked to speak with the manager.

"Nothing's missing that I can tell."

A businesslike male voice responded on the phone. "Yes, this is Mr. Dodson, the manager on duty. How may I help you?"

"The clerks on the front desk gave Ms. O'Malley the key to my room and twice have given a key to her room to other customers."

"I'm so sorry for the trouble, Mister…"

"MacPherson."

"May I speak with Ms. O'Malley, Mr. MacPherson?"

Cameron handed the phone to Faith as she finished looking through her bags. "Yes, this is Faith O'Malley."

Cameron watched the expression on Faith's face change from annoyance to surprise as she glanced up at him. "A complimentary room for the night is fine. Thank you. And can someone send up a room key for Mr. MacPherson in Room 318? He's waiting in my room 317. Thanks." She hung up the phone. "They'll be right up with your key." She motioned to the bed and turned on the TV. "Might as well get comfortable while we wait."

"No one stole anything, I take it?"

"No." But she was back to looking perturbed.

"If you want me to, I'll spend the night."

That got a big smile from her, which brightened her whole expression, her eyes beaming with amusement, her glossy lips turned up in a big way. He figured she wasn't buying it.

"I'll bolt my door after you leave. I should have done so when I was taking a shower."

Cameron was glad *he* hadn't bolted his door when he was taking his shower.

He was quick to settle in the bed with her as she turned on the television and found the channel they'd been watching. He hoped the hotel staff would forget the key, but in short order, someone knocked on the door, probably trying to accommodate them after all the fiascoes tonight.

He wanted to ignore whoever was at the door, but Faith gave him a little smile. He sighed. "We have a date for the morning," he reminded her.

"Six a.m. sharp."

He leaned over and kissed her lips, just a brush of flesh against flesh, her mouth soft, warm, sweetened with lemon-lime, and way too enticing.

Whoever was at the door knocked again. Faith almost looked hopeful the intruder would vanish as she leaned a little into the kiss, her eyes closing slightly, her breathing nearly nonexistent, her hand barely touching his thigh. But when Cameron went to do the kiss more justice, she pulled away. "Tomorrow, bright and early."

His hands cupped her face, brought her to him, and he pressed his lips harder against her mouth. He gave her something to remember him by, just like he'd be thinking about the enticing woman when he was alone in his room tonight, wishing for more. *Then* he left the bed.

When he answered the door, a man dressed in a suit apologized profusely.

Cameron glanced over his shoulder before he left Faith.

He thought she looked like she needed more of a kiss, her lips slightly parted, begging for more attention.

But she quickly said, "Night," as if that would keep her out of trouble.

Smiling, he shook his head. "Night, Faith. See you in the morning." He just hoped he could wake up in time. He had better arrange for a wake-up call and hope the staff would at least get that right, or he'd have somebody's head.

Okay, so Cameron was really a dreamy hunk, but did that mean Faith was supposed to lie awake half the night thinking about his kisses? The first one so light and airy as it promised so much more. And the second one showing he was ready to stay the night for sure. She touched her lips for the hundredth time, wondering how his kisses, as sweet as they were, made her whole body tingle when she'd felt barely anything with Hilson's. Maybe because Cameron was new? Something unexpected?

That was what it had to be. An uncanny attraction that made her whole body heat up again with delicious anticipation.

Breakfast, that was all this was. And then she'd be on her way to find Hilson, and Cameron MacPherson would be on his way to whatever business he had to conduct. And regrettably, she'd never see him again.

With her bag packed and sitting next to the door, Faith glanced at her watch and then the room clock one last time. Cameron MacPherson was twenty minutes late. She couldn't wait any longer, no matter how sexy or intriguing

the guy was. She whipped out a note on the hotel stationery telling him to meet her if he made it in time and was
planning to slip it under Cameron's door when she saw the
tip of a note under hers.

She opened her door and found a folded note. Inside,
the message on hotel stationery said:

> *Sorry to have missed you. Had to leave earlier than*
> *expected. If I return before you have breakfast, I'll meet*
> *with you in the restaurant.*

> Cameron

She sighed, left her room, and closed her door, then
headed for the elevator, rolling her suitcase along behind
her. Probably for the best. Although self-doubt began to
worm its way into her thoughts. Had she turned him off
by one too many rejections? She groaned at herself, always
overanalyzing everything.

After the hostess seated Faith in the mostly empty lodge
restaurant, where the dark-brown furniture and decor
made her feel as if she were in a bear's den, she watched
the entryway. Hoping for a glimpse of Cameron's sparkling
eyes and his roguish smile that would brighten up the place
considerably, she couldn't help wondering what he might
be wearing this morning. From nothing, to a towel, to a pair
of jeans and nothing else, to boxers, and jeans again with an
open shirt, he seemed like the kind of guy better suited to a
hot-weather climate.

She delayed ordering her cinnamon roll for a good
twenty more minutes. But he never showed. Trying not

to feel any disappointment or think anything more about Cameron, she finally gave up, had her green tea and roll, then got into her rental vehicle and drove in the direction of Backcountry Tours. She had business to take care of, after all, and Cameron wasn't part of the deal.

When she reached the office, Faith found that the hotel clerk was right. The carved white wolf sign hanging off the building couldn't be missed. Pictures of snow-covered peaks hung in the windows, and everything was white—the trim, the brick facade, even the roof was nearly white, which made it blend in with the snow accumulated against the buildings as if it were an ice cave in the Antarctic.

A light was on inside, and her spirits lifted. According to Hilson's itinerary, he was coming here first. And maybe she'd finally get some answers to where the hunter guide, Trevor Hodges, was. The man who had taken her father on the tour that had changed his life forever had to have seen something. Or at least be able to confirm that nothing extraordinary had happened. But when her father returned home, he'd begun writing the research paper with such zeal, she suspected whatever had happened here had triggered his need to write it. Besides locating Hilson and the flash drive, she wanted to know the story from Trevor's point of view.

As soon as she walked into the office, she sensed something wasn't right. The place was entirely too quiet. A massive oak desk sat near the entrance, like a fortified barrier to keep the riffraff from going any further into the labyrinth of offices. Or at least that was the way it appeared to Faith.

Then she heard a rustle of papers and a drawer sliding open down the hall. "Hello?" she said, moving toward the hallway leading to several rooms.

The noise instantly ceased. She really didn't have a good feeling about this.

She backed up and was turning around to leave the building pronto when she saw a man's shoe sticking out from behind the massive desk near the entryway.

It's just a shoe, she told herself. A door somewhere else in the building opened, then closed. She hurried around the desk and started, seeing a white-haired old man lying still on the floor, clothed in a suit, missing one shoe, his face gray, his eyes staring at the ceiling, lifeless. She reached for his wrist, felt no pulse. His skin was cold. He'd been dead for a while.

She couldn't see any sign of a struggle or foul play, but if someone had killed the man and was still in the building, she could be next. She headed for the door, jerked it open, and came face-to-face with Cameron MacPherson.

She gave a wispy gasp, threw her hand to her chest, and took a step back.

Tousled by the wind, sandy blond hair fell to the top of his plaid collar, softening his stern look a hint. His parka was open, a soft cabled sweater hugging his broad chest, the sky-blue color electrifying his eyes even more. His eyes widened at the sight of her, and he quickly reached out to steady her.

Her mouth dropped open, and he stared at her with a look of disbelief.

"Faith O'Malley?" he said as if he was so shocked to see her here that he had to confirm it really was her.

"I… There's…" She pushed against him to get out of the building. The killer, if there was one, could be inside and might decide to finish them off next.

Cameron took ahold of her arm and stopped her, the strength of his touch defeating her panic. "What's wrong? You look as white as this building."

"A dead man's in there. Not that I haven't seen a lot of them in the work I do, but the police always call me to the scene after they've dealt with it. I'm never the first one there."

"The work you do?"

"I'm a forensic scientist."

His brows rose a little, but she swore a hint of admiration appeared in his expression.

"Did you touch anything?"

"Sure, the man's wrist. To make sure he was dead. He's been that way for a while. His skin's cold."

"You're sure you're all right?"

"I'm fine. He's not, and if he was murdered, the guy might be still in the building. I heard noises in one of the offices off the hall."

Cameron reached under his jacket and drew out a gun, but he still hadn't released her, as if he feared she'd collapse or something. "Go outside and call 911."

Her lips parted. She stared at the weapon, then looked up at Cameron.

"Private investigator. I have a permit to carry one. Former police officer too." Cameron pulled out an ID to confirm he was a PI.

She closed her mouth, looked back at the other offices, then slipped her cell phone out of her purse. "Then I'm staying right here." She figured she was safer with him—since he had the gun and credentials—than away from him.

"All right." However, instead of checking for the intruder, Cameron did a quick check of the body.

Faith got the 911 operator and said, "I'm Faith O'Malley, and I'm at Backcountry Tours where I found a dead man behind the receptionist's desk."

The operator asked a million questions, or at least it seemed like it, before Faith finally ended the conversation to see what Cameron had discovered about the victim. "Do you see any evidence of a crime?"

He pointed to the man's shirt. "Speck of blood on the front of his dress shirt. I don't see any evidence of any kind of trauma, blow to the head, strangulation, nothing. Looks like he might have been injected with something. No way to confirm my suspicions without stripping him down and looking for a needle mark, then identifying something foreign in the body. Stay here, or go outside and wait for the police. I'll be right back."

Cameron strode off down the hallway.

"Wait! Don't you think that's a little dangerous?"

"That's why you're to wait here or outside for the police." He didn't say another word but headed down the hall.

A cold breeze from the open doorway thoroughly chilled her, and she rubbed her arms, then leaned over the body again and opened the buttons on the man's shirt. Peeling the shirt away just a little, she examined his chest. Cameron was right. He'd been poked with a needle, and the area had bled slightly before the man died. But what was really bizarre was a drip of shiny silver glistening at the point of entry.

A couple of sirens wailed down the road, and she quickly rebuttoned the man's shirt, then wiped the buttons clean with a tissue.

Before the police arrived, Cameron hurried back into the office, took hold of her arm as if he were her knight to the rescue, and led Faith out of the building. Even outside, he didn't loosen his grip on her. She could envision him as a former police officer rescuing women in distress and taking great pride in his work. "Did you see any sign of anyone?" she asked.

He looked a little blank.

"When you went into the back offices. Did you see anyone?"

"No. A door was wide open at the back of the building. He or she probably got out that way."

Instantly, Faith was suspicious. Not just of the person who had been in the building looking for something and who probably killed the old man but of Cameron. Because she could swear he was holding out on her.

As soon as the police arrived, Faith and Cameron showed their credentials to the officers. She thought they acted oddly. She wasn't sure why. Maybe because they didn't seem too surprised. Or because they didn't appear very concerned that Faith and Cameron might be the murderers. Which may have been because the police were dealing with a serial killer and they knew Faith and Cameron couldn't have been involved because they were out-of-towners and both worked—or, in Cameron's case, had worked—with the police. Or maybe it was because the men were jaded— just another dead-guy case.

The one had brownish butch hair, his light-brown eyes glued to her as if he was interested in more than her story about finding a dead body. As if he recognized her or was intrigued with her, but not as a suspect or witness. Officer

Mick Whitson. She couldn't figure out the mixed messages. The other, Bert Adams, moved around the room, his gaze darting about, taking everything in. Several times he sniffed the air. His hair was darker, his eyes hazel, and he had a heavier build. He was the one who asked the questions, as if he was in charge, while Whitson watched Faith's reactions. Not Cameron's, just Faith's.

Officer Adams finished his preliminary cursory examination of the room, then faced Cameron. "And why were you here?"

"Looking for friends of mine, fellow private investigators in a partnership who haven't returned from a hunt."

"With Backcountry Tours?"

"Yes. They made the arrangements with the staff here and are a week overdue back in Seattle. No word, except for a garbled call to our partner there, which isn't like them."

She was impressed. If she worked for an outfit like that, she'd never expect one of her partners to come looking for her. Just a few calls made, and waiting it out a while longer to see if she was just delayed.

Neither of the officers commented concerning Cameron's story, which bothered her. She'd hoped they'd reassure him that his friends were okay. She truly thought they'd say something about a recent snowstorm that might have delayed his partners or how bad communications were out in the wilderness, but they said nothing. Both just seemed to stiffen a little.

Officer Adams shifted his attention to Faith. "And your business here?" Curt, abrupt, businesslike.

She hesitated. Everyone watched her, anticipating her

answer. She was sure she'd alerted them that something about her story wouldn't quite be on the up-and-up.

Well, she could say the same about Cameron. The part about looking for his friends was probably true, but he wasn't just checking for the killer in the building when he went to investigate. And she felt something wasn't quite right about the two cops.

"Can I see your ID again?" she asked the men.

From their nonreaction, she figured she'd stunned them. Although Cameron managed a small smile.

The officers exchanged glances, and then the one in charge, Officer Adams, pulled out his ID. After she looked at it, at him, and at the ID again, she nodded and handed it back. His face stern, he never broke a smile. But the other one did. The smile showed dark amusement. He handed his ID over, made a point to touch her hand, and when she returned the ID, he managed to sweep his hand over hers, lingering a little longer, a little more invasively, as a prelude to something more.

Cameron looked miffed, even stepped closer to her and glowered at Whitson as if to remind him to act professional and stay away from Faith.

Not needing the rescue, she tilted her chin up, was giving Whitson a look that said this was strictly business when Officer Adams reminded her he was waiting for an answer.

"I'm searching for a tour guide who took my father on a hunt last year," she told the officer. "I wanted to take the same trip he'd taken. The guide worked for Backcountry Tours." She spoke matter-of-factly, as if she told the whole truth and nothing but the truth, so help her God.

She thought about mentioning her father's research

paper, that her former boyfriend had stolen it and was close by, but she knew the police wouldn't be interested in any of it. If they had been, they'd ask what the paper was about, and she wouldn't be able to explain. How crazy would that sound? It was better not to bring it up.

More than that and for whatever reason, she didn't want Cameron to know she had a boyfriend. Well, he was an ex, but she hadn't officially told Hilson that. Although she was pretty sure Hilson knew already. And had planned it that way. Unless he was dumb enough to think she couldn't figure out who stole her father's flash drive and hard drive and then intended to come back to her. She couldn't forgive him though.

Cameron's brows rose just a hint. She was certain he didn't believe her.

The officers again exchanged glances, and Officer Adams said under his breath to Whitson, "Kenneth O'Malley's daughter."

"You met my dad?" she asked, unable to contain her surprise.

"No," Adams quickly said. "It's a small town. He was asking a lot of questions, which caught the police department's attention. We discovered he was doing some kind of sociology study, and that was the end of it."

But they seemed to have recognized she was related to her father. Or maybe she was just making too much of their reactions and wasn't correct in her assumptions. So much for keeping her father's business here secret. At least they probably didn't think she'd totally lied. She did want to see where he'd gone on his trip here.

What got to her more than anything was neither officer

asked who the guide was. Maybe they'd talked to Trevor and already knew that he was her father's guide. Small town. Sure.

"If we have any more questions for either of you, where will you be staying for the next several days?" Officer Adams asked.

Cameron, being the gentleman he was, let Faith go first. She cleared her throat, dug around in her purse, then pulled out a piece of paper. Wrong one. List of what she wanted to do when she got here. She dug around a little more, found the slip of paper that she'd written Hilson's itinerary on—after having discovered the password on his computer, teach him to run off with her father's stuff—the receipt for breakfast, one for the hotel, and yes! The information on her cabin rental at Nahmakanta Lake Rustic Resort.

She handed it to Officer Adams, who jotted down the information.

"No telephone service that far out. And cell phones won't work," he warned. "When you reach the trailhead, you have to ski in or get there by dogsled or snowmobile. Snowshoes, if you want to trek ten miles on the unplowed road."

"Yes, that's what the clerk said. But they're the only other cabins near Baxter State Park that still had a vacancy, and hopefully, that's where Trevor Hodges is camping. At least the hotel clerk said she thought he was when I called earlier. I dropped by here first to speak to the staff that employs him to learn more, if I could, of his current whereabouts in the event he moved camp."

"You've made arrangements to get to the resort once you reach the trailhead?" Officer Adams asked.

"Yes. I'm renting a snowmobile."

Cameron smiled a little, and she wondered if he thought she couldn't do this. Not that she was really a rustic type, but the place had two heated shower houses, flush toilets, and a hot tub. So it couldn't be all that rough. And she'd sledded before so no problem there.

Cameron handed Officer Adams a piece of paper and the guy looked at it, then back at Faith. "All right." He jotted the information down in his notebook. "If we need to get in touch, we will. Have a safe trip."

Officer Whitson gave her a slight nod of his head as if sharing the other officer's sentiments. For her, not for Cameron. The officer didn't give him the time of day.

Cameron escorted Faith outside but not before she overheard Officer Adams tell Whitson, "She's intrigued him, and you don't stand a chance."

As Cameron walked her to her vehicle, Faith wondered if the officer thought she and Cameron were already an item, which amused her and seemed to amuse Cameron too.

"What's the name of your cabin?" he asked as they crunched along the crusted snow on the walk, his body touching hers in a possessive and provocative way.

There was something about the way he moved beside her, as if she was truly with him. Hilson would have acted as though he just happened to be there walking in the same direction she was at the same time. She wondered if Cameron acted the same way with all women. Maybe he was a womanizer, well versed in how to make himself more attractive to the female sex. "Don't tell me you're staying at the same rustic resort."

She slipped a little on an icy patch on the snow-covered sidewalk, and Cameron's hand shot out to take ahold of her arm. Hilson would have done the same, but then Cameron went a step further, pulling her in close to his body and wrapping his arm around her waist, making sure she didn't slide again. She hid a smile. If he slipped next, they'd probably both go down. But it was damned cold out, and she enjoyed the heat of his touch.

"Seems we're looking for clues in the same direction. I'm in White Wolf Den."

Now that surprised her. "The cabin I'm staying at is Black Bear Den. Are you using a snowmobile?"

"Yeah, from Skidoo Rentals."

"Guess we *are* headed in the same direction. Maybe we could have lunch together."

Cameron smiled, and the expression was as if he'd found out *her* itinerary beforehand and had this whole thing planned from the beginning, from handing out keys to his and her rooms to leaving his own key by accident in his room. "I thought you'd never ask."

"Yeah, well, after you stood me up for breakfast…" She arched a brow at him.

He gave her a warm squeeze and chuckled. "I knew I'd never live it down if I saw you again. You want me to lead the way?"

"Sounds—" She spied a gray pickup sitting across the street at a barbershop. No driver in the vehicle, and it might not have been the one that she thought had been following her last night, but then again, maybe it was. She had the most awful urge to take a peek in the truck to see if the seats had white dog hair—or make that white *wolf* hairs—on the fabric.

Cameron looked over at the truck. "Something wrong?"

She took a deep breath. "No, no, lead the way." As tinted

as the windows were, she didn't figure she could see inside all that well anyway.

Again he considered the pickup, then patted her SUV. "All right. Don't lose me."

"I don't intend to lose you." Flakes were already falling, and she was sure if they didn't hurry, they might be caught in the middle of the snowstorm. She definitely didn't want to be alone if that happened.

Once he made sure she'd gotten into her vehicle all right—with the pretense he didn't want her slipping again, which was fine by her—Cameron climbed into his rental car. As they drove off, he inched past the gray pickup as if the speed limit was five miles per hour. She swore he was writing down the license plate number. She had done that too.

When they reached the snowmobile rental place an hour later, Faith and Cameron went inside a small grocery store next door to get provisions. Cameron was picking up a few items in another aisle when Faith noticed how much the snow was falling. Too fast.

Last time she was in a snowstorm, she'd been visiting her dad at Portland Community College, taking in the hilltop view as she enjoyed a hot cocoa with him between his classes. The falling snow looked majestic, blanketing everything in a fresh coat of white. Beautiful, until they tried to leave after his final class that day and were trapped with tons of other vehicles attempting to return home in the storm. Pileups. Stuck cars. While she and her father had struggled to get snow chains on the tires. What a mess.

"Hurry up, Cameron," she said, coming up behind him

as he weighed the options of buying one package of tuna over another.

"I always bargain shop."

"That's great, but do it faster. We've got to get out of here before we're stuck staying at the lodge in Millinocket for another night because of the storm. And who knows whose room we'll end up in this time if the same clerk is on the desk."

He chuckled and tugged gently on the tassel of her blue-and-red-striped ski cap. "It would be all right by me if we ended up in the same room again." He eyed the prices again on the packages of tuna. "If I don't choose the right tuna, I could be broke before I return home."

She grabbed one of the packages from him. "Fine. I'll pay for it." Then she hurried to the checkout.

He soon caught up with her with a basket loaded with a week's worth of goodies, and she eyed the snack foods and a couple of salmon steaks in the mix. "If you're so broke, why did you have that gigantic steak for dinner? And room service at that? Plus salmon now too?"

He just winked at her. Yeah, he wasn't so broke. She thought it admirable that he bargain shopped, although about now, all that mattered was that they get on their way.

Then they were off, leaving their rented vehicles in a parking area behind the snowmobile rental shop, bags and sleeping bags loaded onto their snowmobiles, the snow falling way too rapidly. But Faith was sure they'd make the ten-mile trek in time before they lost their way.

She called her father, although she knew he'd still be sleeping at this hour and by the time she reached the cabins, he'd be in the middle of teaching Sociology 101 to a bunch of tired students in the early-morning class, but she wanted to leave him one more message. "Dad, I'm off to the dead zone." Since she never needed a sat phone for deep-in-the-wilderness excursions, she hadn't ever bought one.

She didn't mention how she'd found a body—and a hunk—or how the police officers knew of her father.

She sighed and signed off with "I love you. Call you later when I have a signal again. Don't work too hard. I'll get the flash drive back. And I'll be home as soon as I can. Don't worry."

But now *she* was worried. She'd envisioned getting here, locating Hilson, having it out with him, and him having a conscience and giving the research back to her. Now she was having doubts her plan would work. What if she couldn't find him? What if he refused to give the flash drive back? Or what if he had gotten rid of it already?

What then?

And something she'd been avoiding considering—why did Hilson want the information so badly? And what had he planned to do with it? Plus, what was the research all about that made it so damned important in the first place?

CHAPTER 3

HAVING SPENT THE NIGHT ON SURVEILLANCE OF A warehouse rent-a-cop suspected of worker's comp fraud, Gavin Summerfield finally yanked his bedcovers to his chin at four in the morning in his tidy little condo in Seattle. He closed his eyes, wishing his PI partners would return to help run the business. Since Cameron left, Gavin was being run ragged, and he didn't think he could take much more of these hours.

As soon as he shut his eyes, the phone rang. He ignored the first two rings as he stared at the red numbers on the digital clock. Then he growled and grabbed the phone, ready to strangle the caller if it was a wrong number or an overzealous telemarketer who didn't know what time it was in the Northwest. No phone number listed on the caller ID.

"Hello!" He sounded as grouchy as he felt.

"Gavin?"

Gavin bolted upright. The voice sounded a million miles away and the phone crackled with static, but he'd recognize Owen's voice anywhere. "Owen? Owen, you all right?"

"We're quitting."

"The hunt? Are you and David okay? Coming home soon?"

"Quitting...partnership. Tell—"

The phone sputtered.

"Owen? You're breaking up badly."

"Tell Cameron don't come."

"He's there already. Where are you?"

"Dangerous."

"Owen, Cameron's there. I can't get word to him. What's dangerous?"

"... kill him. We're okay." Crackle. "...go."

"Owen—"

"No!" someone else yelled in the distance on the other end of the line. Then the phone crackled again and died.

"Owen!" Gavin stared at the phone. "Shit." He jerked his covers aside and sat on the edge of the bed, trying to regain his equilibrium. At thirty, he was getting way too old for all-night surveillance without a partner to back him up. But helping his friends if they needed him—and they better damn well need him—he would never be too old for.

He rubbed his tired eyes. If he had the time, he'd drive to Maine. It didn't matter that more people died in car accidents every year than on planes, according to statisticians who kept such statistics. Just taking off in a plane nearly killed him.

He tried Cameron's cell phone, but after several minutes, gave up. Either Cameron was on his way to the cabin resort and couldn't hear the phone above the noise of the snowmobile, or he was already beyond where he could get a signal.

Gavin ran his hands through his hair. At least he could convey the information to Cameron about the gray pickup when he caught up to him. Although he was more interested in the woman Cameron had his sights on rescuing this time.

Gavin shook his head. Cameron would never learn. He punched a few numbers on his phone and said, "When is your next flight to Bangor, Maine?"

The snowstorm intensified as Cameron and Faith drove their snowmobiles slowly along the unplowed road, the visibility less than a quarter mile, the wind blowing faster than they were driving. Pine and spruce trees lining the wide road were draped in white, like snow giants protecting the dwellers of the forest.

Cameron and Faith had considered staying at the lodge in Millinocket for another night, but both of them were impatient to get on with their business. Cameron still wondered exactly what Faith's business here was. He didn't believe for a minute she was here to relive her father's snow-filled adventure. Not in the beginning, and then when Officer Adams mentioned the sociology business, Cameron wondered what that was all about, since the police had taken an interest. Not only that, but Faith had been reluctant to mention it. Curiouser and curiouser.

He was still wondering about his friends too. Were they in some kind of trouble? From what Gavin had told him about the conversation with Owen, it didn't sound like it. With the difficulty Owen was having in talking to Gavin because of the remoteness of the area, that might have been the whole problem. They'd gotten stuck some place where they couldn't make phone contact and were perfectly fine. If Owen and David were quitting the hunt, maybe they'd get home before Cameron could even locate them. Which put a whole different slant on the situation. What if he could make a vacation out of this instead of work? He hadn't taken one in over three years. Maybe he could share Faith's adventure, help her to relive the time her father had spent here.

He snorted. He didn't believe in the least that was what she was here for. And he was determined to learn the truth sooner or later. But another thought occurred to him. Why was she worried about the gray pickup? Even though he'd called the license plates in to Gavin to have him investigate, Cameron knew he wouldn't hear back for a while, what with communications being so spotty where they were going. Faith seemed to think something wasn't right about the vehicle, and he wasn't leaving anything to chance.

And the police officers? That was another concern. Of course every department had its own procedures, and every individual officer had his own way of dealing with a crime scene, but he thought both had acted strangely unconcerned. Almost as if they were trying to cover up their true feelings. He'd observed Officer Adams's expression for the briefest of instances when he'd first seen the dead man, looking as if he had more of a tie to the man than he wanted to admit. But then his look had swiftly changed to all business.

More than that, they had seemed to recognize Faith. From what Cameron understood of the situation, she'd never been to this part of the country. So it seemed odd. Even if they'd heard of her father, it was as if they had a whole dossier on the family, current photos included. The comment about someone being intrigued with the woman threw him too. Even though he shouldn't have made anything of the guy talk, he couldn't help wondering if Adams was referring to Cameron being interested in her or someone else.

Shifting his thoughts to where they needed to be, Cameron concentrated on the road, trying to stay in the center while he followed Faith, unwilling to go first and risk losing her behind him, when he saw a flash of something to his right. Jerking his head that way, he tried to see into the forest, but the snow was blowing so hard, he couldn't make anything out. Probably nothing of importance. But he still couldn't help wondering what it was or if he'd just imagined it.

Watching Faith again, he hoped she was warm enough from the heat distributed from the manifold through footrest grilles and heaters placed on the steering handles on the snowmobile. She was wearing those stretchy, clingy ski pants that, on her figure, were flattering and way too sexy. Even her ski jacket was short-waisted, showing off her curves a little too much.

Not that he didn't enjoy looking, but he could have beaned the guy restocking shelves at the grocery store for eyeing her a little too hard. And the "kid" at the snowmobile rental place made a big deal out of the fact she wasn't wearing a wedding ring and when she returned to Millinocket, he could sure take her out to some fun places. That was until Cameron did his I'm-with-the-lady routine to keep the vultures away. Whether she wanted him to or not.

Actually, she'd seemed a bit amused. If any guy thought he'd make any moves on her at the camp, Cameron would let him know just how wrong he was.

She slowed her snowmobile down a little, and he matched her actions. He suspected they were getting close to the resort when he thought something moved again to his right. But when he looked hard in that direction, all he saw were blowing snow and snow-laden trees, snow piled against them, nothing but white.

He glanced back at the road, and a one-story log lodge

appeared up ahead with a majestic prow-like front and covered wraparound veranda. Cedar rocking chairs sat all along the wooden deck, the arrangement welcoming guests to sit and visit while taking in the panoramic mountain and forest view. But the large picture windows were dark, no light filtering through, and the massive stone fireplace was cold, not a trickle of smoke.

Faith drove up to the porch and paused for a minute, not turning off her engine. He parked beside her and saw what had stopped her: a note pasted on one of the windows from the inside.

Closed due to family emergency. Keys in cabins. Be back later. Charles and Elizabeth Simmons.

Faith pulled her ski mask down under her chin so she could speak more clearly. "Guess we're on our own."

"Good thing we brought supplies with us and didn't count on eating at the main lodge first thing. So, which cabin do we hole up in for now? White Wolf or Black Bear Den?"

"How good are you at starting fires?"

He smiled. "Eagle Scout. Although, I have to admit I always carried a lighter with me on campouts as a boy."

She laughed, and even though her sweet voice was half drowned out by the roaring wind, her laughter warmed him deep inside.

"Come on, Boy Scout, before we freeze our buns off out here. We'll go to whichever is closest."

"Black Bear Den. Yours."

He hoped she'd be amenable to letting him remain for the night. It wasn't that he was so needy, but he didn't like the idea of a woman staying alone in a cabin in the wilderness with no one about. Especially in the midst of a blizzard. Well, truth be told, he was feeling a bit needy too.

They wound their way along a narrow forested trail on their snowmobiles, the trees helping to shield them from the blowing wind, until they reached the first of the small log cabins facing the frozen lake. Through the clearing, bitter cold wind whipped off the ice.

A carving of three whimsical black bears holding a sign that said, *Welcome, Black Bear Den*, attached to the door of the cabin, indicated they were at the right place.

As he recalled from the map Charles had sent him when Cameron booked the reservation, his own cabin was quite a distance from Faith's. Each of the cabins had a screened view of the lake with plenty of trees in between to provide them enough privacy from their neighbors. Which was another reason he didn't like it that Faith would be alone.

Snowdrifts were piled against the side of the cabin all the way to the windows, at least a foot of accumulation covered the deck, and the roof was bearing a heavy load. Although it was midday, the blizzard made everything look gray, cold, and foreboding.

Which made it imperative he start a fire right away to heat up the place. As soon as Faith was inside, he hauled in his stuff behind her. No sense in leaving it out to freeze in this weather even if he wasn't staying the night. When he put his bags down on the knotty pinewood floor, she raised her brows and gave a funny little smile.

"Not snowproof," he said as if answering her unspoken question, then headed back outside before she could retort. When she followed him to get the rest of her stuff, he waved her inside. "Go set up housekeeping, Faith. I'll take care of the rest of your bags. Dressed the way you are, you're way too much of a distraction."

He loved the way the skin underneath her eyes crinkled when she grinned, shook her head, and returned to the cabin. His attention then focused on the skintight ski pants hugging her derriere. The thought came to mind how much fun it would be to ski with her in the great Northwest, share a hot toddy at the ski lodge, and snuggle together with her in a spa, the snow piled up around it. And then work out all the kinks from a day on the slopes in a soft bed made for two. He shook his head at himself, grabbed the rest of her bags, and returned to the cabin, shutting the door against the howling wind.

Faith had pulled off her ski hat, mask, goggles, and gloves but was still wearing her jacket as she looked inside the cabinets. The log cabin was ice-cold, with unadorned large picture windows facing out on the frozen lake. The walls were made of logs but insulated. Cameron didn't feel a bit of wind coming through the walls, which he was grateful for. Once he had a fire going, the place should warm up pretty quickly.

"Have a fire started in a jiffy. As soon as I can find my lighter."

Faith had already started a teakettle on the gas stove. "Fire here," she said, pointing to the flame under the kettle. "Did you bring coffee? I've got green tea."

"Coffee." He knew he'd forgotten something. Although he figured he could have gotten some to drink at the main lodge, the thought crossing his mind that cuddling with Faith early in the morning would negate the need to get up to have any for some time.

"You didn't bring any?"

"No. Forgot all about it."

"How about hot cocoa then?"

"Either is fine." He finally got the fire started in the woodburning stove, turned on the fan to blow heat into the room, and looked around. One double-size bed and two twin beds in two bedrooms off the living room. Although a queen-size suited his height, a double was better for snuggling with a sweet feminine body on cold winter days. No bedding or linens on the bare mattresses, which was why they had to bring their own sleeping bags, and he considered how well his would fit on her mattress.

She caught him eyeing the bed. His ears burned with chagrin, and he smiled. Hell, he was caught in the act, and he was pretty sure she could read his transparent thoughts. Women often could.

"So, I offered to fix lunch. Or have lunch with you. But since it appears this is where we'll be eating, what appeals?" She took off her jacket and laid it on a chair, then started pulling out cans of spinach, green beans, corn, asparagus, salmon, and the package of tuna.

"How about you pick out the vegetable and we can fix my salmon steaks?" He looked around the kitchen. Sink, no running water. "Icebox, but no refrigeration. They'll have to supply us with ice, but looks like no one's around to do that today."

"We could gather up some snow and put it in the ice box. But the salmon sounds good to me."

"No breakfast for me, so it sounds fine."

She cast him an annoyed expression.

He smiled. "Yeah, I know that look. You didn't wait too long for me at the restaurant this morning, did you?"

"No, just ate and left." She turned her back on him and emptied the contents of the can of spinach into a saucepan.

"Ah, good." He didn't believe a word of what she said. She'd waited for him. In fact, he suspected she had gone straight from the restaurant to Backcountry Tours. So she must have waited a good half hour for him at least, which made him feel like a cad to an extent. But he'd believed his partners' welfare had been at stake. "I thought I had a lead concerning my friends so I ran out at five thirty this morning. Turned out to be a dead end. I figured by the time I found that out, you'd have left the restaurant, so I headed to Backcountry Tours. And lo and behold, here's my favorite lady."

She hmpfed. "Panicking over a dead body."

He moved in closer, and with her back still to him, he rubbed her arms, the soft peach sweater sliding a little, her subtle sweet, peach fragrance tantalizing. "You looked a little pale, and you were doing the smart thing by leaving in a hurry when you heard an intruder in the place, but you did it with true grit. Any other woman I've known would have run out of there screaming."

"Not the screaming type. *Normally.* Although when I found a snake curled up in my wet laundry in the washing machine once..." She pulled out a broiler pan for the salmon. "I'm sure you could have heard me all the way to Seattle."

"Fear of snakes?"

She smiled up at him. "Only when I reach for a handful of wet clothes to put in the dryer and feel something solid, wet, round, and slimy that shouldn't have been there." She sprinkled lemon and pepper seasoning on the salmon. "About the dead guy, though, he had a needle mark in his chest. I think you were right in figuring he was injected with something. But there was the oddest thing next to the puncture wound."

Hell, he wished he'd taken a look too.

"A drop of what looked like a silver solution," she continued. "I would have loved to have taken a sample of it and analyzed it. But I didn't want to tamper with the evidence, and besides, I don't have any equipment here to do the analysis anyway."

He admired her for having investigated the situation when he left the office. He never suspected she had. "Silver? Mercury, maybe?"

"Hmm, no on the mercury poisoning. A year ago, we had a case of an attempted suicide who unsuccessfully used an intravenous mercury cocktail. It didn't lead to acute systemic toxicity. Or in laymen's terms, it didn't overload his system causing death."

That was a new one on him.

"But silver poisoning?" she said, raising her brows. "Yes. You can find silver remedies that claim all kinds of health cures. So they're not hard to come by either online or in health food stores. Argyria is the name of the condition when people ingest silver, and silver poisoning can turn skin gray. It's permanent. Slow poisoning is visible to the naked eye; not a good way to murder someone on the sly. In high amounts, though, it can kill someone. I investigated a case where the husband injected his wife with 50mg of silver salts because of the life insurance policy he had on her, and she promptly died. In another instance, a quack doctor injected a pregnant mother with silver nitrate for an abortion and killed the mother too."

Cameron was speechless at first. He and his partners could really use someone like her on their team. "You could be handy in an investigation."

"That's what my coworkers always tell me. Did you see anything in the offices that you checked?"

"Papers strewn all over the place. Looked like someone was searching for records of some sort."

"Anything on your friends?"

"No. At least not that I could find on such short notice. The records were in a shambles, so something probably was there in the mess."

She stirred the spinach. "I hope your friends are okay."

"They're former police officers too. I'm sure they can handle themselves just fine. But I have to be certain. Where had you planned on going exactly? Do you know where your father actually went while he was out here?"

"No. Trevor Hodges knows though. If I can find him. The man who owns this place? Charles Simmons? He runs the dogsledding part of the business here and said he could take me to see Trevor at his campsite beyond Baxter State Park."

"Ah, so then why were you at Backcountry Tours?"

"You know," she said, running her finger along Cameron's sweater-covered chest, then giving a little tug on his belt hidden beneath the sweater, "you sound just like a cop."

Loving the way she touched him with a hint of flirtation, suggesting she wanted more, Cameron was ready to delay the meal. "I've always sounded like a cop. Ever since I was a kid. Heck, one of the Boy Scouts in my troop stole money from several of us. I had to prove who the culprit was." He combed his fingers through her hair, loving the soft texture, enjoying the small smile playing on her lips.

"Didn't you feel like a tattletale?"

"No. I doubt you would have felt that way either." If he had her figured right. He wrapped his arms around Faith, and to his delight, she melted against his chest. He breathed in her heavenly scent, loving the feel of her pliant body pressed against him.

"You're right. If a girl in my Girl Scout troop had been stealing from any of us, I would have set a trap, taken pictures or videotaped it, and caught her red-handed."

Just envisioning Faith in her supersleuthing activities as a kid, he laughed, surprised that she had been a Girl Scout. "Right is right and wrong is wrong. I've never had a problem with seeing the difference. What made you get into the business?"

"The truth?" She pulled away from him and motioned to the salmon. "I'd better turn them before they're blackened."

He didn't care as long as he could cuddle with her longer. He hadn't felt like that toward a woman in eons, but the way she spoke, he sensed some darker reason had catapulted her into her chosen career field. He was sure he wouldn't like it.

"The ten-year-old girl across the street disappeared when I was sixteen. I helped put out flyers, helped look for her in the neighboring communities, and brought food to the distraught family." Faith stared at the spinach for some time before she spoke again. "They found her four days later, dead. The search for Christine was over, but looking for her murderer?" Faith let out her breath. "I couldn't do anything more for the family, so I decided right then and there I'd help find Christine's killer. It took me nearly ten years."

Now that, he hadn't expected. Gavin's father had been on the police force and had died in a robbery shoot-out.

That was what had made Cameron and Gavin join the force. David had always had a sense of adventure, so it was either that or join the military. When the rest of them decided to join the force, he was not one to be left out. And Owen? His father had been in enough barroom brawls that he was always on the opposite side of the law. Owen didn't want to follow in his father's footsteps and much preferred being the arresting officer. But Cameron didn't even like thinking of the danger Faith might have been in, searching for her neighbor's killer.

She offered Cameron a sad smile. "We got him. The bastard was an older cousin who didn't like it that she had loving parents, lots of everything, when his dad was an alcoholic and his mother was never around much. I thought it might have been him, the times I'd seen him treat Christine meanly when he came to visit. But we had to have proof. After I was trained in forensic science, I was able to obtain the proof in the cold case files while sorting through boxes of evidence that had sat idly for years." She sighed. "What about you? What made you go into the business?"

"Nothing as dramatic as your situation. Gavin's father had always been like a surrogate dad to me since my own died in a car accident when I was a teen. When Gavin's dad died in the shoot-out, I wanted to become a cop too."

"I'm sorry about Gavin's father. And yours?"

Cameron shrugged. He didn't want to tell her that even when his dad was around, he wasn't much to brag about. Gavin's father was a different story. War hero, all-around nice guy. His father? Womanizer, carouser, gambler, all-around deadbeat. But it didn't seem the time to talk ill of the dead.

He glanced around at the cabin. Fabric with black

bears on plaid covered the pillow cushions on all the seats. Pictures of real black bears in the woods, fishing in a stream, hung on the walls. And a mixture of real-to-life black bear carvings and whimsical ones sat on a shelf. Cuddly, oversize teddy bears added to the black bear theme of the cabin.

He could imagine what his cabin looked like. The intense amber eyes of white wolves watching every move he made, strategically placed everywhere in the cabin.

Faith motioned to four five-gallon plastic jugs. "At least they left us some water before the staff took off. The jugs of water should last us a while. If we run out, you can go get yours."

Glancing out at the storm, not letting up in the least, he shook his head, having no intention of leaving Faith and the toasty cabin unless they were in dire need. "We'll have to make this last for now." But if he didn't read anything wrong in what she was saying, did she plan to let him stay?

He intended to change her mind if she didn't want him to and made himself useful, setting out the silverware, the plates, only glancing back at her in the kitchen when she stopped rattling pans around. She was watching him, a small smile percolating on her lips. She held his gaze as if measuring him for a job, licking her full sensuous lips as if she was readying them for a well-placed kiss. He was damn well ready to kiss her again.

He hadn't entertained a thought about a woman in such a way for months—not with the self-imposed sixty-hour workweeks he'd been putting in. Not to mention his former girlfriend jilting him several months ago. Just about the time he began working lots of overtime. Yet he was more than intrigued with Faith. Which he thought had something to do with the way she handled herself at a crime scene and how knowledgeable she was in figuring out clues. And not flighty when she came face-to-face with a naked stranger. Her endearing story of her neighbor and the way she had helped out impressed him too. Plus, he'd never have figured her for the kind of person who would manage roughing it in a place like this.

His ex-girlfriend would have thrown a fit not to have an attached bathroom and running water and linens for the bed. And no maid service or room service or television either. Nope, Marjory would have given him notice before they even arrived at the place once she learned she couldn't use the internet or phone her friends. One of whom happened to be the guy she took off with.

Distracting him from his thoughts, Faith turned and flipped the salmon again and switched off the burner.

If his intuition was right, he was certain Faith was considering letting him stay the night, although he was ready to convince her if she had any doubts that it was the best thing for all concerned—for safety's sake, of course.

"Meal's ready." She was beginning to dish out the spinach when they heard someone yell out somewhere in the woods.

He looked out the window but didn't see anything or anyone. Immediately, he worried someone had been ice fishing and fallen through the ice. "Stay here," he said, jerking on his coat and gloves.

"Maybe I should go with you."

He shook his head. "Lock the door after me. It's probably nothing, but I've got to check it out." He yanked on his ski mask and hat, then headed outdoors, hoping he wouldn't find anybody in real danger. He didn't like leaving Faith alone, but he had to make sure no one was in any real trouble.

Faith scooped the spinach back into the saucepan and kept it on low heat. Then she returned to the window to watch for any sign of anyone but mostly for Cameron. She liked that he was a take-action kind of guy but prayed no one was really in any trouble. His story about Gavin's father endeared him to her. It made her wonder what the deal had been with his own father because the concern he shared with her reflected much more sorrow for Gavin's father than his own. She sighed. Maybe his father had been like her mother. Not there to count on for anything.

After locking the door, she began making the bed. Unzipped, his double-wide sleeping bag and her single one fit the double-size bed nicely. Even though it was a bit presumptuous of her to think he would stay the night, she figured he was hoping. They might as well share the place and meals and keep each other company while they dealt with the staff of Backcountry Tours.

Tomorrow, they could straighten out the cost and, well, since Cameron was going to go broke if he didn't choose the cheapest brand of tuna—she smiled—this would save him a little money.

She returned to the stove and poked at the salmon again. At this rate, it would be overdone and cold by the time Cameron got back. Then one of their snowmobile's engines began to rumble, and for a minute, she thought Cameron had come back for it. But when hers started up, she assumed the worst. Someone was stealing their snowmobiles. She grabbed a large cast-iron frying pan, hurried to the door, and opened it, just in time to see two men sitting on the sleds, both backing up from the cabin in the wind-driven snow.

"No!" she screamed, and wielding the pan, she raced out to stop them.

CHAPTER 4

THE FIRE GLOWED IN THE MASSIVE STONE FIREPLACE AS Kintail Silverman paced across his lodge's great room miles from where his new troubles lay, wondering how the hell he was going to remedy this mess, while other members of his pack kept an eye on Owen and David in the den.

Kintail glanced at Lila Grayson. She looked a little contrite for once, and he frowned. "You were supposed to be watching Owen. David will do anything we say, but Owen… he's trouble. How many phone calls did he make before Trevor caught him? And twice, he's tried to escape. The only good things about any of this are that we're too remote for him to get word out, he doesn't know his way around out here, and he doesn't have a clue how to deal with the shape-shifting aspect." Kintail stared out one of the picture windows at the blowing snow, the cold so invigorating that even now he wanted to shift and run like the wolf he was.

He couldn't kill Owen, not yet. He knew the man needed some time to adjust. If only his partner, Cameron MacPherson, wasn't on the way to rescue Owen and David. That was what was causing him all the heartburn.

Lila cocked her head in her arrogant way, yet he knew insecurities about something in her past fed her actions. Given time, he figured she would eventually come around.

"You shouldn't have changed them. Or at least not David."

She smiled. "I don't think Owen's forgiven me for biting him."

Kintail liked it when she smiled, as if a part of her gentler nature was trying to reveal itself. But now wasn't the time to concern himself about his issues with Lila. Neither David or Owen had any family left in Seattle. Kintail hadn't thought one of their partners would look into the situation.

Kintail shook his head. "If we didn't have so many hunting parties scheduled for the next several weeks, we'd leave early for Yellowknife. Take them with us and isolate ourselves. But we can't split up the pack, and we can't leave right now. Not without hurting our business and ruining our reputation here."

He loved living here half the year, flaunting what they were while the locals and tourists didn't have a clue. Except for the Penobscot, Mimac, Wabanaki, and other tribes in the area—they knew, but they revered the wolf, which worked to Kintail and his people's advantage. "I'm sure nowhere else in the States can a werewolf pack show off their pack members in broad daylight, anywhere and everywhere, and get away with it."

Lila stretched her arms above her head, then crossed them. "I agree, and that's what's so much fun about living here in the winter, being around people who are clueless as to what we are, thinking that our wolves are like old good-natured dogs. But what about this Cameron MacPherson? Can't we just change him too?"

Kintail didn't care for the interest in Lila's tone of voice or the expression on her face. He knew her well enough to recognize she was intrigued with the man. Did she think maybe she could convince Cameron to take over the pack and then mate with her just because Kintail wasn't freely mating with her? Cameron? A newly turned *lupus garou*?

She had to be nuts if she thought Kintail would lose against the newcomer. Besides, her secretive past was keeping her from letting Kintail get close to her. He doubted she could get close to Cameron any more than she could with him.

"If he's coming to rescue his partners, he's sure to be an alpha. There's only one way to deal with him."

"Hmm, well, can't we just make an offer first? Then if he says no, whatever happens to him is his own damned fault," she asked.

Kintail gave her a hard look.

She lifted a shoulder and pushed her hair back into a ponytail, and he inwardly groaned at how enticing the woman looked. "You're the boss, of course. But it seems to me if we can get him to join us, that would be the best scenario." Then she curled her lips down, and he knew what was coming next. "What about the woman? She's been snooping around, asking about Trevor. Looking for information on her father's trip here."

"Trevor swore Kenneth O'Malley didn't see anything, but Hilson says he has evidence that her father saw one of us shape-shifting."

Lila sat down on one of the velvet couches. "So…my question, again, is what do we do with her? What we should have done with her father when he was here before is my way of thinking."

Kintail gave Lila a sly smile. "She could make a nice addition to the pack." Lila had only joined his pack two years ago from a group in Finland. He still wasn't sure what her deal was, except she had been born a *lupus garou* like him. But she hadn't allowed any of his pack members to get close to her. Especially not him. Unless she thought she could get him to bend to her wishes. She really didn't know him that well. Yet.

"We have enough females in the pack," Lila snapped.

"We can never have enough females what with the shortages there are. Besides, Hilson wants to deal with her."

"Hmph, if he'd dealt with her when he first staked out her old man, we wouldn't have this new situation. What's your brother's problem? She's not too alpha for Hilson, is she?"

Kintail rubbed his chin and looked back out the window. He wondered why his brother hadn't already taken the woman for his own. Maybe she *was* too alpha for him.

Cameron didn't see anything near the lake where he'd heard the man yell, although the way voices traveled, he might have been much farther away. When the sound of snowmobiles started up at the cabins, his intuition immediately kicked in, warning him something wasn't right.

He trudged through the knee-deep snow as fast as he could manage in the blowing wind, retracing his steps as much as possible to make it easier to run. The snowmobiles sounded like they were leaving the area around Faith's cabin. Which he assumed meant only one thing. At least two people were stealing them.

As soon as he saw Faith racing around the side of her cabin half-dressed, wearing no parka, gloves, or ski hat, shouting, "Bastards!" his heart nearly froze.

"Faith!"

She whipped around, her brows knit in a deep frown,

her mouth curved down, her bare fists held tight at her sides. "They stole our snowmobiles!" She stiffly waved down the road.

"Go inside," he warned as the snow covered her hair and stuck to her sweater, the wind still not subsiding. He figured she'd catch pneumonia the way she was dressed.

She waded through the deep snow, stopped, looked down, then fished a cast-iron frying pan out of a snowdrift, whisked around, and returned to the porch. In disbelief, he watched her. Hell, the woman was lethal. Despite the circumstances, he smiled, then hurried around the cabin and looked down the road. The snowmobiles were long gone.

When he stepped inside and closed the door, Faith was busily jotting down information. "Blue parka, black ski mask, scrawny build but tall, jeans, cowboy boots, black gloves, yellow goggles. Other guy—black parka, black ski mask, heftier, same approximate height, jeans, snow boots, brown gloves, 9mm," she muttered under her breath.

"One of the bastards had a gun?" Cameron pulled off his gloves, parka, and hat, setting each of them on the chair near the woodburning stove, then lifted a blue floral towel she'd hung over the log footboard of the bed.

"Yeah, he pointed it at me when I started chasing them."

"Before or after you pitched the frying pan at them?" He joined her and ran the towel over her wet hair. She melted a little under his ministrations, and he leaned over and kissed her cheek, her skin still cold. "Hell, Faith, didn't they ever teach you not to chase armed men when you don't have a weapon of equal or superior might?" he scolded, dropping the towel on a chair and pulling her tightly into his arms.

She turned her head and frowned up at him. "I didn't know he had a gun at first. Not until he pointed it at me. Bastards."

"The snowmobiles *are* insured."

"Well, yours has a slight dent on the tail end now. But it doesn't make me any less angry knowing they're insured."

"You hit my snowmobile?" He released her and began massaging her tense shoulders, her sweater soft, slippery, and springtime fragrant. She leaned into his touch, and he was ready to carry her off to bed, to sooth his frayed nerves…in his own way.

"I aimed for the guy, but that frying pan weighs a ton so it didn't have the lift I'd hoped for. If I'd had a chance to do it again, I would angle the toss higher." She growled, then purred as he continued to massage. "Good thing you brought your stuff in, or they would have stolen your gear too."

"All I care about is they didn't steal *you* away." Even now, his heart was still racing from worrying she might have come to harm. "Did they do anything other than take the machines?"

"Not that I saw. What about you? Did you find anyone in trouble out there?"

"It might have been a diversion to draw me away from the cabin. They might have suspected that if only one of us was here, they could steal the snowmobiles."

"One of us. You mean the weaker sex." She pulled away and dished up the spinach.

Chuckling, he squeezed her arm to reassure her he didn't feel that way in the least about her, then served up the salmon on hefty-sized dark-brown plates. "Believe me, I don't want to ever make you that angry. Weaker sex? How much damage did you do to my snowmobile with that frying pan?"

She gave an evil smile. "At least if I see it again, I can recognize it better."

When they sat down to eat, Cameron wondered if his insurance or hers would cover the damage to his snowmobile, given the circumstances for the bash, if they ever recovered the machines. He was about to cut into his fish when he spied his couple-size down sleeping bag spread out over the mattress like a welcome mat through the open bedroom door. He tried to conceal his smile before she caught it, but what could he say? His motives were usually crystal clear when it came to women.

"Trying to take all your stuff to your cabin in this storm without the use of a snowmobile isn't a good idea," she said matter-of-factly.

He nodded very seriously as he took a bite of his salmon. But the thing of it was, she had to have laid out the sleeping bag earlier, before the machines were stolen. Had to have, because she wouldn't have had time to do it afterward without him catching her when he came inside.

"I wholeheartedly agree."

"*Besides*, you owe me breakfast, and there's no way I'm traipsing in the cold all the way to your place at six in the morning to have it."

"Six in the morning?" Hell, he thought that was just this morning's schedule, a way to get ahead of the incoming snowstorm.

"Yes, that's when I'm always raring to go."

"I thought this was a vacation for you." Now maybe he'd get the truth out of her.

The sound of her laughter was lighthearted and fun-loving. "My internal alarm clock wakes me at five every morning. It's amazing what I can accomplish by getting up early."

"Maybe you just haven't had the right incentive to stay in bed yet." He was afraid his smile was a little too wolfish when her cheeks blossomed with color, but the coy smile she offered in return made her eyes sparkle with humor.

She saluted him with her cup of green tea. He saluted her back with the awful stuff.

Yeah, he'd make it worth her while to stay in bed until it was a decent wake-up time in the morning. Especially if he couldn't have a cup of coffee first thing.

He was glad he'd brought his made-especially-for-couples sleeping bag. And to think the reason he'd taken that one and not his single sleeper was it would serve more like real bedding while he stayed in the cabin—and truthfully, it was lighter weight and easier to compress than his old one. For the first time, he didn't mind that an earlier girlfriend had ditched him before they'd had the chance to try it out. Or that his latest girlfriend wouldn't have taken a step in any direction that had to do with sleeping bags.

If he could get a good fix on his friends and maybe even help Faith with whatever reason she was really here, this could turn out to be a nice little getaway. Notwithstanding that they had to get word to the police in Millinocket whenever they could that their snowmobiles had been stolen.

After eating lunch, Cameron helped clear away the dishes. Without snowmobiles or the lodge owners in residence at the moment, there wasn't much else to do with the snowstorm still pelting them but hunker down in the cabin…or…

Cameron glanced back in the direction of the main lodge. The cedar hot tub was supposed to be fired up nightly. Two heated shower facilities with flush toilets were connected to it. Since no one was here to object, maybe he'd heat up the hot tub a little early.

"Did you bring a swimsuit?" he asked.

Faith stopped putting some of her sweaters in a drawer of a small three-drawer chest and looked at him as if he'd lost his mind. "Lake's frozen solid. And I'm not a member of the polar bear swim club either."

"I was thinking more along the line of a hot tub."

Her expression brightened considerably. "Oh, I forgot about that." Then she seemed subdued again. "But the owners aren't here." She returned to the kitchen and pulled the cans of groceries from a plastic sack, then tucked them under the cabinet.

"The owners should be in residence. Besides, we wouldn't do anything they wouldn't do if they were here. I figure, why not?"

She shook her head. "I thought you were an Eagle Scout."

"I am, but…" He shrugged. "Do you have a swimsuit?"

Looking thoughtful, she pulled a golden curl behind her ear, which made him want to nibble her lobe, right then and there.

"I wonder how many other guests are here?"

She was going for it! He bet she didn't have a swimsuit.

"Not many. It looked like at least half of the eight cabins were under renovation, closed tight. I saw lights on in one of the remaining ones. None on in the other.

And of course there's mine, which is vacant. Otherwise, that's it."

"One renter. Could be an active family with tons of kids. What if they showed up about the time we did our illegal firing up of the hot tub in the late afternoon? Here we'd be, snuggled down in the hot soupy water, and kids with floaties would pour onto the deck, chattering and laughing and—"

"I'll heat up the hot tub and be right back." He didn't wait for another objection—if she was even going to offer one—just shoved his jacket on and hurried outside.

He thought about what she might wear for their excursion. Something pink and lacy? White, maybe? Daring red? Black and seductive?

The stiff wind hit him with a blast of snow. He wished he hadn't been in such a hurry and had taken his goggles and ski hat. Next trip, when he escorted his date to the spa, he'd be better prepared.

When he reached the deck attached to the shower house, he plowed through the snow and retracted the cover on the spa. Steam rose from the heated water. He pulled off a glove and stuck his hand in. Warm, not really hot. After turning the heat up and the jets on, he pulled his glove back on and rubbed his hands. Billions of bubbles popped up, creating white foam, soon hiding the Caribbean blue marble effect on the walls of the circular tub.

He would have opted for one that was couple-sized, but the spa looked like it could hold six to seven adults, not half as cozy as he would have liked. And the awful thought it could be filled with lots of kids came to mind. He turned on the lights around the edge of the tub, then found a snow shovel in a utility shed and cleared as much of a path as he could on the deck up to the cedar-surrounded spa from the changing rooms. He envisioned Faith in the tub with him and how hot things could get if he and Faith could have more privacy. Too bad they didn't have a hot tub inside their own cabin.

Then he went inside the changing room to warm it up so they could shed the majority of their clothes. He found a switch to heat up the deck so it wouldn't ice over. A gust of bitter-cold wind blew in through the doorway and he turned, thinking Faith couldn't wait to join him. But no, it was some other woman, and he felt a pang of disappointment. If she was a guest, that was the end of his plans to share some private time with Faith. Then he wondered if this woman was one of the owners, ready to give him a dressing-down for heating up the hot tub without permission.

"Lila Grayson," she said, slamming the door shut behind her with a lot more force than needed.

Lila Grayson, the one from Backcountry Tours—it hit him as odd that she'd arrive here of all places. Wearing ski boots, an ivory wool sweater, and ski pants, she looked ready for cold-weather expeditions, minus the ski jacket. Tangled by the wind, her platinum-blond hair drifted past her shoulders. Her golden eyes wary, she was a looker, with skin the same color as her clothes and ruby lips glossed for show. High-angled cheekbones gave her the look of a movie star, but her tiny nose contradicted that image. She pulled off her glove and extended a hand.

"Cameron MacPherson," he said, shaking her hand. "You run Backcountry Tours?" Now maybe he'd get some answers concerning his friends.

She lifted her nose and sniffed. "You were in my office earlier today? Along with a woman friend? You found one of my employees dead, according to the police?"

So Lila hadn't just happened to run across him here. She was investigating him.

"Yeah, I was looking for you or your partner, Kintail Silverman. Two of my friends went on a hunt and haven't returned."

"Owen and David are quitting. Haven't they told you?" She raised a brow and smiled just a hint, but it was icy like her whole demeanor.

"Quitting the hunt."

"No, quitting *your* business. They're going up north with us, joining our hunting-guide team. They're tired of the PI work. Didn't they tell you?"

Cameron stared at the woman as if she'd managed to turn him into a frog. "I'll hear it from them first."

"Owen said he called your partner, Gavin. He said he told him they were quitting the business. Since you were"— she smiled—"checking out our office, I figured you might not have gotten the official word yet."

"I'll get the official word directly from them."

"Hmm," she purred and took a step toward him, and he envisioned a lioness on a hunt, her eyes fixed on him, just waiting for the right moment to pounce and rip out his jugular. She reached her hand out and trailed her fingernails down his sweater. "Maybe you could quit your job too. Come join us."

That was when the door suddenly opened and Faith stalked inside, a frozen smile on her lips, her eyes narrowed in a confrontational way. She looked as though she was ready to punch out her competition, and he loved it. "Forgot your towel, honey." Faith waved the blue towel at him and slid her arm around his waist, snuggling up next to him. She gave Lila a get-lost look.

He was ready to play the lover's role for real.

Lila sniffed the air. "She's the one with you at my office this morning. Are you looking for his partners too? Or something else?" she asked Faith.

Faith stiffened. "Office? You're from Backcountry Tours?"

"Lila Grayson."

"I'm looking for Trevor Hodges. He works for you, right?"

Her smile faked, Lila said, "Not of late. What did you want him for?"

"He guided my father on a…tour. I wanted to see the route they took."

Lila narrowed her eyes. "And you are?"

"Faith O'Malley."

Lila smiled slyly. "Well, old Trevor Hodges could be anywhere out there." She waved her hand around in the direction of Baxter Park and the surrounding woods. Then she glanced outside at the steamy spa. "Don't want to let your water get cold." She smiled again at Cameron. "Offer still stands, if you decide to come work with us."

"Have David and Owen meet me at the lodge, and I'll hear for myself if they plan to quit our partnership."

"I'll be sure to give them the message." Lila whipped around and headed out of the building, shoving the door against the wall as she left the place.

Faith hurried to close the door against the blowing wind.

"Why did she recognize your name?" Cameron asked, pulling off his sweater.

"Dad seems to have made an impression on a lot of people. She might have met him when he hired Trevor to take him on the tour." Faith dumped her ski coat on one of the cedar benches.

"I thought maybe there'd been some trouble when your father came on his trip here. At least the way Lila responded, it sounded that way."

Faith tossed her sweater onto her coat. "What was the business offer she proposed to you?"

The fact Faith changed the topic so quickly made him wonder even more what this was all about. "She wanted me to become one of her guides."

"You don't believe your friends would quit the partnership like that?"

"Nope. We've been friends since grade school. We always talked of having a partnership. Even if they did want to jump ship, they'd never do it like this without discussing it with us and then giving us time to downsize or get a couple of new partners."

"Hmm, so it sounds like Lila Grayson and probably her partner, Kintail Silverman, have something going on."

"Yeah." *But what was the deal with Faith, her father, and Trevor Hodges?* "Do you believe that Trevor Hodges no longer works for Backcountry Tours?"

"Nope. No more than I believe your friends are leaving you and your other partner high and dry without saying so face-to-face." She unbuttoned her blouse.

He felt like a kid in a candy store, waiting to see all the treats. He turned around and pulled off his shirt to give her some privacy. When he tugged off his jeans, the door squeaked open and shut, and he looked around to see she'd left him. Smiling, he hurried to join her outside. The cold wind whipped across his bare skin as she quickly slipped into the hot water with a splash. He got an eyeful of blue bikini panties, a matching blue bra cut nice and low, and pristine peach flesh covered in goose bumps. She lowered herself into the bubbling water, the swell of her breasts lifted above the foam. Her gaze moved lower, her expression bemused; his body was certainly responding. He hoped he wouldn't embarrass himself.

"Warm enough?" Although as hot as she looked, he figured she could heat the water right up.

"Hmm, perfect." She closed her eyes and rubbed the hot water over her neck and shoulders and sank lower into the tub.

Yeah, perfect was right. No matter what the woman wore or didn't wear, she was a sight for deprived eyes.

Cameron climbed into the water and settled next to Faith, wanting to make the night with her something special. The warm water and powerful massaging jets that targeted his lower back and calves were only half the fun. The sound of gentle moving water through amplifiers built into the tub casing covered the noise of the jets. "This makes the cold and the trip well worth it."

Before he could settle in nice and close to her and take advantage of her soft, expressive mouth, a gray-haired old lady waddled from the back side of the building in a coat and short snow boots, her white, hairy legs bare. She smiled. "Be right out, folks." She entered the changing room and shut the door.

Cameron scooted even closer to Faith, his body

touching hers, the image of her half-naked sitting this close to him in the heated water stirring up a raging need. Before the woman returned, he moved restlessly, his gaze switching from the shower house to the object of his most fervent desire. *Faith.* Her lips wore a tentative smile, but her eyes challenged him to take the first step. He couldn't help being irritated with the stranger, to say it mildly. But he wasn't about to let the woman stop what he had in mind to do.

He leaned over and pressed his lips against Faith's mouth, savoring the velvety softness and the way she woke to his touch, lifting her chin to accommodate him, closing her eyes, her hands clutching at his forearms. He touched her supple breasts and she moaned softly, but the moment was all too short.

Shattering the mood, the older woman exited the room, wearing a tent-size bathing suit in hot shimmering pink and the furry boots. "Charles must have fired up the hot tub earlier than usual, although I haven't heard a peep out of his sled dogs. He must've figured we couldn't get out in this weather to ice fish. Always so considerate of his guests. I'm Mary."

"Faith, Cameron," he said, pulling away from Faith, although his leg and hip still rested against hers. His hand shifted to her thigh, caressing, enjoying her silky skin and the way she leaned against him. But even though her eyes were smoky with desire, the newcomer's presence caught Faith's focus. All he could hope for at this point was that Mary would tire of the tub quick enough and leave so he could get back to business.

"On your honeymoon?" Mary asked, smiling as if she were a woman in the know.

Faith said yes as he said no. The old woman laughed. "I've been there, done that myself."

As soon as she had her boots off, the sound of crunching snow coming from the back side of the shower house warned them others were coming. Faith gave Cameron an I-told-you-so look, and he figured it was time to leave before the woman's grandkids showed up with the floaties. Except that the way the newcomers moved, the footfalls sounded more like adults' than overzealous kids'.

Three men around Cameron's age came into view and gave Faith interested looks, then went inside the changing room.

"Do you want to leave?" Cameron asked, figuring she'd want to, as he certainly did.

She patted him on the leg and leaned over to speak in his ear, her whisper-soft voice rousing him even more, which made him wish the others would just vanish in a puff of mist. "I hate to be run off, Cameron. The jets feel so good on my back." She snuggled closer and kept her hand on his thigh.

Hell, now he was really ready to take her back to the cabin and try out his new sleeping bag for two with her. "Are you sure?" He ran his hand over her arm and kissed her cheek, hoping to coax her away so they could have more privacy.

She gave him an interested smile. Yeah, she was game, but she still wasn't leaving the warmth of the hot tub. Couldn't blame her there. The heat and pulsing jets were only part of the draw though. The sexy, nearly naked body snuggled up beside him—soft and malleable and hot and wet—that was what inspired him to stay a while longer.

The raggedy-looking guy with frizzy red hair and a shaggy beard exited the building and gave Faith a wink, his green eyes challenging her to join him—later. Barefooted, the other men hurried out of the shower house and across the heater-warmed deck to reach the tub pronto.

Cameron wrapped his arm around Faith's shoulders and gave her a squeeze, not caring if he was showing his possessiveness. Besides, he was keeping Faith warm in case she needed him to. She responded by leaning her head on his shoulder and caressing his thigh, way too erotic for all the company they had, although with all the millions of bubbles rolling to the surface of the water, no one could see a thing. Speculation was another story, and he imagined everyone was speculating away. "He wasn't no Bigfoot," the redhead said to his companions as he climbed into the sauna and sat next to Mary.

The old lady laughed. "Bigfoot, Chris? When I was a girl, three of my friends and me saw him. Or might've been a her. Twelve foot tall he was. Hairy, slouched over like a bent-shaped man, only naked and bigger. He glimpsed us in the woods, sniffed the air, then hurried into the shelter of the trees and disappeared. I wanted to follow him. See where he went. But the other kids were too chicken."

"You saw him around here?" Faith asked, her body stiffening with interest, surprising the hell out of Cameron.

He really didn't think she'd be interested in hearing about fairy tales, since she was a forensic scientist, dealing in scientific fact.

"North of here. Toward Baxter Park," Mary said, nodding vigorously as if she'd gotten a live one to listen to her tall tale.

The black-haired man of the three shook his head and looked over at Faith. There was something about the way he observed her, not as if he was interested in her sexually but something else. Almost as if he were a cop, watching for her reaction. "Not Bigfoot this time," the guy said. "It's one of those others, and we need to take care of business."

"One of what others?" Faith asked, sounding a little too interested.

Don't encourage them, Cameron wanted to say. Hell, next they'd be talking about little green men and being poked and probed on a spaceship from a galaxy far, far away.

Chris smiled at her, then looked at his friends, but the expressions on their faces said that this was still a secret and they weren't about to share their findings with a couple of strangers.

Cameron was just as glad. But Faith persisted. "What was it you saw?"

Chris cleared his throat and gave her a half smile. "Maybe we can talk about it in private sometime."

"Ah, Chris, can't you see these two are together?" Mary teased.

"Her loss," he said, grinning at Faith.

Cameron wanted to wipe the grin off Chris's face, and although he wanted to take Faith out of here pronto, he couldn't. It had to be her call, or he'd look like a possessive, overbearing lout.

Chris turned to the black-haired guy, who was patting the bubbles on the surface of the water, his nearly ebony gaze still on Faith. "Should we tell her, Matt?"

Matt shook his head. "Privately, if she wants, just like you said." His voice was cold and calculating, and Cameron didn't like it one bit.

Faith stared Matt down and then turned her head and

looked up at Cameron with the most adoring expression. He thought it was faked for their audience's benefit, but he was willing to believe. "Ready to call it a night, honey?" she asked, her tone seductively enticing.

Well past ready, but his heated gaze wasn't in the least bit false.

"It's about that time. Wait, and I'll get your towel." What he wanted to do was kick the men's asses out of here while Faith got out, and he would have, too, if she'd agreed.

He climbed out of the hot tub, grabbed her floral towel, and held it down close to the water so she could leave without showing off her wet bra and panties. No one said a word, and he suspected the guys were watching her in rabid fascination, but he was too busy trying to shield her from them to see. With the towel wrapped around her, Faith headed into the women's shower room, and he entered the men's room.

Once he was dressed, he left the changing room, out of view of the hot tub to wait for her near the path they would take to her cabin, when he saw three feral-looking white wolves in the trees near the main lodge, the blowing snow almost disguising them. Lila stepped out of the forest to join them, her red lips turned up in a half smile. "Kintail told me to bring you to our hunting camp. You can see Owen and David there."

Cameron wanted to speak to them. But not like this. Not off in the wilderness somewhere that he couldn't communicate with authorities if need be. Not without some kind of backup.

"I'll take your suggestion under consideration. In the meantime, I've told the police about my missing friends."

Her lips curved up even more. "Good for you. I imagine they were readying the search parties right away."

The woman had him there.

She snorted. "Didn't think so. See you around, Cameron."

She turned and took a few steps in the direction of the snow-cloaked spruces, still dressed all in white, and he swore she evaporated into the snow-filled wonderland. Her wolves eyed him longer; then one by one, they whipped around and vanished too.

"Cameron!" Faith hollered from around the back side of the shower and hot tub building, sounding distressed and in need of his help.

In full rescue mode, the adrenaline pumping pell-mell through his blood, Cameron dashed around the building to save her.

CHAPTER 5

Faith was pointing at the snowmobiles parked behind the shower and hot tub building, the one snowmobile's back end dented. But that was not what got Cameron's full attention. The wolf lunging in their direction, materializing out of the snow without any warning, made his heart nearly stop. He wasn't sure which one of them the wolf was aiming for, but he didn't have time to do anything but block Faith's body with his own and throw his arm up to protect his throat. She screamed. The wolf bit through his jacket and into his arm.

"Your gun!" she shouted.

"In the cabin." He never thought he'd need it at the hot tub.

He tried to shake loose of the wolf as if it were a friendly old dog with a big bone, playing tug-of-war, growling, eyes narrowed, hair on the back of its neck standing on end, but just in good-natured fun. But Cameron's arm was the bone, and it hurt like hell as the pain radiated up and down through every nerve ending. Plus, he felt the blood seeping from the wound, the tear in his parka letting in the chilled air.

Suddenly, Faith swung a snow shovel, striking the beast in the hip. He yelped, released his hold on Cameron, and jumped back from Faith. For a second, his eyes stared at hers as if he was reading her inner soul and every thought she had.

She stomped at him and swung the shovel in an effort

to hit him again, and this time, Cameron swore the wolf smiled. Then the beast bent down, whipped around, and melted into the snowy woods before she struck him again.

Faith dropped the shovel and grabbed Cameron's good arm. "We've got to get you some help."

The pain in Cameron's arm throbbed even harder now. "You mean, ask for it from those clowns in the hot tub? When Charles Simmons returns, we can get him to send for help. Just take me back to your place for now."

She didn't listen to him and instead helped him to the hot tub. Everyone had left. She opened the door to the changing room, letting some of the heat out. The place was empty. "No one here," she said.

"I guess when you left, the party was over."

"Oh, Cameron, your face is so pale. I'll get you to my place, but I don't have any first aid kit, and I didn't see any in the cabin. What about you?"

"Bandages for blisters, but nothing for wolf-size bites."

"Then we'll have to check out the main lodge."

He was going to object, but Faith had a mind of her own and helped him to the main lodge porch, then up to the door. She tried the handle. *Locked.*

He could have told her it would be. Otherwise, people like him might just wander in and make themselves at home.

"Sit here for a second, Cameron. I'll see if any of the windows are unlocked." She helped him to one of the knotty-pine rockers, put her ski cap on his head—which reminded him he should have brought his own—then started tugging on windows.

Watching for any sign of the wolf that attacked him, Cameron let out his frosty breath, cradled his injured arm against his body for warmth, and tried to ignore the streaks of sharp pains like needles jabbing into the muscle.

Faith tried to open the rest of the windows on this side of the lodge.

When she began to venture around the back side, Cameron said, "No, Faith. I don't want you out of my sight."

She frowned at him. "It'll only take me a minute. If I can find an unlocked window, they might have antibiotics and better bandages inside. I have to try."

"No, it's not worth it. If the wolf's still lurking out there... It's just not worth it to me. Come on. Take me back to your cabin so we can get warmed up." His blood had soaked his shirtsleeve and sweater, chilling him even further. Now, due to the shredded parka sleeve, everything that had been wet was coated in ice. Shivering uncontrollably, he didn't think he could get any colder.

Still frowning, Faith helped him down the steps and back to the cabin. "I can use my towel, maybe, to stop the bleeding. How bad does it feel?"

"Not too bad," he lied, afraid she might still try to go after the windows on the other side of the lodge once he was settled in her cabin. "With as many layers of clothes as I'm wearing, he didn't hurt me too much."

"A German shepherd can crush a bone. I imagine a wolf could do even more damage. Are you sure you're not too bad?"

"I *was* feeling better."

She chuckled a little hysterically.

"Sorry. I guess I shouldn't have told you that."

As soon as they reached the cabin through the path to the woods, she assisted him inside and helped him to one of the dining room chairs, then locked the door. After removing his coat, she pulled off his sweater and stared at the blood and rip in his shirt.

"Not too bad," he said. "It's not even bleeding any longer."

A flitter of concern slipped across Faith's face, but she quickly removed his shirt and wrapped the towel around the wound without saying a word.

"Tetanus shot up to date," he said. But he knew that probably wasn't what was worrying her. Rabies. What if the animal had rabies, and that was why it had attacked?

"We have to go back to town tomorrow if Charles doesn't return to the lodge by then."

He agreed with a nod. Now that their snowmobiles were back, he figured that was the best move, if the weather had cleared up by then.

"I wonder why the men stole the machines, then brought them back," Faith said as if she was trying to get his mind off his injury. "It's really bizarre."

"I don't know. What made you go around that way when the way I went was closer to your cabin?"

"I was drying the edges of my wet hair when I looked out the window and saw the snowmobiles. I didn't really think they were ours. How weird would that be? But I had to check it out. Do you think it might have been somebody joyriding who doesn't have a snowmobile here at the camp?"

"Who first threatened you with a gun?"

"Well, then, maybe somebody stole them from these guys and brought them back." Faith helped Cameron into bed, pulled off his boots and socks, and covered him with his sleeping bag.

"Highly unlikely," he said.

"You're a former cop. What do you think?"

He gritted his teeth against the pain in his arm, but when Faith caught his action and glanced out the window, he started talking to distract her from leaving him to seek help. "It's hard to say why anyone would do what they do. I rode around with some petty criminals once while I was undercover. Their reasoning for not stealing a young woman's purse? She had a kid. Not that morality had anything to do with it. They figured the kid would scream and attract too much attention. Another scenario? A woman was carrying a big purse. Which to them meant she had lots of money."

"You're kidding! A woman with a big purse might not have a bit of money, just lots of useless junk."

"Right. So you see, it's hard to predict what goes on in the criminal mind." He patted his sleeping bag on the mattress. "Are you going to join me?"

She rubbed her arms, her brows furrowed. "I'll add some more wood to the fire."

"Don't go outside."

"Enough wood is stacked in a basket by the stove. Just sleep, Cameron. I'll get you help as soon as I can."

"Don't leave the cabin, Faith," Cameron reiterated in his police officer's voice, obey or else. No way did he want her to risk going outside alone to get help for him. But they needed to get word to the other guests too. Later though. He figured no one would run around much in this weather, and he wasn't in any shape to go anywhere, nor did he want Faith out in it by herself.

Faith's cold hand touched his forehead. She gave him a worried smile. "No fever."

"No, I'll be fine. I just need some rest." Tired beyond belief, he closed his eyes, a dull pain throbbing from the wound and radiating down to his fingertips, the thought of cuddling with her still lingering in his thoughts despite the pain.

She moved away from the bed, added firewood to the stove, and paced across the wooden floor a bit, her footfalls muffled when she walked on the braided rugs. He wished she'd join him in bed, still worried she might leave, but then he drifted off into the world of snow and wolves. The wind howled and then the sound shifted, changed, morphed into the howl of a wolf. One, the alpha male, deep and low and long. Then another joined in, and more until a whole chorus of wolves sang their lonely song. One part of him longed to join them, but part of his conscious mind warned him the consequences could be deadly.

<hr />

"Hmm," Lila said, lounging before a roaring fire in the great room of Kintail's lodge, her bare foot rocking up and down off the sofa, her manner an attempt at seductive, and Kintail wished she really was up to seducing him.

The woman was a master manipulator when she wanted her way, or just plain sarcastic and antagonistic when things weren't going her way. He noted the subtle change in her demeanor since he'd had the run-in with Cameron earlier today.

He knew sarcasm was her ploy this evening before she even spoke further. "So you bit Cameron but you didn't kill him. And his feisty girlfriend struck you with a snow shovel."

Situated at the massive oak dining room table that overlooked the sitting area in the great room, Kintail lifted another spoonful of hot and spicy chili to his lips. Feisty, that was the way to describe the woman named Faith O'Malley. But seeing her in her low-cut bra and bikini panties before she entered the hot tub gave way to more erotic fantasies. He hadn't liked the way Cameron was kissing her in the tub, and Kintail had the notion of biting her instead of Cameron—get it over with, change her, and see what transpired—but she had to call out to Cameron about the snowmobiles. Kintail hadn't predicted the guy would race around the building as if the world was on fire and get in Kintail's way.

Served him right to get bitten first. Still, Kintail couldn't quit thinking about the woman. She might be trouble, but she was damned intriguing. Here she'd just met Cameron, but instead of screaming for help after Kintail had bitten him, she'd slugged Kintail in the hip with a shovel to save the guy.

Kintail hadn't expected that. The bruise would heal up soon, so no big deal. But he liked her character—protective, loyal in the face of danger, striking in the flesh. An alpha female.

He finished the bowl of chili and motioned to Trevor to get him some more.

"Well?" Lila snarled.

He knew she wanted him to kill the woman. Competition. Good competition too. Faith was the first woman he thought might have enough gumption to fight Lila and win. Not that he wanted Lila hurt, but he needed a mate, damn it. And Lila wasn't cooperating one iota.

Trevor set a fresh bowl of chili before him, his gaze shifting to Lila.

"She's intriguing," Kintail said, knowing his words would antagonize Lila. They had sort of a love-hate relationship, and he supposed someday he'd have to take her for his mate. Unless he could find someone else he truly cared for, if he couldn't break the impenetrable barrier Lila had erected around her heart. Miss O'Malley was growing more interesting all the time, even though he'd never considered changing a human to suit his purpose. Those born as *lupus garous* already knew the role they had to play in their society. Much easier to deal with. Normally.

"Intriguing, my ass. She's real trouble. Why did you just bite Cameron and then let him go? I saw the way you looked at that woman and didn't attack her when you easily could have. No damned shovel would have stopped you. Particularly when some weak human woman was wielding it. One lunge and she would have dropped the shovel and fallen flat on her backside. Then we could have been done with her."

Even though Lila sounded tough, he noted a hint of insecurity in her voice, which couldn't help but trigger his interest in her again. He liked her better when she let her vulnerability slip and suspected she could be right for him if she ever let go of her past hurt.

He thought again about the way Faith had clobbered him with that shovel, and it wasn't in the least bit done meekly. She'd let the whole force of her slight body go with the flow. Of course if he'd seen it coming, he would have nimbly dodged the blow, and at most the shovel would have only glanced off him. Next time, he'd be more prepared for the woman's tactics so the outcome would be much more agreeable.

"When have I killed a man for the sake of killing him?" Kintail asked, fingering a slice of buttered French bread. "Even with the intent of keeping our people's secret safe?" He took a bite of the crunchy bread, then scooped up another spoonful of chili.

"I'm sure you used to."

"A long time ago. Before there were that many people. When we had to. Not now. What do you think would happen if someone found his body and thought one of our wolves had killed him? With DNA testing of hairs and saliva left at the crime scene, they could pin it on an Arctic wolf. Who else has Arctic wolves in the region but us? Is that what you want?"

Lila rolled her eyes. "I just wondered if you'd decided to let Cameron join our little merry gang of wolves."

An alpha male? Not on Kintail's life. But he'd draw Cameron into the wilderness where human traffic rarely went, somewhere no one would ever discover his body, and fight him wolf to wolf. Much more sport that way.

The wolves' howls faded into the misty snow, and the moan of the wind returned. Cameron jerked awake, feeling strangely unsettled. Faith was curled up against his chest, her breathing light in sleep, her body soft and huggable. He held her with his good arm, reached over with his bad, and stroked her golden hair. But she was sound asleep, and he didn't want to wake her. His wounded arm didn't even give him a pinch of pain now. Maybe it hadn't been as bad as he thought.

What he couldn't comprehend was the restlessness stirring deep inside him. He'd never felt that way before. On cases he was close to solving, he might not be able to sleep, his mind working overtime in solving the puzzle. This was something more primal, more physical. He was torn between staying with Faith and enjoying her comforting heat, the sound of her steady heartbeat, and her subtle fragrance—and squelching the craving to ditch his clothes no matter how cold it was and run through the snow.

Trying not to disturb Faith, Cameron slipped out from under her, making sure his sleeping bag still covered her, and then he left the bed. He was surprised to experience no dizziness or fever from the wolf's bite. He stretched out his arm, but no matter how he moved it, the ache was completely gone.

After pulling the towel off his arm, he examined where the wolf had bitten him. Except for faded bite marks, dried blood, and light bruising, he was nearly as good as new, although it had seemed so much worse when he was first bitten.

He went to the door and opened it, stared out at the moonlight reflecting off the snow, the clouds having moved away, the storm spent and gone, leaving mountains of snow in its wake. It looked as though the day was already upon them instead of the dead of night. Mystical, magical, even romantic, if Faith had been awake and here to share it with him.

But the moon compelled him to do what no sane man would ever have done. He couldn't repress the urge he had to... Well, he wasn't sure what he wanted to do. Leave. Maybe. But it wasn't exactly that either. Despite not being able to see the actual moon, he could feel its presence. Like the moon's gravitational pull on the tides, he felt an odd connection. A seduction, a caress of wills, his against the moon's. *Come to me, and I'll make your dreams come true. Fight me and you'll suffer.*

He was going mad.

Without another second's hesitation, he stripped out of his jeans and boxers, and stood watching the tree limbs stirring in the breeze. The bitter cold surrounding him shook him to the marrow of his bones, but then dissipated when a strange warmth quickly worked its way through every fiber of his being, his muscles twisting, bones reshaping, all painless, effortless, exhilarating.

He stood on four pads, a thick, double white coat covering his skin, making him impervious to the cold. He stared at his large front paws, black wicked-looking claws touching the wooden floor. He sniffed at his fur, which smelled of spicy aftershave.

The moon again called to him, the branches of the trees waving at him, beckoning him to join them. Without another thought, he lowered his forequarters, keeping his hindquarters straight and did a slight bow, then raced out the door, bounding over the piles of snow left by the storm, and took off through the woods.

Cameron raced through the forest, brushing against the snow-covered branches of towering spruces, shaking loose torrents of snowfall. The snow falling down on him didn't touch his skin though. A thick coat of fur kept the snow from melting, and he felt toasty warm. He expected the snow and cold to chill his "bare" feet, but it didn't bother his paws, maybe, he thought, because of the fur between the pads.

He ran on the tips of his toes, which seemed weird, but it lengthened his stride, and he covered more ground that way. Whenever he began to slip on an icy patch, he instinctively spread out his pads, increasing the surface area that he stepped on, the additional friction preventing him from taking a spill.

A fresh coat of snow, looking to have been a foot or more, covered everything, but he found that he didn't sink into the fluffy white stuff as he would if he was running as a human. The freedom this gave was exhilarating as he raced through the trees, only stopping momentarily to smell a whiff of a rabbit or bird and fresh clean air.

When he came across a fallen tree angled toward the sky, propped against another tree, he would have had to climb slowly over it in his clunky human form, but instead, he leaped, his feet sprawled, gripping the trunk with ease, propelling him over the top. And then he was down again, running on his tippy toes.

He'd run for miles, although it hadn't seemed like any time at all, when he heard the sound of voices. Curious by nature but even more so now, Cameron headed toward them.

"Hell, she was interested," a male voice said, and instantly Cameron recognized it as the guy who'd joined them in the hot tub. Chris, the redhead with the unruly hair.

"Interested in Bigfoot. Sure. But she might not be interested in what we've found. And besides, the fewer who know what we're doing, the better," said Matt, the guy with the cold, calculating voice.

Then a woman spoke up. Mary, it sounded like. "Chris doesn't *just* want her to be on the team. He's looking for something a little hotter than that, Matt, I suspect."

"Her father was writing a research paper about Bigfoot. When we got separated, I swear he saw something like we have since then. Hell, I'm sure she already knows all about them. That's why she questioned us more about what we knew. She wanted in." Chris sounded annoyed with his companions, ready to take them on.

"Says you," Matt countered. "We can't trust just anyone, especially when it's your dick talking for you."

Cameron drew closer to the mammoth-size tent in the small clearing. A stovepipe vented smoke out the top of the tent, while lanterns inside shone through the orange tent fabric, silhouetting four figures sitting inside. Were they talking about Faith? About her father? According to the police, her father was conducting a sociology study. About Bigfoot? Cameron would never have guessed. Was that why Faith hadn't wanted to talk about it? But if he could discuss it with these men, maybe he could find out what they knew. Then, perhaps Faith would have some of the answers she was seeking. Then again, maybe they were talking about someone else, not Faith at all.

He moved in even closer, wanting to clear his throat to warn them he was here before he intruded or startled them too much. But all that came out was an alien huffing sound.

"What the hell was that?" Chris said as all of them began to stand.

"I've got my gun," Matt said.

That was all it took. Cameron was out of there.

CHAPTER 6

HAVING BEEN SHOT ONCE IN THE LINE OF DUTY WHEN he was on the police force, Cameron didn't need to be reminded how much that hurt, nor did he want to be injured way out here in the middle of nowhere if Matt or his buddies decided to shoot him.

Cameron whipped around and headed away from the tent the way he had come, following his trail back through the woods, surprised to find his footpads had left a scent for him to track.

Chris exclaimed, "Shit, it was one of them! One of the wolves. Look at all the damned tracks! Break up camp before they come back for us. Hurry!"

The panicked group hurried to strike camp, but Cameron kept running, following his tracks, keeping his paws in his original footsteps so that he could make better time. The tracks looked huge in the snow, as if his paws were much larger than they were. Which probably contributed to tales of wolves that existed as gigantic beasts.

He raced on and on, realizing he'd traveled a distance much greater than he'd first suspected, yet he felt free and wild, not tired and cold as he might have imagined.

After a good long while, he smelled smoke from a woodburning stove and knew he was getting closer to the cabin resort when he nearly plowed into a wolf. He stopped on the proverbial dime and stared at the wolf, russet in color, his brown eyes shining in the dark, his expression surprised more than anything. As much as Cameron himself was surprised.

He expected a confrontation, but the red wolf just studied him with interest, sniffed the air, and remained standing in place, not moving an inch in any direction, his ears alert, twitching back and forth. His posture seemed relaxed, though, unlike Cameron's. His was stiff, apprehensive, unsure of what would happen next.

He sensed the wolf was an alpha, holding his tail straight out behind him, not tucked, his head held high, not bowed. Cameron was standing in the same manner, waiting to see what the other wolf would do first. He couldn't get over the fact a red wolf would be in the area. Gray maybe, living somewhere in the wilderness. The white wolves, Kintail's, absolutely. But not a red wolf that Cameron thought was extinct in most areas.

Then the sound of snowmobiles zooming off through the woods from miles away caught their attention. Chris and his buddies, Cameron suspected. He twisted his head around to look in that direction. When the snowmobiles headed farther away and weren't driving in his direction, he turned back to observe the red wolf, but he was gone, vanished, like a flake of snow against a snowbank.

Cameron looked around, didn't see any sign of the wolf, sampled the air but couldn't get a whiff of him the way the breeze was blowing. He thought about Faith, about the bed, about snuggling, and felt the adrenaline rush begin to drain off as he loped toward the cabin resort.

When he reached her cabin, he stared at the wide-open door. For an instant, he worried that someone had broken in. Then he wondered if he was the one who had left the door open. He headed inside and nudged it closed with his nose and paws. Then he jumped on the bed and joined Faith, although he didn't attempt to crawl into the sleeping bag with her. Too much trouble and he was plenty warm enough.

Closing his eyes, the last vague thought he had was he'd experienced one hell of a dream.

Faith snuggled closer to him and sighed. The dreams and Faith's touch finally faded away, but before long, Cameron bolted upright in bed and stared at the cabin, the hour still early, his whole psyche turned upside down. Thankfully, Faith's face was cloaked in blissful sleep, and he hadn't awakened her. He swept his hand down her hair, every ounce of his physical being craving her, and yet, now, for some unfathomable reason, another part of him warned she was dangerous and to avoid entanglements with her at all costs.

So why the hell was he wanting to prove she wasn't in the least bit dangerous?

He climbed out of bed and found he didn't have a stitch of clothes on, when he thought he was wearing at least his boxers and jeans when he fell asleep last night. He vaguely remembered Faith carefully removing his parka, shirt, boots, and socks like an angel to his rescue. The braided rugs were wet, too, and he wondered when that had happened. Maybe Faith had spilled water before she retired to bed.

He tugged on a pair of jeans but didn't bother to secure his leather belt or the top button and zipped them only far enough to keep them on his hips as if he might want to shed the pants any moment, so why fasten them all the way? He walked over to the window and stared out at the bleak white landscape, wondering why he was feeling so unsettled. He wasn't feverish, yet he didn't feel right. But he couldn't pinpoint what was wrong. Cabin fever maybe? Too bad the most vivid, unreal dream he'd ever experienced hadn't resolved the bizarre feelings snowing him over. Yet he kept wondering, what if the dream was true? That he'd really heard the guys in the hot tub outside the cabin last night and incorporated their ramblings into his dreams?

He let out his breath. Nah. Just a case of recalling situations he'd been in earlier in the day or past several days and mixing them up in a dream. Although he couldn't account for why he'd envision a red wolf. Then he recalled watching a program about the ones reintroduced into the wilds of North Carolina a week ago, and seeing *Wolf* with Jack Nicholson the night before last, and then *The Howl of the Wolf* after that. And then? Cameron dreamed he was a wolf?

He shook his head. No way had he turned into a white wolf during the night. Being attacked by the one and seeing them with Lila were the reasons for the surreal dream.

Man, he'd had his fill of wolves for a lifetime.

"Are you feeling all right?" Faith asked from bed, her voice silky with sleep.

He didn't look at her. Didn't want to. He hated feeling out of control, out of sorts.

"Much better." Which was the truth, to an extent. His arm did feel better, but his mind was in turmoil.

"What's wrong?" Her voice warned him she understood him as well as he knew himself.

"Nothing. We're snowed in." He pulled the door open, let in the cold air, some part of him wanting to freeze the unwarranted emotions he was feeling now out of existence.

The snow blocked the entryway halfway, except where something had run through it. He stared at the sight, trying to figure out what would have made the impression, and noticed how wet the braided rug was next to the door. Hell, Faith must have left the cabin sometime during the night despite him telling her not to.

He attempted to see beyond the piled-up snow, but it was stacked too high to observe what had happened clearly.

The box springs squeaked, and then Faith's footsteps padded across the floor. Cameron turned to look at her and couldn't help raising his brows. She was wearing a footed one-piece sleeper contraption covered in white bunnies and pink flowers on a lilac background. Her blond hair appeared tangled from a night of restless sleep or a lover's tryst. She looked soft and huggable in the chilly room.

Frowning, she hurried toward him. "Are you sure you're all right?"

His gaze shifted to her bunny outfit and the long, lilac zipper that reached from the neckline all the way to the pubic bone. His thoughts instantly switched from running in the wild to pulling that zipper down as far as it would go. "Plenty of food and firewood. We'll stay warm enough."

The craving to be with her overriding the urge to leave, he shut the door and locked it.

She reached out and touched his hand. "What about your wound? We need to get it checked out."

"Feels good as new." His voice had already taken on a husky tone, and he sifted his fingers through her silky hair, wanting to feel every inch of her, to breathe in her scent, to taste her. Already, he seemed to sense more—her own interest in him—but it wasn't from the expression on her face. She looked worried, not sexually ready. It was her scent that indicated she was interested. A subtle change in the way she smelled was all it took to make him want her even more. As if the scent was a trigger of acceptance and willingness.

Not to be thwarted in her concern for him, she said, "It's still really dark in here. How can you see anything?" She turned on a gas lamp, then examined his exposed skin, her lips parting slightly, looking damned kissable.

As much as he hated to admit weakness, he explained what had been bothering him. "I felt I needed to get out of here."

"Maybe it's cabin fever." Her eyes took in his naked torso, shifting downward to his pants, only partially zipped. Her gaze shot back up to his, but he didn't think she was shocked as much as intrigued. She touched his shoulder in a reassuring way, her fingertips leaving a streak of heat behind, then ran her hand down his arm until she reached his fingers and took hold. "I've been snowed in for a few days, but it doesn't bother me. Maybe we can play games or something."

"Or something." Despite his brain warning him to keep his distance, he wanted to kiss her and much more. He settled his hands on her shoulders, his thumbs caressing them in little circles, his gaze focused on that sensuous mouth of hers, curved up slightly.

Every nerve ending was attuned to the way she felt, the soft, fuzzy fabric of her pajamas, the curve of her shoulders, the swell of her breasts rising and falling with every breath, even her nipples protruding, begging to be fondled, and the way she relaxed under his touch as if she savored his strokes as much as he did stroking her. She tucked her hair behind her ear, the motion surprisingly sensual. Nibbling her creamy earlobe came to mind. His libido ratcheted up another notch.

"I promised I'd keep you in bed longer this morning," he said, his voice deep and raspy as he swept his hands down her arms to her fingers. He lifted one of her hands to his lips and kissed the top of her hand, and then with the same kind of appreciation, the other, her skin delicate like peach velvet.

She smiled coyly, her green eyes narrowed a bit. "Are you sure you're all right?" Her voice was husky with need, too, and he smiled with the knowledge.

"Only one thing will make me feel better." He leaned down and wrapped his arms around her back, pulling her closer, his body barely touching hers, yet every inch that did sizzled with heat. He kissed her lips, gently at first.

But gentle wasn't what she seemed to have in mind as she slipped her arms around his waist, hugged him even closer, molding her sensuous curves against him, and licked her lips, making them glisten in the low lantern light. Her eyes looked deeply into his, challenging him to play with her. He would have dived right in, but he was too intrigued and let her have her way.

In the beginning.

She kissed his lower lip with just enough pressure to stir him up. He intended to do his part, but she kissed his upper lip, her eyes focused on his mouth. He savored the heat and fullness of her sweet mouth, the way she teased him with her light kisses. She opened her mouth and tongued his lips, exciting his senses even more, the scent of her arousal filling him with rampant desire. But when she withdrew her tongue, her lips still parted, offering him a deeper connection, he took the initiative, licking her velvety mouth and taking advantage of her offer. His tongue slipped into her mouth, tasted her, memorized the hot wetness, the softness of her tongue and lips and mouth.

She slipped her fingers underneath his waistband, her nails skimming his naked skin, dipping toward his erection. His skin was on fire, his senses staggered, completely scattering what he had in mind to do next. Nothing else intruded on his thoughts—the cold room, the wet braided rug beneath his bare feet, the aroma of the salmon cooked the afternoon before still lingering in the air. All vanished as he braced for what she would do next, her touch so pleasurable he was momentarily paralyzed into inaction.

Her long nails slid deeper, and she smiled when she discovered he didn't have anything on underneath the jeans. She pulled her hands free from his pants, but before he could again take the initiative, she traced his erection hard beneath the soft denim, making it jump with her touch, the tip now exposed from the zipper riding so low and from her working him up. Despite trying to show restraint, he shuddered with her touch. He'd never had a woman work to pleasure him, and the experience was astonishing.

With one hand, she dragged the zipper the rest of the way down, her fingers stroking his heavy arousal while her other hand slid down the back of his jeans and cupped his ass. Then she pulled his waistband down and exposed him even further, the tip of his penis wet, ready to penetrate her.

Wanting to get her in bed and underneath him, he was slipping his hands down her back, intending to lift the vixen up and wrap her legs around him to carry her to the mattress, when his fingers discovered an intriguing secret. A flap at the back of her bunny britches. Quickly feeling around to determine a way in, he slipped his fingers inside, touching the curve of her naked derriere, and felt her tremble. He pulled his hands free, found the snaps, and with several pops, exposed her sweet, little ass. She smiled and slid her hands down his spine until she reached his waistband and slipped her fingers underneath his jeans, cupping his bare buttocks and squeezing.

Slow and easy, work her up the way she needed, he figured, but she was making it awfully hard on him. And she knew it, the way she rubbed against his arousal, the soft flannel of her nightwear teasing him. He was hard with need, and he wasn't going to last with the slow approach at seduction. He slid his hands over her ass, lower still until he found her drenched curls between her legs. She shifted her feet so he could get better access and he obliged, stroked her deep, bringing forth a moan of uninhibited desire from her. Then he kissed her open mouth with his, speared her with his tongue, and pressed her harder against his erection, wanting to be inside her now.

She groaned and he capitulated. Lifting her off the floor, he carried her to the bed, his hands still cupping her exposed ass, her feet wrapped around his waist. He soon had the bunny gear off and her skin bared to him, peachy silky delight, her breasts perky and full, the nipples pebbled, her legs spread apart, offering him entrance.

He reached into his jeans pocket and pulled out a rubber. "Let me," she murmured, her eyes hot and sassy.

He jerked off his jeans and crouched over her, his engorged penis reaching out to her as he leaned forward. She slid the rubber up his shaft, her hands moving it with a firm stroke. He sucked in a breath, barely able to do anything but concentrate on every touch to the nerves so close to the surface. When she was done, he threaded his fingers through her hair, then shifted his hands to her breasts, his thumbs stroking her nipples, pulling and pinching. She moaned in response, arching her pelvis toward him. Her eyes remained fastened on his cock as if she was ready to devour him. Just her expression of intrigue and the way her hands worked miracles on his arousal nearly sent him over the edge.

Unable to wait a second longer, he nudged the thick head into her opening. Slowly, he penetrated her tight sheath, allowing her to expand to his size, and pressed deeper as she wrapped her legs around him.

"Are you okay?" she whispered as if she suddenly remembered the injury to his arm, pausing as she touched the skin below the bruising.

He groaned in response, eliciting a naughty smile from her lips. For the moment, he felt as if he'd never been bitten, nothing was hemming him in, the world was right again.

He tilted off her a bit so he could reach her most erotic spot, loved the way she tightened her hold on his waist as he stroked her into ecstasy, her pink feminine lips wet with need. She arched into his hand, begging for more, faster, slower, harder. And then she let out a shudder, a satisfied sigh, her face and nipples flushed, her body trembling, gripping his erection with the most erotic sensation as he renewed his thrusts.

Deeper, faster, he found she was the maker of heady dreams, the one he'd been needing to sate his sexual desires since he'd had any interest in the opposite sex. But she'd aroused something more primal, something darker, something that he couldn't identify. He wanted her, craved having her for something longer-term. Crazy. The blood from his brain had slipped into his cock, and that was what was making him feel so light-headed, so powerless under her spell.

Her fingers dug into his butt, and he swore she came again. And that did it. With her hands squeezing his flesh, her inner muscles wringing his erection, he came with a final thrust. Spent, satiated, the most content he'd been in forever, he collapsed on her possessively, spreading his legs over hers, pinning her to the mattress, his erection still inside her. *His.*

"Hmm." She skimmed her nails down his back in tantalizing caresses designed to stir him up again, like a sexy siren bent on seducing him.

She didn't need to make the effort. She'd caught his attention the minute she'd walked in on him when he was naked, towel-drying his wet hair in his hotel room. He'd wanted her then, the offer of dinner only the beginning.

He chuckled and kissed her lips, tonguing her tongue, already wanting more. "If you'd stayed last night, I wouldn't have seen your erotic bed wear."

She laughed and pulled at his earlobe with a gentle tug. "I'll have you know I only wear that on snowy excursions when I'm going to be alone. Or at least think I'm going to be alone. It was a gift from a girlfriend for when…" She paused and a flicker of darkness fluttered across her face. But she didn't say anything further.

Not wanting to ruin the mood although he wanted to know what she was going to say, he kissed her cheek and rolled over, pulling her with him to cuddle against his chest, her legs spread provocatively over his, his hand stroking down her back to the cleft in her sweet little derriere. "Absolutely works for me." In fact, anything she wore—or didn't wear—suited him fine. "I should start a nice hot fire."

The place was much too cold, and although he was still enjoying the heat of her body, he felt her tremble from the chill in the air, and chill bumps were rising on her arm. He was ready to warm up the place and take another long winter's nap with Faith since he'd had such a fitful sleep last night and having sex with her had finally settled his unfathomable desire to run off into the woods.

But she was already pulling away. He should have expected it, because she'd said she was a morning person, but he wasn't, and he wanted to enjoy her in bed a good deal longer.

She glanced at her watch. "I was thinking about running back to the trailhead and reporting Lila's wolf attack and that someone had stolen our snowmobiles. And I can take you in to see a doctor too."

"Since whoever it was already returned the snowmobiles, I doubt the police would care. My arm is fine now." He held her tight, still wanting to keep her in bed, to possess her, to prevent her from leaving. "Why don't you stay here until I get the place warmed up at least?"

That was when the sound of dogs barking in the distance caught his attention.

Instantly, a new primitive need ran amok through his system. The need to dominate the pack.

CHAPTER 7

CAMERON ACTED AS THOUGH HE WANTED TO KEEP
Faith in bed forever, which was a heady feeling she had to
quash before she got used to the idea of having him around.
Already the thought of returning alone to her home in
Portland seemed cold and unappealing, when normally,
being alone suited her fine, once Hilson took off. But God,
she'd never had a man who could send her to the moon
and back like Cameron had done. And despite her usual
need to get up and get to work early in the morning, before
the dogs had gotten Cameron's attention, she probably
would have snuggled with him longer. More, if he'd wanted
more. Which she didn't doubt for a second he would have
wanted.

She sighed. Even though nothing would come of a fling
with Cameron, maybe there was hope she could eventually
start over again with someone new.

As soon as Cameron heard the dogs barking, his whole
demeanor changed. At once, he acted much more interested in where the barking was coming from—probably his
PI instincts. Was it Charles Simmons and his sled dog team?
She imagined it had to be.

The sound of snowmobiles drawing closer filled the air
next. Before Faith could get free of Cameron and the bed,
the snowmobiles parked outside her cabin. A few seconds
later, someone was pounding on her door, giving her a start.

"Maybe it's Charles bringing our ice for the icebox and

some more containers of water," she teased, not believing it, as early in the morning as it was, but if the dogs they'd heard barking belonged to Charles Simmons and he'd returned home, he might be dropping by to complain if he'd discovered Cameron had fired up the hot tub without his permission.

"It's about time we got some service around here," Cameron said with a wink, although he didn't sound like he believed it either as he climbed out of bed and jerked on his jeans.

Faith hurried to get dressed. She quickly ran a brush through her hair as Cameron finished buttoning his shirt and looked over at her. "Ready?"

She nodded.

As soon as Cameron opened the door, she saw two policemen standing beyond their snowed-in entryway— Adams and Whitson. The same ones who had spoken to them in Millinocket when they'd been at Kintail's office and found the dead body. Faith closed her gaping mouth. With them coming all the way out here this early in the morning, it couldn't be a social call.

Officer Adams flipped through a notebook. "Faith O'Malley? Cameron MacPherson?"

"Did you learn anything more about the dead man?" Faith asked, hoping this was good news and nothing more that was bad.

"May we come in?" Adams asked, his tone more of a directed suggestion than a question.

This smacked of an investigation—as if Cameron and she were under the gun.

Cameron motioned for them to enter, although getting through the piled-up snow was a trial.

Then a man appeared in a parka, his fur-trimmed hood framing his darker skin, his dark eyes focused on Cameron as he trudged into the snow piled up on their porch. "Charles Simmons, owner here. I'll bring a shovel and clear the snow away. Return later to talk with you folks," he directed to Faith and Cameron.

Talk to them later about what? The hot tub?

She suspected they were in more trouble than that if the police had anything to do with it. The officers came inside and shut the door.

"Green tea?" Faith asked the men. She was shivering between the cold in the cabin from the fire going out and letting in the frigid air from outside. At least the wind seemed to have died down and the snow was no longer falling.

Cameron quickly shook his head. "I'll have some coffee at the main lodge later." Then he rubbed her arm and kissed her cheek. "You're shivering. I'll start a fire."

"Thanks, Cameron." She glanced at the police officers. Adams and Whitson took deep breaths, then looked from Faith to Cameron. "Tea?" They both declined. Faith started the kettle while the men waited. "So what did you find?"

"Where were the two of you between yesterday afternoon and early this morning?"

Faith put the box of tea bags down and paid more attention to the officers. She and Cameron were suspects in something else now?

Shoving a couple of logs into the woodburning stove, Cameron took the lead, not sounding in the least bit troubled. "We were snowed in here. I left Faith for a few minutes when I thought I heard someone yell out near the lake. But I didn't see anything or anyone. I was heading back to the cabin when I heard a couple of snowmobiles, concerned that someone was taking ours."

"Yes, two men stole our snowmobiles. Here's the description I have of them." She headed to the dining table and offered the note to the closest officer. "We were at the hot tub for a while also. We had witnesses. A lady named Mary, and three guys. One was named Matt and another, Chris. We didn't get the last guy's name."

"Were they guests of yours?"

Faith looked at the officer as if he'd gone mad. "Of course not. Cameron and I arrived first. Then Mary. Then the three guys. We hadn't met any of them before."

"Uh-huh." The officer raised his brows at Cameron, who was lighting a fire in the stove.

Cameron shook his head. "Didn't know any of them."

"Can you describe them?"

Faith poured hot water over her tea bag. "The lady was maybe in her sixties, gray hair, gray eyes, large build. The guys—Chris had bushy red hair, green eyes, scrawny. Matt had nearly black hair and eyes, more muscular, and the last, light-brown hair, blue eyes, medium build, late twenties. He didn't offer a name. They were lightly dressed and wore boxers into the hot tub. Mary had on a bright-pink swimsuit."

"Uh-huh."

"Well, all you have to do is check their stories at the other cabins."

"According to Charles Simmons, the only others staying at the cabins are a Leidolf Wildhaven of Portland, Oregon, and a Hilson Snowdon of the same location."

Faith clamped her gaping mouth shut, set her tea mug down, and sat before she collapsed.

"Does it mean anything to you?" Officer Adams asked, knowing damn well it did from her reaction.

Cameron was watching her just as closely. God. What the hell was Hilson doing here? He was supposed to have been at the cabin resort a couple of miles away that was booked solid, or she would have stayed there instead. And Leidolf? Was he with him? What were the odds that two men would be here from the same city in Oregon that she was from?

"Then where did the other people go? The ones that came into the hot tub?" she asked, hoping the officer would believe that was the reason for her shocked reaction.

"What's this all about?" Cameron asked, rejoining Faith, his hand resting reassuringly on her shoulder.

Not answering Cameron, Officer Whitson pointed at his parka hanging over one of the dining room chairs, the sleeve torn and stained with blood. "Your coat didn't look like that earlier yesterday when we first met. Care to explain?"

Faith really didn't feel good about this. Something else had to have happened if they were being considered as suspects in some kind of criminal activity.

"A wolf bit me. A white wolf. Since I'd seen Lila Grayson with some Arctic wolves earlier in the day near the same area, I figured it had to be one of hers," Cameron explained. "I suspect you don't have any in the area otherwise. I'm glad that you paid us a visit though. Before her wolves bite anyone else, I want to press charges." The officers traded conspiratorial looks, but the impression Faith got from the exchange was that Lila and her wolves were either above suspicion or Lila and Kintail brought too much business into the area to warrant an investigation. Small-town politics. At least that was the way she felt.

"Care to show us your injury?" Officer Adams asked Cameron.

Cameron obliged, pulling up his sleeve to expose his skin, but nothing on his arm indicated he'd been bitten. No bruising, no bite marks, nothing.

Faith stared at his arm in disbelief, his expression just as surprised. "It was bad last night," she said, "but he healed quickly, and this morning, all that was left was bruising and shallow bite marks. You can still see a little dried blood. And my bloodied towel." She pointed to where Cameron had left it on the kitchen countertop. "I'd wrapped it around the wound."

Officer Adams frowned at Cameron. "Mind if we take it with us and have it checked out?"

Whitson continued to be the strong, silent type. Although now he warily watched Cameron, no longer keeping his attention on Faith.

"Why? What's happened?" Faith asked.

"Charles Simmons found a dead body not far from here. He went on in with his dogsled and reported it at Skidoo Rentals at the trailhead. They passed the word along to us since there's no reception out here for phones."

Not believing another dead body had mysteriously turned up, Faith cleared her throat. "Who died?"

"Not sure until we positively ID him. No papers on him."

"Did he die in the same way?" Faith asked.

"Can't say. Ongoing investigation." Officer Adams tilted his head to the side. "You wouldn't know how the other man died, would you?"

She folded her arms. "I'm not sure unless I did lab tests." She was used to being asked her opinion about how victims died, but not as a key suspect!

"You say you saw Lila Grayson with some of her wolves." Officer Adams directed that to Cameron as if he had never mentioned that one of the wolves had bitten him. "Did she tell you where your partners are?"

"Hunting, she said. She told me they were quitting the partnership, but I don't believe it. I want to hear it for myself, so she said she'd let them know. The problem is, I'm not sure she's telling the truth about any of it."

The officer jotted down something, then looked up at Cameron. "Maybe you should have a look at the dead man. Just in case it's one of your partners."

Cameron's jaw tightened, but he didn't say a word.

Faith took hold of his hand and squeezed. "Can I go too? As a courtesy? I can have a look at him and see if I notice anything about the body that might help you in your investigation."

"We have our own investigators on it, but thanks for the offer, ma'am." Officer Adams didn't sound sincere.

"I don't want to leave Faith here by herself," Cameron said, squeezing her hand back. Was he really worried about her safety? Or did he think she might see something he'd miss?

"She can't go. Not without permission from our head honchos, and we can't get it out here. Maybe she can visit with Charles Simmons while we take you out there. You say your snowmobiles were stolen?"

"Yeah, and then they were returned behind the shower building," Faith said. "Really bizarre. When I saw them, I hollered for Cameron, and when he came around the building, the wolf attacked. So we never did have a chance to bring the machines back here to my cabin."

"We'll take a look at them. Are you ready to go with us, Mr. MacPherson?" Adams asked.

"Faith?" Cameron said.

She nodded and pulled on her ski jacket. As soon as Cameron was out of sight, she was going to have words with Hilson and get her father's flash drive back. *Pronto.* Although she wanted to see Trevor Hodges to learn more about what went on, if she could get the flash drive, she would be happy enough to leave and forget about the cold, about Trevor, about everything. Except for Cameron. But what if the spark she felt for him was a case of instant rebound from Hilson's betrayal? What if having a fling with Cameron was nothing more than a way of validating that any man would want her?

That was what she was afraid of as she headed to the lodge with Cameron to see Charles Simmons, when all she wanted to do was find Hilson's cabin and give him a big piece of her mind.

Cameron escorted Faith to the main lodge, despite her telling him he didn't need to take her all the way there. He seemed on edge, glancing back in the direction where he'd heard the man shout out yesterday, and appeared to want to speak to her privately. She assumed it had to do with the reaction she had when she heard Hilson was staying in one of the other cabins, but Cameron hadn't wanted to bring it up in front of the police.

"Do you know either of the men who are staying at the other cabins?" he asked her, his voice hushed as he walked her up onto the lodge's porch.

Yeah, she guessed right. What would he think? He might be pissed that she didn't tell him she and her boyfriend had just split up.

"Hilson Snowdon is my ex-boyfriend. I didn't know he was here."

Cameron stared at her for a second, his face wearing a mask of disbelief. "This was recent? That the relationship was dissolved?"

He seemed more than troubled by the news, as if he had more of a long-term interest in her. No, that wasn't it. Something else seemed to be eating at him.

Cameron added, "If he's followed you here, I assume he wasn't the one to do the ditching."

That came out harshly. The notion suddenly dawned on her that Cameron might have had a relationship that ended badly for him recently too. Great. She hadn't intended to hurt anyone, but she couldn't deal with this right now.

Cameron seemed cold and distant, while the police officers watched them both with too much interest, and although she didn't think they were close enough to hear the conversation, they seemed to be trying anyway. Hell, her affairs were her own and had nothing to do with Cameron's problems.

"Our relationship was…complicated. And for your information, he left without a word a couple of days ago."

"A couple of days ago?"

"Yeah, Cameron. Why don't we just leave it at that for now?" She hadn't meant to sound hurt and angry. But she couldn't help it. Cameron's whole expression was one of accusation. Maybe that she'd pushed Hilson away somehow. Either that or Cameron didn't care for the fact it had been recent and Hilson was here, as if he had followed her and was still in love with her. She didn't want to explain that he'd stolen her father's research in front of the police officers, who wouldn't do anything about it anyway. All she needed was for Hilson to turn up dead, and then they'd figure she really was the guilty party, as mad as she was at him for stealing her father's flash drive.

But then she wondered if Cameron's reaction was tied to worrying if the dead man was one of his partners, and in some bizarre way, he was unloading on her. Pretending that his tone didn't bother her, she said, "I'm sure your friends are safe."

"I believe you're right." He didn't sound convinced, which made her think he probably had a better take on the situation than she did. "Stay with Charles here at the inn, and I'll be back in a while, Faith."

To talk more about her relationship with Hilson? No thanks.

He turned and headed off to where the police officers waited with their snowmobiles. He didn't look back at her or even make eye contact with her one last time, as if she'd already vanished. His attitude? He'd made a mistake in getting to know her even for the brief interval they'd been together; time to cut his losses and run.

Faith rubbed her arms in the winter chill, ground her teeth in frustration, then waited until Cameron was out of sight. She had half a mind to dump his bags onto the porch, move him out of her life pronto, take care of business, and return home just as she intended. She didn't need any more drama in her life that involved men with an attitude.

Hell, she had enough problems.

For a minute, she was torn. Talk to Charles Simmons and find out Hilson's cabin name, or look for it herself? She figured she might as well talk to Charles. She walked inside and found the lodge empty. Figuring Charles must be out with the sled dogs or doing something else for one of the guests, she left the lodge.

With no time to lose, she headed for the tree-lined path beside the lake leading to the other cabins, determined to discover which one Hilson was in and have her say with him, confiscate the flash drive, and maybe even return to Millinocket before it got too late today.

She trudged through the knee-deep snow, some in drifts as high as her shoulders, not that she'd traverse those. Past her place, she finally reached the White Wolf Den, marked by a carved, painted wolf sign that looked like the wolf that had attacked Cameron. Which brought to mind Cameron's wolf bite—she still couldn't believe he could heal that fast.

She peered into the windows of his cabin. The place was dark, and when she tried the door, she found it was locked. She continued on past it, winding her way through the spruce trees until she reached the next cabin, also facing the lake. She was glad her place was closer to the main lodge and shower facility. What would other guests do if they had to go to the bathroom in the middle of the night?

The next cabin, complete with a tower, was called the Eagle's Nest. She went up to the door and knocked. No answer. She peered into the window, hoping she wouldn't see the occupant, Leidolf Wildhaven, staying here instead of Hilson Snowdon. The living room, kitchen, and dining room looked unoccupied. Then again, Hilson was a neatnik, so it still might be his place.

All she needed to find was his bag, clothes, anything to identify this was his cabin.

She reached for the doorknob, but something flashed

by her in the woods. Something. Everything was so white, surely she would have seen if it was a person dressed in something other than white. But nothing. She didn't see anything but the snow-covered firs. Barely a whisper of a breeze caressed the snow-laden limbs. And everything was silent. At least in summer, the lake water probably rippled on the shore, but now, it was solidly frozen. Eerily silent.

Although she was bundled to the hilt, she suddenly felt cold, chilled, like when she'd thought the gray pickup had been following her. She realized she hadn't spoken to Lila about who might own the pickup. One of her employees? Or maybe Kintail, since Faith didn't figure anyone else would run around with a wolf attached at their hip except for the owners.

She stood frozen on the porch, watching for any movement in the woods. *Nothing.* She took a deep frosty breath and turned back to twist the doorknob when she saw movement inside the dark cabin. She pulled her hand away from the door and froze.

Whoever it was had headed out of the bedroom and paused in the darkness as if he suddenly realized a woman was peering in at him. Even in the low light, she could see a mouthful of white teeth. She didn't think it was Hilson. The guy was as tall as Cameron but not as tall as Hilson. And he appeared to be the same build as Cameron, not as husky, as far as she could see in the dim light. She whipped around and meant to leave and look for the next cabin when the occupant of the Eagle's Nest opened the door in such a rush, she gasped.

"Well," the man said, his voice deep and charming, "to what do I owe this unexpected pleasure?"

Faith turned and faced the man occupying the Eagle's Nest cabin, his chestnut hair tinged red, green eyes full of mystery and intrigue.

His mouth curved up a trace, but at the same time, his eyes darkened a bit, and the next question from his lips pinned her with accusation. "Are you lost?"

CHAPTER 8

THE BODY WAS LYING FACEDOWN UNDER A SPRUCE, half-buried in snow. He was the right build and was wearing a gray-green parka that could mean the man was either of Cameron's friends. His heart beating faster than he wanted to admit, Cameron came around to the right of the man to see his face.

He was a stranger, a beard covering his cheeks and chin, now matted with snow, his pale-brown eyes lifeless. Cameron took a deep breath, relieved it wasn't Owen or David. "Not either of my partners."

"So are you certain you've never met Miss O'Malley before?" Officer Adams asked, slanting a glance at Whitson, while a couple of investigators were searching for clues in the snow farther away.

Cameron ignored the question as he leaned over to get a whiff of the dead guy, although he thought Adams's inquiry odd. As though he really wasn't as interested in him identifying the body as he was in prying into Cameron's relationship with Faith.

He considered the dead man further. He was too frozen to decay, but he smelled like a wolf. Which didn't make any sense. For one, why could Cameron smell such a thing, unless it was because of being bitten himself and the close encounter giving him a new awareness? And why would he know that it was a wolf smell and not some other? But he didn't smell exactly like the one he'd had the run-in with either. There was something different about him, but he couldn't pinpoint what it was.

"See anything?" Adams asked, drawing closer.

"No, I just… Nothing. He's not either of my partners, so if you're done with me, I'll head back to the lodge."

"Which wolf bit you?" Adams asked, the question so out of the blue, Cameron stared at him blankly.

Then he gathered his wits and responded. "He was one of Lila's wolves. An Arctic white wolf."

Adams shook his head. "Size? Male? Female? Shorter hair, longer? Full coat? Raggedy? You're a former police officer. What made him different from the others?"

Cameron was used to analyzing people's looks and behaviors, but wolves? "How would I know? He was big. Maybe bigger than the others, but they weren't around at the time so I could compare them. He had a thick coat that made him appear as though he was older, more mature, if that's what you mean. Not a juvenile. Otherwise, they all looked the same to me. No different markings. All pure white. But if you must know, I was concentrating on his bared teeth, not checking if he had balls, when he lunged."

Officer Whitson bit back a chuckle, while Adams gave his partner an annoyed look. "Did the wolf… Was he attempting to kill you? Or did he just bite you and then run off?"

"I didn't ask, but the way he lunged at me, I'd say he went for the throat—for a kill—but I blocked his teeth with my arm. If Faith hadn't clobbered him in the hip with a snow shovel, he might have eventually given up on my arm and gone for the jugular again. So yeah, I think he intended to kill me, not just play with me."

His eyes wide, Whitson cleared his throat. "What did the wolf do when Faith hit him?"

Cameron glowered at the officer, not liking that he still seemed interested in Faith. "After *Miss O'Malley* struck him, he looked surprised. I expected him to growl at her, but instead, I'd swear he smiled."

Whitson shared a look with Adams, who closed his notebook.

Although Cameron figured he wouldn't get a response that would satisfy him, he asked anyway. "So now are you going to put an all-points bulletin out on the wolf and its owner?"

"It's just your word that the wolf intended to harm you. You might have made a move that to him meant you intended to hurt *Faith*," Whitson said, "and he was protecting her. Or he might have thought something you did meant you wanted to play with him. Kintail's wolves are good-natured and wouldn't hurt a soul unless provoked. Did you provoke him, Mr. MacPherson?"

Cameron clenched his teeth, unwilling to get into a pissing match with Whitson. He knew the officer didn't like that he had any kind of relationship with Faith and so was bound to be antagonistic toward him. On the other hand, Adams was looking at the dead body as if he was uninterested in the conversation. But it was only a ploy. Cameron knew that whatever he said, Adams was considering it as important to any investigation.

"If a dog bites someone, no matter its motive, it's considered vicious, unable to live safely among humans. Even if one was provoked, the charges against the animal would be taken seriously. We're talking feral wolf here. Not some centuries-tamed family pet. It wouldn't matter if they'd been raised as a second- or third-generation house pet either. They're wild animals. Period."

Adams finally spoke up. "We'll talk to Kintail about it. But you don't even know which wolf it was. We couldn't very well put down his whole pack, now could we?"

"Whole pack? How many damn wolves has he got?"

"At least two make a pack," Adams clarified. He didn't enlighten Cameron any further about numbers.

"How many *does* he have?" Cameron insisted, figuring from Adams's response that the police officers knew.

Adams's gaze pinned Cameron with warning. "You'd have to ask him. But he's touchy about his wolves. So I'd ask real nice if I were you. You're not from around here. He brings a lot of business into the area, so we take care of our own, if you get my meaning."

"If you mean you can get away with murder if you have enough money and connections, I completely understand. It works that way where I'm from also. Universal policy." Without evidence that he'd been bitten, just Faith's and his word, Cameron figured he didn't have much of a leg to stand on anyway. "Next time, I won't just play with the wolf."

For the first time, Adams offered a slight smile, on the sinister side. "It's your business. Just be sure to stick around in case we need to question you further."

"I'll be here, and if I find my friends and get ready to return home, I'll let you know." Cameron gave Whitson the same icy hard stare, then returned to his snowmobile and headed back to the lodge.

He patted the gun under his coat. He didn't like shooting animals, any kind. He'd never been a hunter, just of the predatory human variety. So killing a wolf didn't appeal. But he'd shoot it if the wolf attacked again, just to make sure it didn't harm anyone else, whether Kintail liked it or not.

As he reached the resort, he saw Charles Simmons putting a snow shovel up at a shed and veered his snowmobile in his direction.

The man turned to look at him. A few gray strands running through his dark hair braided behind his back. His round face, darker skin, and dark eyes looked Native American, and since Cameron had heard many of the tribes felt some kinship to the animals of the wild, he wondered about Charles's take on Kintail's wolves.

"The word is you're looking for Kintail." Charles's gaze quickly shifted to Cameron's bloodied and torn parka sleeve. "You were attacked?"

"By one of Kintail's wolves. Although they were with Lila. Two of my partners went on a hunt with Backcountry Tours. They haven't returned, and I haven't gotten word from them. So yeah, I'm looking to speak with Kintail. I haven't had any luck with Lila."

Approaching snowmobiles garnered their attention. Adams and Whitson headed their way.

Charles responded to Cameron's concern. "Communications in these parts are pretty sketchy."

"I understand, but I have to make sure that they're all right." Which brought to mind another concern. *Faith.* "Can you tell me anything about one of your guests? Hilson Snowdon? Specifically, when he got here?"

Charles looked back at the police officers who were nearly there. "Officer Adams, Whitson," he said in greeting.

"Tell your sister we'll be back when she's made some

more of that chocolate cream pie of hers," Adams said, tilting forward on the snowmobile.

Charles gave them a stiff nod. "Will do."

The officers gave Cameron another hard look. Adams said to Cameron, "We'll keep in touch." Then he and Whitson drove down the road in the direction of the trailhead.

"So what do you know about Hilson Snowdon?" Cameron asked Charles again.

"You can talk to him when he's around. He might be at his cabin now or off on another excursion. Folks come here to get away. I don't ask their business. Does Miss O'Malley still want to see Trevor Hodges?"

Cameron frowned and looked back at the lodge. "Didn't she talk to you about it already?"

"I've been busy shoveling snow so I haven't been up at the main lodge. She's probably talking to my sister while she prepares the next meal, unless she's off seeing to something else. Work's never done around here in the winter." Charles motioned to Cameron's bloodied and torn parka sleeve. "About the wolf that bit you, which one was it?"

"I figure it was a male, as big and aggressive as it was." Cameron couldn't understand why everyone seemed to think that he should know which wolf it was as if they all had names and separate identities.

When he'd raised a litter of Labrador retriever pups, they all looked similar too, although, as they grew, personalities began to appear and some physical differences were noticeable—one was chubbier than the rest, one taller. The only way to tell the difference for most of the rest was to observe them for some time. The brief encounters he'd had with Lila and her wolves were just that—way too brief.

"Do you know how many wolves Kintail has?"

Charles's eyes widened a bit. Then he frowned and rubbed his chin. "No. A few."

"Lila Grayson was with a few of them earlier. They ought to be put down if they attack people, and Lila ought to be brought up on charges."

The old man didn't respond one way or another, so Cameron couldn't get a feel for what Charles was thinking. But he was surprised when Charles asked, "How do you feel?"

"Better. The bite's all healed up."

"Come with me while I feed my dogs. We need to talk."

He led Cameron to a barn where he kept his dogs and sleds. A slew of huskies greeted Charles as soon as he and Cameron entered the building, licking and poking their noses at Charles's hands and legs.

Immediately, Cameron had the overwhelming need to show them who was in charge. Which wasn't like him. Befriend the animal? Sure. But make sure they knew he was boss? Not him. Whoever the dogs' owner was, as far as he was concerned, they served as the boss man.

But this time, the oddest feeling snowed him under, forcing him to acknowledge each and every one of them eye to eye with a glance—not a confrontational stare at first—but then he considered them closer, looking for the leader of the pack. When he found the bigger male, Cameron stood taller, stiffer-legged, and pinned him with his gaze, acting as though he was in charge. As if he instinctively knew this would work with the alpha dog of the pack.

The dogs sniffed Cameron from a distance, looking wary, which surprised him. Dogs and kids always gravitated to him. The alpha leader lifted his head, lowered his tail, and arched his back slightly in submission, and Cameron knew he had won the confrontation. He didn't feel superior to the dog for the rapid change in pack dynamics, just that it was the natural order of things.

Charles turned on a lantern, although it was light enough in the building that Cameron was surprised he would bother. Then Charles opened a hefty-sized canister and poured food into dog trays. "Best sled-pulling huskies in the territory. One of these dogs weighing in at only forty pounds can pull over eight hundred pounds." He pointed to their bootie-covered paws. "The huskies are strong, but their feet aren't meant for this kind of weather. They wear polar fleece booties to keep them warm."

Cameron counted sixteen huskies. "Will Faith be navigating a sled, or are you taking her for a ride when you look for Trevor?"

"She just wanted me to take her to see Trevor."

Cameron glanced at Charles. "I'll be going with you."

Charles looked up at him. "Has she agreed to allow you to go along? I had the impression the matter is personal to her. She wouldn't even enlighten me as to why she wished to speak with him."

"She's agreed." At least Cameron figured she would once he gave his reasoning. "How will we work this?"

"The five-foot-long wooden sled's not big enough for three. We have several sleds and can divide up the dogs, but I doubt either of you are trained in mushing. Although, that's what I do. Give rides and teach folks how to handle a team. Faith can snuggle up in the sled bag on my sled, but of course if the going gets tough, we'll all be walking. How are you with dogs?"

Charles gave Cameron a look as if he were judging him for the job.

"Good. I've never found one that didn't like me." He reached down to pet one of the darker-faced huskies. The animal bowed its head to him as if she was afraid.

"That's Nikki. She's a real beta and pretty shy, but for her to greet you first indicates she really likes you." Charles packed the rest of the dog food into a sturdy can. "Bear-proof. A bear can smell dog food through anything. One broke into my barn and tore it up good, but at least he can't get into one of these. There's nothing worse than reaching my place and having no food for the team."

"I can imagine. Have you ever tried a husky-wolf breed?"

Charles snorted. "These dogs love to pull a load and they love to please humans. Plus they get along with each other great. A wolf mix?" He shook his head. "Wolf blood makes the wolfdogs skittish and aggressive with one another. Mostly, they like their freedom. Pulling a load for a human? Forget it." Charles took a deep breath. "What I wanted to talk to you about was the wolf that bit you. Normally, when a wolf like that bites someone, the pack takes the person in."

"A wolf pack?" Cameron wasn't following him.

"Has anyone talked to you about, well, ahem…" Charles looked back at his dogs and began stroking one of them on the head. "Has Kintail talked to you since you've been bitten?"

"I haven't met the man."

Charles looked up at Cameron. "Seeing the extent of damage to your parka and the fact no one's talked to you about what's happened, I'm assuming something else is going on."

"You mean that Kintail has trained wolves to attack certain people? Like attack dogs?"

Charles shook his head. "No, that's...not exactly what I'm trying to say. I'm Penobscot, if you were wondering. In ancient times, my people believed that when the aurora borealis danced across the night sky, magical or divine wolves came to earth. In many Native American cultures, wolves have been revered. Wolves take care of their packs, much as we take care of our families, our tribes. My people much admired wolves' superior hunting skills in cooperating with one another. Like the wolves, in ancient times, we would keep outsiders from invading our territory." Charles smiled as if he was remembering the stories passed on by his elders.

Then he sighed. "The Inuit tell the story of an old lady, abandoned, who became a wolf. The Navajo believed a man or woman who wore a wolf's skin would transform into the wolf. The Sioux believe the wolf has a powerful spirit. The Pawnee were often known as the Wolf People, who, like some other tribes, stored their magical tools in wolf skins. Unless I'm mistaken, one of these wolves has infected you."

In disbelief, Cameron raised his brows. "A magical wolf?" The wolf was big, but there wasn't anything magical about it. Just one mean-spirited beast, although the way Cameron had healed so quickly was pretty bizarre.

"Have you...experienced any changes? Heightened senses? Or feel anything out of the ordinary, like cabin fever?"

Hell, that was what was making Cameron so antsy. His senses were on higher alert. Everything from seeing well in the low light of the barn before Charles turned on the lantern to smelling the differences between the dogs.

Normally, they would have all smelled like wet dog, period. But now he noted subtle differences—one had rolled in something. How he should know that beat him. Another's breath smelled bad, although the dog was not anywhere close to him. It was even more than that though.

It seemed as though every gland associated with each hair follicle produced an individual odor signal that he could easily recognize. And pheromones that cast off a different smell—more of a form of communication—like when one of the bigger dogs, the alpha male, maneuvered closer to the food that was left. As soon as he did, the dog next to him lifted its nose, sniffed the air, and moved out of the bigger male's way.

Sounds were more pronounced also, now that he thought about it.

Charles eyed Cameron closely. "Do you feel any different?"

Yeah, although Cameron wasn't a runner, he had the worst urge to stretch out his legs and run for miles. Hiking, swimming, and skiing were more his style. "Nothing that can't be explained."

"Don't you have any...empathy for the wolf now? More so than you might have had before?"

"What I feel is irritation that anyone would stick up for a wild animal that bites people unprovoked."

Charles just shook his head.

Cameron took another tack, figuring that wolf lovers couldn't understand unless maybe one bit them. "So what is a magical wolf's bite supposed to do to me?"

Charles cleared his throat again. "Have you had any cravings to rip off your clothes and run like the wolf?"

—••—

Faith considered Leidolf Wildhaven as he stood in the entryway of the Eagle's Nest cabin, his amber eyes studying her just as much in return. "Um, no, I'm not lost. I'm looking for someone," she said.

"Ah. Did you knock? I didn't hear you."

"Yes." She had, although probably not hard enough and wearing her gloves, which had muffled the sound.

He wore a hint of a smile, as if he was saying he knew very well she was planning on searching his place without his permission. Then again, maybe she only thought so because she was feeling guilty.

"I'm sorry. I'm at the wrong place."

She was starting to step off the porch when Leidolf said, "Watch out for the Arctic wolves, young woman. They can be troublesome in these parts."

She turned around. "You've seen them? My friend got bitten by one. But the evidence of the bite marks are already gone. Do you know Lila Grayson? She owns the wolves. And Kintail Silverman, I guess. They run Backcountry Tours."

"I'm Leidolf Wildhaven. And you are?"

"Sorry, Faith O'Malley." She walked back over and extended her hand.

He studied her way too closely, took a deep breath, and smiled a bit ominously, belatedly shaking her hand with a firm touch. "Your friend? The one who was bitten? Is he a very *close* friend?"

Closer than she would admit to a perfect stranger. "We just met."

"Ah. So you have separate cabins."

The statement was more of a question, but she treated it as a statement, and none of his business. "You didn't say if you knew Lila Grayson."

"No, I don't know of the woman or this Kintail. But I've seen their wolves. Your friend, where is he staying?"

She hesitated. Hell, she was lousy at lying. "He's at White Wolf Den."

"Appropriate. His name?" When she hesitated to say, Leidolf added, "I've been bitten by a wolf before, so maybe we can swap stories. Sometimes it helps to air our concerns with someone who has experienced the same...trauma."

Faith hadn't even considered that Cameron might have been traumatized by the attack and thought it was a great idea, warming up to Leidolf instantly. "Cameron MacPherson. I'm sure he'd love to talk to you."

"You said he was your friend, that he's staying at White Wolf Den, which means you were looking for someone else?"

"Yes. I thought maybe this was his cabin. But obviously not."

"He wouldn't happen to be Hilson Snowdon, would he?"

"Uh, yeah, do you know him?" From Portland? Friends? She hadn't known Hilson to have any friends in Portland. It seemed like too much of a coincidence that they both were from there and now here at the same time.

"I ran into him while he was pacing down by the lake. He seemed to be bothered by something. He didn't like it that I intruded on his privacy. Although from what I understand, he's the only other one here right now. I assumed he was either Hilson or Cameron. Since White Wolf Den isn't occupied yet, or I should say wasn't until more recently, the one I met must have been Hilson."

"Dishwater blond hair? Amber eyes?"

"Yep. That would describe him. And irritated. I'm not sure he's in the mood for company. Would you like me to walk you back to your cabin? Or to the main lodge?"

"No, thank you. Is his place in this direction?"

"Next cabin over. Porcupine Cove. The other four places are under renovation. Or at least will be when the spring thaw comes."

"Have you seen three men in their late twenties and a gray-haired older lady around? Or had any trouble with theft?"

Leidolf looked darkly amused that anyone might try to steal from him. "No. Why?"

"They were at the hot tub last night, but apparently they aren't staying here. And two guys stole our snowmobiles, then parked them behind the shower facilities."

"Sounds like pranksters to me. Using the facilities but not belonging here."

"But in the storm last night? Where would they have been from?"

He seemed vaguely interested. "I don't know. But I'll keep an eye out for them. Are you sure you don't want me to escort you back to—"

"Thanks, but I've got to run." She hurried off the porch, not having any doubts about what she had to do next and not wanting to delay the inevitable.

"Be careful, young lady," Leidolf said, his voice a warning.

Something about the man seemed mysterious. She couldn't put a finger on what made her feel that way. Something inherently protective. Even though he seemed intrigued with her, he seemed just as willing to help out her "friend," Cameron. Which she so appreciated. But considering how Cameron had reacted to her having a recently ended relationship, she wasn't sure she could still call him a friend.

That bothered her a lot more than it should have for just having met the guy. She felt some kind of connection with Cameron and... Well, hell, she was not willing to dwell on that issue, because once she got the flash drive from Hilson, she could just pack her bags and go and get her life back together where she belonged.

She thought about something more that Leidolf had said. Hilson was pacing and agitated. Why? Had he learned she had followed him here? Or had he tried to sell her father's research and hadn't been paid?

She couldn't imagine he would want to use the research for himself, no matter what it was about. He was a stockbroker, although because of the stock market, he'd lost a lot of money recently. Enough to make him want to steal her father's work for a tidy sum? She hadn't thought about that.

Plowing through the fresh snow and getting way too much of it into her boots, she noted that no one had walked anywhere in this area since the blizzard had subsided. Everything was perfectly pristine. Which meant Hilson should be home and hadn't ventured out. Or he had left during the blizzard or before it began. She should have asked when Leidolf had seen him last.

What of the men and woman who had dropped by the hot tub? What if they were staying at one of the cabins that was closed due to renovations? It would make sense that they would be from some place close by and slip into the hot tub. Something else she should check out. But a nagging worry warned her she should have Cameron with her for that excursion.

When she finally reached Porcupine Cove, she stared at the bristly, fat little critter carved on the sign. The place was dark, just like Leidolf's cabin had been. Maybe Hilson was taking an afternoon nap. He often did because he was such a night owl. Before she reached the porch, she saw dog tracks. No, not dog tracks. She'd bet her IRA that they were wolf tracks. All around the area, into the woods, up to Hilson's porch. Lots of wolf tracks. She thought it had to be several wolves or one very antsy, hungry one.

She glanced around, suddenly feeling a flush of adrenaline, worried a wolf might be watching her. Not any wolf, but the one that had bitten Cameron. Not seeing anything, she hurried up onto the porch and raised her hand to the door. And hesitated.

Steeling her back, she wondered if Hilson would hand over the flash drive without a fuss. He'd always seemed to genuinely care for her. But how could she be sure of anything where he was concerned now? She growled, then banged on the door as hard as she could.

No answer. *Hell.* She twisted the doorknob. *Locked.* She hurried around the place, trying every window, peering inside. Everything was sealed tight. Just like Leidolf's place, this one was neat, bed made, no dishes on the kitchen counter, no sign of any bags, as if no one had ever stayed here. But Leidolf had said he'd met Hilson, so he had to be around. She looked back in the front window. If she broke a window and managed to get inside, what would that accomplish? There was no sign of any of Hilson's belongings. But what if his bag was under his bed and his clothes in the drawers?

She wouldn't know for sure unless she made the effort. If she could find the flash drive, she would have done what she came here to do—make her father proud and learn what he had been up to for so long. He would have enough time to prepare his presentation, and that was all that truly mattered. Plus, she'd make a million copies of his research in the meantime, in case Hilson had a mind to snatch it again before her father gave his presentation.

She searched for something to break a window, then spied a log stacked on a rack, half buried in snow. She struggled to get one of the logs off the top, where it was frozen to the others. After several minutes of trying, she broke it loose, stumbled back, and lost her footing. Landing in a pile of snow, she was glad it softened her fall.

She scrambled to her feet, grabbed the small log, and headed for the porch. As soon as she readied it for a good, hard, window-breaking swing, she heard someone rapidly approaching from behind.

CHAPTER 9

HOLDING THE LOG IN HER CLUTCHES LIKE A WEAPON, Faith whipped around, her face white with fright. Then she let out a frosty breath as if she'd found an angel instead of the devil.

"What are you doing?" Cameron asked, closing in on the porch. He'd followed her trail here, although a stop at Leidolf's place had given him the information that she had gone to see Hilson at the next cabin on the path around the lake.

He assumed she might have decided to return to the ex-boyfriend to renew her relationship with him, which didn't sit well with Cameron, even though he shouldn't have cared one way or another. On the other hand, he thought she might be planning to have words with Hilson. Although it wasn't any of his business, he wanted to make sure she was going to be all right. That this Hilson Snowdon wasn't a violent type. He never expected to see her like this.

She lowered the log and frowned at him. "What are *you* doing here?"

He chuckled darkly and joined her on the porch, then took the log from her. "Apparently, I'm here to stop a breaking-and-entering criminal trespass in progress. What's going on, Faith? What's the deal with you and Hilson and Trevor Hodges, your father, everything?"

"I thought you were pissed off at me and didn't want to talk."

He tossed the log into the snowbank off the side of the

porch and reached out to run his gloved fingers over her cheek, red again now from the cold. "I want to know what's going on. Maybe I can help."

"The...the man who was dead that you went to see... He wasn't one of your partners?"

"No. I have to believe they're both fine." He appreciated that whatever issues she was dealing with, she was still concerned about his situation, even if it meant she tried to sidetrack him about her own troubles. For some reason, he wanted to talk to Faith about the strange way he was feeling and about the odd conversation he'd had with Charles. Something about Faith made him want to share things with her that he didn't even want to disclose to his partners. Not even with his former girlfriends had he still been dating them. "Faith, we've got to talk. Hilson doesn't appear to be here, so why don't we head back to your place and get warm and discuss this?"

"You were angry with me over Hilson." Her eyes flashed annoyance along with the accusation.

He wrapped his arm around her shoulders and held her tight as he guided her off Hilson's front porch. Angry, yes. He couldn't help thinking she had unfinished business with Hilson that meant she might end up going right back to the bastard. The first girl Cameron had dated had done that to him. He sure as hell didn't want to fall into the same trap again.

But somehow this whole scenario was different. He wasn't willing to let her go back to Hilson, if she had half a notion to get sidetracked in that direction. Why he was even thinking along those lines, he wasn't sure. Maybe it was because he figured the guy didn't deserve a second chance.

He noted the wolf tracks all over the place and eyed the woods, looking for any sign of the wolf or wolves. Nothing. Yet a trickle of concern wormed its way into his blood, the feeling that any second now, the wolf that had bitten him might materialize out of the snow-filled scene and attack. But he didn't worry about himself as much as he worried about protecting Faith.

As they crunched through the snow back toward her cabin, Cameron kept an eye out for trouble, trying not to alarm her. But he wanted to know what her deal was with Hilson, so he figured he might as well share his own story first. Maybe that would encourage her to talk. At least he hoped so.

"One evening, my girlfriend, Marjory, was talking to me about a vacation we'd planned to Canada, and then the next morning, she called it quits."

"I'm so sorry, Cameron."

He shrugged, although he hadn't gotten over the hurt. Not exactly. "My fault."

She looked up at him, her eyes filled with tears.

"Ah, Faith, I didn't want to upset you." He figured she must have been through the wringer with Hilson recently, and the parallel was making her feel bad, but he wanted to get this out in the open. "Later that night when I was on a stakeout of a house where a guy who'd been skipping child support payments lived, he grazed me with a single shot fired. Marjory decided she couldn't deal with the life-and-death dangers I might be involved in. I could understand that to a degree. But there was someone else."

Faith shook her head. "Like my mother."

Cameron looked down at Faith, not expecting that. She

didn't say anything more, just watched her boots as she navigated the trail of tracks they'd left in their wake the first time.

When she didn't speak, Cameron figured he'd have to coax it out of her later and continued. "Gavin, one of my partners, discovered the truth. He'd just happened to see Marjory at Starbucks with another man. He didn't think anything of it at first, but the guy was acting a little too intimate, hand on her thigh, head leaning in toward hers to whisper something in her ear. Although I didn't know it, Gavin began following her, assuming I'd be pissed if I learned of it. He's like that and can't let a notion go. He wanted to prove to himself she wasn't being unfaithful. He didn't want to see me going down the same road again."

"This happened to you before?"

"Yeah, I guess I'm just a magnet for cheating women." Cameron squeezed her tight as they trudged through the snow, loving how her body warmed his, wishing that he hadn't upset her. He wondered if this was what rebound was all about. He supposed that Marjory had been the reason for such a whirlwind romance after Katie had dumped his butt. Now was Faith the same to him? There to fill the void in his life, but when he had his act together and she did, too, they wouldn't suit?

Getting way ahead of himself, Cameron cleared his throat. "Gavin followed Marjory and her boyfriend to the guy's apartment. After that, every time she said she was supposed to be one place or another, Gavin would jot down exactly where she'd been. And learned she'd been with this guy."

"Who was he? Anyone you knew?"

"Gavin wouldn't tell me at first. I warned him I'd find out

myself. So he explained who it was, but only on the condition I wouldn't kill the bastard."

"Someone you knew?"

"A former police officer friend."

"That sucks."

Cameron kissed her forehead. "Yeah, so she was trading me in because she was afraid I'd get shot in the PI business when this man is still on the police force."

"He can't be half the man you are, Cameron." She smiled up at him, her expression much brighter.

"No. He's a loser. But then I guess that's what she needed. Someone she could boss around, and I'm not very bossable." This time, he smiled down at Faith, feeling much more lighthearted than he had since Marjory left him several months ago.

He hoped Faith would feel like sharing her story with him. When she opened her mouth to speak, she was back to being concerned for him. "Did you see Leidolf? He's staying at the Eagle's Nest cabin. He said he was bitten by a wolf, too, and wanted to talk to you about it. He seemed real nice."

Cameron gave her a heartwarming squeeze. "He didn't say a word about it when I came looking for you. He seemed a little amused but not surprised that I was chasing you down. He also was worried that you were alone and didn't say anything except where you were headed and that he'd tried to talk you into letting him go with you to keep you safe."

"I told you he was a nice man."

As long as he wasn't *too* nice. As they neared the Eagle's Nest cabin, Cameron suddenly thought back to what Faith had been saying. "Did Leidolf tell you one of Lila's wolves had bitten him?"

"No. Just that a wolf had bitten him." Faith's eyes grew big. "You think he might collaborate our story, that the same wolf bit him that attacked you? Or one of Lila and Kintail's other wolves?"

"Yep, that's exactly what I'm thinking. Let's pay Leidolf a visit." He led her up the steps to Leidolf's deck, but when he knocked, there wasn't any answer.

"Maybe he's gone to the lodge." Faith glanced at her watch. "They should be serving early lunch there now."

"Okay, let's go. You can talk to Charles about finding Trevor too."

Faith didn't say anything, and he got the impression she had other things in mind. "You still want to go, right?"

"I...thought if I could talk to Hilson, I might not bother with Trevor."

Cameron stopped walking and pulled her to a stop. "What's really going on, Faith?"

She let out her breath. "Hilson stole my father's flash drive containing his research. Hilson's been gone from Portland for a week, but I located him in this area by discovering his password and finding his itinerary."

Research, like the police officers had mentioned her father was doing. Cameron shook his head. "Breaking into someone's computer and..."

"Hey," she said, poking his chest with her gloved finger, feigning annoyance, "did you hear what I said? Hilson stole my father's research paper. And Hilson's computer was at my place, and he abandoned it *and me*. So fair play."

Cameron took her hand and wrapped her arm around his waist, then hugged her tight, looking down into those sparkling green eyes. "What am I going to do with you?"

She gave half a shrug. "Treat me to lunch."

"We've got some other business to take care of first." Cameron didn't often use his lock-picking kit, but every once in a while, a situation justified the use. He turned her around and headed back toward Hilson's cabin.

"What are we doing now?"

"We're going to see if Hilson has your father's flash drive."

Faith frowned at him. "But the place is locked tight. I didn't think you believed in breaking and entering."

"Not the way you were going about it. That would add charges of destroying property."

She tightened her hold on Cameron and gave a relieved smile.

"So, Faith, what's the research about that's so important Hilson wanted it?"

"I have no idea why it would be so important. Something Dad had witnessed while he was on his sociology research project with Trevor Hodges was what spurred him on to write the paper. He's supposed to be speaking on it in just a week. I have to have it to him before then."

"He didn't have any other copies?"

"On his hard drive, but Hilson stole that, too, and Dad wouldn't tell me what it was about. Super hush-hush. All I know is that initially he went on a hunt for Bigfoot out in this area with a group who really believed in the elusive creature. My dad didn't. He was just doing a study of the group's behavior, how they goaded each other on, how that affected what they might find. Of course they didn't know he was a nonbeliever and that he was studying *them*.

"But something happened while he was out here. He

was shaken when he first came home, wouldn't talk about what he'd seen, thought he was being followed even, and then dove into writing the paper with such enthusiasm, I was thrilled to see him interested in his research again. No matter how many times I asked, he wouldn't tell me what it was all about."

"Hilson must have known."

Faith didn't say anything in response, and that was when it dawned on Cameron. The guy had used her to get to her father's research. Then again, maybe not. Maybe he'd just learned of it while he was seeing Faith and thought he could make a quick buck off it if he could find a buyer.

"How long ago did you say Hilson stole it?"

"About a week."

Cameron frowned.

"I know. Hilson's probably already sold it. But I still have hopes I can find it. If not, Trevor's my next best bet. Maybe he can help me reconstruct what happened. I thought if I learned what happened from Trevor's perspective, I could help my father put the pieces back together in time for his lecture if I couldn't get the flash drive from Hilson."

"I'll help in any way I can."

She looked up at him, her smile dazzling. "Thank you, Cameron."

He shook his head. "That's another of my problems. Helping women in distress."

She chuckled, the sensual tone triggering another bout of deep-rooted need. "Seems I have the same problem, except I help men in distress—rescuing my father from failure and you from a wolf."

"For which I'm grateful." He didn't think his friends

would ever let him live the fact down if the word got out that a petite lady like Faith had saved his butt from a big, bad wolf attack.

When they reached Hilson's cabin, Faith acted as lookout, and Cameron used his lockpick to unlock the door. But inside, the place was empty. No bags, nothing out of place. Either Hilson had already vacated the place, or he hadn't actually moved in. Faith's shoulders slumped forward slightly.

Cameron rubbed her back. "Come on. Let's get some lunch and talk to Charles about leaving to see Trevor."

He locked the place up and escorted her in the direction of the lodge. They hadn't gone very far when they saw Charles stalking toward them on the path. "I've gotten word that Trevor is at a campsite about three hours from here and wishes to see you, Faith, concerning your father's trip."

Faith took in a deep breath, exhaled, and smiled. "When can we go?"

"Now, if you want to grab a bag." Charles looked at Cameron. "Still going?"

"Yep."

"Are you certain, Cameron?" Faith asked, looking worried, but he noted a hint of hopefulness in her expression that he truly wanted to go with her. "What about your partners?"

"Trevor works for Kintail as a guide, and maybe he knows something about David and Owen. Plus, I can help you gather information about your father's research while we're at it." He just hoped Trevor would enlighten him and not give him the runaround like Kintail and Lila.

"Are you a friend of Kintail's?" Faith asked Charles

as they trudged back through the snow, and Cameron wondered why he hadn't thought to ask. Faith was really good at this investigative work, and he couldn't help but admire her for it.

"I…respect him. He's taken a ragtag group of people and given them purpose, jobs, an income. I do business with him from time to time. He takes hunting groups out, but sometimes he has inquiries from people looking to go dogsledding. Since he has a bigger operation and much more business, he directs interested clients my way. Nothing more than that." He looked at Cameron's torn parka sleeve. "But sometimes one of his wolves gets a little cantankerous."

"Cantankerous? He could have killed Cameron. He *would* have if I hadn't clobbered him." Faith folded her arms. "Kintail's wolves might be okay where some people are concerned, but not with us."

"You hit the wolf?" Charles stroked his chin. "I'm not one of Kintail's men. I respect what he does, who he is, but I don't work for him. But he's superprotective of his wolves. I wouldn't want to be on his bad side and…" Charles just shook his head as if he thought better of saying anything further. As if he wanted to warn Cameron of trouble, but he was afraid, or maybe just loyal to someone who sent business his way, who he respected and who lived nearby.

But the connotation was there. Cameron was on Kintail's bad side. He smiled a little. No one wanted to get on Cameron's bad side either.

"Do you know Trevor Hodges very well?" Faith asked Charles.

"He's an old-timer who's worked with Kintail on hunting excursions forever. Get your bags and join me at the barn." Charles eyed Cameron for a minute. "You sure you feel all right?"

Cameron thought it odd he'd ask again. "Yeah, I'm fine." For the moment, he was ready to get this show on the road. Maybe just the notion he could get somewhere where his friends were concerned and help Faith with her difficulties was all he needed to make him feel right again.

When Faith and Cameron entered her cabin, she packed a bag with a few items of clothing. "Do you really think you'll locate your friends through Trevor?" Faith asked, heading for her sleeping bag.

Cameron hadn't unpacked his bag, so he just set it by the door. "I think he'll have seen them and reassure me they're just fine." He wasn't about to speculate any further than that. Before Faith could roll up her sleeping bag, he halted her. "We don't need to take your bag, if you don't mind sleeping in mine again with me."

"Sure, we'd stay warmer in the cold that way. Okay, I'm ready."

He handed her his sleeping bag since it was lighter and more compact, then he grabbed the bags with their clothes and other items and headed outside. She locked up the place, but way before they even reached the barn, the sound of dogs excitedly barking made them both smile.

"Sounds like the dogs are ready to go," Cameron said, but just their enthusiasm was making him feel the unfathomable urge to run again.

"We used to have a standard poodle, and when we said the word 'go,' whether we were talking about taking her for a car ride or walk or anything, that dog would act crazy, hopping around, poking her nose at us, ready to go."

"Sounds like a Lab I had. He would sit by the truck if I mentioned taking a ride."

She smiled. "Someday, I wouldn't mind having another dog, but I'm living in an apartment right now and no pets nor children are allowed."

Cameron raised his brows a hair, wondering if he'd read Faith wrong. "A swinging singles place?"

She chuckled. "Not sure about the swinging part, and there are a lot of couples…working couples."

"Ah. Just sounded kind of interesting." He winked and she grinned back at him. But again that strange feeling of possessiveness washed over him, of not wanting to hear that a ton of single guys were hitting on her where she lived.

Trying to quash the unreasonable feelings bubbling up inside him concerning Faith, he led her into the barn where Charles was harnessing one of the teams. "If you can, Cameron, just copy what I'm doing. I'll check to make sure you've done it right after I'm finished here."

Cameron strode across the floor and began harnessing the first of the dogs, but they were so excited about running, wriggling and thrashing about so wildly that it was hard to do the job right. In the oddest way, Cameron knew the feeling of wanting to run so badly, he could taste it. As if he were a runner in a competition, and yet he'd never been interested in competitive sports before.

Nikki poked her nose at his bare hand and gave him a warm, wet kiss on the cheek while he was working on aligning two of the males. "You get to be on my team, Nikki."

Faith rubbed one of the dogs between his ears. "Looks like you have a new girlfriend already." She raised a brow, her lips curving up slightly.

Cameron gave her a small smile in return. No way was a pooch stealing his interest away from the tantalizing woman.

"At least they're well fed and had a little rest." Charles hitched the first team to the sled.

When his dogs were ready, Charles came over to check the harnesses Cameron had used on the team, then helped him to hitch them to the sled. "A couple of tips. When we start out the team, you say, 'Hike.'"

"In the movies, they hollered 'mush.'" Cameron wondered if that was another Hollywood-ism.

"The sound is too soft, not a distinct enough command for the dogs. Make a loud kissing sound to get the dogs to speed up. 'Gee' means turn right. 'Haw' is for left turn. 'Whoa' means stop. 'On by,' to pass another sled team or some other kind of distraction. And just remember, to the sled dog, you're the leader of the pack."

Cameron didn't need to be told that. Dogs naturally seemed to want to please him, and these even more so. Plus, now that he had come to an agreement with the leader of the pack, Cameron was it.

"Also, we don't talk while we're sledding, unless giving orders."

The dogs were so hyper, the air felt electric with their zeal—ready to run, ready to gratify their masters. The thrill of the impending trip electrified Cameron's blood, and in the worst way, the craving to run with them grew.

"Faith will ride with me up ahead so I can show the way, and if you take a spill, she'll be safe," Charles said.

Cameron's jaw tightened. He couldn't pinpoint why he was feeling so acutely possessive of her when he knew Charles wasn't interested in anything but her safety.

Although no matter how much he tried to crush the feeling, the stirrings of wanting to protect her nearly strangled him.

"He's at a campsite located twenty miles northeast of here that will take us about three hours to reach. That's where Trevor is planning to be for the day and overnight. I've packed lunches, dinner, and food for the dogs for the trip."

"Good," Faith said, but the unsettled sensation that raced through Cameron's blood hadn't gone away, he had to admit, and he barely heard what Charles was saying.

Despite realizing how crazy the notion was, Cameron had the most awful urge to rip off his clothes and run through the snow, not as a naked human, but as a... *wolf.* As if something alien possessed him, or someone had slipped him a drug that was making him feel so strange. Yet the vivid dream he'd had during the night reminded him he'd felt the same way before and then it was as if he had stepped into his dream and made it real.

He thought back to Charles's comments about this. How had Charles known how he'd feel? Cameron's attention shifted to the way the dogs were bouncing around, which stirred his own compulsion to get on with business.

Faith climbed into the heavy canvas bag filled with wool blankets on Charles's sled. She looked warm and cozy, but most importantly, safe. He should have been satisfied. She looked over her shoulder at Cameron and smiled—sexy and siren-like. He wanted her on *his* sled, and he couldn't conceal the annoyance he felt as he glowered at Charles.

Charles looked from Cameron to Faith and gave a slight shake of his head.

Cameron felt he could drive a sled well enough and that Faith's safety wasn't an issue, but he gave in to the older man's decision. Cameron climbed onto the two ski-like blades attached to the bottom of his sled and grabbed hold of the horizontal bar in front of him, his body tensed for the new experience. The dogs continued to bark, their muscles taut like tightly coiled springs, readied for when he gave them the magic word.

Charles glanced back at him. "Ready?"

Cameron bowed his head slightly and lifted it. Charles's eyes widened. Then Charles turned and yelled to his team, "Hike!" and his dogs took off.

Cameron shouted, "Hike!" and his team yanked the sled in the direction Charles was moving. A rush of adrenaline instantly flooded his veins. Losing his balance, Cameron quickly compensated for the sudden movement by crouching a little and gripping the bar tighter.

The sleds sped across the snow with a soft, creaking sound, away from the resort and down an unplowed road, the snow-laden spruces and pines stretching out to them from either side of the road. The dogs barked, bellowed, and yelped starting out the trip. As they journeyed onward, they grew quiet, all business, the crisp sound of the sled runners whooshing, no noisy, sputtering engine roar like when they rode the snowmobiles. The dogs' booty-covered paws thudded gently on the snow while their frosty breaths wafted in the air.

Every bump shot through the blades and up Cameron's legs to his hands, every dip making his heart drop and rise again. *Exhilarating*. Then Charles picked up the pace and they practically flew over the snow. Cameron was glad his mask and ski glasses protected his face from the bitter-cold wind.

One of the dogs turned and nipped another, and Cameron immediately yelled, "No, Trigger!"—glad Charles had introduced him to each of the dogs by name earlier. The dog instantly minded. "Good dog!"

As soon as he said the words, the whole team perked up. He smiled. The team was a dream to work with.

Then Charles made a sharp turn onto a narrow path through the forest. Cameron tried to copy the maneuver, but he nearly tumbled off his sled. So much for thinking he could keep Faith safe. Quickly shifting his posture to lower his center of gravity, he regained his balance and again wished he was running alongside the team on his own power.

The soothing whispered sound of the skis crunched on the snow, but everything otherwise was softly silent, filling him with awe as he thought about his friends and the next step he would take if Trevor didn't have any clues for him. He was sure Lila was right, that the police wouldn't do anything unless something indicated his friends were in real trouble.

An hour and a half into their journey, Charles suddenly called out "Whoa!" and stopped.

Up ahead, a tree had fallen and blocked the path. Charles checked it out while Faith climbed out of her snug sled bed and joined him. Cameron crunched on the snow to reach them as Charles had gone a way into the woods. He looked up at Cameron and pointed to where the tree had been cut, the trunk over forty inches in diameter and branches spread out several feet in every direction. "Recently," he said, touching the trunk. "Still warm from the chain-saw blade." He looked up at Cameron. "Can you smell who did it?"

CHAPTER 10

CAMERON TOOK A DEEP BREATH, SAMPLING THE BREEZE, but he didn't smell any sign of who might have cut down the tree in their path. "Did you get a whiff of cologne or after-shave or something?" he asked Charles as Faith took a deep breath, her chin tilted up.

Charles shook his head at Cameron as if he was hopeless.

Not sure why Charles should think he would smell something when the old man couldn't, Cameron glanced around at the woods, looking for tracks in the snow. Boot prints could be seen all over the place. "We have axes, right? We could cut up the tree to clear the road."

"It would take too long. Too much work. We'll go another route. Through there." Charles motioned to a narrower path.

Cameron didn't like it. They had switched from a major unplowed road to a smaller one, and now to just a trail from the looks of it. "Are we being railroaded?" He wondered if they were being forced to take this route for some sinister reason.

Rubbing his chin, Charles stared at the downed tree. "No reason I can think of that someone would do such a thing. We don't have to go if you don't like it. We can always return to the resort."

"No, I want to see Trevor," Faith said, frowning. "As long as this trail will get us there, I'm all for it. Don't you think it'll be all right, Cameron?"

He studied the trail. "If Charles thinks it's all right, it's fine by me."

Charles headed for the sled, and everyone took their places and then they were off again. Only this time, the woods reached out so close to the trail that they sometimes touched Cameron, calling to him—every shadow as the day drew on, every whisper of movement, a bird startled by their presence, fluttering off, the breeze making the branches tremble, a rabbit bolting from underneath a spruce close to the trail. Instead of riding down the man-made path on the sled, he wanted to explore the woods on foot, smell the scents of animals and plants, identify everything with his senses that seemed to be so much more highly attuned.

Conquering that urge, he continued to follow Charles and avoided thinking of anything but what he had to do when they reached Trevor. After half an hour on the trail, they came to another downed tree, cut in the same manner, only it had been sawed down earlier. Charles peered into the forest and didn't say anything for several minutes.

Another trail branched off from this one, but where would it lead? A dead end? The wrong direction?

From Charles's reaction, it appeared that wasn't a good thing.

"Can we cut this one up?" Cameron asked.

"Too big. It would take too long. We go back and try another way."

"Who would do something like this?" Cameron asked, walking with Faith and Charles back to the sleds.

"Someone who doesn't like snowmobilers, possibly. Cross-country skiers maybe." Charles pointed to ski tracks. "They can easily traverse the tree. Hard to say."

Faith looked disappointed, although she tried to hide the expression. They'd already been delayed over an hour. This would add another hour to the trip.

The most worrisome concern was whether they were being delayed on purpose, and if so, why. Or if the situation was more a case of being forced to go in a different direction, which again led to the question of why. Although the downed trees might not have had anything to do with them at all.

When they reached the small road again, Charles motioned to the tree lying prone in the road. "We'll cut it up."

About time. Cameron grabbed the ax off his sled and stalked over to the tree. For a quarter of an hour, Charles and Cameron chopped off branches, and Faith hauled them into the woods. Another hour and Charles and Cameron had chopped enough of the trunk away to maneuver the dogs and sleds through the partially cleared path.

When they were on their way again, Cameron mulled over everything that had happened since he'd met Faith. He couldn't stop thinking about the way she'd beaten the wolf off him or how she'd taken care of him afterward with such a tender, caring touch. Then this morning, the way she'd wanted him like he'd wanted her, settling his strange desire to leave the cabin and run through the woods with a few well-placed kisses and… Well, hell, he had to admit she wasn't anything like the other women in his life. He even admired her for hauling off the branches while he and Charles chopped away at the tree. Marjory would have looked at her long fingernails and said, "No way." Katie would have pouted.

From roughing it, to trying out the spa in the bitter cold, to investigating a crime scene, to nearly creating her own as she readied a log to bash in her ex-boyfriend's cabin window, to standing up to Lila when she thought she was making moves on him, Faith was the kind of woman he could really go for. Even though they barely knew each other, he felt a connection between them that made him feel as though he'd known her for so much longer. And yeah, he wanted to be there for her, to help her father out in his time of crisis while he searched for clues concerning his friends' whereabouts.

Cameron shook his head at himself. He just hoped he wasn't being a sucker for lost causes again.

It didn't seem like another two and a half hours had passed when Charles called out to his team, "Easy!" His dogs instantly slowed to a walk.

Cameron surveyed the two-story lodge in the distance and gave the same command to his team. Surrounded by spruce, the place looked like a rustic dwelling, probably having been inhabited for a couple hundred years. Even Charles's main lodge had been built in 1860, according to the brochure.

"Trevor's campsite is about another hour west of here since the secondary road we took moved us out of the more direct route. This is Kintail's lodge. I thought you might check in with him to verify that Trevor was still at the campsite, although he might not know. But it looks like nobody's home." A hint of warning was in Charles's voice, and Cameron wondered why.

It probably had to do with Cameron threatening to press charges about the wolf attack.

Like Charles's lodge had been when they had first arrived at his resort, the windows were dark, no lights on inside, and there wasn't any smoke coming out of the chimney.

It didn't look like anyone was home, which rankled. He'd really hoped to talk with this Kintail and get some answers about his friends.

When they finally reached an outer building, Charles pulled his sled to a halt, a good three hundred yards from the main lodge situated on the banks of a frozen lake.

Charles said, "Wait with the teams. Since Kintail and his people know me, I'll check the place out first. He wouldn't like it if strangers were snooping around the place without permission if they're not home." He handed Cameron a canvas bag. "Give the dogs treats while I'm at it, and they'll love you for life."

Without a backward glance, Charles hurried to the lodge while Cameron helped Faith out of her canvas bag.

She watched Charles trudge through the snow to the lodge. "He seemed kind of on edge, didn't you think?"

"He thinks I have issues with Kintail. And why wouldn't I? The guy's wolf bit me, and he likely knows my friends' whereabouts but isn't forthcoming with the location. At least his partner, Lila, isn't."

Faith shivered and Cameron reached over and rubbed her arms, but she turned her attention to the metal building. "I wonder if it's locked."

"Why?"

She looked up at him. "After we feed the dogs, we could stand in there out of the wind."

But the expression on her face was much more devious, and he assumed she had it in mind to do a little investigative snooping. Just his kind of woman.

He glanced back at Charles as he neared the lodge and hoped Kintail was home despite the way it looked.

"Sounds like a plan to me." Cameron gave her a handful of doggy treats, then headed to his team while Faith offered her portion to Charles's team.

Faith assumed Cameron had figured out her real reason to visit the outer building. Just the slight glint of recognition, the tilted-up chin, his eyes lighting just a bit, and then the devilish smile. Yeah, he was all for it.

After giving Charles's dogs their treats, Faith stalked across the snow to join Cameron as he gave the last dog on his team a hug and back rub. She shook her head. "You're just one of the pack."

"The alpha leader."

She grabbed his arm and hurried with him to the barnlike building. "Did I tell you I like alpha males, and I love the way you handle the dogs, firmly but kindly?"

"If I didn't know better, I'd say you were ready for another kiss."

And more, if the circumstances were more suitable. She smiled as they entered the outbuilding, but as soon as he closed the door, she headed for a stack of crates underneath a window that was about eight feet off the ground. "Looks like just some camping supplies," she said, lifting the lid of one wooden boxes. "Probably for their hunting excursions."

Cameron was checking out a box across the room, situated next to a couple of snowmobiles with the name *Backcountry Tours* painted on the side with a white wolf logo.

"Tents here." Cameron poked around some more as Faith pulled out a sleeping bag.

A little crinkling noise from inside the bag caught her attention, and she unzipped it to find out what it was. A candy wrapper. But deeper down in the bag, a receipt.

"Finding anything?" Cameron asked, surrounded by a growing mound of tenting gear.

"You sure know how to make a mess." She smiled when he did. She opened the receipt. The handwritten note listed food and other items from the grocery at the trailhead. "Nothing that would help. This receipt is dated yesterday for food supplies. But it only has the last numbers of a credit card, so no telling whose it could be." Something shiny caught her eye, and she reached in to pull out a can of pepper spray. "This could come in handy."

"Good as a deterrent for some wild animals if the wind's blowing in the right direction. Why don't you hang onto it? Nothing in this mess." Cameron began gathering up the tents and shoving them back into the box. But something hard in one of them stopped him. He pulled out the tent again and fished out a credit card from an inside pocket. "Trevor Hodges. I bet he doesn't even know it's missing."

"What are the last four digits on the card?"

"Four, nine, nine, two."

"Not the same as this receipt." She was about to drop the receipt in the bag and zip it back up when something leathery caught her eye. She reached in and pulled it out. A gun holster. "David Davis," she read, engraved on the inside.

Cameron dropped the tent he was about to shove in the box and stalked over to join Faith.

"David's," Cameron said, and the way his voice hitched a little, Faith knew this wasn't real good news. "He'd never leave his gun or holster behind. I don't like this."

The door lock made a clicking sound. Cameron raced to the door and twisted the knob. It didn't budge. "Shit."

Outside the building, Charles suddenly hollered, "Hike!"

"Son of a bitch!" Cameron rushed across the building to join Faith as she scrambled to climb on top of the crate to look out the window, but it was too short to reach.

"Was it Charles who locked us in?" She got back down and assisted Cameron in sliding another crate over, then helped him lift it on top of the other.

"It looks that way." Cameron sounded pissed.

He gave her a little boost up on top of the stacked crates. Using her gloved hand, she wiped away the dust on the window and peered through the still-dirty glass. All she could see was the lake from this angle, not the dogsleds or the lodge. "Nothing." She hated to ask but wanted to know what they were up against. "Did you bring your gun?"

Cameron patted his side, glad he'd been prepared. "Always." Except for when he went to the spa with Faith. But on an excursion like this, absolutely. No telling what they might have run into. Although he was thinking more of wildlife problems, like an attack wolf, not real human troubles.

Trapped in a snare is the way Cameron felt, and his blood heated with anger. Just like the time he and Gavin were locked in a storage building when they discovered illegal smuggling. Only that time, the building had no windows, just metal walls that were weak and rusted. After a few well-placed kicks, he and Gavin had managed to knock out part of a wall.

At least for now there wasn't a soul around outside of this building. Although before long, Cameron figured he and Faith would have trouble.

Faith suddenly looked below. "Holy crap," she whispered. "Two wolves are pacing beneath the window."

Hell. Cameron searched the building for another weapon. Finding a shovel, he returned to the crates and handed it up to Faith, then climbed up to the top to join her. Slowly, he slid the window up, but the wolves looked in their direction, their ears perked, alert and ready.

"We can climb down to the ledge below, and from there, it's an easy drop," Cameron said.

"But the wolves—"

"Use the pepper spray. You make a run for the sled. If I don't make it, you leave me, Faith. Do you understand? If my friends have come to harm because of Kintail and his people, we're sitting ducks here. You leave if you can and return to the cabins. Take the snowmobile and get to the trailhead. Once there, grab your rental vehicle and report this…" He reconsidered. "If you report it to Officers Adams and Whitson, they'll no doubt discount our claims, unless we find a body. Leave Millinocket and go to Bangor. Get outside help."

She shook her head. "You have it all planned out, I see."

"Yeah, well, you're a forensic scientist. I'm a former police officer. You're not trained for this kind of work." Although he had the most awful urge to take the wolves on wolf to wolf.

She climbed down, muttering something that sounded suspiciously like she wasn't leaving him. But that *wasn't* an option if things didn't turn out well. She waited on the ledge, clinging to the side of the building, and shivered. He joined her.

The wolves watched them. Anticipating their move. Ready.

"I'll go first, swinging the shovel. You jump down right after me. Spray their faces and run for the sled."

As soon as he jumped, one of the wolves lunged. Cameron swung the shovel and connected with the wolf's nose. It yelped and darted away.

Faith jumped down next to Cameron, sprayed the other wolf in the face, grabbed Cameron's arm, and ran with him. The wolf sneezed and pawed at his nose and eyes. "Come on, hero of mine. I'm not leaving you behind. What if I need you again?"

The sled dogs barked like crazy, wanting to run too. Charles had taken off with the sled Cameron had used earlier. What the hell was he up to?

As soon as Cameron got Faith to the sled and she was safely in the sled bag, he jumped on the runners. Throwing the shovel aside, he yelled, "Hike," and made a kissing sound to get the dogs to hurry.

One wolf was still pawing at his face, sneezing and coughing, and the other was limping toward them but not making any real effort to chase after them.

"Maybe Charles didn't do this to us. He couldn't have locked us in," Faith shouted over the dogs' excited barking.

Cameron chastised himself for going along with her on this trip. He felt *he* was the reason for her being in danger. "Maybe." But he wasn't convinced. Maybe Charles figured he'd better cut his losses and run since he was in business with Kintail. Although Cameron couldn't believe Charles would leave his other sled team behind.

They shot across the snow in a madcap race to catch up to Charles. But Cameron couldn't help worrying that Kintail's men would learn of their escape soon. Hell, he should have done something to mess up the snowmobiles in the shed so they couldn't use those at least.

Riding snowmobiles, how long would it take for Kintail's people to catch up to them?

After an hour, Faith and Cameron still hadn't caught up with Charles, yet she saw his sled tracks clearly. The sun was fading, and the dogs needed to rest. She was glad Cameron had so quickly mastered handling a dogsledding team, but she still couldn't believe Charles would have left them behind and not waited for them somewhere along the way.

When Cameron finally pulled the team to a stop, Faith frowned at him. "We're not going any farther? What if it snows in the middle of the night? Or the winds pick up even more and we lose his trail?"

"I'll find it. The dogs are naturally crepuscular, most active at dawn and dusk, and they need a rest."

Cameron seemed sure of himself, but she wasn't as positive. "I'm not certain we even have a tent."

"Underneath that bag you're sitting in. I noticed it earlier when he pulled out his ax."

"Why would he desert us like that? Leave the rest of his dogs, his sled? They're his livelihood." She crawled out of the bag and felt chilled to the bone. "Not to mention I'm sure he's really attached to them."

"He likes wolves too. They're…magical, powerful," Cameron said sarcastically. "But if you want to know the truth, I think he was attempting to draw the wolves away from us. Or he figured we'd have a better chance if we left separately, one not blocking the other's escape." Although he wasn't sure either scenario could be the truth.

Who had locked them in the building? Unless Lila had done so and hightailed it back to the lodge until Kintail and his men arrived, leaving the wolves to guard the place in the interim so Faith and Cameron couldn't escape.

He began unloading the sled and found food for the dogs while Faith pulled out the double-walled tent, red and orange, like a brightly colored pergola he'd seen at a Renaissance fair.

"Hope there's something for us to eat on this sled. I'm starving since we missed lunch and breakfast." She searched on the sled while Cameron erected the two layers of tents, then went about setting up a stove and pipe to vent the smoke.

"Food! Salami, ham, cheese, cookies, bread, bottled water." She sighed. "Charles gave me a book to read on how to take care of a team on a race while we were traveling. It's a good thing I read it, because we're sure going to need the help." She glanced up at Cameron as he paused to watch her. "It's almost like he figured we'd need to know how to do this alone."

"I'm sure he was just being prudent, making sure that if we got in a bind like this, at least one of us would know the ropes."

"Yeah, but I was with him, not you."

Cameron didn't say anything, and Faith could tell by his darkened expression he'd already had the same thought. "What do we do with the dogs while we lie down?" He carried his sleeping bag into the tent while she dug around on the sled.

When she found what she was looking for, she grabbed a handful of straw just as Cameron reemerged from the tent.

"The book said to lay this down for the dogs, take off

their tug lines and booties, and massage their feet and leg muscles."

"I'll take care of the dogs. Why don't you carry the food into the tent, and I'll join you when I'm done? Maybe I'll even massage something of yours." He raised a brow.

She chuckled. "It's too cold to remove anything." Although if it hadn't been, she'd sure take him up on it. "I'll help you with the dogs so we can get done with the chores faster." She handed him a tube of ointment. "For their feet."

Then she grabbed the cooker to heat some snow. Once it melted, she mixed it with bits of chicken. She glanced at Cameron as he pulled off the dogs' booties while they licked his face.

He massaged their feet as the ones waiting for his attention continued to bump him with enthusiasm. She smiled. He fit right in.

He grinned at her. "See how much they appreciate me?"

She laughed. "Yeah. Snuggling I can do. Licking your whiskery face, um, not tonight."

"I guess that's why a dog is man's best friend." He rubbed one of the leader's legs and glanced up at Faith with a wicked look on his face.

"And diamonds are a girl's best friend."

Cameron shook his head as he fed the dogs the kibble and melted snow. "We haven't even had a real date, and she's already talking wedding rings."

"Who's talking weddings? I just like diamonds." She brought over the cooked food for the dogs. "Here, earn some more brownie points with them, and I'll cook us something hot to eat. Might not be five-star restaurant worthy or as good as the dogs' food, but it won't be cold."

She cleaned out the cooking pot and melted the cheese over the ham and sausage, then served it between two slices of bread. "Ready?"

Cameron gave her a look like he was interested in more than just eating but took a bite of his sandwich and nodded, his eyes smiling. "Good stuff. Where'd you learn to cook on campouts?"

"Truthfully? I didn't. I just used what we had available. Except for day hikes, I've never camped out."

"You could have fooled me."

Yeah, she wasn't used to this. At least there were no bugs. But camping in snow and ice was for the bears, and even *they* had sense enough to hibernate. She'd prefer a nice, warm hotel room, comfy bed, and room service. Her thoughts shifted to Charles. Although she didn't want to undermine Cameron's plans, she wondered if they should be following Charles or just heading back to the cabins and doing what Cameron had outlined for if she had been on her own.

She cleared her throat. "You think this is the way to go? Not return to the cabins?"

"I have to believe that Charles didn't steer us wrong. That he wanted us to follow him this way, and I figure eventually, we'll locate Trevor or end up back at the resort."

But his expression said he wasn't completely sure that was the case.

They finished their meals, checked on the dogs one last time, then retired to the tent, which was nice and toasty inside from the stove's heat.

"What are we going to do if Kintail comes for us? We don't have much in the line of defenses," she said, pulling off her jacket, gloves, and boots.

"The two wolves weren't in much condition to run off and alert Kintail. I doubt he was around, or we would have seen him when we escaped." Cameron slipped off a boot, then the other, watching her snuggle in the bag, and she hoped to hell they wouldn't have any trouble while they napped. He climbed into the bag with her and pulled her into his arms, then stroked her hair. "Get some rest. We'll leave in a couple of hours and run by moonlight."

"Are you sure you can find the way at night?"

"Yeah, we'll make it now."

She sure hoped so because she didn't relish sleeping out in the open another night. At least a building would offer them further protection.

Then she nestled tighter against Cameron's warm body. If Kintail or his men tried to follow them, they didn't have sleds or dogs, and Faith and Cameron would hear snowmobiles from a mile away, forewarning of their approach. That was if they used snowmobiles and not skis.

Faith tried to close her eyes, to rest, to shut off her mind, but she couldn't. His eyes closed, Cameron was still touching her hair with one hand, his other stroking her back, his fingers drawing lower to the tip of her spine, stirring a compulsion to feel him deep inside her again. She lifted her head and he looked down at her, his expression half-quizzical, half-hopeful, and she wanted him. She reached up and kissed his lips, his mouth soft and warm. His skin smelled soap fresh, and his body heat wrapped around her in an enjoyable way. A shiver of pleasure stole through her. His blue eyes were what caught her attention the most—dark and beautiful, and quickly turning from intrigued to lustful. She nibbled his lower lip. His mouth curved up slightly.

He closed his eyes, slipped his other hand around her back, and pulled her tight against his chest. His full-blown erection speared her belly, and she rubbed her body gently against his arousal. A low moan escaped his lips and he took charge, licking the seam of her mouth, tugging at the waistband of her pants, trying to lower them past her hips. She responded, touching her tongue to his, licking his lips back, pressing her mouth to his. Her hands jerked up his sweater and then his shirt so she could feel his skin.

The aching need he'd awakened in her pushed her to roll off him and reach for his jeans. Verging on panic, she yanked at his belt buckle, but he quickly unbuckled the belt and continued the sensual onslaught, pressuring her mouth with his, getting her worked up, her panties growing damp in response. His breathing and hers were labored, her body burning with need. Every touch sent her head spiraling, making her want more. Before she knew it, their tongues were mating again in a teasing, heated dance as she struggled to pull off her pants.

They bumped heads as he tried to help her remove her panties, his actions just as frantic as hers. The air from the stove kept the tent warm, and a slight breeze brushed against the silky walls and rustled through the branches of nearby trees, but mostly all she noticed was Cameron, his hands yanking at her sweater to remove it, his fingers fumbling with her bra and making her wish she hadn't worn one.

She struggled to help him remove his sweater and shirt, but he wasn't cooperating. Instead, his hands were on her breasts, weighing them, massaging them, playing with her nipples, his smoldering gaze slipping from her nakedness to her eyes. Something about the look on his face warned her their relationship had taken a drastic turn, that he didn't plan to let her go anytime soon. Which was crazy. They didn't even live in the same state.

For the moment, she didn't care. And when he drew her down onto her back and pressed her legs apart with his knees, nothing mattered but feeling him deep inside her. The tautness in his actions fed into hers, her hands reaching to touch his skin, to feel the muscles in his arms beneath her fingertips, tensing as he centered himself between her legs.

Then he thrust deeply with raw desire, no measured moves, no gradual accommodations. Too late for anything but primal fulfillment. She surrendered to his frenzied pace, drove herself to meet it, her pelvis angled to feel the urgency, to glory in the experience. For the first time in her life, she felt wanted, needed, loved, as crazy as it might sound.

She felt the exquisite peak of the sexual experience just beyond reach, and then as if he instinctively knew, he slowed his pace, slipped his fingers between her legs, and touched her. Just that simple touch nearly pushed her over the edge. But she wanted more and pushed against his fingers, begging for fulfillment. And he obliged, rubbing and stroking, and didn't let up until she moaned with pleasure.

He watched the expression on her face, as if her orgasm was the most precious thing he could have ever done for her. Her lips curved up a bit, her skin flushed, her fingers instantly grappling for him to finish what he'd begun.

He didn't hesitate, diving into her again and again, his mouth on her lips, the nape of her neck, her breast. Then he groaned out loud, "Sweet love of…"

He didn't say another word as he tackled her mouth one last time, thrusting again until he was done. Spent and looked totally satiated, a small smile lifted his lips, his eyes saying she was the best thing in his life right now. Rolling over on his back, he pulled her tight against his heated body. "I don't…think…we needed the heat from the stove," he said, brushing her damp hair behind her ear. "God, you feel good."

"And you," she whispered, loving his sentiments, not wanting to break the spell. She hugged him tight, wondering where their relationship was headed, but despite feeling he wanted something more, she wasn't sure if it was still just a case of rebound—for both of them.

That was when she realized that in their enthusiasm, they had forgotten to use a condom this time.

Faith slept half on top of Cameron, snuggled in his double-wide sleeping bag. He was torn between staying with her and enjoying her comforting heat, the sound of her steady heartbeat, and her subtle fragrance, with the tantalizing smell of her arousal still lingering—and quashing the craving to ditch his clothes, no matter how cold it was, and run like one of the sled dogs.

The dogs were quiet and he planned to leave in another hour or so after they'd had some rest, concerned Kintail or his people might still catch up to them. Plus, he worried about losing Charles's tracks if the winds grew. But he couldn't suppress the restlessness growing in his blood again.

Trying not to disturb Faith, Cameron slipped out from under her and ducked out of the tent.

He wanted to run in the worst way, to stretch his legs, and—something new—to claim the area while they stayed here as if he were a conqueror and wanted to leave his mark.

Giving in to the urge, he started pulling off his clothes as if it was the most natural thing in the world to do. At once, he had the eerie feeling he'd done this before. The cold chilled him instantly, the dogs all watching him with interest, expectant, their eyes alert, ears perked. Then heat sifted through every muscle, through every blood vessel, and Cameron stretched his arms out as if he were reaching for the moon, visible in the distant sky.

In the next instant, he was standing on all fours, his fur white, his body perfectly warm, his elongated snout sampling the crisp, cold air. His footpads felt fine against the snow, which made him look back at the dogs, all sitting up now.

Why would they need booties when he didn't?

When he started to leave the campsite, the dogs ran after him, but he growled at them to stay behind, to protect Faith. They stopped and stayed.

He swung around and raced off again. He didn't have to look to see their reaction. They were silent, standing there still, waiting, like he'd commanded them.

It didn't take long for him to cover about a mile. His toes digging into the snow, he lifted his nose and smelled the scents—a rabbit, fishy odor of the frozen lake they'd left behind, even the dog's food, and—Nikki's scent. What the—

He whisked around, and she bowed her head slightly to him. She hadn't been with his team. Initially, yes. But now she was supposed to be with Charles.

Hell, Charles and his team had to be close by. Cameron

opened his mouth to ask where Charles was, but as soon as he tried to speak, his words ended up sounding like a huffing noise, not quite a bark, more like a woof, a breathy cough. Nikki circled around in front of him as if she was trying to tell him something, but he wasn't sure what she was attempting to say. She gave a little bark and pranced around some more. He huffed back, wondering why his bark didn't come out the same. Then Nikki headed away from him, and when he didn't follow, she returned, wagged her tail, and turned and headed in the same direction.

Follow her, that was what she was trying to tell him. But as soon as he ran up behind her, the dogs in his team began barking, warning of an intruder.

Faith. His heart in his throat, he raced back toward camp in hunting-to-kill mode.

It was only another dream, he reminded himself. A really vivid dream, but he couldn't help feeling Faith was in danger. And what about Nikki? How had she found Cameron? Was Charles in trouble?

More dogs barking. Hell, it was the other team from somewhere in the distance. *Charles's team.*

His heart wildly pounding, Cameron had another eighth of a mile to go when he spied Faith emerging from the tent. Four wolves were skulking toward her.

His blood on fire, Cameron would kill every one of them before they touched her. The dogs circled the wolves, barking and growling in a mad frenzy, protecting Faith, protecting their territory. Cameron bolted for the wolves.

Faith dove back into the tent, but the lightweight fabric designed for cold-weather conditions wouldn't deter the wolves. She reemerged with the pepper spray and Cameron's gun, and he couldn't believe her tenacity. She was no match for a pack of feral wolves. Neither were the dogs. She had a chance against one of the wolves, maybe. But she couldn't fight this many.

Racing toward them as if his life depended on it, he vowed to reach her before any could hurt her.

One of the bigger wolves tried to cut Faith out of the pack. Cameron's heart pounded even harder. *Hold on, Faith. Hold on.*

She hesitated to shoot the predator with either weapon.

The wind is blowing the wrong way. Don't use the pepper spray!

And the gun. She couldn't aim with any accuracy without using both hands.

Faith.

The wolf separated her from the huskies, snarling and snapping his jaws, his nose puckered, his hackles raised, pelt bristling, creeping closer, ready to lunge.

Cameron did what he never thought possible, leaped nearly sixteen feet into the air at his prey, his own fur raised, his canines bared—ready to kill.

CHAPTER 11

WITH HER HEART IN HER THROAT AND NO SIGN OF Cameron, Faith backed away from the Arctic wolf targeting her. Her chances of survival were slim at best. The way his narrowed amber eyes pinned her with promise—glowing menacingly in the moonlight—she'd be dead within seconds.

But she had to save herself, the dogs, and find Cameron.

The wolf crept toward her, separating her from the dogs that were charging and growling at the other wolves. Like a predator singling out the weakest link, the wolf bared his daggerlike teeth, snarling, crowding her. Her heartbeat spastic, her hands trembled as Faith tightened her grip on the can of pepper spray in one hand and the gun in the other.

The damned wind was blowing in the wrong direction. She couldn't chance choking herself or the dogs with the spray. If she could work her way around to have the wind at her back… But dogs and wolves blocked her path, and the tent was hindering her in the other direction. Plus, she was unable to fire the gun accurately without using both hands. She shoved the pepper spray in her pocket and wrapped her hands around the gun. Having had weapons training in her line of business, she knew how to shoot, but practicing at targets was one thing. Killing a live animal or a person…

The aggressor wolf paused, his expression changing. No longer growling, he smiled—if a wolf could smile. Her finger on the trigger, she hesitated to fire the weapon.

Since he'd quit pursuing her, she hoped she could scare him away—although she figured it was a futile exercise—but giving it a try, she stomped her foot, yelling, "Ha!"

He crouched in response. An icy shiver stole down her spine. Readying to leap, he behaved just like her standard poodle would when he was a puppy, crouching before the pounce.

But more than that, she envisioned the wolf that had lunged at Cameron, then bit him in the arm.

She aimed the weapon again, took another step backward, and stumbled on a pile of snow. Her heart nearly seized. Falling on her butt, she dropped the gun.

Everything seemed to freeze in time. The dogs and wolves quit growling and barking, their mouths snapped closed, their attention diverted to something behind her. The one ready to leap on her straightened, his ears perked, his gaze focused to her left.

She didn't have time to turn to see what was coming when a huge wolf sailed past her shoulder, nearly hitting her. She jerked away from the great white beast and rolled over the mound of snow.

The new wolf, bigger than any of them, pounced half on the wolf's shoulder, his hind feet landing firmly on the ground. He knocked the other down. The pinned wolf tried frantically to get to his pads before the newcomer seized his throat.

Not wanting to see any of the animals fighting or injuring each other, she feared the outcome should either win.

The other wolves and the huskies all observed the pair as if the newcomer was attempting to become the pack leader of a mixed bunch of wolves and huskies, and they wanted to see who came out on top.

Faith scrambled to her feet and shoved her gloved hands into the piles of snow until she located the gun. She shook the snow off her gloves and aimed the weapon at the fighting wolves. Their incisors bared, they were snarling, lunging, and biting, and the ferocious sound chilled her blood.

Patches of blood covered both wolves' fur and stained the snow in places.

Desperately, she wanted them to give up fighting and run off. But the two continued to circle each other. Then the biggest wolf attacked the other, tore his ear. When the wolf yelped and jumped back, the biggest one went for his throat like an animal possessed by the devil. The newcomer seized the other's throat, and the wolf went down.

The victor's head swiveled around to look at her. Immediately, she raised the gun and pointed it at him. But she couldn't pull the trigger. If they were all Kintail's wolves—which she believed to be so—why did the biggest one kill one of the others?

For an instant, the animals were silent. Then the other three wolves began to growl low. So, they didn't accept the newcomer as the pack leader. At the same time, the dogs began to bark at the wolves, growling and lunging. The big wolf's chest heaved for a few minutes while he stood still, turning his attention toward the rest of the animals.

Although he had helped her and the dogs, she worried he still might turn on them.

The dogs pounced on one of the wolves while the other two wolves shied back, then ran off. They'd tell Kintail. That was what she figured. They'd alert him to where they were, leading them back here like bloodhounds on a prey's trail. Then she and Cameron would be in bigger trouble.

Bleeding at the shoulder, the big wolf crouched low, targeting the last of the aggressors. The beast continued to show his aggression, his ears straight up, his tail stiff behind him, snarling at the dogs. The huskies ran at him, snapping their jaws. He lunged in retaliation. They darted out of his path.

The victor wolf growled threateningly low. The sound made the hair on the nape of Faith's neck stand at attention, even under her parka hood.

The final aggressor had been fierce and full of bravado when facing the dogs, but she swore he looked like he was about to die now. His tail suddenly lowered, his ears flattening as he turned to face the real threat—their wolf savior.

The big wolf crouched. His tail was slightly raised, the tip twitching to one side, his ears and fur erect. As soon as he made his move, he would kill the other. The smaller one had to also be a male, aggressive and single-minded in his urge to fight. Because of his size, the larger wolf had to win.

Without further warning, the victor lunged. The two slammed into each other. Their front legs lifted off the ground, their teeth clanking as they bit each other's mouths. They landed on their pads, but the victor didn't hesitate to attack again. He grabbed the aggressor's throat and killed him. The animal dropped to the ground with a thud.

Everything was whisper-soft with the breeze blowing against the tent and the animals now standing silent. The victor quietly watched Faith. He stood still, panting, his white muzzle tinged with blood, his eyes amber, the wildness in them softening. Her heart was beating hard and she felt panicked, unsure what to do, but she didn't want to kill him. Not after he'd saved them from two of the wolves. And not while he didn't act threatening toward the huskies or her.

For a minute, no one made a move. Then the dogs barked in excitement. Jumping at each other, they licked him in the face in greeting. He continued to watch Faith's reaction, his tail now pointed down. She barely breathed and wanted to get the huskies away from him before their overexuberant attention irritated him, and he attacked them. The dogs treated him as if he were a war hero and they were cheering the wounded veteran. He didn't seem bothered by them but eerily kept his attention on her.

Then a husky nuzzled its face against the wolf's ear. Recognizing the husky, Faith's mouth dropped open. "Nikki?"

Nikki. What had happened to Charles and the rest of the team? And Cameron? Faith's gaze searched for any signs of him and saw Cameron's parka and the rest of his clothes piled up on top of the sled.

"What the…?"

The wolf lifted his nose and sniffed the air, then turned his head south. With the dogs still yipping, he tore off. Nikki followed him, along with two of the other dogs.

Dashing to the others to grab their collars and make them stay with her, Faith hollered at the rest to come back. But the wolf's influence overrode hers, and the dogs ran with him until they disappeared from sight. She prayed they'd come back and that Charles and his team were all right. That the wolf wasn't leading the dogs into an ambush like a wolf did in one of Jack London's wolf tales.

But what of Cameron? She had to locate his tracks in the snow. Something surely had gone wrong with Charles and his team too. She glanced at the dead wolves, their blood coloring the snow red. What if the blood attracted predators? She shoved her outer gloves back on and hurried to the sled to search for a shovel.

In the distance, an eerie howl sounded.

After he killed the first of the wolves, Cameron reluctantly concluded he wasn't living a dream or a nightmare. The taste of blood and fur was too real. The smell of dogs and wolves. The way he recognized their fear, anger, and jubilation in every action—the raised tails and the drooped ones, the ears forward or back or flattened, the eyes narrowed or widened. Every action signaled a defensive or aggressive or excited posture. The way he understood their barks, growls, and yips. The feel of the cold breeze whipping across his face and the burning in his shoulder from the new wolf bite. The iron smell of blood—of his and the ones he'd killed. All were very real and too unreal to ponder more closely.

Still in shock over the whole changing-into-a-beast scenario—had to have been twice now—he couldn't figure out what the hell had happened to him. Except it probably had something to do with Charles's comments about magical wolves coming down from the aurora borealis. But he didn't want to think about his bizarre situation beyond that for now. All he knew was he had to locate Charles pronto, make sure he was safe, and find out more concerning the magical wolves.

He was a white Arctic wolf, just like the one that had bitten him and the ones he'd killed.

Right now, more than anything, Cameron hoped the older man was all right and the dogs were too.

Nikki ran with Cameron, then turned west. He followed her along with the other dogs and heard Charles's team barking in the distance again. The sound was in greeting, not warning of danger. Which gave him a small sense of relief.

Then it occurred to him that the other two wolves had taken off before he could kill them—the one howling their whereabouts. What if they circled back around to the camp and Faith? Hell, if only he could be in two places at once. He had to hurry, not wanting to leave Faith on her own for long.

When he neared the camp, his original husky team raced to greet him, but there was no sign of Charles, just his sled, tent, and the bed of straw he'd made for his dogs. Cameron loped toward the erected tent, the door flap blowing in the wind. He poked his head inside and saw Charles lying in his sleeping bag, deathly quiet. After walking inside, Cameron nuzzled Charles's face with his nose and pawed at his chest, but Charles didn't wake. Cameron concentrated on the man's breathing, his heartbeat. And he smelled blood. But Charles was alive, thank God. Although he needed help and Cameron couldn't give it to him—not like this.

Then a blood-curdling scream shrieked across the snowy woods from the direction of Cameron's campsite. The dogs began barking. His heart thundering, Cameron raced out of the tent. *Faith.* Kintail's other wolves. Or maybe Kintail and his men had arrived.

Hell, what next? He had to take care of Faith and then Charles, but how could he take care of anyone while he was in the form of a magical wolf?

Cursing his situation, he tore off across the snow again, heading straight back to Faith. A couple of the dogs had followed him from the other team, and so did his own, making him truly feel like the alpha leader of the pack.

When he finally reached the campsite, Faith was gone. Or maybe she was hiding inside the tent. There was no sign of anyone else, and he realized there had been no sounds of snowmobiles approaching the area. The wolves had to have returned.

The dogs that had remained behind greeted him and their teammates. It wasn't until he got around them to head for the tent that he saw what probably had shaken Faith.

Kintail's men lay naked in the snow where Cameron had killed the two wolves. He stared in disbelief. That could have been him if they'd gotten the best of him instead. Shaking loose of his surprise that they had the same affliction he had, Cameron rushed over to the sled, wishing he could turn back into his human form and dress and see to Faith. They had to get the team together and take care of Charles.

Cameron closed his eyes and concentrated. *I want to be human again.*

He opened his eyes. Nothing had changed. Hating not being in control, he growled low. He nudged at his clothes with his long wolf's snout, pawed at them, wanting to put his things back on, to be himself. But still, he didn't change.

Without another plan, he loped toward the tent, hoping Faith was all right inside. But when he pushed the flap aside, he found the tent empty. *Hell.* Trying not to panic, he attempted to smell where she'd run off to. Or *had* someone managed to take her?

He found no signs of any tracks other than wolf prints and the impression in the snow made by her small boots. He raced after her, hating not being able to holler her name.

When he found her, if he found her, what then? She'd think he was the same kind of wolf that he'd killed, most likely. Some type of alien aberration.

The sound of footfalls followed him, and he whipped his head around to see all the dogs chasing after him. His breath frosty in the breeze, he paused and sniffed again. Straight ahead. He bolted in that direction, his tail straight out. The tracks indicated she'd stumbled and fallen several times, running at first, then slowing her pace as if the need for flight had dissipated.

When he finally saw her not very far from camp, she was sitting in a pile of snow, her white parka and clothes nearly blending in. She looked back, her eyes widening when she saw him with the teams. The dogs raced to greet her, and Cameron moved in close with them, hoping she wouldn't shoot him or attempt to with the other dogs surrounding him.

Tears sparkled in her eyes, and streaks of tears trailed down her cheeks. The dogs were so enthusiastically licking her and poking her to go with them that their actions stirred her from where she sat. He wanted so badly to take her into his arms and hold her tight. Damn what he'd become.

Warily, she watched Cameron, then patted some of the dogs and rose to her feet. She didn't pull the gun on him, *yet*, but she kept her eyes on him as she headed toward him in the direction of the camp. *Good.* Maybe he could nudge her into hitching up the team and joining Charles until Cameron could figure a way of changing back. *If* he could. Hopefully, he wouldn't have to die first. Damn, what if Kintail somehow changed people through these attack wolves and then once they changed, there was no turning back?

No, Cameron had done it before. Damn, that meant that he really had seen Chris and his friends in the tent that one night. Oh hell, if they hadn't seen Bigfoot, had they seen someone like he was now?

When Faith neared him, she made a wider circle around him as the dogs escorted her back, some racing ahead, some running by her side. Cameron inched in closer and nudged her gloved hand with his nose in greeting. She looked like she was about to run.

Don't run, Faith. He'd take chase. He could already feel the urge rising in his blood. He didn't want to scare her, but the instinct was too great.

She was already walking as fast as she could, trying to get away from him. He stayed close. *Don't run, Faith.*

But as soon as she got near enough to camp, she dashed for the tent.

Had she left the gun in there?

Hell, maybe. His shoulder already hurt like the devil, and he didn't need her shooting him too. Beyond that, he had to convince her to take care of Charles, who could be dying for all Cameron knew.

He bolted for her, the thrill of the chase coursing through his blood. The dogs barked with glee, and Cameron lunged for her.

He pounced on her back, and she screamed and fell face-first in the snow. And then lay very still, but he didn't move either. If he released her, she'd go for the weapon. She continued to remain motionless. From the sound of her too-rapid heartbeat, her heavy breathing, and her slight trembling, he knew she hadn't passed out but rather was playing possum. He wanted to smile at her clever deception.

The playful urge to take her down gave way to something deeper, more primal and possessive. How could he want her now when he was a wolf? The more he tried to deny his feelings, the greater his need to have and protect her surged through him.

The strange feeling that had consumed him rushed through him again, the heat, his muscles and bones stretching, until he was butt naked and his backside was freezing as he pinned her down.

How the hell did he change back? Worse, how was he going to explain to her what had happened to him?

He cleared his throat. "Faith, I'm going to let you up, and we have to get the team hitched. Charles is not far from here, but he's been hurt and isn't responsive. We need to hurry and give him first aid."

"Cameron?" Her voice was muffled in her ski mask, kind of a squeak.

"It's me. Cameron." He spoke close to her ear, huddled against her for warmth. From the surprise in her voice, he guessed she was thoroughly confused. Why wouldn't she be? He still couldn't get over the change himself.

Then a new thought occurred to him. What if she thought he had bolted out of nowhere and shoved her down, protecting her from the big bad wolf that was chasing her?

He groaned. Then what? Tell her, or keep it a secret a while longer if she hadn't put two and two together?

"I have to dress. Why don't you take down the tent while I do that, and then I'll get the dogs together." Cameron let her up and raced over to the sled, trying not to think about how cold he was, hoping she didn't go after the gun and shoot him in the back. But if he didn't get dressed quickly, he was going to lose some body parts to the frigid air. Beyond that, his new wolf bite shot streaks of throbbing pain from his shoulder straight to his brain, and he was having trouble concentrating on much else.

When he'd donned everything but his parka, he looked back to see her staring at him, her eyes dark and wide. He hoped she'd realized what had happened so he wasn't left trying to explain or keeping his strange condition secret. Deep inside, he knew he shouldn't tell her what had become of him, that it would be safer for him and for her. "Hurry, Faith. We've got to help Charles."

Her expression changed slightly, from still in shock to all business. She whipped around and went into the tent. He hesitated to do anything, his first thought she was going for the gun. But she came out holding his rolled sleeping bag up and headed for the sled. "Hurry, Cameron. You have some explaining to do."

Well, that decided that. He closed the distance between them and pulled her into his arms to give her a comforting hug.

At first, she was stiff, but then she melted, wrapped her arms around him, embracing him as if she had found her long-lost love and never wanted to let him go. Still concerned that she might be in shock, he leaned down and kissed her forehead, then ran his gloved hand across her cheek. "Let's get you settled in the sled bag. I'll take care of everything else."

"I'll pack the tent." Her gaze fixed on his, making her seem determined to get through this on her own.

He leaned down and kissed her cold lips and hugged her with a bear of an embrace. He still worried she might be in shock, but when he tried to steer her toward the sled, she shook loose. "I'm…I'm all right." He could tell by the hesitancy in her words that she was putting on a front.

He let her go, but while he rushed to get the dogs' booties on and harnessed the team, then hitched them to the sled, he watched Faith dismantling the stovepipe from the stove, then working on the tent, to ensure she truly was all right. She seemed to be, and afterward, he packed the stove and tent on the sled. But then he caught Faith's gaze focused on the dead men lying in the snow.

"I'm sorry, Faith."

"You're injured," she said, changing the subject, her voice more sure now, and he was glad to hear it. "We have a first aid kit, and I'll take care of you after we see to Charles."

"It's a deal." The burning in his shoulder from the fresh wolf bite hurt like hell now, and every move added a twinge of excruciating pain through the muscles.

He wondered if Faith was in denial—if she truly didn't believe he was the wolf, or if she did and just couldn't acknowledge it. He sure had refused to believe it. Well, still did to an extent. Now that he was back to his normal self, he couldn't imagine being able to shape-shift again. At least the urge to run as a wolf was gone for the time being.

Glancing at the dead men, Cameron took a deep breath. "I'll clean up the camp a bit. Be right back."

He grabbed the shovel she'd dropped in the snow and buried the two men. It was as proper a burial as he could give them, but he figured Kintail and his men would come for them eventually. For a moment, he stared at the mounds, wishing it hadn't come to this. Figuring he'd killed a couple of wolves, wolf to wolf, he never imagined…

The wolf part of him felt no remorse. He had to protect Faith and the huskies. That was a given. The human side of him...

Then he remembered Faith's terrified expression. The wolf would have killed her. The man-wolf. It didn't matter what form they had taken. Cameron wouldn't have let any of them harm her.

Letting out his breath, he hurried back to Faith. He slipped the shovel on the sled and climbed onto the runners. Even if she couldn't see that he was one of them, she knew the others were. No words could express what had happened to make it any less unreal.

In pain and worried about Charles's condition, Cameron shouted, "Hike!"

The dogs took off and raced past the grave mounds.

"Haw!" he shouted, steering them left, toward Charles's camp.

He hoped Faith could deal with all that had happened and that she wasn't too traumatized. She needed to manage the other team if they were going to get both sleds home. He prayed Charles would be all right when they got him to Millinocket. *And* Cameron hoped that he didn't have a sudden urge to turn into a wolf again *ever*.

He made kissing sounds at the team, encouraging them to run faster.

When they reached Charles's camp, Cameron hollered, "Whoa," and the dogs came to a halt.

"What's wrong with Charles?" Faith climbed out of the sled bag and seemed much steadier now.

"Not sure. I couldn't rouse him." Cameron grabbed the first aid kit and hurried into the tent.

Charles was sitting up, his eyes glazed.

"Hell, you're alive." Thank God for small miracles. Cameron knelt beside him and took his wrist to feel for the strength of his pulse, although he concentrated more on listening to Charles's heartbeat, but he couldn't let Faith know that. Strong, steady pulse, not raspy like he'd feared.

Charles's gaze shifted to Cameron. "What…what happened?"

Cameron glanced at the sleeping bag and saw blood where Charles's head had been.

"You tell me. You took off and left us to fend for ourselves." Cameron examined the back of Charles's head as Faith knelt beside Charles and held his hand.

"Ambush," Charles said and started to lie down.

Cameron stopped him. "Wait, let me see where you're injured." He found the bloody swelling centered on the very back of his head. "Who struck you?"

Charles moaned and closed his eyes.

"Kintail? One of his men?"

Charles didn't respond, and with the way he was struck from behind, he might not have even seen who hit him. Cameron pulled bandaging out of the first aid kit and wrapped it around Charles's head, trying not to hurt him any more than he was already. Charles winced and groaned.

"What's wrong with him?"

"Someone struck him from behind." Cameron eased Charles down on the sleeping bag and covered him with the blankets.

Faith rubbed her arms. "He wasn't bitten, was he?"

"No, he wasn't bitten. Here, you can feel the knot on the

back of his head. Probably got a concussion. He's pretty out of it."

"Kintail's men?" she whispered.

"It's a good bet."

"What do we do now? Find our way by ourselves? Wait until he's better?"

"We'll be right back, Charles." Cameron took Faith's arm and led her from the tent to the sled. "We can't go the way we came, or we'd have to run by Kintail's lodge. We'll have to find our way to the main road that had been blocked. Since he's in bad shape, we'll stay here, let the dogs rest, then head for the cabins. I'll set up our tent and—"

"I'll stay with Charles. To make sure he's okay during the night."

Again he wondered if she had a clue about the wolf and him being one and the same, about him being naked in the snow. And why she hadn't asked him anything more about it. "All right. Go to him then. Let me know if he gets any worse." He headed for the dogs.

"I'll help you with the huskies."

He thought she'd ask him what had happened at their camp. Instead, she talked lovingly to the dogs and helped get them settled. Then, much to his surprise, she assisted him in setting up the tent. When they were done, they shared an awkward moment of silence. He wanted to kiss her and give her a hug, to reassure her that they'd all be fine. Before he could take her in his arms, she said good night, whipped around, and quickly escaped to Charles's tent.

He couldn't reproach her, although he couldn't stifle his desire for her, no matter how much he tried. Normally, if a woman wasn't interested in him, he wouldn't have followed up. Although no woman had ever acted afraid of him. Except for when he'd questioned a woman who had everything to hide—including a dead husband and stolen money from work—but he hadn't thought he would get involved with a woman who feared him. So what the hell was making him want Faith even more?

The need to prove he was the same person as before? The same man that she'd found as desirable as he found her? But he wasn't the same either. He was some kind of aberration. And he still wanted her. Craved her as if she was his lifeline to reality.

Inside the tent, she asked Charles, "Are you going to be all right?"

Cameron hesitated to hear an answer. Charles didn't respond, much to Cameron's disappointment, so he ducked into his own tent.

His shoulder was throbbing with a deep ache, and after settling into his sleeping bag, he tossed and turned, reliving the night's events. He thought about Kintail and his wolves and how they were not at all what they seemed. Which meant?

Hell, Kintail was probably one too. And David and Owen?

Cameron raked his hands through his hair.

If they'd seen Kintail's people shape-shift, had he had them killed? Or were they now one of them too?

CHAPTER 12

UNABLE TO SLEEP AFTER ALL SHE'D WITNESSED, FAITH rolled over and felt Charles's pulse again. Normal. His breathing was steady. She sighed and hoped in another couple of hours, he'd be feeling well enough to make the journey. And that she could drive a team without any problem.

She bumped against something plastic, wondered what it was, then realized it was the first aid kit. *Damn.* She'd meant to tend to Cameron's wound.

She couldn't get the look of hurt in Cameron's expression out of her mind—although he'd quickly hidden it when she'd chosen to stay with Charles instead of him—but she had to watch over Charles. Beyond that, yeah, she couldn't have stayed with Cameron. She just couldn't have—not in light of what had happened. She didn't want to think about why he was naked or how he could have survived in the cold that way for long. She could only come up with one conclusion, and that was too bizarre to contemplate. The wolf had been chasing her, and then all of a sudden, she was pinned beneath Cameron's naked body. He hadn't shouted that he was coming to save her, nothing. Just one pounce and she was facedown in the snow, and then he was on top of her, heating her backside.

Not only that, but their savior wolf had miraculously vanished. If he hadn't, she still would have wondered what Cameron was doing freezing his naked ass off in the Maine wilderness. And how had he been injured? Wolf bite for sure. But when and where? He sure hadn't freely offered any explanations, and that didn't bode well.

Even so, she'd meant to treat his injury.

Grabbing the first aid kit, she crawled out of the sleeping bag and tent. Several of the dogs lifted their heads and watched her. She shushed them before they ran to greet her.

She peeked inside Cameron's dark tent, but she couldn't see anything. She hesitated. Maybe this was a stupid idea if he was sleeping soundly, and she should just skip it. But his bite wound had looked nasty, she'd promised, and besides, it might soothe his pride over her not staying with him.

She crawled into the tent, opened the first aid kit, and pulled out the ointment and bandages. Then she reached for Cameron's arm to shake him slightly and wake him so she could ask him to turn on his lantern, and she'd doctor him.

Bad plan. Her fingers felt fur and lean, mean wolf instead. As soon as she touched him, she about had a heart attack. He growled, whipped his head around, and bit her.

She screamed, and fluorescent amber eyes peered at her in the dark; then the shine in them faded. Her heartbeat pounding, she jumped back, favoring her throbbing hand, and ran into one of the tent poles. The pole toppled and the tent collapsed.

Feeling suffocated, Faith scrambled away from the center of the tent, trying to extricate herself from the tomb of polypropylene fabric. Her hand touched fur again and she jerked back, afraid he'd bite her once more. She thrust her hands out madly in another direction. The canvas elevated near her. He'd slipped in front of her like a dangerous predator, unwilling to let her escape.

A tongue licked her injured hand, and she gasped. *The taste before another bite?*

Again, she crawled toward what she hoped was the tent opening, but all she found was more tent, and then Cameron's soft bedding. Her heartbeat thundered in her ears as she scrambled over his blankets and sleeping bag and tried to locate a way out.

Then she touched bare skin—Cameron's thigh?

Before she could jerk away, a large hand grabbed her wrist and held on tight. "Stay."

God, Cameron. Barely breathing, she didn't move.

"I'm sorry, Faith. I didn't mean to bite you." He sounded remorseful but worried too.

Her hand was stinging so badly, she was sure he'd broken the skin. Her heart pounded like a sledgehammer while she tried to come to grips with the truth. *He* was the wolf. It made the only sense and yet no sense at all.

But he was the wolf. He admitted biting her, had been chasing her earlier, had saved the dogs and her from the other wolves, so that was the only reasonable explanation that fit. The dead men—the ones who had been wolves before Cameron had killed them—were like him. He was one of them.

She groaned and collapsed onto the bedding. Could Cameron's bite have transferred whatever he was to her, and she'd be like him now?

"What were you doing in here?" He pressed her hand against his face and breathed deeply.

She swallowed hard, trying to calm her racing heart, to drum up the courage to speak. What *was* she doing in here? Oh yeah, his wound.

"I was going to put some salve on your injury."

"Do you still want to?"

What a disaster. She closed her eyes to still the pounding in her head. "We need to erect the tent first. But I can't see anything."

As if he was afraid she'd escape, he didn't release her but moved away slightly and turned on a lantern. She wasn't exactly afraid of him. Not after what he'd done for her and for the dogs. He'd risked his life to protect them.

That was when she saw every muscled naked bit of him as he elevated the tent with his free hand, then released her and pushed the lightweight fabric upward with the other—like Atlas, only the world wasn't on his back.

She'd gotten an eyeful when he went to dress in the snow, but that was only his remarkable backside, toned from his back to his butt and legs. Now, she got to see all the goods again, from his corded chest all the way down to his well-toned thighs. Despite the cold, he was fully aroused. Her gaze shifted to his face, and he raised his brows, waiting for a response.

She cleared her throat, glanced back at his glorious erection, and said, "I'll get the tent pole."

He smiled a little and pointed with his head toward the bedding between his legs. And sure enough, there was the pole lying between his feet.

"Oh."

His wolfish grin made the heat rush through every nerve ending.

She hurried to set the other tent pole, knowing his injured shoulder had to hurt something awful, and he had to be freezing.

He released the tent with a groan, sat down on the bedding, and pulled his wool blanket over his lap.

She examined the bite as he watched her. "It doesn't look half as bad as the other bite did."

He didn't say anything but reached up to touch her cheek. His gentle caress felt like a prelude to something much deeper.

This was *so* not good. She knew he wanted her and she knew it wasn't right, not when he was whatever he was. "I'll just cover the wound with this salve."

When she smeared the smelly stuff on, he hissed, and she looked up at him. He gave her a half smile. "Stings."

"I'm sorry. Hopefully, it'll kill any germs." She instinctively clasped her hand on his forehead, but his skin was normal and not feverish, thank God, and she hoped it stayed that way. She pulled the bandaging from the first aid kit and began wrapping it around the injury, trying to be gentle, although his muscle was rigid as she worked, and she feared she was hurting him.

"Hasn't anyone ever told you not to touch an injured animal?" He relaxed a little and leaned his head closer to hers, his face touching her hair with an amative hint of a nudge.

"You're not a wolf now." She couldn't help that her voice was tinged with annoyance. What did he think? She was stupid? Of course she knew to be careful around an injured wild animal. Even a pet that had been hurt could react viciously to helping hands. "*Furthermore*, how could I have known you were a wolf when I came in to take care of you? Besides, it's too late for the warning."

"Do you often go into dark places without regard to your safety? What if I'd thought you were one of Kintail's men?" he scolded.

"I smell too nice. Besides, I've got the gun and pepper spray."

His brows rose in a roguish way. He tenderly touched her cheek with the back of his hand. "You'd actually use those on me? I know martial arts and could have you just where I wanted you in a matter of seconds."

The vision flitted across her brain of him flipping her onto her back with an expert martial arts move, the can of pepper spray tossed one way, the gun the other, and the aroused hunk landing squarely between her legs, pinning her to his soft bedding. Just the images that brought to mind started an ache between her legs. She grabbed his wrist, stopping him before things got out of hand. Before she changed her mind and let him get out of hand, rather.

When they'd made love before, it was one thing. She didn't know what he had become. Now, she did. She frowned at him. Had he already known?

His eyes were clouded with desire, his voice coated in lust. He definitely had sex on the brain. Not that she wasn't having a tough time keeping her own mind on business. Trying to take care of his injuries, she had every intention of returning to Charles's tent before she got herself into more trouble.

"Stay with me. For a little while?" He took her face in his hands, his brain definitely now residing in the lower part of his anatomy.

She closed her eyes and breathed in the cold air, the slight cologne Cameron wore, and opened her eyes. "Do I have a choice?"

"About what's to be? I doubt it. About staying with me? It'll always be your choice."

Before, she had been afraid to become too attached to the

hunk because they'd go their separate ways. But now...now how could she knowingly make love to someone who was part wolf, part man? On the other hand, what if she was half and half now too? She didn't feel any different except that her hand throbbed with a vengeance. She didn't feel like she was having any symptoms of cabin fever like he'd had, which she was now thinking had all to do with what he was. Then again, he had experienced those symptoms several hours after the first wolf had bitten him.

"Do...do you have any control over it?"

"When I'm around you, I want to be human and it seems to work."

"Seems to? You don't know for sure?"

"I've only changed three times, and every time when we were close to each other, I changed back."

Close. She didn't think it had to do with him being close to her as much as him lusting after her, at least as far as she could tell. The first time, he'd pinned her to the snow. The second time after he bit her, she'd thought it was more because he felt bad and the emotions swamping him precipitated the change. Unless it had to do with her being on his bedding, and he wanted her again. "Three times? When was the other?"

"The middle of the night. I thought I was dreaming. Oh hell, Faith, I overheard Chris and his friends talking in a tent. They might have been discussing you."

"What about? Why didn't you say so before?"

"I thought it was a dream." He sighed. "They were talking about a man doing research and how Chris believed his daughter would join them."

"Join them? In what?"

"Finding the magical wolves? They were looking for

Bigfoot when your father went with them. He must have gotten separated from them when he saw what he did. Then he was shaken up—and no wonder—and returned home to write his paper."

"What if Kintail learned of it and sent someone to spy on my father? Hilson." She let out her breath in exasperation. "Do you think he could be one of Kintail's people?"

"Maybe."

Well, that decided that. Hilson had wanted the research and not her.

She looked up at Cameron. "I need to return to Charles. To watch over him."

"Lie down with me, Faith, for just a little while."

He half pleaded and half commanded. The commanding made her think of Hilson. Always in charge. Always bossing her around. The pleading, *that*...was another matter entirely.

She came to her senses and shook her head. "You'd better get something on before you freeze." Hating to reject him further, she decided she had to leave because she was certain she'd hate herself more if she stayed.

Besides, Charles needed her, as badly injured as he was. She'd never forgive herself if he got worse, and she wasn't there to monitor him closely. And they required some answers from him soon.

Before she exited the tent, Cameron groaned, and she glanced back at him. He'd slipped into the sleeping bag, his face white with pain. Then she was really torn. Stay with Cameron for a little while, just until he fell asleep?

Or return to Charles pronto and save herself?

CHAPTER 13

FAITH'S WISHFUL EXPRESSION MADE CAMERON THINK she was trying to decide whether to stay with him longer or not. Her soft green eyes shifted to the opening of the tent, and he knew he was losing her.

He reached out and touched her uninjured hand, wanting desperately to pull her into his embrace, to hold her tight, to make everything that had happened in the last several hours fade away, but he couldn't force her. Her jaw clenched.

"Faith." He meant to say her name softly, but it came out as lust-drenched pleading to his ears.

"Just for a little while. I've got to go to Charles before long." Her gaze flickered to Cameron's, and she looked down at the bedding.

Then she crawled into the sleeping bag with him and laid her head on his chest, her arm over his waist, and even one leg propped over his. For an hour, she rested with Cameron, his hand stroking her hair as he held her tight. She seemed tense. He could tell from her breathing she wasn't sleeping, her body stiff, but she lay against him just the same, her body heating his. This had to be enough for now, and he was grateful for any concession on her part, but then she pulled away so tentatively, he was certain he could still keep her close if he just pushed a little harder, even though he didn't want her that way.

She had to accept him for what he was, even if it killed

him to see her go. He was certain her reluctance didn't mean she hadn't wanted to be with him. Maybe that she was truly worried about Charles. Or maybe that she was unsure of being with Cameron. That bothered him as much as her not staying with him for a little while longer.

She rubbed her injured hand again, then slipped out of the tent, leaving him to face the bitter cold. With her there, the tent had seemed so much warmer, full of her light. He ground his teeth and sank against the bedding.

The damn pain from his injury wouldn't subside, and he wanted her. Every inch of him was freezing. He growled and jerked his sleeping bag aside, then yanked his clothes on, feeling like he was sitting in his freezer. He couldn't understand why he desired Faith so badly. Not that he hadn't been interested in her from the beginning, and he admired her tenacity and resolve despite all that they'd been through. But everything about her triggered a deeper interest, a need to possess, to make her his, when he hadn't thought he'd ever feel that way about a woman.

He doubted her resolve to tend to his injured shoulder had everything to do with it. His hangdog expression had upset her, and she'd been feeling bad about abandoning him. Come to think of it, no one had ever nurtured him so far as he could recall, which endeared her to him even more.

Then he'd had to change into the blasted wolf again and, worse, bite her. He'd tasted her blood and knew he'd broken the skin. He prayed he hadn't infected her with the magical wolf's virus, or whatever the hell it was.

Damn the change and his lack of control over it! He jerked the sleeping bag to his chin and slammed his eyes shut, but sleep wouldn't come. Not with the way his mind kept working over all that had occurred since he'd first met her. All he wanted was the siren curled beside him, her head resting on his chest, his arms wrapped around her bundled body, listening to her steady heartbeat, breathing in the fragrance that was all Faith—a hint of something floral, and definitely something sexual. More than anything, he desired her acceptance. And now what? Had he changed her too? Annoyed with himself for his lack of restraint, he curled his fingers into fists.

Unable to sleep, Cameron wanted in the worst way to look for David and Owen and search the area to ensure none of Kintail's wolves lurked nearby. Or Kintail and his men either. He wondered if they were all one and the same.

But he needed to rest too.

He rolled onto his side, then his stomach, the pain in his shoulder giving him fits. He tossed onto his back and stared at the tent ceiling. "Hell," he growled.

He stripped off his clothes and willed himself to shift.

It didn't happen right away. He thought of claws and teeth, of fur and a long menacing snout, of ears sitting atop his head that twitched back and forth, listening to sounds. Then he felt the heat circulating through every blood vessel.

This time when his fur coat covered his bare skin, and he was standing on the bedding as a wolf, a new sensation filled him with an uncontrollable need. The urge to howl.

Faith woke with a start, unsure what made her stir. She hadn't thought she'd ever fall asleep, as upset as she was about Cameron biting her. Well, more than that, that he was whatever he was and Kintail's wolf had turned him that way.

She thought back to when she was in the camp alone. Most of the dogs had run off with the wolf that had killed the others. Fearing the dead wolves' blood would attract a predator, she'd meant to bury the wolves. But when she'd found the two naked dead men in the wolves' places, she'd nearly had a stroke. It didn't dawn on her that Cameron was the wolf that had killed them either, just that he'd vanished. Even when he'd pounced on her, then began talking to her in his human form again, trying to reassure her, her brain had a hard time assimilating the information. He was human, a bit of a rogue, dangerous even, if someone threatened his safety, but a man who could turn into a wolf?

She ran her hands through her tangled hair. Even now, it seemed more like a dream, well, nightmare, especially once he'd bitten her. Although the bite wasn't hurting any longer. Hopefully, it was only that—a small bite that wouldn't amount to anything.

Charles mumbled something. That was what had woken her. She sat up and touched his cheek. "Charles? Can you hear me?"

He didn't respond.

His temperature appeared normal, his breathing too.

Glad he wasn't in distress, she sighed. They still needed to get him to a doctor.

Not wanting to leave her warm sleeping bag, Faith finally crawled out, the call of nature too great. The worst part of winter camping in the middle of nowhere, besides the constant cold, was that there were no outhouses. She slipped out of the tent, glanced at Cameron's tent and the dogs, but Cameron must still be sleeping. The dogs lifted their heads. She shushed them, then walked away from camp. She headed deeper into the woods, but not too far, perfect for privacy in case Cameron exited his tent. Although she was surprised he wasn't up already, tending to the dogs. Then again, she was the morning person, and he seemed to be more of a night owl.

Then she worried about his new wound. Hell, what if the bite had made him terribly ill? No way could she manage taking two injured men back to Millinocket, maneuvering two sleds and all the dogs. Planning to check on Cameron as soon as she took care of business, Faith found the perfect spot, a huge spruce shielding her from the campsite. She was about to get on with business when something moved in the woods off to her left. She jerked her head that way. A big white wolf with light brown eyes stood watching her. *Don't run*, she warned herself, the image of Cameron flattening her against the snow in his wolf form flitting across her brain. Yet the instinctive urge was there—to flee the danger.

On the other hand, maybe it was just Cameron in a magnificent ice-white coat, same tall stature, longer legs, and healthy body, unlike the scrawnier wolves he'd fought. She folded her arms and faced him down. He paused some distance from her, panting, his ears twisting back and forth, probably listening to sounds only he could hear, his tail slightly wagging, and his mouth almost smiling.

Then the sound of one of the dogs running up behind her caught her attention. She turned slightly to see another white wolf. Her heart nearly seized. The two wolves were matched in size and looked very similar.

If the one coming from camp was Cameron—must be because the dogs didn't react—then—

She glanced at the other.

He'd vanished. Her heart racing, she stared at the trees, the snow piled up against them. Any one of them could be hiding the white wolf.

The wolf behind her nudged her hand, and she swallowed a scream. "Cameron?"

He bowed his head.

"Jeez, I thought the other was you." She rubbed her arms, her whole body trembling. "I need some privacy."

Instead of returning to camp, he took off to check out the woods in front of her, and then she wished she hadn't wanted him to leave, fearing he'd find the other wolf and tangle with it.

After taking care of business in a hurry, she waited for Cameron to return. When he didn't, she hurried back into camp. Once she'd retrieved the gun and pepper spray—which she scolded herself for not carrying with her all along—she rushed back to the woods.

Silence greeted her. Not even a whisper of a breeze. Her heartbeat pounded in her eardrums, the can of pepper spray in her gloved hand as she took a few steps in the direction Cameron had taken.

What if she found a wolf? What if it was the wrong one? She pushed forward, her boots sinking knee deep in the soft snowdrifts. If she had to run, she'd be in a world of hurt. But she wouldn't abandon Cameron either.

Growling pierced the frigid air and she stood stock-still. And then another sound, snowmobiles? The engines' roar in the distance…headed their way?

Rescue? Her heart lifted. Or Kintail's men? Her hopes took a dive. She stared at the spruces, figured she'd better get back to protect Charles and the dogs, and prayed Cameron would be all right.

With no sign of the snowmobiles yet, although they were headed this way, she raced to feed the dogs, who pranced and danced around her, eager for breakfast.

Hurry back, Cameron. Now, she silently pleaded.

After putting food out for the dogs, she returned to Cameron's tent to get the first aid kit and change Charles's bandage before the snowmobiles arrived, three of them, she thought. They continued to roar toward them, and as they drew closer, the dogs let out a chorus of wild barking.

Listening to the noisy snowmobiles, Faith loved how much quieter and in tune with nature dogsledding was. Then, as she saw the three machines in the distance, she felt the heavy metal gun in her pocket and held onto the can of pepper spray.

The three men drove into camp, wearing ski masks and snow goggles, their fur-trimmed hoods hiding their faces so she couldn't see their expressions. Then Cameron, or at least she hoped it was, loped back into camp as a wolf. He eyed the newcomers, sniffed the air, and moved in closer to her in a protective mode, bumping her leg, nuzzling her. She was glad to have him on her side.

"Where's Charles?" one of the men asked, climbing off the snowmobile. He glanced at the wolf, but he didn't seem surprised.

He knew Charles? He had to be a friend, the way he sounded worried. Which would have eased her concern, but the fact he didn't act shocked to see a wild wolf in camp meant he knew Kintail and his wolves. Then again, it seemed everyone knew of Kintail and his wolves.

"He's been injured. How do you know him?"

"I'm his cousin. He didn't tell us he had paying customers for an overnight sled ride, and he's late arriving home. His sister is worried sick about him. How was he injured?"

A cousin. Relieved, Faith motioned to the tent. "It's a long story. We became separated from him, and when we found him, he'd been hurt. He was struck on the head and appears to have a concussion."

"Separated?" The man frowned at her, then stormed inside the tent and spoke in French, but she couldn't understand what he said

At once, she felt as though they thought Cameron and she were party to a crime.

The other two men dismounted and began taking care of the dogs, putting on their booties, packing up the sleds. The dogs' barking was nearly deafening.

His brow deeply furrowed, Charles's cousin exited the tent. "I'm Michael Simmons. Charles is conscious and said you need to return to the cabins, pack your bags, and leave for Millinocket at once. You and my brother, George, can take the snowmobiles in. The rest of us will follow with the sleds when we've finished packing."

Cameron loped past them into his tent and, after a few minutes, reemerged in his human form, dressed for the weather. Faith closed her gaping mouth. *Guess he had the wolf change business under control.*

Michael and the others took notice but didn't say a word. They knew. She wondered how many other local area residents knew about Kintail and his wolves. Or were

Charles and his cousins also some of the same kind of creatures?

Cameron hauled out his sleeping bag and Faith's and his bags, avoiding looking at anyone, appearing uncomfortable as hell. Faith hurried to help him.

"You must be with Kintail," Michael said to Cameron as he worked on the dogs' harnesses.

Faith felt her blood pressure rise.

Cameron sliced him a glare. "Not in this lifetime."

Michael and the other two men stopped harnessing the dogs, and he glanced back at Charles's tent and swore under his breath, "Damn, Charles." He considered Cameron's torn parka sleeve. "When did it happen?"

"A couple of days ago."

Michael considered Faith. "Were you bitten also?"

"Not by one of Kintail's wolves." Faith avoided eye contact with Cameron.

Cameron threw their bags on one of the snowmobiles. "Yeah, she was…*by mistake.*"

Michael shook his head. "It would be best for the two of you to leave the region pronto, if you know what's good for you."

Cameron gave him a caustic look. "I'm still looking for two of my friends."

"We admire you and your kind." Michael bowed his head slightly in reverence. "Kintail and his people have been here for centuries—magical creatures, powerful and at one with nature. They have always lived in peace with our people, the tales passed on from generation to generation, while we have honored their ways. Which means we don't interfere in their…your business. What goes on with

Kintail's pack—territorial disputes, internal encroachments or external ones—will be decided by you and your kind."

Faith closed her gaping mouth. Kintail *was* one of them. For centuries, this had been going on? It had to have been what her father's research was all about!

What about what the men in the hot tub had said? They hadn't found Bigfoot, but something else? The man killed in Kintail's office…with silver. Hell, he was a…werewolf?

The fairy tales were true? But then again, silver in high amounts could kill anyone.

"We appreciate your helping us out, and we'll take it from here." Cameron took the gun from Faith and shoved it in his pocket.

The notion they were out on a twig of a limb without a safety net crossed Faith's mind. This was so not good. Wanting to thank Charles and say goodbye, she stalked into his tent, but his eyes were shut, and when she crouched next to him and spoke, he didn't respond.

"Thank you, Charles, for everything." She kissed his cheek and pulled the blanket higher. "We appreciate everything you did for us, and if I can ever pay you back…just contact me." She hoped he was really awake or enough so that he could hear her. But she intended to check on him after they returned to Millinocket.

When she reemerged from the tent, she asked Michael, "Will Charles be all right?"

"That hard head of his has taken a lot of knocks. Yeah, he'll be fine, but he shouldn't have gotten into Kintail's business. He knows better."

"I can't understand how you can treat Kintail as if he should get away with this"—she waved toward Charles's tent—"as if you don't care." Faith's voice was much higher-pitched than she meant it to be, but she couldn't believe Charles's family would allow such brutality to one of their own. Maybe they didn't care about Cameron's friends, but Charles was their cousin! "You act as though Kintail's a god!"

"I'm certain you'll come to understand Kintail's ways before long. All I can say is that we were not put here to judge him or his kind." Michael turned to George. "Get them to the resort, and make sure they leave for the trail-head after that. We'll be headed that way shortly. And don't talk to anyone. We don't want any more trouble."

George barely let Faith and Cameron mount their snowmobiles before he took off. He drove so fast she wondered if it was because he didn't want Kintail or his people to catch him aiding them, he hoped to lose them, or he just wanted to get back as quickly as possible to help Charles.

She glanced at Cameron driving behind her. Was he getting the wolf change more under control? She hoped so, or he'd have to live like a mountain man. He'd have to find a job where he could work out of his home. No dealing with people on a regular basis. Only private-eye investigations under the cover of dark.

Then she worried about her own situation. What if *she* began to change? There went her job too.

She didn't feel any urge in that regard though. Thankfully. Through her balaclava, she smelled the air: crisp, clean, and cold. Nothing unusual about it. Maybe the only time someone like Cameron had the wolf sense was when he was a wolf. That would be understandable. At least as much as turning into a wolf could be believable.

The whole time back, she worried about what they would report to the police. That a wolf attacked Cameron and changed him into something mythical? And maybe she was in the same boat? That he'd killed two wolves defending her who also happened to be men? That Kintail or one of his men had nearly killed Charles?

Officers Whitson and Adams would believe every bit of it. *Right.*

In half the time it took to travel with the dogs, they arrived on the snowmobiles back at the cabins. As soon as they dismounted at the lodge, Faith hoped to understand more of what they were up against. She asked George before he could run off, "What do you know about Kintail's wolves?"

He cast a disgruntled look her way. "You're not one of the Penobscot, and you're not an accepted member of Kintail's pack. If I were you, I'd do what my brother suggested. Get out of here before Kintail or his people make you vanish for good."

"But Cameron *is* one of them," Faith insisted.

George shook his head and took the keys to the snowmobiles from them. "Kintail hasn't made him part of his pack, and none of his people will welcome him here while the leader wants him dead. My own people won't willingly take sides with an outsider who's one of Kintail's kind but on his terminal list. Cameron will have to leave and"—he lifted a shoulder—"maybe start his own pack. Since Cameron bit you," George said, his lips lifting slightly, "for all practical purposes, he's already claimed a mate."

Faith's mouth gaped, and she quickly looked at Cameron.

He cleared his throat and took her hand. "We don't know that you've been infected."

George looked like he didn't believe she'd escaped Cameron's fate. "Kintail's pack rules this territory. The best thing for the two of you to do is return to your own region. Although blending in someplace else might be hard to do when the shift occurs. There are no Arctic wolves in the States, except for Alaska. Unless you manage to win the populace over like Kintail and his people have here, pretending that the wolves are pets."

George's expression darkened. "The problem if you go to Alaska is it's the only place in the United States that animals can be shot from an aircraft, through some loophole in the law. So hunters will either kill from the air or run the wolves or other hunted animals down until they're too exhausted to escape, then land the aircraft and shoot their prey. A magical wolf would be just as much at risk of being hunted down while in its wolf form. Many hunters oppose aerial hunting because it violates the ethics of fair chase, but the ones who don't..." His jaw taut, George shook his head.

"You can leave the keys to the cabins on the kitchen counters." George went inside the lodge and shut the door.

"You might be all right, Faith," Cameron reiterated. "You might not have contracted my...condition."

She wasn't just concerned about herself. "What will you do? And what about your friends?"

Cameron took Faith's uninjured hand, walked her past the shower facility, and headed for the path through the woods to her cabin. "I can't leave until I find them. It appears you don't need to stay here any longer though. It seems your father might have seen something of what I've become while he was doing his research. I doubt that even if the flash drive still exists, Kintail will want your father sharing the information with the world. In fact, it's too dangerous for you here. Until I can get you on a plane out of here, you'll stay with me, but then you need to return home."

She frowned at him. "I agree that my dad probably found out about Kintail and his people, and that's what he wrote about. Maybe someone was following him like he thought because of what he knew." Faith pulled Cameron to a stop. "What if Hilson is dead? If he tried to blackmail Kintail with the information, he or his people most likely would have killed him. Maybe that's why he's no longer at the cabin. Or maybe he's one of them." She took a deep breath. "Even so, I can't go, not now."

"Listen, I've got to find my friends and free them from Kintail's clutches if they're still alive. *Somehow*. It's not going to be a walk in the park. But I can't be watching your back too. It's too dangerous."

She humpfed and headed off to the cabin. "For your information, Cameron MacPherson, I may already have your, um, problem, condition, whatever. I'm not about to get on an airplane and fly home before I know for sure. What if I changed in the middle of the flight? No pets allowed, and certainly no feral wolves.

"I could see myself having an *episode* and having to hightail it to the bathroom. Then the seat-belt lights go on, and I'm stuck in the privy as a wolf. The stewardess is pounding on the door, trying to get a stubborn passenger to retake her seat. And I can't say a word. The stewardess uses a key on the door, afraid there's something terribly wrong. And there is. I've got big, sharp teeth, an extraordinary sense of smell, and better vision—all the better to see, smell, and eat her with. So I'm staying here until I know the whole story."

He didn't say anything for quite a while, his hand still tight around her arm as he held her close, helping to keep her warm from the bitter breeze. Then he cleared his throat. "Okay, but you continue to stay with me for the time being. And," he turned to look at her and added, "if you don't show any signs of what I have, you go home, pronto."

She glowered at him. "It would be my pleasure." Although she didn't mean it in the least. It had to be a case of immediate rebound. Hell, she was ready to settle down with a wolf-man?

"What if this *condition* affects people differently? What if I take longer to change?"

Cameron let out his breath in a frosty huff and hurried her faster toward her cabin but didn't reply. Then he mumbled, "I shouldn't have gone with you and Charles. I put you at risk."

Surprised, she glanced up at him. He was feeling this was all his fault? "Right, you protected me from the big, bad wolf behind the shower room."

When he raised his brows at her in disbelief, she frowned. "He was coming for me. You got in his way. So you just delayed the inevitable. He still got me, only through you." She gave a half smile. "Besides, I've been in worse predicaments."

He opened his mouth, and she figured he planned to contradict her.

She shook her head. "Okay, maybe not anything worse than this. Although I did have a mad killer after me once."

He snorted.

"I did. In my line of work, sometimes the crazies go after the forensic scientists. He didn't want me to learn how he'd murdered three of his victims."

A look of admiration crossed Cameron's face for a second, then he was back to being annoyed. "Okay, so that was one mad killer. This is a pack of them. And I'm serious about sending you home." Cameron took Faith's hand and continued walking her down the path to Black Bear Den cabin.

He stepped on the deck, paused to smell the air, and frowned.

She smelled something too. A hint of spice, and something else.

Cameron pulled the door open.

Leidolf Wildhaven, his brows lifted, stood in the middle of the cabin among Faith's colorful bras and panties, which were strewn about the floor.

CHAPTER 14

"WHO THE HELL TOLD MY MEN TO GO AFTER CAMERON and the woman at their campsite?" Kintail asked Lila, suspecting she had everything to do with it as he glowered at her, and then he switched his deadly look to the rest of his pack.

Twelve males and six females stood around his great room, their expressions wary, looking rebuked. The only two who didn't seem that way were David and Owen. But they wouldn't have had anything to do with it. If anything, they seemed pleased to hear that things had gone so well for their partner and friend.

Kintail growled. Two people murdered at the hands of fanatical killers and two more dead because of this damned Cameron MacPherson. Although Kintail didn't blame him. The newly turned wolf was protecting what he felt was his property. She wouldn't be for long.

"Who?" Kintail asked again, his voice just as hard. No one spoke. He motioned to one of the older women. "Katina was the only one who did what she was told. Well, she and Vance and Luke." He bowed his head slightly to them, glad they'd been so quick thinking when Charles appeared out of the blue with his sled teams and Cameron and Faith. Katina locking Cameron and Faith in the barn while they were snooping around couldn't have been better planned, and Vance and Luke guarding the building in their wolf forms was the perfect touch. Even if it didn't work to keep his hostages where he wanted them, at least some of his people were making the right *effort*.

"Despite that he's newly one of us, Cameron is an alpha, folks, if any of you are too shortsighted to see that. He's not one to mess with. From what I could see of the track marks at their campsite, Baker targeted Faith. To kill her? Or to have her? Since he's dead, the case is moot. If anyone else tries to touch the woman, you won't only have her newly turned protector to deal with but me. Understood?" He gave Lila a hard look.

Her expression sulky, she lifted one brow, not to be cowed.

David and Owen exchanged glances.

"As to the ones murdering our people without provocation, I want them brought to me alive. Understand?"

Officers Whitson and Adams shifted a little in their stances. Hell, why have a couple of his people on the police force if they weren't going to learn who the murderers were pronto? Except for getting his wolves out of hot water when need be, this was the first real test of trouble, and they hadn't been able to do anything about it.

Although Kintail suspected Faith might have a clue. "Get the woman to share her theory about the killings, Adams."

"But you said not to involve them."

"They're involved up to their hairlines, damn it. Find out what Faith suspects. Maybe as a forensic scientist, she can uncover the truth."

"She'll cause problems." Lila sounded as if she hoped the woman would.

Kintail suspected she was going to be trouble, but in a different way than Lila was. He had every plan to keep Faith under his control better than he had Lila.

"And Cameron? He's a private investigator and former police officer. We checked his credentials, and he's been at this a lot longer than we have," Adams said.

Kintail should have gotten Adams and Whitson on the force and trained a long time ago instead of just six months ago. "How long has he been in the business?"

"Eight years."

Hell, no way did he want to solicit the outsider's help. On the other hand...

Kintail nodded. "Yeah, see if he can shed any light on the situation." Once they located the murderers of his people, Cameron wouldn't be needed any longer.

"What about that nosy red?" Adams asked.

"Leidolf? You were supposed to question him. What did he say he was here for?"

"He explained he was on vacation. He wouldn't say anything further."

"Vacation, my ass. And where's Hilson?"

"He's around. But he's making himself difficult to locate." Adams looked back at David and Owen. They both perked up. Adams turned his attention to Kintail. "We have another situation."

Before Adams said what it was, Kintail knew.

"Their partner, Gavin Summerfield, booked a flight and is on his way to Bangor."

Owen shook his head. David raised his brows at his friend.

Kintail pondered the situation before he spoke. "Where are Cameron and Faith now?"

"Michael Simmons told us he sent his brother George with them to return to their cabin rentals. Charles wants them gone. He figures he's upset you."

"None of my people better have injured Charles." Kintail looked over at Trevor. "Faith wants to speak to you about her father's work. They won't fall into the same trap twice. Go to her. Make up a Bigfoot story. Appease her. Unless she's learned what we are. Then tell her whatever satisfies her. I want Cameron and Faith to stay right where they are. It's easier to monitor their movements than if they're back in Millinocket. Until we have some answers about the murders committed recently, I want their help. Gavin's, too, if he can provide it."

"What about them?" Adams asked, motioning to David and Owen.

"They stay here, out of sight and away from harm. The four men together would be too much of a risk. Not when they're still learning pack rules." Kintail cast a small smile at Owen.

The guy was trouble, but at least he had David in line.

"I can't believe Gavin's coming here," Owen said to David as they were locked in the basement again, the windows barred, the room smelling of mold. Owen sneezed again. "I'm afraid I really blew it this time." He slumped on a mattress resting on an iron bed frame that looked like old army issue—olive-drab blanket, scratchy bedsheets. Hell, he was used to the kind with the silky high-numbered thread count—courtesy of a former girlfriend who'd hated his own rough sheets. Now he couldn't get used to anything else.

"Don't be so hard on yourself. You were only trying to save Cameron's ass. You can't help it that communications are so spotty out here. And you know Gavin would have come out anyway if he never could get hold of Cameron. Besides, together, they'll be able to do more." He sighed. "You know, the more you create problems, the more they watch you."

"Yeah, and while you're doing nothing, they figure you're a real beta, complacent, willing to do whatever they say." Owen couldn't help sounding disgruntled. He was always a man of action who would take control of a situation, push for a solution no matter how difficult the trials. In that respect, he was more like Cameron. David? He was the ultimate laid-back kind of guy. Owen couldn't be like that, no matter how much he tried. And who has the heart attack? The no-stress guy. On the other hand, maybe David's no-worries attitude was all a facade, and all this time, he'd held the stress in.

"What do you think they'll do when Gavin reaches Cameron?" Owen asked, clenching his hands into fists, wishing the hell he had his gun but recalling belatedly it wouldn't help anyway. Not against these wolf types. Unless real bullets did work and silver bullets weren't really needed—just part of the mythology.

David reclined in the bed, arms beneath his head, and stared up at the concrete block ceiling. "I'm not sure. Sounds like Cameron's got his hands full, protecting some new little lady in distress. I'm kind of surprised after the way Marjory stiffed him. I just hope Faith doesn't put him through the wringer too."

"Hell, what about these werewolf hunters? At least if Kintail would let us, we could put our heads together and deal with them." He growled, hating to be locked in the basement most of the time. At least he'd gotten the shape-shifting business pretty well under control. He wondered how Cameron was taking it. "Cameron's been turned," Owen said, tapping his fists on the bed frame. "He's got to be pissed."

David closed his eyes and yawned. "No more than you are. As for the werewolf hunters, we can't do anything about it. As many people as Kintail has guarding us, we shouldn't have to worry. Relax. If we seem like we're not going anyplace, Kintail and his people will get sloppy. Then we'll make our move."

"What about Elizabeth?" Owen raised a brow at David. When David ignored Owen, he persisted. "She's got the hots for you. You might use it to our advantage." Although he knew David was the kind of man who wouldn't use a woman, no matter what the circumstances. Owen took a different approach and shrugged. "Once we get out of here, you could always send for her if you're that interested." He knew David was. He'd seen the shared glances. The shy intrigue on Elizabeth's part. The way David tried to hide his interest in her. Owen recognized she meant something to his partner.

David slipped his hands behind his head. "Lots of guys in Kintail's pack are interested in her."

"Yet she only has eyes for you. You heard that police officer, Adams. He was peeved as hell. She said she hadn't made those fudge brownies or that special stew of hers for anyone in the pack until the two of us arrived."

David smiled. "Damn good too. But who says she made them for me and not because of some whim of hers? For you, even?"

"She watched you to see what you thought of her cooking. Of course you made a big impression when you went back for thirds."

"They were good."

"Yep. And she has the hots for you. So you ought to use it to our advantage."

Don't jump to conclusions, Faith warned herself as she stared in disbelief at her clothes strewn all over the cabin while Leidolf Wildhaven stood on the braided rug among a pink bra and four pairs of panties ranging from matching pink to black. He didn't look like a guilty man caught in the act, which may have been the reason for her thinking he had nothing to do with messing with her stuff. But he did have a hint of a smile on his lips and in his gaze, which irritated the hell out of her.

She noted, too, that not one thing of Cameron's had been touched.

"What are you doing in my cabin?" She stormed into the place and started to grab up a sweater when she smelled the odor of urine.

"You've made an enemy," Leidolf said matter-of-factly. "Female. She left her calling card."

Now, Faith was *really* ticked off. "Who?" As soon as the word was out of her mouth, she figured out who. *Lila Grayson.* Despite being the type who was always civilized even under the most uncivilized conditions, Faith wanted to pay her back.

"I don't know the woman to match her with the scent."

Leidolf sniffed the air and raised his brows. "We need to talk."

"You don't smell like one of us," Cameron said, yanking a plastic bag out from under the kitchen sink. "What's your story?"

Faith stared at Leidolf. He was from Portland. He couldn't be an Arctic wolf too.

"You saw me the other day. In my wolf form."

"A red wolf?" Cameron's eyes widened.

"A red wolf?" Faith parroted, helping Cameron to pick up her things. Clothes that hadn't been peed on, she deposited on the bed. The rest of the stuff went into the plastic trash bag, while she cursed silently to herself. "You said you were bitten by a wolf too. Not one of Kintail's?"

"No. He and his people are Arctic wolves. I'm a red. Then there are grays. Arctic wolves are a subspecies of the gray. Beyond that, I wasn't bitten and changed like the two of you. Not that I haven't been bitten before. That comes along with the territory as a pack leader."

Faith snapped her gaping mouth shut.

Cameron flicked his gaze Faith's way.

"The two of us? You know for sure I'm also one now?" She collapsed on one of the dining room chairs. She didn't feel any differently, well, except for a sudden bit of light-headedness, but that wasn't from *being* a wolf but *being told* she was one. "How...are you certain?"

"It's subtle. You have a special scent. You're one of us. Guaranteed."

—⁂—

Faith looked a little ill. Cameron had prayed he hadn't infected her. He guessed it was as she'd said—everyone's system reacted differently to the change—although he'd been trying to sense anything about her that might have been altered. He'd hoped since her wound had been nearly superficial, she might not have been infected. But he couldn't break free of the gnawing at his gut that he was responsible for her condition.

Part of him felt like he had to keep and protect her, since she was like him and he'd made her that way. Part of him worried she'd hate him for what he had done to her. Since they had both recently weathered dissolved relationships, he figured that might create even more problems. Yet he couldn't deny how much he wanted her.

He joined her and rubbed her back. She relaxed a little but just stared at the floor, and he assumed she was thinking about how much this was going to affect her. At least for himself, he couldn't quit thinking about how he could live among humans and continue to work with his partners the way he was now.

"How could you have been born this way?" he asked Leidolf.

"My mother and father and all their ancestors, or most of them, were *lupus garous*. So that makes me one too. Or rather a royal, one who has barely any human genes." He gave a small smile, arrogant, as if everyone could figure that out.

Faith looked up at Leidolf. "Why are you here? Charles's cousin George said that Kintail's pack controls this area. Since you're a red from Portland..." She didn't say anything further.

Portland, where Faith was from. As much of an alpha as Leidolf appeared to be in his wolf form, Cameron assumed he ran his own pack in Portland.

"You've seen the killings. The one at Kintail's offices, and the one out here. What did you make of it?" Leidolf questioned in response.

"You're investigating them? With Kintail's permission?" Cameron asked, not figuring that Kintail would have given it unless Leidolf had special qualifications to deal with something like this.

Leidolf offered another subdued smile. "Not exactly. It's my business because it also involves my pack, so..." He shrugged.

Cameron frowned. "Your pack out of Portland?"

"That's where I'm from now. Do you want her?" Leidolf asked Cameron, but before he could answer, Leidolf responded for him. "It's obvious you do."

The pheromones Cameron was giving off must have clued Leidolf. Cameron could smell Faith's too. Although he wasn't sure if that was purely a biological issue or if something deeper down triggered it.

"What I'm getting at is do you want her for your mate? *Permanently?* We take a mate for life, no adulterous affairs, no divorces. Once we've mated with one of our own kind, that's it. Although in a couple of rare cases, researchers discovered pack leaders among the wolves with two mates at the same time; it's not the usual case with us. Partly, it's an inborn thing—one mate at a time, no desire for another. Maybe our genetic predisposition evolved that way because we haven't had enough females to go around as it is. I've always suspected it goes a lot deeper. My sister would say it has to do with finding your soul mate. Although I'm not certain I'd go as far as believing that."

Leidolf seemed deep in thought for a minute. "Then again, maybe she's right. With our werewolf kind, if we can find one, we're able to select a mate. It's not just left up to the alpha leaders like in most real wolf packs. And if we're able, we can have our own offspring. Like with real wolves, in a rare instance, one of our kind might deviate from the norm and take a second mate while already having one. Just like with any species where one of its kind does something that isn't normally done."

From Leidolf's glum expression, Cameron assumed he knew someone who *had deviated from the norm*. Which made Cameron curious as to the outcome.

"I take it you know someone who had a couple of mates at the same time. What happened?"

Leidolf's face darkened. "Let's just say it didn't have a happy ending." Taking a deep breath, he added, "Before you're mated with one of our kind, you can have sex with any number of humans. We're immune to their sexually trans-mitted diseases and normally can't get a human pregnant. As long as we don't get ourselves killed off accidentally, we live long lives, aging a year for every thirty once we reach eighteen. So be sure of what you want. I only mention all this because I assume the one who bit you and intended to kill you didn't give you any insight into the way we live."

Not saying a word, Faith left her chair and began heating the water in the teakettle.

Cameron wondered what kind of a mess he'd gotten himself into. He figured there'd be a big learning curve but not that he would have to adapt that much. Mainly, control the timing of the shifts, but the werewolf politics was another matter.

As far as taking a mate for life…he glanced at Faith and saw the vulnerability in her sparkling green eyes. Whether it was right or wrong, he craved having her for his own. From the moment he had walked out of his bathroom and seen her standing in his hotel room, her boots on the floor as if she was getting ready to stay, he'd wanted her.

"I don't know how it is with Arctic *lupus garous,* but with reds and grays, we have a severe shortage of females. So"—Leidolf shrugged—" finding another mate could be difficult if you and Faith aren't itching to become mates. Once Kintail's bachelor males discover a new, unclaimed female *lupus garou* is in his territory, better watch out. Of course, that's saying there's a shortage of females in his pack."

Crap, what else? He had intended to send her home for her own protection from Kintail and his people as soon as Cameron knew for sure she hadn't been turned. He'd never expected that the unmated population of Arctic magical wolves in the area might try to claim her for their own.

"If a pack leader had it in mind to kill me and I was newly turned, I'd be leaving this area pronto." Leidolf removed his parka. After folding it over the couch back, he took a seat on one of the kitchen chairs. "What can you tell me about Kintail and his people?"

The concept was probably preposterous, but Cameron had to ask. "There's no cure for this condition?"

CHAPTER 15

FAITH JERKED HER HEAD AROUND TO SEE LEIDOLF'S response, but the smile on his lips told her all she needed to know. No cure existed for the werewolf condition.

"There's no sense in fighting what we are. You are what you are. Of course being a red would be preferable to an Arctic wolf. It limits where you can live in some regards."

"Red wolves aren't all that common either," Cameron said, sarcasm in his voice. Faith smiled at him, thankful he'd had a swift comeback when she couldn't think of one for the life of her.

Leidolf shrugged. "You're right of course. I'd still rather be a red than anything else. You'll both have a new lifestyle to an extent, but for the most part, I'm sure you'll adjust well enough. However, you'll need to live with an established pack while you learn our ways. You might have to go to Alaska to find one. Since Kintail's from the Canadian Arctic, from what I understand, you won't be able to join his pack up there. Unless there are others in the area."

"So why exactly are you here?" Faith asked, offering Cameron a cup of hot cocoa, then another to Leidolf. She was not the least bit interested in joining a werewolf pack in Alaska or anywhere else.

"Have you heard of the Dark Angels?"

Faith already didn't like the sound of them as she sat down at the dining table and sipped her cocoa, then shook her head.

"I discovered them on the internet, describing some group that searches for abominations—Bigfoot mainly. No problem. But then there was some interest in werewolves. Usually someone in the pack monitors stuff like that. This group listed some information about real werewolf trials, which in itself could mean nothing. But they are extremely focused on the possibility we exist."

"Real werewolf trials?" Of course Faith knew about real witch trials, but trials for werewolves?

"Sure. For centuries, trials have been conducted all over the world. It was really bad in France during the witch hunts in medieval times. One of the documented cases was about a John Grenier, only thirteen, who confessed to being a werewolf. There was no torture involved. At the time, a reddish feral dog had been attacking villagers. Because of the boy's age and that he came freely to the court to confess, they didn't sentence him to death." Leidolf shook his head. "The boy wore a wolf skin and confessed to killing a dog, a baby, and a young girl. He tried to kill another, but she beat him off with her staff while she was shepherding. He tried to murder a young boy, but his uncle rescued his nephew."

"But…werewolves aren't supposed to kill just for the sake of killing, are they? If he was a real werewolf…"

Leidolf drank his cocoa and set the cup aside. "Most of our kind believe he wanted to be one of us. He probably saw a *lupus garou* changing and thought killing innocents was what it took to become a werewolf. He was nothing more than a murderer, a cannibal."

"But they released him? How could they?"

"The president of the court said that lycanthropy—the ability to change into a wolf, and kuanthropy, someone who changes into a dog, were hallucinations, that the boy was of too tender an age, and that he was too dull-witted to know what he had done was wrong. Instead, he was incarcerated for life at the monastery of Bordeaux, where he could learn morals and Christian teachings. They say he ran around the cloister and garden on all fours, devouring a bloody pile of offal—you know, the entrails and internal organs of a butchered animal."

Cameron shook his head.

"He died when he was twenty, his mind completely gone. That's why we figured he wasn't truly one of us, just a mad youngster who wished to be."

Faith let out her breath. She'd never considered people would turn to cannibalism in the guise of being werewolves. "Still, he wasn't really a werewolf."

"Right, but the problem is that people like that give us a bad name. Some think that we truly exist. Some think those tried for being werewolves truly were werewolves, but the authorities wouldn't believe it because of church doctrine. Then hunters of werewolves suddenly appear from time to time, reciting these old trials. Another case was Gilles Garnier," Leidolf said, getting up from the table and making himself another cup of cocoa. "He was a poor farmer who had been a hermit, then married and moved his wife to an isolated home. But he wasn't used to feeding more than himself, and he couldn't afford to feed a wife, so he started foraging for food. That's when he killed a girl, a boy, wounded another girl who was rescued but died later, and again was caught after murdering another boy. What shocked the court the most was that he planned to eat the boy on a Friday, against Catholic doctrine."

When Faith's mouth gaped, Leidolf explained. "Fish only on Fridays. There never was any sign of wolf attacks. Just a human claiming, under torture, that he was a werewolf. His story changed so many times that who knew what to believe. He was found guilty of lycanthropy and witchcraft and burned at the stake. It's interesting to note that in one place in France, the president of the court didn't believe in lycanthropy, and in another, he did."

"But he really wasn't one," Faith said.

"No, he wasn't. In another case, a man in Russia was accused of being a werewolf, and he told the court that he and his werewolf pack killed demons. He was sentenced to ten strikes with a whip for idolatry and superstition, then released."

"Was *he* a werewolf?"

"No. If he had been one, he wouldn't have admitted it. None of us would ever willingly give our kind away. Remember that. Now it seems we have a group that believes we exist, maybe who have even seen our kind shape-shift, and are killing us. They are trying to start a cell in Portland. That's why I'm here. To get at the root of the evil. Eliminate it here and stop them from causing trouble in my region."

"And Kintail knows this?" Cameron asked. "I wouldn't think he'd like your interference."

"He doesn't have to like it. I'm here to get the job done, then return to my pack, not before that."

"What if you help us and we help you?" Cameron asked.

Leidolf studied Cameron, then glanced over at Faith, who was watching his expression closely. Could he be trusted?

"You want me to help free your friends from Kintail's pack?" Leidolf asked.

"That's the gist of it," Cameron said.

Please, please say yes, Faith said silently to herself.

"I can't." Leidolf leaned away from the table. He exuded confidence in his mannerisms, the way he smiled, the intensity of his look, all alpha and just as arrogant. He might seem relaxed, but Faith was quite certain if he was threatened, the man would be the devil to deal with. That was why she figured having him on their side would help significantly in confronting Kintail and his people.

"It has to do with pack politics. I'm here about my own situation concerning the danger to my pack. It has nothing to do with Kintail or his people. I can't interfere with his pack or how he runs it."

"He's taken Cameron's friends hostage! They weren't part of his pack, and he can't claim them." Faith scowled at him. "We'd help you!"

Unruffled by her outburst, Leidolf bowed his head slightly. "If you located the men who are doing the killing, you would help yourselves. Any of us are at risk. If you want to get right down to it, both of you belong to Kintail's pack."

"Because his wolf bit me," Cameron said.

"Right."

"But Cameron bit me," Faith said, still frowning at Leidolf.

Leidolf smiled a little. "Then it seems you're Cameron's, if you're agreeable. Or if not, Kintail will surely want you. As for Cameron? I suspect Kintail doesn't want him, or he would have taken him into the pack right away once one of his people bit him."

Faith looked over at Cameron, not liking any of this one bit. Cameron was masking any reaction, making her feel he wasn't part of this or was afraid to show what he was truly feeling in front of her.

Leidolf cleared his throat. "Mate with her, and she's yours. If you don't, she's considered available. If you do mate with her and Kintail or one of his people desires her, they'll have to kill you before they can have her."

"That's barbaric." The more Faith heard about the pack rules, the more she thought they needed major revamping.

"We mate for life. The wolf's instinct is ingrained in us. It's our way." Leidolf rose from the table. "I'm going to do some exploring in the woods, then return to Millinocket for a time. I think that's where these men are from. Either of you want to come with me?"

"As a wolf?" Faith asked, hoping not but expecting the worst.

"As a wolf."

Faith gripped her mug tightly. "I haven't changed before. I don't plan to if I can help it."

Leidolf appeared mildly amused, then he looked at Cameron. "You?"

"We're returning to Millinocket. Charles wants us out of here." Cameron got up from his chair and joined Faith. "Good luck on your hunt." He offered his hand to Leidolf, and they shook on it.

"Thank you. Good luck on yours." Leidolf headed out of the cabin and shut the door.

Faith wished Leidolf would have helped them, figuring he knew the wolf ways a lot better than they did. Since it wasn't an option, there was no point in worrying about it.

"We can't leave here," Faith said, tugging at Cameron's hand. "What about your friends?"

"Like I said, we return to Millinocket. We can use the internet there, and I'll get in touch with Gavin. I'll find David and Owen and get them back. I don't need some red's help."

Faith wasn't so sure they couldn't use Leidolf's help. And she noted she was left out of the equation, but she figured as soon as she shape-shifted and Cameron was assured she was an Arctic werewolf like him, he'd change his mind. Maybe it was fate that had thrown them together, or maybe it was a total mistake. The idea she'd return without Cameron and live like this on her own, well, hell, he needed her as much as she needed him, and she had no plans to return home alone!

She started to pack her bags, then considered throwing out the items that Lila had sprayed with urine. Yeah, no sense in taking them with her. There was nothing that she couldn't replace. She dumped the trash bag on the floor next to the door. "I'm ready, Cameron. Let's go."

She hoped they wouldn't encounter Kintail or his people on the ten-mile trip to the trailhead and have more difficulties again. The way things were going for them, she halfway counted on trouble.

Leidolf's words rattled around in Cameron's brain, over and over again, like a computer program attempting to make a connection. Cameron had bitten Faith. She was his. That much he got, whether Leidolf had said so or not. No matter how many times Cameron told himself Faith was as much his to keep and protect, he didn't like her being with him and being in more danger. Although there was nothing he could do about it for now. He had to get her safely to Millinocket. From there, he hoped to get her to Bangor and on a plane for home. Werewolf killers and mate-hungry bachelor werewolves all made it too dangerous for Faith to stay here. Later, he'd hook up with her, and they'd work something out. For now, the priority was leaving here and getting a safe place in Millinocket.

Faith was too quiet as she packed up her snowmobile, and he figured it had something to do with the fact she was just like him now. The concept still hadn't completely sunk into his own brain that he was now a werewolf. He could imagine how she was feeling. Or maybe not. Being a woman, she might feel a little differently. Especially the part about how a bunch of werewolf males might be after her, and Kintail was leading the pack at that.

Before Cameron could say anything to her, she got on her snowmobile, pulled her ski mask up and her ski glasses down, then headed down the road toward the trailhead.

All he could think of when they first ventured to the resort was how he wanted to ensure his friends were all right. Now he was pretty sure they weren't. He was a werewolf, the woman he'd traveled with was one too, and werewolf hunters had killed two of his kind. He shook his head at the whole nightmarish and unreal concept and hurried to keep pace with Faith. At least this time, they weren't traveling in a blizzard.

A few miles from the resort, Faith suddenly sped off into the woods. That was when he saw that a tree had been felled across the road. *Hell.* Cameron veered into the woods to follow Faith. She'd slowed down to maneuver between the trees. He heard the snowmobile in pursuit of them.

What next? Kintail's men? The Dark Angels? Only one thing he could think of to do—set a trap to stop their pursuers. He slowed his snowmobile, turned it around, wished he could flip off the headlights—but he dared not turn off his engine and waste even more precious time—and waited, hoping Faith wouldn't get too far ahead of him. The sound of the engine grew closer, the halo of light widening in scope.

After removing his outer gloves, he readied his gun—time to terminate the pursuit. Thankfully, he had plenty of bullets. At least enough to put an end to this madness. Not that he wanted to kill anyone. A minor injury would be enough to make his pursuer cease and desist. At least he assumed.

Then the sound of two more snowmobiles pelted the vicinity, much farther off, headed this way. Cameron clenched his teeth. *Damn.* Well, he could get rid of the first driver and then take down the next two. Good thing they weren't any closer to the first one. All three at once could take some fancy maneuvering. The sound of the snowmobile's roaring engine drew closer. And closer. He aimed his gun straight ahead.

The engine sound grew louder. The vibration in the ground sent shimmers of the stalker's pursuing vehicle through Cameron's snowmobile and up through every one of his nerve endings. He responded by tightening his grip on his weapon, his finger poised on the trigger.

"Let's get this over. Come to Daddy."

He hated the delay. Every precious moment he idled his vehicle, the sound of Faith's machine faded away. "Come on, damn it."

The stalker didn't deviate from his course. Cameron gave a bitter smile. As soon as he appeared in his sights, Cameron would have his man.

—⁓—

Fearing whoever had felled the tree wished them harm, Faith tried to find a way back to the main road around the downed spruce, but the forest didn't cooperate. The farther into the woods she drove, the farther it seemed she was headed away from the unplowed road. She glanced back for a second to see if Cameron was keeping up with her, but all she saw was her tracks in the snow, trees laden with the white stuff, and no sign of Cameron. Although she could hear him in the distance. She slowed to a stop and waited.

Faith heard the snowmobile headed for her from the opposite direction. "Shit."

She glanced back Cameron's way. Still no sign of him. If she drove off in a different direction, she was afraid she'd lose him, not to mention she might lose her own way. Navigating by street maps, no problem. Navigating her way through woods was not her forte.

The snowmobile in front of her grew closer. She reached into her pocket and gripped the pepper spray. And waited, praying Cameron would hurry up and join her.

She heard a snowmobile behind her but still too far away. She thought a couple more were behind that one. Damn it, they were being hemmed in from all sides.

The snowmobile appeared in front of her, moving slowly, the driver male, tall, bulky, and if she wasn't mistaken... But no, the ski mask and hat hid his hair color and face. It couldn't be.

The man pulled in front of her with several feet separating them. She tightened her grip on the pepper spray still in her pocket.

"Faith, honey. What are you doing way out here? Looking for me?" His voice was deep, dark, and full of warning.

Hilson. Come a little closer. She was afraid that the pepper spray wouldn't have any effect on him while he was wearing a mask and goggles that protected his face.

"Hilson?" she asked, trying to sound clueless, as if she truly didn't know who he was in his wintry gear. Although she didn't recognize the clothes. Then again, he'd never worn winter clothes like that before. Suits, yes, as a stockbroker. In fact, he'd never worn anything much casual. Jeans were out. Sneakers? No way. She wondered now if he even was a stockbroker or something else.

Hilson fell for her ploy and drew the mask under his chin and pulled up his goggles to rest on his ski hat. "It's me, honey. In the flesh. Missed me, eh?"

At least her glower was hidden behind her mask and ski glasses. She was sure her voice would give away her ire once she spoke. He had to know damned well that she was madder than hell at him.

"You weren't supposed to follow me here. I would have come back for you eventually. Didn't you get my note that said I would return in a couple of weeks? That I had some important brokerage deals I had to handle?" He folded his arms and leaned slightly back on his machine.

Thankfully, he didn't approach. Maybe because he thought she looked ready to bolt.

"I must have missed the note." She'd found it all right, but she hadn't seen it until she'd discovered he'd stolen her father's flash drive and hard drive. She hadn't believed for a minute that he would return.

As much as she wanted to take another glance in the direction of the trail off to her right, she didn't want to give away that she was considering detouring in that direction. She figured if she kept heading that way, she'd eventually end up at the frozen lake. Probably not the direction she wanted to go.

"How did you manage to find me so quickly? Break into my computer? I left it there so you would know I was returning to you. I hadn't expected you would learn my password. Kintail says you're an investigative genius."

She didn't care what Kintail said about her, and she didn't say anything in response, stalling for time, hoping Cameron would hurry and arrive with the backup weapon. Even though the bullets he had weren't silver. Not that she wanted Hilson dead, just stopped in whatever he had in mind to do.

"You've really caused some problems coming here, you know?" Hilson leaned forward, his amber eyes narrowed, the same look he'd give when he caught some guy hitting on her, and he meant business. "Lila wants you dead. Kintail wants you, period."

"What do you want, Hilson? I thought I meant something special to you." It sounded like Hilson had given up all claims to her. She desperately wanted to look behind her. Wanted to see if Cameron was nearly there. Had to stall Hilson before he did anything she'd regret.

"I know. Whirlwind romance. Three months of great times. You're lucky I didn't just eliminate your father. That's what we do when someone learns what we are. We terminate them or turn them. There wasn't any good reason to make him one of us."

Her father. She felt sick to her stomach. They hadn't killed him, had they? "My father," she said, half-angry, half-choked with emotion.

"He's not the one you have to worry about right now. You know about us, don't you? Kintail says that prick Cameron told you." He sighed. "Damned newbie *lupus garou*. Don't know when to keep their mouths shut. It's supposed to be instinctual, a preservation-of-the-species type of thing." He shook his head. "I knew it would come to this eventually." He pulled off his ski mask and goggles.

"What are you doing?" She tried to sound scornful, but her armor was slipping. She guessed what he was doing, just as soon as he began unfastening his coat.

He was getting ready to shift. And then he would bare his teeth before the bite.

The snowmobile roared around the bend in the trees and slid some distance to a stop. Goggles and a black ski mask hid the driver's expression, but Cameron could pretty much guess the gun was a deterrent in the man's pursuing them. Cameron hadn't heard Faith's snowmobile in some time now and hoped to hell he could locate her quickly once he dealt with their pursuers.

Then the driver of the snowmobile jerked up his goggles and pulled down his mask and grinned like a lunatic. *Gavin.* His red brows raised, he motioned behind himself, and Cameron instantly lowered his gun.

"Cavalry's coming. Where's the little lady?" Gavin asked.

"Up ahead."

"Let's set up a roadblock. They're not far behind." Gavin hurried off his idling snowmobile, and Cameron did the same. Gavin glanced at Cameron's shredded parka sleeve. "You all right?"

"Yeah." Switching the subject, Cameron warned, "No ax."

"Looks like we have enough fallen trees that together we can create a makeshift stopgap."

Cameron always liked that about Gavin. He was an optimist extraordinaire, and he could MacGyver anything together if he had the time and resources. Sometimes even when he had neither. Their current predicament reminded Cameron of some of the missions they'd been on.

"What's she like, Cameron?" Gavin asked as the two of them hauled a heavy tree onto the trail behind Gavin's snowmobile, but he glanced again at Cameron's torn coat, and Cameron figured he'd have to start making up stories to appease his friend, as much as he hated doing so.

Looking at the mess they were creating, Cameron hoped to hell they wouldn't have to backtrack this way anytime soon.

Gavin dumped another armload of branches on the trail. "Faith O'Malley, the woman you've hitched up with this trip. Believe me, I was surprised as hell. She must really be something."

"Faith O'Malley?" How the hell had Gavin already learned so much about her?

"When I arrived at the lodge where you stayed for the night, the clerk gave me an earful about giving the key to your room to a cute blond, that she suspected you were now friends with since her room was across from yours. The clerk sounded a little wishful that she'd had the key to your room instead. Then I learned Miss O'Malley had some business with Lila Grayson and Kintail Silverman concerning Backcountry Tours also. That made me wonder if it had anything to do with you calling and having me check out the license plates for a gray Ford pickup."

Cameron paused as they pulled another tree in place. "What did you learn?"

"It belongs to Backcountry Tours in the name of Kintail Silverman. Since you were investigating the same outfit, I figured you might have hooked up together in the romance department. Although the way you were feeling about Marjory, I wasn't sure you'd take the plunge again so soon—even if it's been several months. So what's the story?"

The information about the registration for the pickup didn't help much, although it looked like Kintail had been following Faith's progress all along. Cameron was damned glad Gavin was here, but the realization hit him again that he couldn't explain all that had happened. He wanted to, as close as he'd been to his partners. But internal warning bells went off concerning what he was now. Instinctually, he knew for the preservation of his kind, he couldn't reveal the truth to Gavin.

He didn't answer Gavin but considered the tangle of trees and branches they'd gathered now blocking the trail and figured it would take their pursuers a while to clear a path. "She's up ahead. Let's go."

Gavin would assume that Cameron was in a hurry to protect the woman. Soon, he suspected more would be at stake. He just hoped the reason there was no sound of a snowmobile's engine grumbling in Faith's direction was because she was stopped, waiting for him to catch up.

As soon as he climbed onto his snowmobile, he tore off toward Faith, Gavin following a distance behind. No matter the bizarre set of circumstances now, Cameron was glad to have his partner at his back. He just hoped Gavin wouldn't learn the truth about the werewolf business, or they'd have a hell of a new mess to deal with.

Trevor stalked into Kintail's lodge, and the hangdog expression meant things hadn't gone as planned. Kintail at first thought the problem was that Faith wouldn't speak with Trevor. But Trevor quickly explained, "Before Officer Adams and Whitson could reach the cabins, Cameron and Faith had left. The officers are in pursuit, but they wanted me to report back to you to tell you what had happened. Once they convince Cameron and Faith to return to the cabins, I'll visit with her there." He stroked his gray beard, his gray eyes watching Kintail's reaction.

Kintail ground his teeth. Couldn't anyone in his pack do anything right? He wanted the woman to discover who the killers in their midst were, and then he wanted her. Period.

"Another thing."

Kintail refocused on Trevor, the man's posture defeated, and Kintail knew he wouldn't like this other thing.

"Or, a couple of things, I should say. The red, Leidolf, was seen exploring the woods near the lake. We think he's investigating this matter of the *lupus garou* killers also. But why, we don't know."

"Fine. He's welcome to help in the investigation if that's all he's here for."

Trevor cleared his throat, and Kintail knew the next bit of news would not set well with him either. "Hilson's after the woman."

Kintail drew himself taller. "My brother didn't claim her. He didn't mate with her. He didn't eliminate her father, who could be a real threat. He has no right to the woman."

"He's been with her for three months," Trevor reminded him.

"Only to get closer to her father, to learn what he was up to, despite *you* saying Kenneth O'Malley hadn't seen any of us shape-shift."

Trevor didn't flinch. Kintail liked that in him. No matter how many times he'd questioned Trevor, he hadn't been able to bully him into telling a different story. Either Trevor really didn't think Mr. O'Malley had seen them change, or he was protecting him. If it was the latter, it meant something about O'Malley's actions must have triggered a sentimental side of Trevor to appear suddenly. Where kids and pets were concerned, he had a soft spot. But adult human males?

Kintail just couldn't figure the situation out. His gut instinct told him Trevor saved O'Malley's ass from being eliminated. Hilson had thought the same and of his own accord moved temporarily to Portland to watch O'Malley. Observing him from a distance had been getting him nowhere. Then he'd targeted the daughter.

Trevor took a deep breath. "Lila cares for you."

Kintail stared at him as if he'd lost his mind.

"I overheard her talking tearfully to Katina about losing her mate and son."

Kintail clenched his teeth, not sure he wanted to hear how much she had loved someone else, telling himself that was why she couldn't love him. He held his tongue and waited.

"She's scared she's going to lose you, and she's scared she can't show you how much she cares before it's too late. As an alpha female, she puts on this act to hide her true feelings, afraid to show her vulnerability."

Kintail looked out the window. Maybe so, but would she ever come to grips with her past? She wouldn't even speak to him about it.

"As to Faith, she wants Cameron and he wants her. You won't ever change that. If you kill Cameron, Faith will want to kill you."

Glancing at Trevor, Kintail wouldn't be thwarted in his mission. If Lila could come around before it was too late, so be it. Otherwise, Faith was his. "Where the hell is Hilson now? No one's been able to get ahold of him."

"He's after the woman. George Simmons told us that when we were looking for Faith and Cameron, Hilson had arrived twenty minutes before us, looking for the woman, then he headed into the woods to find a way to stop her."

"She's mine to turn, damn it." Kintail began jerking off his clothes. "Where the hell are they now exactly?"

Standing against the wall, waiting for the door to swing open and hide him in their basement prison, Owen warned David, "It's now or never."

The aroma of beef, potatoes, gravy, and spinach wafting

down the stairs made his stomach rumble in anticipation. But he wasn't planning to eat the lunch this time, no matter how much it appealed. This morning, only an older woman, Katina, had brought their food and no guard. If it happened again, they'd be in luck.

David reclined on the bed, looking perfectly relaxed like he wasn't about to go anywhere. But the effect was an illusion. Owen could see the tightness in David's face, even if others couldn't. He noted the tension in David's body and knew that if the chance availed itself this time, he'd spring from the bed and aid their escape.

When the door opened wide and David's placid face turned to a frown, Owen knew the circumstances weren't exactly right for an escape attempt. But damn it, Owen was ready. And he'd already played his hand, so they'd be wary of another trick in the future.

As soon as Elizabeth entered the room, Owen wondered what the difficulty was. Although she stopped short to see Owen wasn't in the bed or anywhere else in the basement. David quickly smiled at her and reached for the tray, trying to distract her. Owen figured they could tie her up and take off. Or take her with them. Right after that, a man followed her into the room and turned to see where Owen was once he saw he wasn't anywhere else in the small basement room.

With no time to lose, Owen clobbered him with his fists, bringing him down, but he was carrying the other tray of food and the dishes clattered to the floor. Worse, a second man came in right behind the first. David was up and out of the bed in an instant, knocking the second man out. Elizabeth looked like she was going to die but quickly set the tray on the bed and moved out of Owen and David's path.

"Do you want to come with us?" David asked, taking hold of her hands.

"Hell," Owen said, hating that they'd made such a racket and hoping whoever else was in the lodge hadn't heard. "This isn't the time, David. Let's get a move on."

"Do you?" David asked.

"They'll kill us," she said but nodded. "I can guide you."

"All right, let's go." Owen raced up the stairs as Elizabeth followed him.

David locked the door to the basement and hurried to join them at the top step. "The place is quiet," he whispered, suspicious.

"Maybe they're out looking for the killers." At least Owen hoped they were.

"Several are, but not everyone. Lila's here, too, taking a nap," Elizabeth warned.

Even though Elizabeth was petite and seemed shy, she'd targeted David from the beginning. As if she'd wanted him and when the time was right, she'd have him. Well, the time might not be right, but he was all hers, for now. Owen just hoped she would be a help and not a hindrance.

Heavy footfalls headed their way. Owen bolted through the kitchen and jerked open the door that led outside to a small garden, with David and Elizabeth following on his heels. The garden was covered in snow, but from what he'd overheard, Kintail and his people left here before the weather got too warm and returned to their native stomping grounds in the Canadian Arctic, so Owen imagined the garden never was planted. Unless a small contingency of his people remained behind.

"Somehow we've got to join forces with Cameron," Owen said, racing through the snow in the direction of the outer building and wishing he at least had gloves and a hat. Kintail's people had confiscated their parkas, gloves, ski masks, goggles, anything they could use to keep warm outdoors if they managed to escape. He glanced at Elizabeth. Wearing jeans and a soft sweater and boots, she wasn't in any better shape clothing-wise than they were. Already he was having misgivings about this.

"As much as I don't want to, we may have to shape-shift," David warned.

Elizabeth stayed close to him, not saying a word.

"I thought you liked being a wolf," Owen shot over his shoulder as they made their way through the deep snow to the barn. "Maybe a couple of the snowmobiles are still in residence and some of our gear is in there."

"Being a wolf is fine. I love the freedom, the hunt, the attuned senses we have. Trying to communicate with Cameron is another thing. And what do we do about getting some clothes in case we decide to shift back? Even though we're getting better at this, we still don't have the shifting completely under control. I can imagine us in the middle of nowhere, stark naked."

"Yeah, well, that's true enough." Although Owen hated that it was and that they still hadn't gotten the shifting under complete control.

"If you can control it, I agree we'll need to shift," Elizabeth said, "but there may be some spare clothes in the barn in the event either of you can't."

Trevor had warned them it might take months to get the hang of shape-shifting and sometimes years, depending on the personality of the newly turned *lupus garou*. The phase of the full moon forced them to shift, but during the new moon, they could only be human.

Owen jerked open the outer building door and hurried inside, briefly noting the empty place where a couple of snowmobiles had sat. "Damn." He started rummaging through a box, but it appeared to contain just tents. And a credit card. He lifted it up and smiled. "Trevor Hodges's. Might come in handy if we can use it where no one knows him."

"He's probably lived here for eons, and everyone would know him. But sure, take it just in case. It might come in handy."

"Everyone knows him," Elizabeth said, digging through another box.

David dove into another one. "Sleeping bags in here. Yours and mine, too, Owen. But no sign of any winter clothes."

"Well, hell. Let's get out of here before someone sounds the alarm."

They heard angry shouting from the main lodge.

"Too late for that," David grumbled.

David grabbed Elizabeth's hand, and they bolted out of the barn with Owen and ran straight for the cover of the nearest woods.

CHAPTER 16

THE WOLFISH GRIN ON HILSON'S FACE TOLD FAITH HE meant business as he jerked off his jacket. She was afraid he intended to turn her when she'd already been turned! She didn't relish getting bitten again. Then she heard two snowmobiles headed in her direction. Cameron! But someone else, too, and she didn't think it could be anyone who would help them. Kintail's men, or...

Something crashed some distance behind her, and curses carried through the woods like a long-distance echo. Thank God, not Cameron's voice. Hilson glanced in that direction, his expression turning from wolfish intent to red-faced anger. "Adams," he growled under his breath.

The police officer?

Then another crashing sound and more curses. Some from the same man, some from another.

"Hell, and Whitson," Hilson said.

She didn't know what to think if the men following them were the police officers. All she knew was if she waited for Cameron and Hilson changed before she could leave, he'd bite her. Even if she tried to outrun him, he'd be able to keep up, as slowly as she had to maneuver between trees on the snowmobile. In his wolf form, she figured he'd have the advantage.

Then she swore she saw a red wolf's amber eyes peering between spruces, watching her, watching Hilson. Leidolf? If it was him, would he come to her rescue if she needed him to?

Hilson had stripped down to his shirt and pants and boots. She made the decision, right or wrong, turned her machine, and headed in the direction of the lake— unfortunately, farther from her destination.

Hilson swore at her, and she was sure he was ripping off the buttons on his shirt as he tried to finish undressing quickly, although she couldn't hear that over the roar of her machine and didn't dare look back. When she'd gone some distance, the vehicles behind her stopped suddenly but then turned in her direction. Cameron to the rescue. She and he could stop whoever was following them next. But in the meantime, she pulled her snowmobile into the woods off the trail and waited for Cameron, hoping Hilson would run off in another direction, afraid of what could happen if he messed with Cameron.

Except for the approaching snowmobiles, the woods were quiet and still and deeply shaded. They smelled of evergreen and a chilled wetness. She glanced back at the white woods, the sudden urge to blend in with them overwhelming her, as if a wolf guardian angel was nudging her in the right direction. Before she could control what she was doing, she began yanking off her own clothes. The cold tightened her skin as she tossed her sweater and shirt. Chill bumps raised up on her arms. She jerked off her boots and then her pants. Cold, freezing cold. Standing beside her snowmobile, completely naked, she knew the wolf bite had made her insane.

When she thought she'd die from exposure, her body began to warm. A heat, like what she imagined a hot flash to feel like, invaded every inch of her body. Cameron suddenly came into view on his snowmobile. Just before her body twisted painlessly, effortlessly, like giving a good stretch to knotted-up muscles. Then she dropped down on four paws and stared at her black claws against the white snow in disbelief. Her legs were skinny and long and covered with white fur. This was just too damned unreal.

"Faith," Cameron yelled, right before Hilson—or at least that was who she assumed it was—lunged as a wolf and knocked Cameron off his snowmobile.

Her heart nearly quit beating. Before she could come to his rescue, a man driving a snowmobile behind him shouted, "Cameron! Damn it!" He jerked his machine to a stop, drew a gun from beneath his parka, and fired at the wolf, hitting him four times before the wolf bolted into the woods.

Faith stood stock-still as the man turned his attention to her, afraid he would shoot her next, although she wanted to make sure Cameron was all right. The man held his gun aimed at her but didn't fire. Faith didn't move, just whimpered at Cameron, wanting reassurance he was all right.

He stirred from his prone position, face-first in the snow. He raised his head, groaned, and saw her. "Faith," he whispered, and she noted the deep regret in his voice.

Yeah, well, he'd done this to her, but it was her own damn fault too.

Cameron turned to the other man. "Don't shoot the wolf, Gavin. She's all right."

Gavin? The partner Cameron had left back in Seattle? She hoped Hilson would survive Gavin's bullets, but she was glad he was here to help Cameron locate their other partners.

"Why are Arctic wolves out here?" Gavin asked, his

voice full of disbelief as he holstered his gun, then climbed off his snowmobile. "Are you all right?"

"Yeah." Cameron shook his head, dislodging some of the snow from his hat and ski mask, and glanced back at Faith.

She wanted to approach him, lick his cheek, and nudge him to see that he truly was all right. He appeared a little dazed. Certainly, if he'd been perfectly all right, he would be on his feet already.

"How do you know this one's okay when the other attacked you?" Gavin asked, helping Cameron to stand.

Cameron leaned in toward Gavin, and she knew Cameron had been hurt.

"Faith," Cameron said, reaching his gloved hand out to her, his attention focused on her eyes, his concern for her evident.

Appreciating his gesture, she still didn't move. Gavin could have killed Hilson, and she didn't relish getting shot too. Just one wrong move and the cowboy would pull his gun. Guaranteed.

"Faith," Cameron said again, and he tried to move toward her, but he seemed to be in pain. His face was hidden by the mask and goggles, but he was leaning so hard against Gavin that she assumed he must have hurt his leg or hip or something.

She inched toward him, ready to bolt if Gavin reached for his gun. She probably couldn't outrun the first bullet, but maybe subsequent ones she could. Hilson seemed to have been too focused on taking Cameron down to notice Gavin had hit him right away. She wouldn't have that problem.

She smelled a hint of wolf nearby, carried to her on the breeze. A hint of…red wolf. *Leidolf.* Was he just curious what would happen? Or was he watching out for her in case she needed him? She liked to think he was there for her, if need be. Although he seemed kind of mysterious— willing to help, but then again, not wanting to get mixed up in Cameron's and her affairs.

"Are you sure…" Gavin said, his hand reaching under his parka.

"Don't shoot her," Cameron ordered, his voice angry. "She's mine."

Gavin chuckled a little under his breath. "You haven't had a dog since old Dusty died. But at least she was a Lab. An Arctic wolf?" He shook his head. "I'm sure there's a story behind all this. Can you make it, Cameron? Can you ride?" He glanced back at the clothes lying behind the snowmobile and frowned. "Was Faith driving this snowmobile? Hell, what happened to her?"

Cameron just shook his head. "She's okay. She'll be fine. We need to get to Millinocket," he said, his gaze focused on Faith's. "That's where Faith will go."

How could she go there dressed in her wolf coat? What if she decided to change back all of a sudden out here in the middle of nowhere without a stitch of clothes. She'd freeze to death. Not to mention embarrassing herself to death. If anyone saw her shift, she'd put the whole werewolf world in jeopardy—which she still had a hard time believing existed beyond Kintail's pack, and now maybe Leidolf's.

"You have to follow us, Faith," Cameron said, pleading with her.

"You named the wolf after the woman you're running around with?" Gavin asked, his voice incredulous. "Does she know?"

"Grab the clothes and bags off the snowmobile. We'll have to return for the machine later." While Gavin did as Cameron asked, Cameron crouched, groaning with the effort and reached out his hand to Faith.

She couldn't reconcile the emotions swamping her. She was a wolf now, and no matter how she looked at it, this was just plain bad news. Usually, she felt pretty well in control of her life. Not now. Now she was a danger to others of her kind and a danger to herself. And there was nothing she could do about it. She didn't move toward Cameron, as much as his eyes pleaded with her to draw closer. She didn't want to be petted like a damned dog. She didn't want him to hug her and try to reassure her everything would be all right, because it wouldn't be. Leidolf might have been right in saying they were what they were now. But having been born a *lupus garou*, he couldn't know how it would feel to someone like Cameron or her.

She took a step away from Cameron, hating the look of hurt in his eyes. But she couldn't accept his comfort. Not like this. Not as a damned vicious Arctic wolf with teeth that could crush bones.

She lifted her nose and sampled the air, smelled Leidolf drawing closer but still out of sight. She understood why. He probably had seen what Gavin had done to Hilson.

Gavin was watching the two of them, her clothes and bags in his arms. "She's still a feral wolf," he said, his voice gentled. "Let her go."

"You're mine," Cameron said softly. "You have to go with us, Faith. You can't stay out here alone. Kintail's men…" He rose unsteadily, his jaw clenched, eyes narrowed. "You can't stay here. Follow us."

She waited for him to limp to his snowmobile, waited for him to climb on, waited for him to look back at her once more, pleading more than demanding that she obey him. Then she decided what she would do. She'd follow him for a brief time, then find Leidolf. She couldn't run to the trailhead and risk turning into a human somewhere along the way. If she could make it to their rental vehicles, maybe. But not out in the open like this.

She followed Cameron for a little while as he drove his snowmobile and tried to find a way back to the main road. He kept glancing back at her, making sure she was still there, loping slightly behind his snowmobile, while she kept looking for the best place to bolt where the trees wouldn't allow a snowmobile passage.

Gavin was an even further distance behind, and she noted he was watching her too. Wary, she suspected. If one wild wolf could knock Cameron from his machine, why not another? But she was female and not half as big as Hilson. Although she assumed if she bared her teeth, she could scare the most stalwart of men.

She glanced back at the woods, knowing Gavin had figured out what she was up to. Cameron, too, but she hoped he wouldn't see her take off until it was too late. Then she spied a flash of red fur. *Leidolf.* He must have realized she might need help. At least she hoped that was why he was stalking them.

With one last look at Cameron, she silently wished him well, then bolted for the woods. She half expected Gavin to warn him that she had taken off, but he didn't. He probably figured she needed to run wild, and Cameron shouldn't have interfered with her natural instincts. In any event, it worked well for her.

Cameron would no doubt give him holy hell for it. But Faith didn't think she could make it to the trailhead as a wolf. She couldn't risk it.

She ran deeper into the woods, suddenly realizing that no matter what else was wrong with her life, she enjoyed the sense of adventure she was experiencing, the freedom to move as a wolf, the way her fur coat protected her against the elements without her having to wear tons of clothing to keep warm. Freedom, that was what she felt.

But it would be short-lived if anyone from Kintail's pack caught up with her. Or if she ran into the werewolf killers.

―⁂―

Cameron was certain Faith would run off, but he hadn't expected his good friend Gavin not to tell him the moment she did. He glowered at him again as the two trudged through the trees on foot, pursuing her tracks, unable to follow on the snow machines. He had to admire her ability to solve problems, no matter what the circumstances. He only hoped they wouldn't find her naked, freezing to death along the way. And he hoped that if they did catch up to her, she wouldn't be in any other trouble and would be willing to follow his lead this time. Frustrated with his own inability to take care of her while she was a wolf in the wilderness, he was damned thankful Gavin hadn't seen her shape-shift and that he could avoid the problems that would have entailed.

A blurring of two exquisite shapes, like the northern lights mixing in surreal colors, that was the way she had appeared to him, blending from the beauty of a naked woman into that of a furred white wolf. The woman one instant, the wolf the next. Even though she shifted quickly and even if he hadn't chanced to see the blurred effect, she wasn't the same after the process was done. The woman vanished, the wolf took her place. So there was no mistaking it if Gavin had caught a glimpse of the switch. Although he probably would have assumed he'd been hallucinating.

"I don't understand why you feel we have to chase after the wolf, Cameron. She probably took off after a rabbit, and she'll be back."

Cameron sliced his friend another glare.

Gavin looked back at the tracks. "You already bit my head off about not warning you sooner. But hell, she's a wild wolf, and this is what they do." He paused and leaned over a little. "Damn, there are two tracks now."

Cameron stared at the impressions in the snow. "Broader paw, larger wolf. Male." He swore under his breath.

Gavin chuckled. "She could be in heat and interested in him and having little wolf pups in the spring."

Cameron hauled off and socked his friend in the jaw. He didn't know what came over him to knock Gavin off his feet. Except that the raw emotions he felt toward Faith were sitting at the surface, and he couldn't contain them any longer.

Gavin winced and stared up at him. "Hell, what is wrong with you? I know you've got to be tied up in knots over the guys' disappearance, but this wolf? What's gotten into you?"

Cameron couldn't even make the effort to apologize like he should have. He wanted to shift. In the worst way, Cameron wanted to go after her, tear into the male wolf who was with her, and show the world of wolves she was his.

After the male wolf met up with Faith, her paw prints

disappeared, and he knew she was following the male, using his tracks to make her journey easier. Incensed, he wanted to shake her, make her realize he was the only one for her.

He vaguely noticed Gavin rejoining him, still caressing his jaw. "You still have a damned hard punch. Want to tell me what's going on?"

Cameron wanted to. They'd never kept secrets from each other, except for Gavin's clandestine operation watching Marjory's extracurricular activities. He knew he couldn't disclose this part of his life to Gavin. Now he was afraid he might have to dissolve the partnership or get his friend into the trouble he and Faith were in already.

But *after* they located Owen and David. After they made sure they were safe.

Which brought another troubling thought to mind. If Owen and David had been changed, and he suspected at this point they had been, the three of them could continue to be partners in their business. How would they be able to eliminate Gavin from the partnership, as close as they had all been over the years?

He shook his head. No matter the scenario, he couldn't think of an uncomplicated way out of the mess.

Gavin followed behind Cameron. "I guess you don't want to discuss it. I could understand you not wanting to tell me about your new girlfriend. But hell, your relationship with a wolf?" Then he hurried to catch up. "Did the wolf rescue you?" He shook his head. "Knowing you, you rescued the wolf and now you feel this connection, like you always do when it comes to rescuing damsels in distress. I never thought in a million years the situation would have extended to a wolf."

"They've headed back to the cabins," Cameron finally said, noting the path the wolves' tracks were taking. "Let's return for our snowmobiles and find a way back to the main road. It'll be faster that way."

"What about Faith, the woman?" Gavin asked, taking a handful of snow and holding it against his jaw.

That was what Cameron worried about more than anything. Faith, the woman, and the mess she could be in now.

"It'll be faster if we shed our clothes and run like wolves," Owen said, racing through the woods ahead of David and Elizabeth, half freezing to death, rubbing his numb fingers, then shoving them back in his jeans pockets, his trouser legs stiff with clinging snow. "You still think we should go straight to the cabin resort where Cameron is staying?"

"Yeah. I know that Officers Adams and Whitson and Trevor Hodges are on their way there, but it's the only way we can get to Cameron. They'll stop him from leaving for Millinocket, and we've got to let him know we're all right. Although Kintail will most likely assume we're headed that way, too, and try to have us intercepted before that." David looked at Elizabeth. "What do you think?"

"I agree with everything you've said." Elizabeth had kept up with their longer strides, while David's hand remained wrapped around hers the entire time—pulling her along, making sure she didn't fall—and she hadn't once complained. She looked worried, of course. She knew Kintail better than they did.

Owen had been surprised when David asked her if she wanted to come along. He'd figured David would be more concerned for her safety. Maybe he was using her a little as she'd kept them headed for Charles's cabin resort when Owen had accidentally steered them wrong. Deep down, he didn't think so. Maybe David had the hots for her as much as she did for him, only as usual, he was hiding his feelings.

Suddenly, David asked, "Do you think we can start our own pack in Seattle?"

Owen shot him a get-real look over his shoulder. "We'll be lucky to find a place in Alaska where we will fit in as Arctic wolves. I doubt we'll be safe there either. What if the areas are tied up with packs already, just like Kintail's, and they don't relish the idea of two more full-grown males joining them?"

"Kintail's got the people here believing his pet wolves are perfectly tame, so everyone's used to seeing them around, off leash and completely compatible with the human populace. Why couldn't we do that back home?"

"In Seattle?" Owen shook his head. "Can you imagine dropping into Starbucks for your favorite cup of coffee with me in tow as a guide wolf?" Owen let out his breath in a puff of frigid smoky vapor. "Do we do it or not? Can you force the shift?"

"I can do it. I'm just not sure I want to."

"When we arrive at Cameron's place, he'll have a change of clothes for us. He's already one of us. He'll recognize us. His girlfriend, Faith, should have clothes for Elizabeth. We'll be warmer. My hands are already numb. I'm losing most of the heat in my body through my head without having a parka, a hood, or a hat to keep me warm. I can barely see because of the sun reflecting off the snow, except where the trees shade the area. Plus, trudging through the snow is slowing us down. We'll be able to run a hell of a lot farther and faster with our lighter weight as wolves situated on top of the snow rather than in our human forms plowing through it. And we'll be a lot less visible in our white fur against the snow-filled backdrop than we are now."

"He's right," Elizabeth said.

David said, "All right, all right. Cameron just better have a change of clothes for both of us." He gave Owen a disgruntled look as he began pulling off his wool sweater.

Owen and David turned their backs to Elizabeth while they stripped. Even though it was a natural occurrence for the members of the pack to shed their clothes in front of each other if the occasion called for it and no one paid any attention to it, David and Owen weren't there yet. Even now, Owen was feeling a little self-conscious with exposing his backside to Elizabeth.

"At least his clothes will fit you. With my height, it'll look like I had a growing spurt and haven't had time to buy new clothes," David added.

Owen smiled and finished ditching his clothes. Once he was stark naked, he hurried to bury his things underneath the snow before he felt the shift taking place. He hadn't even willed himself to do it. He figured it might have been a need for self-preservation, that once his skin grew too cold, the wolf coat kicked in.

David was soon at his side nudging him with his long wolf snout, and the two greeted each other like a couple of old wolf pals, noses touching, tongues licking, a show of camaraderie, of solidarity. They did the same with

Elizabeth, only David was a little more amorous, and if Owen could have laughed, he would have. Then he took off at a run.

Kintail had told him they could run flat-out at forty miles per hour tops for several miles and easily cover sixty miles in a night at a trot. He loved the way he felt as a wolf, capable of anything. His paws gripped a fallen tree and he bolted over it, knowing David and Elizabeth were right behind him. The three headed down a trail where dogs and sleds and Cameron had once traversed, their scents still lingering behind. They'd find him soon. And then?

They'd return to Seattle changed men. Poor Gavin—odd man out now. If they made it home safely, what could they do about him?

CHAPTER 17

AFTER AN HOUR, CAMERON REACHED THE BLACK BEAR Den with Gavin, but the place looked lifeless, deserted, just as he and Faith had left it. His heart in his throat, he hurried to enter the cabin, smelling Faith's sweet fragrance still lingering in the air, but there was no indication she had returned here.

"Maybe she's watching us from the shelter of the woods," Gavin said, glancing at Faith's soiled clothes in the garbage sack.

Maybe. But Cameron figured she'd show herself now that he was here. Maybe Gavin was the one who scared her. Hell, sure he did. He'd shot the wolf that had attacked Cameron and then pointed the freshly fired gun at Faith.

"Listen, Gavin, why don't you go up to the main lodge and see about Charles's condition. Say that Cameron's asking, but don't tell anyone I've returned."

"Are you sure? I know that look in your eye. You're going off to investigate Faith's disappearance on your own. Why don't you let me come with you? If nothing else, I can watch your back."

Cameron shook his head. "She may be afraid of you after you shot the other wolf. Just check on Charles. I'll return to this cabin after a while. You can meet me back here."

Gavin looked a little worried, but Cameron motioned to the lodge. "I'll be fine. See you in a few minutes."

"All right, but if you're not back here in half an hour, I'm coming for you." Gavin trudged off, muttering under his breath about friends and not keeping secrets.

Cameron got back on his snowmobile and hurried off toward his own cabin, calling out Faith's name. She wasn't at his place either, although unless she'd shape-shifted, she wouldn't have been able to get inside. Then he thought of Hilson and his place. Damn, why hadn't he thought of him before? Cameron raced toward the Porcupine Cove cabin but was in sight of Leidolf's place when the man opened his door and waved to him to come inside without saying a word.

Faith. Cameron parked and jumped off his vehicle, then rushed up the steps to the deck.

Before he could step inside the cabin, Leidolf warned, "She's here and she's sleeping. We've got problems."

Hell, tell him something he didn't know. Cameron shoved past Leidolf into the cabin and headed straight for the bedroom. "On your way out, run by the lodge, will you? My partner Gavin Summerfield's there, but I want him to know where I am and that I'm with Faith, the woman, so don't want to be disturbed."

Leidolf gave him a knowing smile and didn't seem to be offended that Cameron was ordering him about, then closed the door to the place and locked it from the outside. He strolled on past the window in the direction of the main lodge.

Thank you, Cameron said silently and opened the door to the bedroom as quietly as he could. Faith looked like an angel, sleeping soundly on the bed, her shoulders bare. Hell, she was still naked? Leidolf didn't give her anything to wear?

The place was comfortably warm, though, and she looked like she was sleeping well. Still, he wanted her to know he was here, and although he was pissed that Leidolf had had to rescue her, he was glad the red wolf had done so and seemed to have her best interests in mind.

Cameron sat next to Faith and leaned over and kissed her cheek, his hand caressing her shoulder, wanting to make the contact, wanting to assure himself she hadn't come to any harm. "I'm here," he said, his voice soothing, low and dark, not wanting to wake her but just to reassure her he was with her again.

She stirred, her eyelashes fluttering. He ran his hand over her hair and kissed her lips this time. Her eyes popped open, her expression startled, and then she smiled, the most delightful smile he'd ever witnessed. Then she frowned and reached out to take his hand, her fingers grasping his protectively. "Are you all right? You were injured."

He sighed and stroked the nape of her neck. "Seems the werewolf genetics heals minor sprains and twists quickly enough. Why didn't you keep following me?"

"I didn't think I could keep from shifting again. I couldn't chance it. I barely made it to Leidolf's cabin. Where's your friend Gavin? He didn't see me shift, did he?"

"No. If he had, I'd never have heard the end of it."

Frowning, Faith touched Cameron's stubbly cheek. "We're in trouble. Officers Adams and Whitson? They were following us and were injured when Adams's snowmobile plowed into a hastily constructed barricade across the trail and Whitson slammed into him right afterward. They'll live, according to Leidolf, who got the news from Charles's cousin George, but they both were injured pretty badly.

Broken arms, legs, Adams has got a concussion. The worst of it all?"

"They want to arrest Gavin and me?" Cameron couldn't believe this could get any worse.

She shook her head. "They were trying to catch up to tell us Kintail needs us on the investigation. Whatever it takes, he would like us to find out who the killers are, and then he'll deal with them. And he wanted us to stay here at the cabins while we're doing the investigation."

Cameron cursed under his breath. "Kintail fancies having you. If he wants both of us on the investigation, why did a wolf try to kill me in the woods just a half hour ago?"

Faith's cheeks turned a little pink. "That most likely had to do with me and nothing with Kintail's orders."

"You?" Before she could say what she meant, he cursed again. "Hilson. Hell, the ex-boyfriend scorned?"

"Yeah, well, he's an Arctic wolf, too, although I had guessed he might be after I learned they existed and that their kind—well, our kind—wouldn't want to be exposed. That was the reason he stole my father's research. What will we do about my father? We have to make sure he doesn't try to put another paper together about werewolves, or others of our kind will most likely kill him."

"It seems we only have two choices—change the person who witnesses the shift or kill him or her."

"Will you bite him?" Faith asked, running her hand over Cameron's.

He took her hand in his and squeezed. "After biting you, I wouldn't want to be responsible for turning another soul."

Faith looked away from Cameron. "Hilson will live, too, according to Leidolf. He said he'll go off and lick his wounds, and it might take a few days, but he'll be as good as new as long as the bullets Gavin fired at him didn't hit anything vital."

"Hey, Cameron!" Gavin shouted outside the cabin, banging on the door.

"Damn it, Gavin," Cameron said to himself more than to anyone else and then added for Faith's benefit, "I'll be right back." He stalked out of the bedroom and closed the door, then headed for the front door.

Unlocking it, he scowled at Gavin. "I told you to wait for me. Leidolf was supposed to tell you—"

"A Trevor Hodges is at the main lodge. He said Faith wanted to talk about her father's research concerning Bigfoot." Gavin raised a brow, then gingerly touched his swollen jaw again. "Anything you want to talk to me about?"

Bigfoot, my ass. Then again, the hunter guide might know David and Owen's location. That was the leverage they needed. If Kintail turned over their friends, they'd locate the killers. Working as a team, they could do it. Except now they had a new partner, much prettier than the rest of his partners. If Leidolf wanted to come along for the ride, he was welcome to tag along. "Tell Trevor to meet us at Faith's cabin. We'll be right there."

Lila fumed as she paced across the great room at Kintail's lodge. She'd just managed to overhear some of what Kintail and Trevor were speaking about and knew for sure Kintail planned on taking that damned O'Malley woman for his mate. What did he think? That Lila would just go along with it? A newly turned *lupus garou* would become the alpha leader's mate?

She didn't think so. She couldn't believe Trevor had overheard her crying when she'd talked to Katina. Wasn't anything she did private? At least she knew Katina hadn't said anything to anyone about her distress.

How was Lila to thwart Kintail from taking Faith for his mate? Then again, Cameron was looking more appealing all the time. She smiled at the thought he'd put Adams and Whitson in their place. Once Kintail had gotten them on the police force, the two had thought they were better than anybody else, not accountable to anyone—except Kintail. They knew where they stood when it came to the pack leader.

But damn it, before that, they'd listened to her too. Probably because they'd initially thought she'd be Kintail's mate. Now they weren't sure.

She stalked to the picture window and stared out at the woods where a few of Kintail's men were still searching for David and Owen. Kintail might think he was in charge of those two, but she could have told him David wasn't as willing to go along with the scheme of things as he put on. She knew that he wasn't being just thoroughly grateful that he was still alive after suffering a massive heart attack. They were a lot alike in many ways—she was openly honest about some aspects of her life and secretly dishonest about a lot more. She couldn't help it. She just didn't want to expose some of her past life and didn't want to deal with.

David seemed that way to her too.

But Elizabeth? She'd never suspected the woman would turn traitor and run off with the men. Yet she should have seen the signs. She'd seen a glimpse of Elizabeth observing David when she thought no one was watching her. But Lila hadn't put two and two together. Too wrapped up in her concern over Kintail. Yet in Lila's heart, something stirred. A desire to be like Elizabeth. To do what the woman had done—defy an alpha pack leader to choose a man she wanted to be with. Not that Lila truly wanted anyone but the pack leader. She wished she could show that side of herself again—that she wanted him, no other, and would stake her claim. What if she lost him? That was what she thought she couldn't handle the most. Another mate's death.

She glanced down at the statue of an Arctic wolf sitting on a chest—a gift she'd given to Kintail. She tried to show she cared about him. He was the typical, arrogant alpha-male leader who ran the pack, made the decisions, and was in total control of everything that went on. And that appealed to her. But her past thwarted her when it came to having any kind of a relationship with a man.

She suspected he sensed that, maybe concerned she'd never grow to love him. Which was probably why he hadn't mated her in the two years since she joined the pack. There were several other available women, but none of them was alpha enough to lead the pack like her. She'd hoped that when Trevor told Kintail on her, the leader would have understood her better since she was having a devil of a time explaining herself to him. Even though she hadn't wanted Trevor to tell him her secrets like that. What did Kintail do? Said he was going to take Faith for his own anyway. She jammed her hands in her pockets and growled.

Lila had liked Cameron. Instantly. There was just something she admired about him. And she wanted him.

But what if that attraction had to do with her not knowing him that well and him not knowing her? What if she could only want attachments that weren't real? That once she got to know him, she'd have the same difficulty showing him affection as she had with Kintail?

She ground her teeth, irritated that she couldn't get on with her life. She had to get rid of the cute little forensic scientist who was a constant reminder that both Kintail and Cameron coveted her. And neither desired Lila. Yet.

Eliminate one threat, and maybe Kintail would come around and give Lila another chance.

Baker had missed his calling. She didn't know how he'd botched his assignment so badly, failing to kill Faith at their campsite, but he had. She ran her fingers down the condensation on the window and stared out at the snowy setting, the forest perfectly still. Not a soul in sight. The lodge itself was eerily empty. The few men left here who weren't trying to locate the killers of their pack members were running around in the woods, searching for their escapees.

Time for her to change into the wolf and see if she could somehow isolate Miss O'Malley away from the others and do what Baker had failed to do. She was reaching for her sweater when snowmobiles zoomed up to the kitchen on the other side of the lodge, and she hesitated. Should she stay and see what news the others had? Maybe they'd located David or Owen or both. That would give her a good reason for going to Charles's resort, if she ran into Kintail there. With news of the men's recapture. Or news of their escape and continued success at evading recapture, if no one had gone in search of Kintail to apprise him of the situation yet.

She'd warned everyone who had seen Elizabeth take off with the men that the woman had been forced to go with them. Even though a couple of the men seemed reluctant to spread that tale, she'd finally convinced them that David had ahold of Elizabeth's hand and was tugging her along. That she hadn't gone of her own free will. Kintail would forgive Elizabeth if Lila asked him to.

David and Owen? They were another story. She didn't think he'd listen to her about them. Even though she'd speak up for them again. Kintail hadn't liked it when she'd let Owen get away with phoning Gavin. She thought maybe Owen hadn't gotten the message across that they were quitting the PI business and Gavin should let them go. It didn't work, but she'd tried to help.

A door creaked open to the kitchen. She didn't hear anyone speaking, which she thought odd. Whoever they were noisily tromped on the tiled kitchen floor, and then loud male whispers reached her ears—but not of anyone she recognized. And no one she knew would speak in hushed voices at the lodge.

The hair on her neck stood on end.

Kintail had one thought in mind when he arrived at Charles's cabin resort—turn Faith O'Malley before his brother did. When he focused on a single area of interest, he got results. Plain and simple. Until he reached Charles's lodge and saw Charles's cousin George, his eyes widening at the sight of Kintail as a wolf. George knew him and knew Kintail wasn't any threat to George and his people.

But the expression on George's face meant Kintail could expect trouble.

Except not as much as he ever bargained for.

Silently, George waved for him to come into the lodge. Kintail loped inside, his temper already rising.

"In here." George motioned to Charles's office. "I'll get you a change of clothes."

Kintail paced. What the hell had happened now?

It seemed to take forever for George to return with a handful of clothes. He set them on the leather love seat by the window and then bowed his head slightly and left the room, closing the door behind him.

Kintail shifted faster than he thought possible and quickly shoved on the trousers, not bothering with the shirt or sweater. "Come in," Kintail hollered, not liking any of this one bit.

George pulled the door open and hesitated to enter until Kintail motioned him to the love seat. "What's happened?"

George was Charles's younger cousin, definitely not an alpha, and if Charles hadn't still been at the hospital under observation for the blow to his skull, Kintail was certain George would have much preferred to have Charles talk to him. George's older brother, Michael, was always in charge if Charles was absent, so Kintail wondered where he was. Maybe he was with Charles.

"Tell me."

George took a seat and wrung his hands, his eyes avoiding Kintail's glower. "Officer Adams and Whitson were injured badly in a snowmobile accident. Michael took them both to the hospital. We couldn't wait to get word to you to send your people here to take care of them. They'll both be all right, but they suffered several broken bones, Adams had a concussion."

Kintail stared at him in disbelief. "How did it happen?"

George shook his head, still not looking Kintail eye to eye.

"Guess."

George's gaze flicked his way and then returned to study the floor. "They were following Cameron and Faith. We think they might have run into a barricade."

"A barricade."

"Yes, hastily made on a trail through the woods. A felled tree had blocked the main road, probably dropped down by whoever is doing the same on other roads and trails in the area. It appeared Cameron and Faith took a trail into the woods to go around the obstacle. Adams said that Cameron was joined by another man. I later found out it was his partner, Gavin Summerfield."

"Where's Faith now?"

"She's at Leidolf's cabin, but she and Cameron are returning to the Black Bear Den to talk with Trevor."

The way George fidgeted, Kintail suspected there was other news. "What else?"

George rose unsteadily from the chair. "Your brother's been shot. He was in his wolf form and knocked Cameron from his snowmobile. Cameron's partner, Gavin, shot Hilson four times, afraid the wolf planned to kill Cameron. Hilson's resting in Charles's bedroom, some of the wounds superficial, and he's feeling well enough to demand three meals already, but one of them wasn't and he's not in any shape to go anywhere. At least it didn't hit anything vital and he didn't bleed out. Because they're bullet wounds, we couldn't risk transporting him to the hospital and facing the questions that would follow."

Kintail clenched and unclenched his fists. Half the time, he was perturbed with his brother, and he couldn't help being annoyed that Hilson had gone against his wishes, but when it came right down to it, he was Kintail's brother. Damn it.

Cameron and Gavin were dead men.

Kintail hated to ask, although he couldn't imagine anything else could have gone wrong. "Anything else?"

George paused at the office door, his gaze finally focusing on Kintail's. "Cameron's partners escaped your lodge. Elizabeth's with them."

CHAPTER 18

As soon as Owen and David heard snowmobiles, they darted deeper into the woods with Elizabeth, knowing Kintail's people wouldn't give up on trying to return them to Kintail's lodge. They'd dodged them several times already, and Owen was slightly worried the men were trying to corral them. He was pretty sure he, David, and Elizabeth were getting closer to Charles's resort.

Then he thought something was different about the men in pursuit of them. The snowmobiles were plain noisy, no masking the sound. They had never heard a peep out of the men stalking them in silence, just like wolves on the hunt. Owen felt a kinship to them and understood their ways.

Now he heard shouts of glee, "Woo-hoo!" "There they are!" like kids at a circus. He felt in his bones that the predators had changed. They might sound like silly-ass kids, but his gut instinct told him they were a hell of a lot more dangerous than Kintail's people.

David tensed, his hackles raised, his ears twitching back and forth. He recognized the change in their circumstances too. Elizabeth appeared almost frantic, running between David and Owen, panicked. He didn't believe she'd feel that way about her own people.

They had to reach the cabins. There, they could join forces with Cameron and Gavin, if he'd already arrived. There, they stood a chance.

—◆◇◆—

"Trevor can't be here to speak to us about Bigfoot," Faith said, getting dressed while Cameron watched her in Leidolf's bedroom. Cameron looked like he could devour her in one wolfish bite. She raised a brow at him as she pulled on her pants.

He smiled back, the look just as devious.

"Pay attention, Cameron. We can't allow Gavin to be in the same room with us when we talk to Trevor."

Cameron ran his hands down Faith's sweater-covered arms, then held her hands tightly. "I don't want to ever lose you, Faith."

She gave him a coy smile back. "I have news for you. You're not getting rid of me that easily."

He pulled her into his embrace and squeezed the breath out of her, his hands sweeping down her back, his body pressed against her, already hard and wanting. If they hadn't had important matters to take care of, she would have been willing to relieve both his needs and her own right this very minute.

"I thought I might have lost you. I even clobbered poor Gavin when he mentioned you running off with Leidolf and having wolf pups."

Faith's lips parted slightly. "Wolf pups? What next?" She didn't even want to think about that scenario. Although if Leidolf's assumption was right, the mistake she and Cameron had made with not using a condom the last time wouldn't have mattered, not if a werewolf couldn't get a human pregnant.

Cameron held onto her tightly as if he was afraid he truly

had lost her, and she loved the way he was—protective, desiring her and only her, and a little bit jealous that anyone else might want her.

With Gavin in the next room and unable to focus on much more than getting this business with Kintail over with, she pulled free from Cameron's embrace. "Let's see what Trevor has to say."

Cameron slipped his hand over hers and held it tight, his gaze saying other issues were at stake and just as important to him. For her, business always came before pleasure, although she snuggled up against him to reassure him she was just as willing. That seemed to relieve some of his tension, and he hugged her close as he opened the bedroom door.

As soon as they left Leidolf's bedroom, the appraising look Gavin gave her and the small smile that sparkled in his eyes told her he approved. She noted the bruise on the side of his jaw, though, and hoped he and Cameron weren't too mad at each other. He probably couldn't figure out what had set Cameron off like that. If only he had known.

She squeezed Cameron's hand, and the three headed outdoors.

"So," Gavin said as he mounted his snowmobile, and Faith climbed onto Cameron's with him, "I understand Cameron named a female wolf after you."

Faith smiled, closing her arms around Cameron's waist, hugging him tight. "Yes, sweet of him, wasn't it?"

Gavin looked to see Cameron's reaction, but he seemed deep in thought because he never said anything in response. She wondered if he'd made the slip inadvertently, or deep down, he wanted his friend to know she and the wolf were the same.

When they arrived at the cabin, Leidolf and Trevor were standing on the deck, watching their approach. At least that was who she assumed the gray-haired man was. His gray eyes seemed wary when he observed Gavin, but he seemed pleased to see Faith, although his eyes widened a bit and then he appeared surprised as she, Cameron, and Gavin joined him on the deck.

"I wish a word with only the young lady if you don't mind," Trevor said, speaking to Cameron.

Cameron put his arm around her shoulder. "We stay together."

Trevor flicked a glance Gavin's way, then said to Cameron, "It's private."

"I'll talk to him." Faith wanted to hear the news Trevor had from Kintail, and if the hunter insisted, she'd speak with him alone. They couldn't include Gavin; that much was clear.

"Leidolf and Gavin can wait out here for us, but I stay with the lady," Cameron said, his voice a barely controlled growl.

She was beginning to think losing her for a while when she turned into the wolf had affected him more than she'd first thought. "The two of us then."

Trevor bowed his head slightly, although he looked displeased.

Cameron opened the door for them, and after closing it behind them, they took seats at the dining room table.

"Who bit you?" Trevor asked first.

Cameron tensed at once. She folded her arms. "You were supposed to tell me about my father's trip out here."

Trevor took a deep breath and leaned back in the chair. "All right. I suppose it really doesn't matter who bit you, but

Kintail will be displeased." His eyes remained focused on Faith's as he continued. "I really liked your father. He had a great sense of humor and spoke privately to me about his real purpose here—to observe the Bigfoot hunters while he did a research paper.

"On the hunt, we spotted nothing but a bird occasionally and a rabbit. Until the guys on the expedition found wolf tracks and thought they might have been a small Bigfoot, although from what I've ever heard, the footprint is supposed to be more like a human's print, not a wolf's. But since we weren't finding anything else and the prints were old, I allowed the men to follow them. At the same time, your father took copious notes on the group's behavior, casting me small smiles unobserved by the others on the team. Although they were grown men, they behaved like excited teens playing a video game."

"But my father saw something he shouldn't have."

"I was supposed to perpetuate the Bigfoot myth with you, but Kintail doesn't know you're one of us now. So yes, your father and I became separated from the team. They'd run off wildly into the woods after the old wolf trail. Your father got a stitch in his side, and I waited with him, figuring I could catch up to the team members if they got lost, when I spied Lila in the forest. She was stripping out of her clothes, then shifted into the wolf. I don't know what she was up to, didn't want to tell Kintail in case it was something he didn't want to hear, and I didn't speak of it to your father. I hoped he had been too busy writing notes to have noticed. Well, he was busy writing, and I hoped it was about the team and their behavior rather than anything he had seen with respect to Lila."

"You didn't ask him?"

"I'm not dumb. Self-preservation for our kind is tanta-mount. I did like your father, but exposing our kind to the world is not something any of us want. So when every-one was asleep in the tents that night, I read through your father's notes. He said nothing about what he'd seen. But he was strangely quiet the rest of the time. As if he had seen Lila shift. As if he had seen me observe her. I had said nothing. Which for him—for a sociologist—was just as telling as if I had. I couldn't know that for sure. Just speculation on my part."

"If you didn't tell anyone, how did Hilson learn of it?"

Trevor snorted. "Here I was afraid to get Lila in trouble, and she managed to turn the trick. She probably figured she'd better do so before I did. Anyway, she wasn't supposed to change in the open like that, and certainly not with so many humans close by. I denied that your father saw anything. Hilson took it upon himself to watch your father, following him all the way back to Portland."

"When he couldn't get enough information from him from a distance?"

"I imagine he approached you."

"So what do we do? My father is at risk, isn't he?"

Trevor didn't say anything.

Faith took in a deep breath. "I don't want him killed."

"It's not up to you."

But it was, damn it. Fine, no way did she want to bite her father and turn him into what she was, but she didn't want him dead either. "What about Cameron's friends?"

Trevor had been sitting so regally, so confident, until she mentioned that part of the equation. Then he fidgeted a bit, his hands on the table, then back off the table, on his lap, hidden. He glanced Cameron's way and looked back at Faith. "Both of you are in danger if you remain here. Kintail…"

"Where are they?" a man roared to Leidolf and Gavin, stalking across the deck outside.

Immediately, Trevor rose from the table and said under his breath, "Kintail."

The door flew open, and a giant of a man barged in, as tall as Hilson, but instead of being an overstuffed teddy bear, this guy looked like an enraged polar bear standing in the entryway, filling it, and blocking out the sun. Blond hair nearly white, square jaw clenched, his narrowed pale-yellow eyes shifted from Trevor to Cameron…to Faith. Clenched fists swung at the polar bear's sides as he strode into the cabin where Cameron had already pulled Faith to his side, close, protecting her. The hulking man got in their space. Maybe it was fine for a wolf or the way an alpha showed dominance, but it was much too close for Faith's liking, and as tense as Cameron was, she knew he didn't like it either.

Faith felt the heat of Kintail's body, the smell of the fresh wind on him, saw specks of black in his eyes that seemed to expand and consume the pale-yellow color as he turned his angry gaze from Trevor to Cameron.

Cameron didn't move until the man flicked a look Faith's way, the same kind of threatening expression—yet there was a hint of something else, interest maybe? Intrigue? Garnering her attention again, Cameron tightened his hand on Faith's back, squeezing her closer.

The man growled something under his breath, jerked his lethal eyes back to Cameron, then turned to look at the open doorway. Both Gavin and Leidolf had moved inside, waiting, anticipating trouble, ready to be of service.

"This is private," Kintail snapped at Gavin, ignoring Leidolf.

Faith felt bad for Gavin, who wanted to stick by his partner's side but was being dismissed by everyone he came in contact with, even his own partner.

"Do you want me to talk to Gavin about the situation?" Trevor offered, his voice rather meek, and Faith hated that he seemed cowed before the great Kintail.

"Yes, take him up to the lodge." Kintail glanced at Gavin. "We have a pack of serial killers on the loose. We could use your services since you and Cameron put two of the police officers working the case in the hospital when they were coming to ask your aid in solving this crime."

Gavin looked a little gray. Cameron motioned for him to leave with Trevor. Kintail glowered at Leidolf. "He can go with you too."

Leidolf gave Kintail a sinister smile, then bowed his head slightly and left with Trevor and Gavin, shutting the door behind them.

"Where the hell are my partners, Kintail?" Cameron asked, his hand rubbing Faith's shoulder but his whole body vibrating with anger.

"They're gone, slipped away. My people haven't located them yet."

"You want our help finding your killers, then we do this my way," Cameron said.

"Our way," Faith corrected him. If she was going to be an alpha pack leader's mate, it would be an equal partnership. She smiled at Cameron when he frowned down at her.

For the first time, a hint of amusement crossed Kintail's face. Then he was back to being dour again. "You can't have your men—"

"I want them here with me. With the four of"— Cameron paused—"five of us—well, six if Leidolf wants to still help—we'll catch these killers. We won't bother otherwise. Our sole focus is locating my partners and getting them out of here."

"Are you quite finished?" Kintail asked, folding his arms.

"I don't want my father killed," Faith said, choking a little on the words when she had planned to sound as firm and forthright as Cameron.

"It's not up to me," Kintail said, his words softening.

"What do you mean, it's not up to you? You sent Hilson after him, right?"

"No, he went on his own, but Kenneth O'Malley is in Leidolf's territory. He'll have to deal with him now."

Faith just stared at Kintail, the words sifting through her brain but not making any sense. Why didn't Leidolf say anything before this? Because he thought she would be upset if she heard what he intended to do? She was torn between racing to the lodge and forcing Leidolf's response or staying with Cameron to provide a unified front until they got Kintail's concession concerning his partners.

"We'll talk to Leidolf, Faith," Cameron said, then kissed her cheek. The threat in his voice indicated they'd get their way on this, so not to worry. But she did worry. What if they weren't in time? What if they were already too late?

Cameron focused again on Kintail. "Do we have a deal? My partners will be released to me in exchange for our help in finding your serial killers?"

"I told you, your partners escaped. They're on their own, most likely headed in this direction."

"You have men trying to recapture them, don't you?" Cameron asked.

Kintail abruptly sat down at the table and drummed his long fingers on the oak top, his gaze fixed on Faith, his unspoken words speaking volumes. He wanted Faith, and he was bound to have her. As for Cameron's partners? He didn't seem willing to give them up easily either. Which meant?

Cameron was a dead man.

She refused to back down from Kintail's impertinent gaze, furrowed her brow, and gave him the devil back. His lips lifted slightly.

Very softly, very darkly, and very meaningfully, Cameron said, "She's mine."

She squeezed his waist, glad he'd stand up to Kintail.

Kintail slowly switched his conceited, all-knowing gaze to Cameron as if he were an insignificant gnat. "You're a newbie, don't have a clue what you're doing, or the ramifications of what you are now. She needs someone with experience. Someone like me." He didn't emphasize the *someone* as much as he did the *me*.

"We're mated," Faith said.

Kintail raised his brows at her.

"Leidolf said that if wolves are mated, they can't seek anyone else. Cameron and I are mated. You'll have to stick with Lila or someone else who can put up with you."

This time, Kintail's smile was slightly more than a hint, as if she'd really amused him and as if he wasn't used to showing a lighter side of his personality and didn't know how to do it. The smile wasn't a good indication because it meant—at least to her way of thinking—he either didn't believe she and Cameron were mated, which according to their werewolf traditions, they weren't, or he didn't care. In which case, that reverted back to Cameron being a dead man.

The snowmobilers were running David and Owen ragged as they tried to protect Elizabeth, but to no avail. If the two men hadn't had such healthy hearts after they'd been turned, Owen figured they'd have been run to death by now. When he smelled woodsmoke and the lake, he guessed they were close to Charles's resort. But they couldn't move any closer. Every time they tried to dive through the spruces, another snowmobiler hemmed them in.

Then one of the men pulled in front of Owen and yanked out a gun. If they were the guys who were killing werewolves, the bullets would be silver and the three of them were good as dead. Though Owen couldn't imagine that if they were regular bullets, they wouldn't also be dead. Kintail's men never resorted to guns, except on a hunt. Never to track Owen down, even the last two times he'd escaped.

He lunged, ready to kill the man, when something hit him in the flank with a sharp stab of pain. He yelped. And fell in midair, landing on his belly. What the hell, he thought, his mind drifting like the sparse clouds in the darkening blue sky.

David nudged his face with his nose as if telling him to get up. He could smell David's fear, but then a shot was fired again, and David collapsed against his legs. Elizabeth growled and lunged for one of the shooters, and a third shot was fired. She yelped and collapsed where she was. David growled softly from his prone position in the snow. Owen wished David had been given the chance to have a life with Elizabeth. Owen had always figured he and a partner might die together on a mission. He only wished they'd accomplished it, ensured Elizabeth's safety, and seen Cameron and Gavin one last time.

Incarcerated at some unknown location, Lila stalked back and forth across a basement that smelled like wet cement, musty and moldy. If she'd suffered from allergies, she figured she'd be sneezing her head off. She glowered at David, Owen, and Elizabeth sleeping still as wolves in the big cage against the wall, angered they wouldn't wake up, as many times as she'd poked at them through the bars with a cane she had found behind a bunch of old crates.

She began pacing again. Fourteen steps led to the door to the basement. Forty steps across the main floor both ways. The windowless room was dark, but she could see just fine. She stopped and listened. Traffic noises. They were in a town or city. Millinocket maybe?

She paced again. Thankfully, they didn't think a female werewolf was as dangerous as a male, so they'd taken her without drugging her. She hadn't fought them, because a female in human form was no match for three human males. So they'd treated her like a lady. She knew they had to be the ones who'd killed Sutter at the pack's tour office in Millinocket from the scent the redhead had—deodorant not working and aftershave smelling like pine floor cleaner.

Once Kintail and his men got through with these killers, she'd be ready to return to the frigid Canadian Arctic for a vacation. At that instant, she realized Kintail was the one she was looking for to rescue her. Not Cameron, the newly turned wolf. But Kintail, centuries-old Kintail, who would locate her and free her, and if she played her cards right, she would show him just how much she appreciated the rescue. Some part of her finally recognized she'd been holding onto the past, unwilling to let go, feeling as though her mate and her child's deaths were her own damn fault. Yet deep down, she knew they weren't. Knew her mate had wanted the role of alpha pack leader, knew he couldn't win it. She'd only wanted him, but he hadn't been happy as the second-in-command. And he'd died for it.

She paced across the floor some more. So why did she feel at fault? She was an alpha female, and he felt inferior not being the alpha leader. She knew he'd never make it against the leader. And little Tristen had just gotten in the way when the two men fought. No one could protect him while her mate and the leader tore into each other.

Lila closed her eyes and rested her hand against the wall for support. It wasn't her fault. She hadn't pushed her mate to fight the leader. She'd been assisting another female in labor, so her mate was supposed to have been watching Tristen. It wasn't her fault.

Wiping away tears, she climbed the creaky stairs again, pressed her ear against the wooden door, and listened.

Kintail still had a thing for that Faith O'Malley. If Lila eliminated her, Kintail would know it. He'd condemn her to death or send her far, far away.

Which made her take stock of what she had…a winter

lodge here, a summer lodge up north, a bunch of pack members who treated her like the alpha pack leader's mate, even if she wasn't Kintail's chosen mate yet. And what of Kintail?

Two years ago, he'd tried to encourage her interest in him after she'd fled the pack where the politics were brutal, her mate murdered, and her child killed. She hadn't known how to live. Or love again.

Kintail had been so patient with her, waiting, watching, and finally giving up on her when Faith O'Malley suddenly appeared. She wondered if some of his attraction to Faith had to do with his brother wanting her first. Lila didn't really think Hilson loved her, or he would have turned her and mated with her three months ago. Or maybe Kintail's interest in her only had to do with Lila's refusal to show him any real affection.

She growled at her inability to change back to the person she had been, the person before her beloved mate and son were murdered.

She reconsidered Faith and what she had to offer Kintail. The woman was a neophyte. It would take eons for her to understand their ways. Kintail couldn't want that. Maybe he was trying to get Lila to give up her loss, her secrets, to move on, forcing her by showing an interest in another woman.

Then she heard movement somewhere in the house, footfalls walking from one room to another. No voices though. She wanted to hear voices, to get details. A house number and street name would be nice. A warning to the others that Kintail was on his way to free her would also be welcome news.

She waited, just as if she was on a hunt, patient, all ears, waiting.

She thought back to how she'd gotten here and tried to recollect anything that might help her pinpoint the location. They'd pulled a black hood over her head, but she'd memorized the amount of time she'd spent on a snowmobile and then in a vehicle, the roar of the engine sounding like a pickup, and the amount of time on the road. That was why she thought she was in Millinocket. Not too far away, but far enough. The killers' home base.

She knew how many steps it took from the front door of the house, or a back door, into a long hallway and then to the basement door. Waxed wooden floors that were a little slick, the smell of gingerbread cookies baking in the oven, the sound of New Age music drifting from another room had greeted her when she arrived. The place had been almost uncomfortably warm, but not the basement.

As soon as she was taken to the basement, the temperature had dropped a good thirty degrees. When she had asked if they could give her a coat, the redhead just smiled. "Grow a fur coat," he said, his companions all laughing, then they left her alone in the basement in darkness.

Which suited her just fine.

About two hours after that? They brought in this huge cage bearing the Three Stooges. Sleeping a long winter's nap like a bunch of damned grizzly bears. David, Owen, and Elizabeth. Kintail's people didn't recapture them... Nope, the killers had to have.

Lila let out her breath as she stared down into the basement at the three wolves, glad the killers hadn't eliminated them or her yet. She wondered why the killers had taken the three into custody this time. Why didn't they just kill them outright?

Hopefully, they didn't plan to dissect them or torture them into telling the truth about their existence. What if that was what this was all about now? The Dark Angels didn't plan to rid the world of the scourge of werewolves but wanted to make a real name for themselves. The famous Dark Angels who discovered the real existence of werewolves.

She ground her teeth and listened again at the door, figuring if she could ever wake up the sleeping beauty trio and conjure up a way to get them out of the cage, they'd show the Dark Angels how dangerous it was to deal with darkly angered *lupus garous*.

CHAPTER 19

CAMERON DIDN'T TRUST KINTAIL ONE BIT, BUT MAYBE, just maybe if Cameron could help the pack leader with his troubles, Kintail would change his mind. If Kintail didn't, Cameron assumed there was only one way to deal with it—wolf to wolf. Ancient or not, Kintail would not win this battle. Not when Cameron had so much to lose.

"All right," Kintail said and rose from the table. "I'll call off my people and let Owen and David make their way here under their own power. From the time they left the place, they should be here within the next hour or so, if they're running as wolves. Find the bastards who killed my men, but let me deal with them in my own way."

Cameron shook on it, although he didn't know what he'd do when the time actually came. The idea of just killing the men in cold blood didn't appeal. Yet if he and his kind were exposed, he was sure that they would have an even worse nightmare.

Kintail whipped around and headed out the door, slamming it behind him.

Faith let out her breath and wrapped her arms around Cameron's neck, her gaze worried. "What do we do first?"

"We're going to have a problem with Gavin." Cameron stroked his hands down her sides, attempting to reassure her. "We can't tell him what we're up against. He'll think these bastards are crazy, and he can help us locate them, but beyond that, it'd be too easy for one of us to slip up and show our true nature."

Someone walked up onto the deck and knocked at the door. "Yes," Cameron hollered.

"It's me, Gavin."

"Come in."

Gavin opened the door, smiled when he saw Faith and Cameron in a hug, then closed the door. "I don't understand what's going on. Trevor said David and Owen are still hunting and that communications are just not available where they are. Which is understandable. I researched the place and read that the owners of several lodges told guests to leave laptops and cell phones behind because they don't work out here. No landlines, nothing. This Kintail has asked us to search for serial killers, but from what I gather, he's a winter resident here, not even a permanent year-round one. He's not a police chief or anything. So what's the deal?"

"Which as private investigators is why it's right up our alley," Cameron said smoothly, offering Gavin a chair. "The two men who were killed were employees of his. That's why he's so concerned. He's afraid someone is targeting his people, and if we don't catch these bastards soon, there'll be more deaths."

"Want some green tea or cocoa?" Faith asked, moving to the kitchen to turn on the stove.

"Cocoa," both men responded.

"So it's not an official investigation?" Gavin asked.

"The police are definitely looking into it. They've had two murders, one out here by the lake and one at Kintail's office in Millinocket. But they don't have the resources to analyze all the clues or find the killers."

"Then it must be connected to his hunting business." Gavin looked in Faith's direction. "What about Faith? Isn't this kind of out of her area of expertise? I mean, this could get dangerous, and I wouldn't think you'd want her involved."

Faith didn't look in his direction but smiled a little.

"She's a forensic scientist, working for the police in Portland."

Gavin stared at her. "Well, hot damn. Beauty and brains all in one package. Send you on a rescue mission, and instead... Hey, wait, so what was the deal with the guy in the gray pickup stalking her?"

"Just Kintail's people wanting to get in touch with her about her father's research here."

"Which was about Bigfoot?" Gavin smiled. "Did Cameron tell you we went on one of the Bigfoot hunts in Washington State once?"

"You did?" She raised her brows at Cameron.

He shook his head and joined her at the stove, resting his hands on her hips and kissing her cheek. "Yeah, but they're not real, you know."

"All four of us went," Gavin continued. "We were actually tracking down a deadbeat ex-husband who owed child support. We heard he was on one of those Bigfoot hunts so we hoped to catch him."

"Bigfoot or the deadbeat husband?" she asked.

Cameron wrapped his arms around her waist and pulled her snug. "The deadbeat husband. We always catch our man...or woman."

She smiled back at him. "And Bigfoot?"

Gavin cleared his throat. "Missed him completely. But

you know, hunters can go on hunts looking for known prey in an area and still not run across it. Even if the prey really exists. So what's the plan now? Trevor said you'd already been to both crime scenes, so what's the verdict?"

"I've only been to the one at Kintail's office." Faith stirred the cocoa into the mugs, then handed them to Cameron. "At least that one appeared to have been killed by silver poisoning."

When Gavin stared at her in disbelief, Faith shrugged. "Lots of silver remedies claim all kinds of health cures. So you can get them either online or in health-food stores. When people ingest silver, the condition is called argyria. But it's not a good way to kill someone. Slow silver poisoning can permanently turn skin gray."

"Sounds like you've got a keeper, Cameron," Gavin said with a wink.

Cameron knew from the slight sarcasm in his partner's tone of voice that Gavin didn't think Cameron had what it took to make this relationship work. But he and Faith had more in common than they'd ever thought possible. And he planned to hang on to her. The problem was retaining Gavin in the partnership. He wondered if David and Owen had changed any personality-wise after being turned. Would they be able to stay together as a team after all this was over with? If his friends were even all right?

"So what's next?" Gavin asked.

"I think the three men who were in the hot tub with us the one night are the ones who killed the men," Faith said.

Again, Gavin looked surprised.

Cameron smiled a little. "Like you said, she's a keeper."

"What makes you think the three men had anything to do with it?" Gavin asked her.

"They said so, in so many words. If Trevor didn't tell you already, the killers are werewolf hunters. They believe that werewolves exist just as much as Bigfoot does. They injected at least the first of the two men with silver, believing that he was a werewolf and it would destroy him. The only thing is, it can kill anyone, so his death isn't really proof that the guys are werewolves. They've seen Kintail's Arctic wolves and believe they're werewolves and anyone who has anything to do with them is too."

Gavin switched his attention to Cameron. "Did you ever find your wolf?"

"She's back with Kintail's pack."

Gavin leaned his head back and opened his mouth to speak, then looking as though he thought better of it, he closed his mouth and said, "Hmm."

Yeah, that would take some explaining. First, Cameron was frantic about "his" wolf, and now he didn't care anything about her because she was back with Kintail's pack. Cameron could see how complicated things were going to get without telling the whole truth of the matter.

"So what do we do first?" Gavin asked.

Faith pointed the spoon she'd been stirring the cocoa with at Cameron. "What if the guys in the hot tub were the ones who stole our snowmobiles? You said that the man yelling was a distraction that drew you from the cabin so that while you were gone, they could steal the machines."

"Because you were the weaker sex." Cameron smiled when Faith did. He turned to Gavin. "You should see what she did to my snowmobile."

"You mean that huge dent in the back side?" Gavin asked. His expression showed even more admiration for Faith.

"She wields a heavy cast-iron frying pan like an Olympic discus thrower."

"Ha! If I could do that well, I would have hit the driver, not the vehicle."

"It probably would have killed him. I take it you had another theory about them stealing the machines?" Cameron asked.

"Yeah, what if they were afraid you were going to find the body, so they took off with our machines to divert our attention. That way, if the man was still alive, he would have frozen to death overnight. The police came in the morning and asked us where we'd been during the night. After the men stole our machines, they got in the hot tub with us, and voilà! The machines are around the back side of the shower building. They probably had... Wait! I was thinking, what if they were staying at one of the cabins while it was closed for renovations? I didn't want to check it out without you being there. Then we got distracted when Charles said he'd take us to see Trevor."

Cameron rose from his chair. "Where did Leidolf go, Gavin?"

Gavin motioned to his cabin down the trail. "He said if we wanted his help to come get him. He was up a lot last night and went back to the cabin to take a nap."

"Let's go. Weapon reloaded?"

Gavin nodded. "When I was listening to Trevor. I wanted him to know that I was armed and dangerous if he was on the wrong side of the law."

Cameron wondered if Kintail knew yet about Gavin shooting Hilson. He set the mugs in the dry sink and poured water into them. "I'll wash them when we return." He pulled on his parka while Faith got hers on.

Gavin looked again at Cameron's sleeve. "Faith, the wolf, wouldn't have had anything to do with the way your sleeve looks, would she?"

"No," Faith said, walking out ahead of the men. "She's the one that saved Cameron's butt."

Cameron shrugged at Gavin. "Actually, you're looking right at her. Faith, the woman, clobbered the wolf with a healthy swing of a snow shovel. That little lady is not someone you ever want to piss off."

Gavin chuckled. "Sounds like you've met more than your match." He climbed onto his snowmobile and turned to Cameron. "So what's the real story about David and Owen?"

Kintail had barely returned Hilson to his own lodge when six of his people hurried to greet him, every one of them looking like he was going to beat them within an inch of their life. "What's happened?" He suspected it had to do with David and Owen and that they hadn't been recaptured.

Well, that was one bargaining chip he'd lost. Although he hadn't intended to give them up, ever. They were much better off with him since he knew the ropes and could keep his people safe. Normally. The *lupus garou* killers were another story though.

"Lila's gone. They came through the kitchen. You can smell their scents," Whitson said, limping around in a walking cast, one eye blackened, but at least Cameron hadn't killed him.

"Wait, what? Some damned human came here, and Lila went with him?"

"No," Whitson said, his expression more than concerned. "From the smell of them, there were three, all male. One of them was the same we smelled in your offices in Millinocket where Sutter died. When the men took her, Lila was alone while the rest of our people were trying to track down David and Owen. Elizabeth went with David and Owen, if you didn't get word."

Kintail stared at Whitson, shook his head, and stormed down the hall to the kitchen. He walked into it, lifted his nose, and smelled. The humans' scents were unmistakable, sweaty with fear, doused with heavy, spicy colognes, mixed with the lingering aroma of roast and gravy still clinging to the air.

His voice fierce, he growled, "Where'd they take Lila?" He stalked back into the great room where Hilson was sitting on one of the couches, still looking pretty beat-up from the gunshot wounds.

Whitson shook his head as he hurried after him. "We're not sure. A couple of our men think maybe they also grabbed Cameron's partners and Elizabeth. They saw some snowmobilers, not any of our own. Our people backed off when they saw these guys had guns. Immediately, they worried they might be the killers. Since the wolves they were after weren't part of the original pack and Elizabeth chose to go with them, they didn't feel any need to go getting themselves killed over them."

Kintail swore under his breath and gave the men gathered a steely-eyed glower. "We're a damned pack. So act like one. One for all and all for one. Whether we have new men or women or we were born that way. Hell." He stared out the window. "Did you see any bodies afterward?"

"No bodies," one of his men said. "After they left, we searched the area and found where the wolves had lain in the snow. We think they carried the bodies away this time. Maybe thinking they have proof we're werewolves? The tracks led toward Millinocket. We didn't want to get too close. We heard gunshots, three of them, and figured the men and Elizabeth were dead. They shouldn't have run off."

Unable to shake loose of the misery he felt, Kintail said, "It wouldn't have mattered, it seems. They took Lila."

"Because they ran off, we were out looking for them. That's how they got Lila."

Kintail didn't think it would matter to him one way or another, as detached as Lila had been toward him ever since he'd brought her into the pack. He knew she'd had difficulties where she was from, but she'd never discuss it with him, and he'd never wanted to pry. After what Trevor had told him, he was rethinking her plight, and he couldn't help worrying about her. She didn't deserve to die at the hands of these lunatics. She was a member of his pack, to protect always, even if she didn't want to be his mate. "Where did they take her?"

"The snowmobiles reached the trailhead, then the tracks disappeared. We think they're somewhere in Millinocket."

"Gather all our men. Send word to Cameron and his partner, Gavin, that whoever's doing the killings has either taken his men hostage or killed them. And make sure they know these men have Lila and another of my females, too, that they're probably alive and hostages for now."

Hilson held his side where Gavin had managed to shoot him. "I'm going."

"Like hell you are. Just stay here and recuperate."

"You can't have her, Kintail," his brother growled.

"What? You never changed her and never mated with her. It's too late for you to have her."

Hilson gave him a sour look. Kintail knew his brother well. If he really had wanted her, he would have taken her. Which meant the woman was up for grabs. Although, he was seriously considering giving her to one of his other bachelor males, any of whom would be eager to have the woman. "You shouldn't have gone after Cameron against my orders."

"I couldn't let him have her. But damn it, someone had already turned her."

Kintail suspected Cameron had done it—but of his own free will or by accident?

Whitson limped over to the couch. "What do you want me to do?"

Kintail shook his head. "Babysit my brother. The two of you are a pair." He stalked out of the house, hoping to hell he could end this nightmare in short order once and for all, and Lila would be so grateful, she'd have a change of heart concerning him.

<hr>

Owen woke from the worst nightmare he'd ever had, about being pursued by wolves on snowmobiles, to a nightmare he was still living as he realized he, David, and Elizabeth were caged and locked in a basement. Not Kintail's either. He poked his snout at David, who looked up sleepily at him. Then they both considered where they were, a large cage in a moldy, wet basement. David hurried to nose Elizabeth's face, trying to wake her.

And Lila?

Eyes widening, Owen stared at her. How the hell did *she* get here?

Sitting on the bottom step of the stairs leading out of the basement, she leaned against the wall, her eyes closed. It looked as though she was every bit as much a hostage as they were. Which was probably good. Kintail would want her back, even though they seemed to share a lot of animosity. Still, she was his pack member, and he seemed really protective and possessive of everyone in the pack.

Everything was dark in the room, but they could see as if it was a cloudy day. Traffic noises could be heard—not a lot, but a horn blew—and cars rushed nearby, speeding up at a traffic light and slushing through melting snow on the roadways. They were in town. Maybe Millinocket? It wasn't far from the cabin resorts, maybe an hour and a half at most.

What they needed was a window. Well, that and a crowbar. Too bad their pursuers had taken only Lila hostage. She had some wicked teeth when she was in her wolf form, but they needed a couple more guys with muscle instead.

Owen stood, stretched the kinks out of his wolf's body, then walked over to the padlock on the cage. Looked like an old one, slightly rusted, and...it was a combination lock. Like an old school lock. If he could shape-shift, although he was rather reluctant in the event he couldn't shift back before the killers returned, he figured he could decipher the combination. If they caught him in his human form, he'd have proved their theory if they had any doubts. But also, he'd be naked and freezing.

He made a little woof sound. Lila didn't stir. He did it again. David and Elizabeth joined him and looked at the padlock.

Lila's eyes snapped open. "Jeez, it's about time you three woke up."

Owen poked at the padlock. She stared at him, then the lock. "I can't open it. I tried."

He poked his nose at the lock again and looked at her. "All right, but it won't work."

She crossed the floor and lifted the lock, then twisted the knob around real slowly. As soon as he heard the telltale click of the tumbler being in place, he nudged her hand with his nose.

She smiled, then twisted it in the opposite direction for the next number. Closer this time. He nudged her hand again. "Good boy," she said.

He growled and she chuckled. She turned the knob in the same direction as the first time. When he heard the click, Owen pushed her hand, but he was afraid either he'd moved too slowly or she was a little too enthusiastic and moved too quickly this time, not allowing him time to react.

She paused and looked at him. He shook his head, but she pulled on the lock anyway. Nothing.

"It's okay, I've got the first two numbers down, and the third was just a couple before that, I think." She tried again, but twisted the knob even slower on the third number.

He bumped her, and this time when she pulled, the lock opened, and she jerked it off the cage. He wanted to howl! Howl. That was how they could get word to the others. If anyone heard them, it would most likely be Kintail's people, but only if any of them were nearby and could hear a wolf howling from a basement without windows. If the men who took them prisoner heard them? Either they'd shoot them with tranquilizers or shoot them with silver bullets. Neither a good scenario.

Lila pulled the cage door open and motioned for them to come out. "I haven't really been a good pack member as far as the two of you are concerned, but believe me, right about now, all of you are the closest thing to a dream come true." She gave each of them a hug, and they licked her cheeks in response.

One thing about wolf pack members was they made up easily enough, and since she was the one with the human hands, Owen felt pretty good that she was in the same boat with them. It served her right for being one of the ones who kept them in captivity too. Now she knew what it felt like.

"Except to bring you here after they dumped me here, I haven't seen any of them. I don't even want to think about what they plan to do with us."

Kill them, if what the murderers did with the others was any indication. Owen didn't plan to die anytime soon. He doubted David, Elizabeth, or Lila felt that way either.

But what were they to do now?

"Someone's walking around up there. Someone's making gingerbread. Otherwise, I haven't heard a soul talking. I think we're in Millinocket. We've been here about an hour. I'm hoping Kintail will be sending the cavalry soon."

But to where? Unless Lila had left a trail of wolf tracks, Owen doubted Kintail would ever find them. Or if he did, it would be too late.

As soon as Faith, Cameron, and Gavin reached Leidolf's cabin, he hurried outside, but before they explored the renovated cabins for evidence the hot tub guys had been there, she wanted to speak with Leidolf *alone*.

"I have to talk to you." She grabbed his arm and led him back inside his place. She glanced at Cameron, and his expression said he understood and would stay with Gavin while she had her little discussion.

Her heart was beating so hard with concern over her father that she was sure Leidolf could hear it. She closed the door and moved across the sitting area to the other side of the cabin to ensure that Gavin would not hear their conversation.

Sure of himself as usual, Leidolf crossed the floor to join her. "If this is about your father…"

She scowled. "It is."

Leidolf shrugged. "He should've kept the *lupus garou* secret until the day he died, Faith. As a sociologist, he should have been aware of how important keeping our identity hidden is to us. He should have realized we couldn't have allowed him to publish his research or give a lecture on it."

She felt the blood drain from her face as her eyes watered and her stomach hit the wooden floor.

"He's not dead. I didn't mean that. He is in my jurisdiction, and I couldn't allow him to threaten our kind with exposure. He was working on the speech again after you left, still hoping you'd get the flash drive back to him because he was afraid he might have omitted some important details."

"So…what are you going to do? About my father?" Her voice sounded ghostly faint, as if she hadn't the strength to fight him on this.

"It's done, Faith. He was a loose cannon. Now he's one of us."

It took a minute or more for that particular news to soak in. "A red?" she squeaked. "You made my father a red wolf?"

Leidolf smiled in his arrogant way. "It's the best kind of wolf there is."

Her head swam with the notion as she tried to gather her wits and recall previous conversations with her father. "But I talked with him. He seemed himself."

"I gave the order once you arrived here. Once I realized you were still in pursuit of the flash drive. That was the reason you wanted to see Hilson. I tried to warn you he wasn't in a good mood. I wanted to prevent you from seeing him, afraid he'd turn you. As it was, he'd already left the area for the time being."

She didn't give a damn about Hilson. Her father was who meant the world to her. "Where is my father?"

"One of my older females is staying with him, taking his classes at Portland Community College, a devoted listener. He's really quite all right with it."

Faith leaned against the wall, not comprehending any of it. Her father. A werewolf. A red werewolf. And she was an Arctic wolf? On top of that, he had a girlfriend? Who really served as a guard to keep him in line?

"She genuinely cares for him, Faith. And he adores her. Who wouldn't when a woman acts like the ground the male walks on should be worshipped?"

"But it's all a lie."

"Catherine lost her mate ten years ago. None of the males in my pack have impressed her in all the years she's been with the group, according to others. I haven't been in charge all that long. She truly cares about your father. She has one of those nurturing personalities, and she needs to feel needed. They're perfect for each other. He's worried about you, though, knowing now that Hilson was an Arctic wolf who had stolen his research. Catherine's reassured him I'm looking after you."

"You could have told me, damn it. You could have let me know what you'd done."

"You weren't a *lupus garou* at first, although I suspected Cameron would soon change that. Not on purpose. That's why we don't like to have newly turned *lupus garous* running around on their own. They're too unpredictable. They make dangerous mistakes."

"My father's a red werewolf," she said, her voice soft and rife with disbelief.

Leidolf touched her arm. "He's going to be just fine. Better than fine. He's giving a speech on the observations of a group in search of Bigfoot in the wilds of Maine instead. He's really happy, although he wants to hear that you're all right."

Faith glowered at Leidolf, then headed for the door. "You could have let me turn him. Then he would have been an Arctic *lupus garou* like me. What's he going to think when he learns I'm a white wolf when the urge swamps me?"

"I'm sure he'll love you just the same."

She growled and paused at the door. "If he's disappointed in me..."

"If it's any consolation, he talks nonstop about you to Catherine. She's dying to meet you."

"Your kind don't mix. You said so."

"We'll make an exception just this once."

Faith watched Leidolf's expression for any hint he was lying to her. "He really is all right?"

Leidolf smiled. "He's fine."

She frowned again and grabbed the door handle. "He should have been an Arctic wolf." Because then he would have joined Cameron's and her newly formed pack. Now her father was going to be in Leidolf's pack? She told herself if he was happy, she was happy, but it wasn't really sinking in. Until she realized what the matter was. She always took care of him. He'd expected it of her ever since her mother left him. Now Faith had been replaced by another woman.

Faith looked back at Leidolf. "I'm not needed anymore."

"I'd say someone else needs you more now." Leidolf shrugged. "It's just the way of things."

"He'd better be as happy as you say." Then she yanked the door open, and when Cameron and Gavin saw her scowl, she figured she'd better let them know everything was all right in a hurry and smiled. "Ready to find the killers?"

Both Gavin and Cameron looked like they thought they'd missed one hell of a conversation, and she knew Cameron would be dying to find out what she learned once Gavin wasn't listening.

When they reached the first of the cabins under renovation, the party climbed onto the porch where the windows were all boarded up.

"Charles said they'd had some vandals break the windows and tear up the cabins, which is the reason for the renovations." Leidolf peered through a couple of slats.

"Ah, there," Faith said excitedly as Cameron lifted her high enough that she could peek between the upper slats of wood covering one of the picture windows. "There's all kinds of stuff in there."

"Renovation materials," Leidolf said.

"No, there." She poked her finger at the window. "See on the floor next to the sofa? An empty package of chips."

"I don't see anything from this angle. Besides, the workmen could have left it," Leidolf said.

Faith didn't believe it. Well, Leidolf could be right, but she didn't want to believe him. "Let's find a way in."

Before Cameron could put Faith down and use his lockpicks on the door, Leidolf pulled out a set of his own.

"Standard key set?" Cameron asked.

Leidolf gave him a warning look, then opened the door.

Both Cameron and Gavin pulled guns. Leidolf and Gavin entered first while Cameron stayed with Faith on the deck. Then Gavin shouted, "All clear."

Faith entered with Cameron, but before she could check out the potato-chip bag, she smelled something else. The redhead named Chris. She turned to Cameron, but the look on his face said the same thing. Not only Chris's scent was in there but the other two men and the woman and the smell of gingerbread also.

"Do you sense anything?" Leidolf asked.

"They've been here," Faith said, barely breathing, thankful now that she hadn't gone looking for these men alone.

"How long ago?" Gavin asked.

"Not today. Maybe yesterday." Cameron looked under the cabinets.

Faith smelled gingerbread next to the couch. She looked under the couch. Nothing but dust balls. She pulled out the cushions. The second one hit pay dirt. An empty package of gingerbread cookies from Specialty Cookies, Millinocket.

"Is this a processing plant in Millinocket? Or a small business? Maybe a family-run business?"

"The cookies might just be sold at the grocery stores. Anyone could buy them," Leidolf said.

Faith cast him a frown. "Let's ask George Simmons. Maybe he'd know."

First, they explored the other cabins under renovation. Every one of them had evidence that someone had been eating in them. Maybe sleeping here. Watching the comings and goings of the guests and owners?

Suspecting that maybe Charles and his family were in with the werewolf culture? And that brought something else to mind. "When Charles was injured at his campsite, we thought it was Kintail or his men. What if it was Chris and his thugs instead? Maybe because he does business with Kintail, and Chris and his Dark Angels believe that he's in on the werewolf business."

Gavin shook his head. "I've heard some crazy things in the police business and in our private eye concerns, but this really takes the show for the most bizarre."

Leidolf exchanged looks with Cameron as if he was warning him the trouble he could be in by keeping his friend on the mission.

They mounted their snowmobiles and headed back in the direction of the lodge, but when they reached Cameron's place, Trevor drove toward them, waving for them to stop. He seemed so agitated, she knew the news couldn't be good. Because he was here to tell them, she figured it had to do with David and Owen. Cameron's whole body went rigid. She imagined Gavin's did too.

"They've got them," Trevor hurriedly said. "They've got David and Owen and Lila. And one more of our females."

Faith didn't have to ask who had taken them. She felt

light-headed, as if the knowledge Cameron's partners were at death's door delivered a blow to her brain. Instantly, her thoughts switched to the day the little neighbor girl ended up missing. About how hard they'd tried to find her before she was murdered. About how they were too late.

She broke the silence first. "Are they in Millinocket?"

Trevor's eyes teared up, and he wiped his nose with his gloved hand. "We think so. We think they're not dead yet. But every second they're gone…"

"Let's go," Cameron said. "We'll tear the town apart."

"Wait." The men all turned to hear what Faith had to say. "Is there a place called Specialty Cookies in Millinocket?"

"Near the library. Yes," Trevor said.

"All right. We'll check the place out while we're at it."

Cameron waited for her to speak further, and she could have hugged him for believing in her. "Let's go," she said and reached out to squeeze his hand.

His grip was gentle, but hers was not. She wanted him to know she was in this for whatever it took, damn the consequences. He seemed to understand.

The five of them took off for the trailhead, first dropping by the location where she'd left her snowmobile when she'd had the urge to shape-shift. She hoped the hell she wouldn't do that again anytime soon.

From the snowmobile rental shop, they could pick up her SUV and Cameron's rental car. Although her SUV fit five, the back seat was awfully small for three adults, so she figured they would divide up and a couple of the men would take Cameron's vehicle.

And then like Cameron said, they'd tear the town apart.

CHAPTER 20

EVEN THOUGH KINTAIL AND HIS MEN WERE SCOURING Millinocket, he hoped the hell Trevor had gotten word to Cameron and the others since they were more equipped to handle investigations. Kintail, although normally in control and never rattled, felt like the proverbial chicken with its head cut off as he searched down every side street, drove past every home. But there wasn't anything to say, "Here's the house where your wolves are being kept hostage," and he didn't feel he was getting anywhere—totally useless, at a complete loss as to what to do. More than anything, he couldn't help worrying about Lila. She'd really gotten under his skin.

He pulled his gray pickup off to the side of the road. Even though he'd intended to leave Hilson and Whitson safely behind at the lodge, they both had insisted they come along to be part of the pack despite their injuries. Since he'd arrived in town, even Adams, suffering from his concussion, had called him on his cell phone from the hospital, wanting to join in the search.

Kintail said no to that, but if Adams acted anything like Hilson and Whitson, Kintail doubted he had any control over his pack members, all of whom wanted to help save Lila and the others and knew that in his present state of mind, no meant maybe and that was all they needed to hear.

His phone buzzed, and Kintail saw it was Trevor. Thank God. "Yes."

"We just made it to town. We're on our way first to Specialty Cookies. Faith thinks it might be a lead."

"We're on our way there now." He hoped to God the woman was right, and they found Lila and the others before it was too late.

"There it is," Faith said, pointing out the window while Cameron drove her SUV. They'd meant to split up the passengers, two in Cameron's rental, and the rest in Faith's because the seat was really crowded for three men to squish in back.

Everyone—Leidolf, Gavin, and Trevor—did just that, squished together in the back seat, because Cameron wouldn't let Faith ride in the back with them, and the men all wanted to stick with the woman who seemed to be in the know.

"I know it's a real long shot." Faith didn't want them to think she knew for sure, but she was used to following dead-end leads in her work, and she figured both Cameron and Gavin would realize that. Trevor and Leidolf might not.

"It's the best shot we have right now," Cameron said, his voice attempting reassurance, but an edginess was evident.

All that kept going through her mind was a little girl with dark curls and dark eyes and a winning smile who drew pictures on the sidewalk in colored chalk across the street from Faith's parents' home, annoying the eighty-year-old next-door neighbor who claimed it was graffiti and hosed it down every chance he got.

The day of her disappearance, he hosed down the last

memory of her, and that was the last Faith remembered of the smiling little girl. Faith stared out the SUV's window and fought the tears. She thought she'd gotten over the memories so long ago. But every time she had a case like this where the victim was still possibly alive, she felt the same cloud of doom and feared the same ending.

And all she was left finding was the killer on the loose, the victim sacrificed for yet another meaningless cause.

"Faith?" Cameron said, touching her shoulder.

She clenched her teeth and looked at him.

"We're here."

"Right." She grabbed for her door handle, but Gavin was already opening the door for her. She saw the quaint little house with the gingerbread trimmings like lilac lace and the rest of the house painted in garish pink. It reminded her of Hansel and Gretel and the witch who lived inside with her big oven and children made into gingerbread ornaments in the front yard. Here a white picket fence enclosed the small front yard, and a sign hanging between white porch columns said: *Specialty Cookies, Open Mon-Wed, 1–5 p.m.*

It was Thursday, so no problem there. Cameron led Faith up to the front door, but none of them bothered to knock. Leidolf whipped out his lockpicks and opened the door without a sound as if he were a master thief. Thankfully, there wasn't any alarm to let the occupants know someone had come in through the front door. Gavin gave Cameron a look, and Faith assumed he wanted to know what business Leidolf was in where he carried lockpicks wherever he went. That made her curious too.

The entryway had a quaint little parlor filled with two antique love seats, curved mahogany legs and seat backs, and bright-yellow floral fabric. A counter with an old-time cash register sat nearby. A plastic display next to it contained chocolate fudge of various kinds—vanilla, with nuts, without, chocolate, the aroma mouthwatering. Deeper inside the house, the fragrance of gingerbread filled a kitchen decorated in yellow, bright and cheerful. Antique platters and plates and paintings gave the place an old-world feel, but the splash of constant color made it more Alice in Wonderland in appearance, when ironically, Faith thought it could be a front for a bunch of Dark Angel lunatics bent on killing werewolves.

While Faith investigated each room thoroughly, Gavin, Trevor, and Leidolf hurriedly explored every room throughout the two-story house and the basement, looking for any sign of hostages or hostage takers.

Cameron stayed with Faith, his gun ready, protecting her while she looked in every kitchen cabinet, in every drawer for some kind of clue.

Just cooking supplies and cooking utensils, nothing else. Then she found a drawer full of receipts. Again, for cooking supplies, shipping orders, nothing that would indicate whoever owned this place was involved in hunting werewolves. She moved on to the basement, but she didn't smell any of the men who had visited them at the hot tub.

"You don't smell them here, do you?" Cameron asked.

She shook her head.

She walked to the second floor, up the creaky wooden stairs covered in an old worn tapestry that muffled her footfalls, and examined the two bedrooms and bath when she got there. All were very feminine with frilly curtains, frilly bedspreads, and frilly lace pillows in frilly pink and purple colors. She looked in the drawers. In one, the folded sweaters were big and bright. In another, she found underwear, all white. In another, she noticed a bright, neon-pink strap of bathing suit fabric beneath a pair of denim shorts. She reached for the strap and pulled the bathing suit out and stared at it. The woman in the hot tub. The woman who had seen Bigfoot. Mary.

In the other room, the chest of drawers was completely devoid of clothing. Downstairs in the office, they didn't find anything but billings to customers and to grocery stores in the area.

"I'll…" Trevor started to say when the front door swung open and Gavin and Cameron pointed their weapons at the entrance.

Kintail held up his hands in surrender, his amber eyes darkening, narrowed. "Just me. Find anything?" he asked Faith, looking at her as if she was the only hope he had in the world.

"A swimsuit," Trevor eagerly said. "She's one of them. A woman."

"Older, gray-haired, heavy-set, Mary McNichol's her name," Cameron said, holding up an invoice.

"And the men?" Kintail asked.

"It appears they've never been here. We couldn't find any trace of their scents." Faith looked back at the kitchen. "There was an empty bag with her cookie company's name on it at one of Charles's cabins that's under renovation. We smelled all of them there. So they work together, but the men must avoid her house for some reason."

"Do you have another clue?" Kintail asked.

"No, but if we split forces, we could ask various business

owners, like these grocers," Faith said, pointing to a list of the places Mary sold to wholesale, "if they know Mary and have any idea about a redheaded Chris and a dark-haired Matt. It's worth a try. Surely someone's seen the woman with the men, and they'll know last names and an address."

"I'll go to the grocery store here," Trevor said.

Kintail waited for Faith to say where she planned to go. "I'll be checking out the lodge where Cameron and I first stayed. A clerk I talked to knew a lot about you and your wolves. Maybe she knows something about Mary and her friends," Faith said.

Kintail looked like he wanted to go with her, but she handed him a list, thwarting him. "You might want to have your people check out these other businesses that dealt with her. Before long, everything will be closing. So we need to hurry."

Almost in panic, Kintail immediately began snapping orders to his men while Cameron escorted Faith back to the SUV, with Gavin and Leidolf joining them.

"If we make Faith one of our partners," Gavin said, walking with them back to her SUV rental, not leaving Faith and Cameron's side for an instant, "we could sit back and watch her work, and she could solve all our cases for us. Of course we'd provide her with protection. Think that could work?"

Cameron opened her door for her and shook his head at Gavin.

"I don't know," Gavin said, smiling. "I really think she's worth taking a chance on."

She wondered if he'd think so if he knew what she and Cameron had become. She climbed into the front passenger seat and watched as Leidolf came around to the left side of the car and climbed in. She thought he was going to go sleuthing on his own. He'd been so quiet all along, she wondered what he was thinking.

When they arrived at the hotel, she saw what he intended to do. After getting a room so he could use the internet and one of the lodge's guest computers, he sat down at one in the lobby and began searching through websites, looking for the Dark Angels. Gavin remained with him while Faith and Cameron got a room for the night.

Unfortunately, the clerk who'd been on the desk the evening they had arrived wasn't here tonight. When Faith described her to the man at the desk, he said, "Sissy? Yeah, she knows everybody's business. We learned a long time ago if we wanted a rumor spread, tell Sissy. If you don't want the world to know, mum's the word around her."

"But she'll be on duty here in the morning, right?"

"First thing, six in the morning."

"Good, that's my kind of time." She took Cameron's hand and led him to Leidolf's table as he surfed the Web, barely pausing to see what she wanted. "We'll be in Room 213. What's your room number, Leidolf?"

"It's 442. Gavin can stay with me."

"If you find anything, let us know, okay? We're going up to the room to discuss plans."

A small smile lifted Gavin's lips, but he didn't say anything. Leidolf glanced up from the computer screen and frowned at Cameron. "Remember what I said, Cameron. We do things differently. Once you reach a certain point, there's no turning back. Not for us."

"I'll keep it in mind, Leidolf. Thanks for the advice." But

Cameron sounded like he was peeved that Leidolf would mention it.

Faith understood. Being a pack leader, Leidolf was used to taking charge of a situation. He probably didn't trust Cameron and her to follow the rules of their society yet. And he was probably right not to trust them. At least she figured some of the rules might need to be broken.

Cameron walked back out to the vehicle to get a single bag for each of them, then led her to the elevator. "You really were talking about discussing plans to locate David and Owen, right?"

"Absolutely. I have to assimilate what I've seen. I categorize everything in my mind, run over it mentally, back and forth, until I come up with another idea. There's no one way to do this. Something triggers something, and then that triggers something else. And then we've got our man or woman."

"Or three men and a woman."

As they walked to their room, Faith said quietly, "Or more."

Once they were settled in the room, Faith pulled off her parka, hat, and gloves, kicked off her snow boots, and climbed onto the bed. "Do you want to order some room service?" She leaned against the pillow and closed her eyes.

"Are you going to sleep?"

She didn't open her eyes. "This is how I think, Cameron. Really. I have to have absolute quiet, shut down everything but my mind so I can think."

"What do you want to eat?"

"Salmon. If they have any."

"What did Leidolf say to you?"

Faith opened her eyes and narrowed her gaze at Cameron. "My dad's a red wolf, damn it, and he has a red wolf girlfriend. And he's happy with everything that's transpired." She snapped her eyes shut.

Cameron moved in close to the bed and kissed the frown on Faith's forehead. "He's alive and well, and that's all that's important, Faith, honey. That's all that matters."

Afraid that her father might have been eliminated or would be soon, Cameron was damned relieved her father was fine.

She quit frowning. "You're right." And then she didn't say anything more.

He watched her, worried that she was going to fall asleep on him when every minute that passed meant his partners were at risk. Then he gave up and ordered the salmon dinners. Every officer, every investigator had their own methods for working things out. Some looked over evidence a million times, some had to visit the crime scene to visualize what might have occurred; everyone did something a little bit differently. Combing through the physical evidence was more his style, so just thinking about random happenings didn't work for him.

For a while, he stared out the window at the parking lot, trying to figure out where they could look next, hoping that Kintail's people would pick up another lead or that Leidolf would. He glanced at Faith. Her breathing seemed shallow. Hell, she *had* fallen asleep.

He kicked off his boots and joined her in bed, pulling

her against his body, her head resting on his shoulder, her hand planted on his stomach, her inner thigh pressed against his thigh. Breathing in her subtle lavender fragrance, he felt the shaft of desire slamming into him. Every sense on higher alert—the sound of her soft intake as she took a deep breath, her fingers spread across his belly in a tantalizing touch, her leg draped over his as if screaming *I'm yours, take me*—keenly affected him. Ever since he'd felt he'd nearly lost her when she was in her wolf form, he'd been forced to realize how much the woman was already part of his life. How much it would kill him if she no longer was.

He stroked her hair, his other arm wrapped around her, holding her close, enjoying the moment of silence, of peace, wishing he didn't have to worry about his friends being in trouble at a time like this, when there was a knock at the door.

"Room service," a man cheerfully called out.

Cameron slipped out from under Faith and headed for the door. When he opened it, the man rolled in the cart, the same one who had brought him the steak the first night Cameron had been here. The man glanced at Faith, and Cameron expected him to smile at the sight of her sleeping on the bed, figuring he'd have remembered her slipping on her boots while Cameron was wearing only a towel and that the lady was more or less a permanent guest of his, when Cameron noted a tattoo on the man's hand.

The words *Dark Angel* in small print stood out as if the letters were as visible as a billboard on a high-speed highway.

Faith opened her eyes and took a deep breath. "The food's here."

The man was already edging toward the door, his eyes

wide. Something clued him in about who Cameron and Faith were, or maybe just Faith, but he wasn't waiting for his tip, and that confirmed Cameron's suspicions.

The man turned to bolt. Cameron tackled him to the floor. The guy was wiry, flailing with arms and legs, trying to connect with anything that might help him break free, but with his stomach pressed against the floor, he didn't have much leverage. If Cameron hadn't needed him to be coherent, he would just as soon have knocked him out.

"Who is he?" Faith asked as she hurried to get Cameron's gun from his holster on the bedside table.

"One of them."

The man's green eyes widened even more when he saw Faith pointing the gun at him. "Where are they?" she asked in a voice that bordered on dangerous.

He grew very still.

Someone knocked on the door, and Faith called out, "Yes?"

"It's me, Gavin."

Cameron nodded, still pinning their Dark Angel conspirator to the floor. Faith went to the door but had the gun poised in case Gavin wasn't alone.

She might not be a police officer, but she sure knew what she was doing.

Gavin said, "Leidolf found their website and—" He stared at the gun Faith was wielding, although she lowered it quickly, and then he saw Cameron sitting on the Dark Angel. "Holy hell, who's he?"

"He brought our meals, but he gave us the wrong brand of tartar sauce," Cameron said sarcastically, pointing at the man's hand bearing the tattoo. "He recognized us and started to book before he had his tip. Now the question is, what kind of torture should we use on him to get him to reveal our partners' location?"

Gavin closed the door, stalked into the room, and stood with his boots pressed against the top of the man's head. "We're werewolves, right? So why don't we turn into wolves and start eating body parts? Slowly."

The man began to tremble. He might think he was a killer, but he wasn't anything more than a scared pup, probably talking big when he was with his *gang*. Without them as moral support, egging each other on? He was nothing.

Faith crouched next to him. "Gavin's teasing. He's got an *insanely* sinister sense of humor. Werewolves don't exist. But their partners' lives are at stake, and right now, I doubt I can keep them from torturing you so they can learn their location. If you don't think they'll do it, believe me, they've used some techniques even I can't stand to watch. I've seen some pretty hideous stuff, being a forensic scientist."

Gavin raised his brows at Cameron. Cameron gave him a small smile back. The woman was worth her weight in diamonds.

"We've seen you change," the man bit out, his words muffled with the way Cameron was pressing him against the hotel's carpeted floor.

"Me?" she asked, and Cameron detected a hint of alarm.

"Not you specifically. But some of the others."

Cameron figured Gavin wouldn't believe any of it, so he assumed the best way to get the truth out of the guy was to play along with it. "My partners?"

"They're wolves right now. The bastards are in a cage nice and safe and sound—for the moment."

Hell, that didn't sound good. Did they have the shape-shifting trick down pat? Or would they inadvertently shift at the wrong time?

Gavin grunted. "Hell, you've got some of Kintail's wolves and think they're David and Owen?"

"We saw them shift, damn it. Them and some woman they had with them. They buried their clothes and shape-shifted near where Kintail's lodge was. Surprised the shit out of us. We were watching the lodge, ready to get any of his men who ventured out of the place alone, when these three ran for the barn like the devil was after them. Then in a few minutes, they headed for the woods as others from the house shouted they'd escaped. At first we assumed the three of them were prisoners, and we thought to rescue them from Kintail's people. Then we'd solicit them to join our group."

He squirmed a little, but Cameron tightened his hold on him.

The man groaned and quit resisting. "After they started tossing their clothes, we changed our minds. You sure as hell turn fast. One minute a man or woman, the next a wolf. If I'd looked away for a second or two, I would have missed the whole episode. But it wasn't the first time we'd seen it happen. When we were on that trip with the hunter guide, Trevor Hodges, looking for Bigfoot? We got separated from him, and then we saw Kintail's woman shape-shift. We wanted to tell Trevor and Kenneth O'Malley, the weird dude who kept taking notes. But then we thought they wouldn't believe us. We kept them out of the loop and changed our focus from hunting Bigfoot to werewolves. For a long time, we just watched Kintail and his wolves. Then we decided to act. Why should they pretend to be normal people like us? So we tried to kill them with silver and it worked."

"Anyone can die from a lethal injection of silver. Even anyone as stupid as you," Faith said.

The man's eyes widened, then narrowed. "Says you."

"If you're so well read up on stuff, you could easily find out that what I'm saying is true. In fact, we could run to the health-food store tonight and get some silver supplements to feed you. See how long you live. Hell, how do we know *you're* not a werewolf?"

He scowled at her. "We wanted you to join our team. We thought you'd understand us. It seems you're one of them now. Either that or just clueless." He didn't say anything for a few seconds, then took up his story again. "Here are your friends, running as wolves through the forest in the direction of Charles's resort. We figure he's either a wolf, too, or a friend of theirs. The next thing we knew, Kintail's men were in hot pursuit of your partners and that woman. At first, we just observed them, not sure what to do. Then we figured, what the hell. We have what it takes to show who's superior. Who shouldn't exist. We showed off our guns, and that made their pursuers run away like scared little rabbits. So much for them being badass wolves. It didn't take long for us to run your partners and the woman down and dope them up. We got Kintail's main squeeze too."

"Where are they?" Cameron growled.

"If I tell you, you'll kill me."

"Quickly, mostly painlessly," Gavin said. "Believe me, you don't want a wolf eating at your organs while you're still alive. That's got to hurt, *lots*."

"I don't know where they are exactly. They took them to

one house, but Chris said he'd moved them to another later. Just in case anyone might have tracked us."

"Why not kill them like you did the other men?" Cameron asked, still puzzled why they'd keep Owen and David alive this time.

"Hell, we could just kill all your sorry asses. But we'd have to do it secretly, and someone would eventually try to arrest us for mass murders. So we have to prove you're werewolves. Then we can become famous for finding the first real werewolves. Fame, fortune, we'd be able to make public appearances on all the talk shows, maybe even get honorary degrees. If we were in England, the queen would even knight us."

"Lead us to the house where Chris had taken them," Cameron said.

"Change into a wolf. You're not going to shoot me with that gun. You can't scare me like this. Shape-shift, growl at me, bare those wicked teeth. Then I'll take you there. But I can't guarantee they'll be there."

"Sorry, we're all newly turned. We can't just shape-shift any time we want to," Faith said, shrugging.

"But I can shift anytime I want to," Leidolf said, and everyone turned around to see him standing in the doorway, his amber eyes lethal.

CHAPTER 21

HOW IN THE HELL HAD LEIDOLF UNLOCKED THE DOOR? Cameron's lockpicks wouldn't work on key-card slots. And how long had he been standing in the room listening? The guy moved like a phantom.

But he got the Dark Angel's attention.

"Do it, tough guy," the man sassed back as if he didn't really have the faintest idea how dangerous Leidolf could be.

Maybe it was Cameron's heightened senses that clued him in, besides the threatening tone Leidolf used or the look of aggression on Leidolf's darkened face. A scent of a coming battle hung in the air. Of murderous intent. An alpha who would show the beta he wasn't one to be messed with.

"Gavin's not one of us," Leidolf smoothly said, his voice still deep and dark, his fierce gaze locked on the man's eyes. "I can't do it in front of him."

The man studied Gavin, who was looking every bit as menacing. "He said he was one."

Leidolf smiled, but the look was pure evil. "He might wish he was, but he isn't. Trust me."

"Whatever. Have the dude leave then."

"You won't like what you see when I shift."

"It's the only way I'll feel intimidated enough to tell you where they are."

"Fine." Leidolf glanced Gavin's way. "Leave, before it's too late." The way Leidolf said it wasn't so much an order as a challenge.

"Sorry, I'm staying for the show."

Hoping to encourage him to leave before his partner lived to regret it, Cameron said, "Gavin."

Gavin shook his head. "We're all on the same team, no matter the circumstances."

Cameron knew his friend would not believe this one iota, but Leidolf wasn't waiting, wasn't about to try to talk any sense into him, and began stripping out of his clothes. Faith looked like she was going to be sick. She caught Cameron's eye. He knew what she was thinking. If Leidolf went through with this, Gavin had to be changed. And the man who had tried to sound so brave would die once they located the house where their partners were being held hostage.

She left to put on her boots, not bothering to watch Leidolf get naked and shift.

Cameron watched the man, saw the stupid smirk on his face. Gavin observed the Dark Angel's expression, too, probably wondering how Leidolf stripping out of his clothes was going to force this man to reveal anything to them.

But as soon as Leidolf growled, baring his teeth, his nose and face wrinkling, his eyes narrowed with dangerous contempt, and his hackles raised as a highly pissed-off red wolf, he garnered everyone's attention. For a moment. Cameron quickly glanced at Gavin to see his take. Faith was watching him too. Gavin was still observing the man's posture, seeing if Leidolf's threats were working, as if he didn't need to see what Leidolf had become. As if he already knew.

The man had quit smiling, and he was trembling again, but even so, Cameron didn't feel as though he was ready to spill his secrets. He released his hold on him. The man started to sit up, and Leidolf lunged at him with a fierce snarl that made Cameron both respectful and proud to be one of them.

Faith quickly turned on the television to help drown out the sounds in the room.

The so-called Dark Angel threw up his hands to instinctively block his face. Leidolf clamped down on one of his hands, and the man screamed out in pain.

He looked as if he was about ready to faint, his skin turning ashen, his eyes rolling into the back of his head. Leidolf quickly released him, then stepped aside, shifted, and dressed. "He's one of us now," he said with menacing conviction. He glanced at Gavin. "You should have left the room when you had the chance."

"I wouldn't have dreamed of being left out of this little adventure."

Cameron suspected Gavin had seen Faith shape-shift on the trail. So his partner had truly already known.

Leidolf gave Gavin an evil smile. "He'll make a good pack member." Then he turned his attention to the Dark Angel passed out on the floor. His hand was bleeding, but Leidolf hadn't crushed the bone like he could have.

"Are you sure he's one of us now?" Faith asked, pausing to pull on her parka. "What if he isn't?"

"He's one of *my* kind, I should say," Leidolf said in that arrogant way of his. "Which means I'll either have to eliminate his sorry ass if he causes me any grief or take him back with me and make him part of my pack. Although there is a slight chance I didn't change him. He still won't be sure either way. So he's ours, pliable once we revive him."

"I'll get some ice," Faith said, but Gavin stopped her.

"I'll get it."

Faith looked at Cameron as if she feared Gavin was getting ready to run. Cameron knew his partner better than that. He handed him the ice bucket. "Fill it to the top."

———

Kintail knew they were getting closer to finding Lila, Elizabeth, and Cameron's partners. He smiled at Trevor, unable to hide his own deviousness. He still had it in mind that Faith would be his if Lila wouldn't change her tune and David and Owen would remain with the pack, although he couldn't stop thinking about Lila and how him taking Faith would affect her. Some distant niggling kept warning him he couldn't do it to her, that he had to give Lila more time.

As far as Leidolf went, he didn't believe the red would interfere in his plans, since this wasn't his territory, he was a red, and he wouldn't want to mess in Kintail's pack business.

Cameron and Gavin were another story. He didn't believe he could let them live if he wanted to keep Faith and their partners.

"We've found six leads, but this looks like the best one yet?" Kintail asked Trevor, raising the list of leads he'd scratched off.

"Yeah. Just waiting for your go-ahead."

"Let's go."

"What about letting Cameron and the others know?"

Kintail smiled again, and Trevor shook his head.

"Kenneth O'Malley saw Lila shift, didn't he?" Kintail asked Trevor for the hundredth time.

"At the time, I didn't think he had."

Finally, his pack member was being honest with him. "That's just what I thought."

They climbed into his truck, and Kintail glanced into the back seat of the king cab. Hilson was sound asleep. Whitson was dozing but snapped his head up. "We got a lead?"

"Yeah, this time, it's got to be the right place." But how to kill the bastards without the residents of Millinocket believing Kintail's wolves had done the deed?

Owen figured if they could maintain their wolf form, he and David would be a hell of a lot more intimidating than as naked humans if the men tried to come into the basement. Armed with guns, though, the werewolf killers would be a hell of a lot more menacing. Still, they had to chance rushing them if nothing else. Somehow, they had to get upstairs and out of this place. Once they did, he figured they could hightail it back to Charles's cabin resort, meet up with Cameron and Gavin, and take it from there.

Lila was standing at the top of the steps, her ear to the door again listening. She looked back at them and shook her head. "Kintail will be here soon to rescue us," she said, her voice hushed and more hopeful than trusting.

For the first time, she seemed vulnerable and, Owen thought, a little bit frightened. He knew this could all go badly for them in a split second. He didn't have any illusions. The werewolf killers were trigger-happy nutcases, and if he and David didn't do what they needed to do to make the outcome right…they could all be dead.

"Someone's coming," she whispered, her voice half-excited, half-worried.

Showtime.

———

Sarge—so named because he'd been in the army before he had been dishonorably discharged for illegal drug use—held his injured hand, now wrapped in a hotel hand towel, the blood spotting the white terry cloth. His face wore a scowl, but he was trembling hard as he climbed into the SUV seat between Leidolf and Gavin.

"You didn't have to bite me, damn it," Sarge said to Leidolf. "You were only supposed to growl."

"I growled, and you weren't talking," Leidolf said, his voice darkly amused.

"Yeah, but hell, now I'm one of you."

"Yeah, you are. Now your buddies will want you dead," Gavin said. "So start talking. Where'd they take them?"

"If I tell you, they'll kill me."

"You're alive with us so far. It's the only chance you've got," Cameron said, glowering at him from the front seat. "Either start talking, or Leidolf will bite you again."

Sarge looked at Leidolf, probably figuring he wouldn't dare change in the vehicle.

"Windows are darkly tinted, Sarge. Better do as everyone says," Faith warned.

Sarge tightened his wounded hand against his chest. "It's 200 East Dover. I can't guarantee that they're there. I told you that already. Chris said they'd move them after a time."

"Which way?" Cameron asked.

"Take a right at the next light. Head straight for six blocks, then turn right on Amy."

Cameron roared off, then made the six blocks in record time. Faith wanted to tell him to slow down or they'd get picked up by the cops, and then what? But they reached Amy without incident and after turning right on the street of little brick homes, Sarge said, "Next street is East Dover. Seventh house on the right."

"Whose home is it?" Faith asked.

"Matt's. He lives with his girlfriend, but she's working late at a hamburger joint tonight."

They pulled up six houses down from the brown brick house. Then, with Sarge in tow, they headed for the house. Cameron had wanted Gavin to wait in the vehicle with Faith, but she opted to stick with the group. Gavin had a gun, and they might need all the firepower they could get. Faith didn't need to be protected in the SUV.

Cameron didn't argue with her, although he didn't like it that she'd go along. Gavin did argue with her, but he wanted Cameron to stay and protect her. Leidolf didn't say a word. And Sarge started to say something about staying behind with her, but all three men cut him a glare and he shut up.

Cameron and Faith went around the back, where birdbaths covered in ice and bird feeders filled with snow were hanging in a number of trees. Gavin went to one side of the house. Leidolf took Sarge to the front door and knocked.

The place looked dark and quiet. No lights, no chimney smoke, no movement, nothing.

Faith was pretty sure no one was home. Which meant that either Sarge was lying, or Chris had moved their hostages like Sarge said he would.

Within minutes, Leidolf was opening the door to the backyard. "No one here. Why don't you come in and see if you can get a clue."

Faith, Cameron, and Gavin hurried into the house and began searching the place. In the basement, she and Cameron got a whiff of Chris and his companions. And they smelled wolves. Since Faith and Cameron had not smelled David and Owen since they'd been changed, they couldn't tell for sure that it was them. Although they suspected it was.

"Wolves have been here," Faith said, lifting a couple of white hairs off the cement floor.

"Where to now?" Cameron asked Sarge, glowering at him as if he was ready to change into the wolf himself and bite him somewhere new.

"I told you—"

"Where!" Cameron snapped.

"We can check Chris's house. It's on the other side of town," Sarge rattled off really quickly.

"Let's go." Cameron grabbed Faith's arm and hurried her up the stairs.

Barely able to keep up with his long stride, she said, "It might be quicker if you just tossed me over your shoulder and hauled me to the car."

Gavin chuckled.

In a deviously sexual way, Cameron smiled at Faith. "If you're asking me to do it, I'd be happy to oblige."

"No, it was a subtle way for me to say, 'Slow down,' so I could keep up."

But he didn't slow down, and she had to run to keep up, although she couldn't blame him. She didn't want him telling her she should have stayed in the vehicle.

Suddenly, the headlights of the SUV flicked on and the vehicle drove in their direction. When it stopped, she wondered how in the world Leidolf had gotten to the rental vehicle that quickly. Then she recalled he had already left the basement before Cameron began dragging her up the stairs.

"Where is Chris's house?" Cameron growled.

Sarge hesitated only a second before he began giving the directions in a hurry.

The door swung open into the basement, and at that instant, David and Owen jumped from the top steps where they were waiting in rabid anticipation and knocked down the blond-headed man who was in their direct path. He didn't have time to squeal or shout, his blue eyes round with shock when Lila came out of the opening and swung a cane at him, striking him in the head, either knocking him out cold or killing him. Owen didn't have time to check him out or even care. David made sure Elizabeth stayed behind him, protecting her as if she were his mate already.

Freedom loomed in front of them, the door to the outside just down the long hall that opened onto a living room. Before Owen could navigate it, a redheaded man stepped in front of the door, wielding a damned gun.

Owen didn't hesitate. Kill or be killed, and he leaped, farther than he ever thought he could manage. Except leaping and dodging bullets was another thing. The weapon discharged, and Owen felt the damned projectile lodge in his chest at the same time he slammed into the redhead. At least Red couldn't shoot David or Elizabeth or Lila.

He grabbed the man's raised arm and bit before his mind faded into darkness, his last thought that he'd saved them. He'd saved his friend and the two women. Then his thoughts dissolved into oblivion.

Kintail looked at the damn list again, his blood boiling with fury that Cameron and Faith had already been here in this house, already searched every inch of it, and without sending him word. "Where the hell are they?"

Trevor jumped in the truck. "They've been at this house. All of them. That Gavin, Leidolf, Cameron, Faith, and some other man I've never smelled before. Do you think it's one of the Dark Angels? Do you think he's guiding them to the members' houses?"

"Hell, yeah. From the blood we smelled, I'd say that one of the *lupus garous* resorted to pressure to convince the guy to make the right choice."

They drove off down the street and headed west. Trevor looked over the list. "Here's a house we haven't checked yet. It's on the other side of town. It's supposed to be Mary's nephew's place. Maybe we should check there?"

Kintail drove in the direction Trevor gave him. The moon was waning, lights in the town winking out for the night, but the aurora borealis lit up the dark sky in a flashy display of greens and mauve almost as an omen. The wolves would win tonight.

"Chris's house," Sarge said, pointing at a white clapboard that blended in with the snow.

As it grew darker, the aurora borealis flowed across the sky in an unbelievable array of colors from a blending of mauves and greens, dizzying and magnificent. Faith felt as though she was witnessing a dreamlike light display, as if she had fallen into a fantasy world where the sky was full of shifting, flowing, colorful lights and the ground a palette of ice-white frozen whipped cream. A world where men and women could turn into wolves. That was when she realized that she had changed when the moon was waning. So the tales of how werewolves could only shift during the full moon weren't true. What of when the new moon was present? Or did they never get a break from the threat of shifting?

"He'll be well armed," Sarge warned, breaking into her thoughts. "He'll kill every one of you."

"He can try," Cameron said, jerking his door open. He glanced at Faith, but she was already getting out of the vehicle.

"No, Cameron. I'm not staying behind." She hurried with Leidolf and Gavin, who wedged Sarge between them in case he tried to bolt.

Cameron slipped his arm around Faith's shoulders and held her close, his touch protective and caring. "You can't blame me for wanting to keep you safe."

She smiled up at him. "I'd worry if you didn't."

Gunfire rang out inside the house, and Faith's blood chilled. Before anyone had time to react, a green all-terrain vehicle barreled out of the driveway and sped down the road. Cameron released Faith and rushed for the door with

Gavin and Leidolf, his hand firmly on Sarge, as she caught the license plate number. Their guns drawn, Cameron and Gavin kicked the front door open, then rushed inside with Leidolf and Sarge.

A gray pickup rumbling toward her caught Faith's attention. *Kintail.* She frantically waved at him to follow the green ATV, and Kintail gunned the engine and tore off after him.

Seeing Chris's fuzzy red hair sticking out the front entryway where he must have fallen, Faith hurried up the front steps. Inside, she saw Lila hiding behind a grandfather clock, a cane readied in her hands while she watched down the hall where Gavin, Cameron, and the others must have run.

A white wolf lying motionless next to Chris appeared to have passed out but was coming to. Faith saw the gun lying on the floor next to Chris's injured arm.

She bolted for it but not before he grabbed the weapon and pointed it at her, his green eyes on fire. "You're one of them, aren't you? We thought you could be one of us." He scooted himself up to a sitting position against the wall, but he was losing a lot of blood. "You're my ticket out of here."

She froze only a couple of feet away from him. If he shot her, she'd be dead. He couldn't miss at this distance.

"Out the back way," Cameron shouted to the others from deeper inside the house, oblivious to her plight. The door slammed open and banged against a wall.

Faith figured Lila had seen what was going on with her. She could have helped. Then again, maybe not. She only had a cane, and from where she was standing, she couldn't easily reach the lunatic. "If you shoot me, you won't have any leverage," Faith reasoned.

He dragged himself up the wall, leaving a streak of blood in a wide stripe on the rose wallpaper. "If I don't take you hostage, I'll never make it out of here alive. Come closer."

She didn't move an inch in his direction. He seemed so wobbly, she didn't think he could walk. He was having such a difficult time even standing against the wall.

"Come here!" he snapped.

She wasn't going anywhere with him, no matter how much he commanded her. Then without warning, a wolf snarled and snapped behind her. Where Lila had been, only the cane and her clothes were left behind and a wolf now stood, with light-brown almond-shaped eyes narrowed in contempt. At Faith.

Then she realized what the woman, wolf, wanted. Faith moved out of the path of Chris's gun, and Lila leaped. The bastard got a shot off and Lila yelped, but she still managed to tear at his throat. Chris slid to the floor and let out his last breath. Her heart pummeling her ribs, Faith closed her eyes. What would they do now? Wolves would be accused of killing a man. Even if in self-defense. And Lila and the other wolf were dead—which one was he? David or Owen?

Then she saw the first wolf stir. He wasn't dead? She rushed to him and ran her hand over his body, leaned over and listened to his heartbeat, steady, tired, but he wasn't dead. She searched the wolf's body again and found a dart. A tranquilizer dart. Thank God.

She reached over and ran her hand over Lila's head. "Thank you, Lila." The wolf that was Lila stared at her for a moment, closed her eyes, and growled sleepily.

Then the gray pickup roared back in front of the house, its front grille crumpled some. Had the werewolf killer gotten away? Kintail stalked out of the truck, up the walk, and into the house, while Trevor rushed to keep up with him.

"Lila," Faith said, stroking the wolf's head, although after she said who the wolf was, she figured Kintail would have already known and thought she was an idiot for telling him. But hell, most of the wolves all still looked the same to her.

Kintail's hard face looked sick with grief, but Faith quickly explained, "They've been shot with tranquilizers."

"Owen too?" Kintail said, crouching to lift Lila into his arms.

Faith thought his tenderness toward the woman indicated he'd had a change of heart concerning taking Faith into the pack. "That's Owen?" Somehow, she'd figured he'd be bigger, taller. Less furry. She wondered what Gavin's take would be on all this when she suddenly realized there was no sign of David or the other woman who was supposed to have been taken hostage.

"Where are Elizabeth and David?" Kintail asked.

"Cameron and our friends are with them." She hoped.

Kintail grunted, then he headed out to the truck with Lila. Trevor opened the truck's door for Kintail. Then Faith worried that Kintail may just still try to take her and Owen with them. She slammed the front door closed and locked it. Kintail glanced back at the house, his look treacherous.

He could look mad all he wanted, but she wasn't going with him while Cameron and the others were chasing down the killers. Still, she wanted to see if David was all right. Then Kintail stormed up the walk, his expression still furious, and she figured he'd huff and puff and threaten to blow the house down.

"Open...up...Faith," Kintail growled, and he sounded as if he could knock the house down with his fierceness.

CHAPTER 22

HER HEART RACING, FAITH HOLLERED TO KINTAIL through Chris's locked door, "Cameron's hunting down the other killers. You've got Lila back. You can take care of how to deal with the cleanup/cover-up, whatever you want to call it. Cameron and his partners are all returning to the Northwest, and I'm going with them. Like it or not, that's what's going to happen." She wasn't sure about the woman he called Elizabeth, so she left her out of the equation on purpose.

She halfway expected Kintail to act civilized. To let them alone. But when the cedar chair that was sitting on the front porch crashed through the picture window, she realized he didn't mean to play by her rules at all. She considered the cane. If she swung it just right, she might be able to knock him out. Then again, what if he was expecting her to do something like that? Not like when she hit the wolf with the snow shovel the last time. He hadn't expected it. Kintail most likely would.

She glanced at Chris's gun. As soon as she lunged for it, Kintail jumped through the window frame as a wolf. She screamed but grabbed the gun and didn't hesitate to shoot him at the same time as she heard footsteps at the back of the house. Kintail knocked her down, the dart not putting him out like she'd hoped. She didn't dare shoot him again and risk killing him with too much tranquilizer.

Kintail's front paws pinned her chest down, his weight

suffocating, but she couldn't see who was running down the hall. What if it was a Dark Angel?

Kintail looked back.

Cameron swore under his breath. "My bullets might not be silver, but they're like Gavin's. They can give you some heartburn if regular bullets do the same trick on us as they do on humans. Move away from Faith, and I'll pretend this didn't happen."

She swore Kintail almost smiled. Maybe because Cameron didn't take any crap off him? She wasn't sure. He did step away.

Afraid he still might leap at Cameron, she held her breath. Would Cameron shoot him? She suspected he would.

"You've got to take care of Lila and your pack. You have to take care of this mess so your wolves aren't blamed for it," Cameron said.

Kintail looked back at Chris. Then he turned and jumped out the window, stumbled outside, and landed on his belly, the drug finally taking effect. Hilson and Whitson hurried out of the pickup, and with Trevor, the three of them managed to carry their wolf pack leader out to the truck.

"Are you all right, Faith?" Cameron asked, his long stride eating up the floor to reach her.

"I'm fine. Where are David and the other woman?"

Cameron pulled Faith off the floor and into his arms. "He runs faster than we do. He chased Matt down and dropped him. The woman stayed with him. I think he's found someone to call his own. The blond guy? He took off in the ATV."

"What will we do with Matt?"

"Turn him over to the police."

"Adams and Whitson? But they're Kintail's people."

"Officer Adams is out back. He's willing to turn Matt in to take the blame for the killings, saying that they were fanatics who murdered some of Kintail's men. None of them can prove werewolves exist, and the police department needs to resolve the crimes."

"What about Chris?"

"Kintail can say his wolves were protecting him. Is Lila okay?"

"Sleeping like Owen…and Kintail."

Gavin hurried into the house with David and Elizabeth, Faith guessed, still in wolf form, and Leidolf and Sarge. "Is Owen all right?"

"Sleeping," Cameron said. "Let's get him into the SUV. Leidolf?"

"I'm staying a while longer to ensure there are no more of them." He patted Sarge on the shoulder. "He's going to help me."

Sarge looked as though he was going to be terminated at any minute. She wondered, given Leidolf's expression, if he recognized the man hadn't been turned. If so, he'd be up on murder charges too.

"Gavin?" Cameron asked.

"I'm ready to get back to Seattle and the job. Do you think we could rent a bigger SUV and travel that way instead of by plane?"

Faith wrapped her arm around Cameron. "As far as I'm concerned, that's the only way we should travel, considering."

"A woman after my own heart," Gavin said.

"Only she's got mine," Cameron said, giving her a comforting squeeze. "Help me lift Owen, and let's head back to the lodge. You can make the reservation for a full-sized SUV for our return trip. Leidolf, we'll see you around?"

"Find a pack to join, Cameron. You can't do this on your own as newly turned *lupus garous*."

"I guess this means you owe me a diamond ring and marriage license, Cameron, if we're going to make this official," Faith said.

"No jewelry, no weddings," Leidolf said, his voice slightly amused. "We can't wear jewelry. It's too difficult to shift quickly if we're wearing rings and the like. And we don't marry, we mate. That's why you need to be with an established pack, so you can learn our rules. Though some wolves have been marrying, just to have the paperwork because of their offspring."

Faith glanced at Sarge. "What about Mary?"

"Mary McNichol? Chris's aunt? She's harmless, a big believer in Bigfoot, and that's why she was running around with our gang. She never was one of the Dark Angels and didn't believe in werewolves, no matter how many times we tried to convince her they were real. That's why we never let her in on the killings. She would have turned us in. She just wanted to be with us in case we spotted Bigfoot. Chris, especially, hoped she'd change her mind."

Faith sighed, glad to hear the older woman hadn't taken part in the murders. "Why did you do it, Sarge? Why kill them?"

"We thought we were doing the world a good deed. That's what we thought. Then we figured if we could get money, it would be even more of a good thing. We didn't think we'd get caught."

"What about the trees cut down on the trails?" Faith asked.

Sarge shrugged. "We were trying to create a mess for Kintail's people. Harassing maneuvers."

"And Charles?"

"Hell," Sarge said, scowling, "he's either one of Kintail's people, or he helps them conceal who they are. So he *is* one of them, no matter what. We just wanted to give him a wake-up message. Watch out who your friends are. Could be dangerous for your health."

Faith hoped the bastard didn't turn and was tried for murder. Someone as evil as that didn't deserve to be in Leidolf's pack or anyone else's.

Leidolf's expression was revealing though. The more he listened to Sarge bury himself with the deeds they'd done, the darker Leidolf's face became. Then he turned to Cameron and said, "I told Gavin he could have my room for the night, share it with David and Owen. I'll be sticking with Sarge until I'm assured we've finished with business here. And, Faith? You're one of us, even though you'll be with an Arctic pack. Anytime you visit your father, you're part of my extended pack."

Faith pulled Cameron close. "And Cameron and his partners?"

Leidolf gave them an elusive smile. "Sure, as long as no one plans to stay long. Only one alpha leader per pack. Anything else would cause real problems."

Faith wondered how that would work with Cameron and his partners. Owen and Gavin both seemed to have real leadership tendencies. She wasn't sure about David, but he might be more the emergent kind of leader. When the others weren't around to take charge, he'd step right in. None of them seemed very beta to her.

"I'll see you again soon then," Faith said with promise, because she had every intention of seeing the woman her father had hooked up with and making sure he really was all right. Although as soon as they returned to the lodge, she was calling him.

"Let's go then," Cameron said. He carried Owen out to the SUV as David and Elizabeth trotted next to him, and Gavin got the door.

Faith slipped into the driver's seat and Cameron looked at her, his eyes a little rounded.

"My rental SUV, and last time you drove, you were speeding. I thought you were an Eagle Scout and always obeyed the laws." She started the engine.

He smiled and buckled his seat belt. "Always. So no diamonds and no marriage license, I guess. Uncomplicates things and makes for a cheaper union."

She hmpfed. "We're getting married. I can see Leidolf's point about the jewelry. I suppose in a few years if we've got the shape-shifting business under control, you can get me a ring. There's no reason we *can't* get married." She drove back to the lodge at the correct speed.

Cameron chuckled. "I told my partners I'd never get married. *Ever.* Not after all the girlfriend problems I've had. I really thought I'd be keeping my promise."

"There won't be an engagement, if that will help."

He leaned against his seat and smiled.

Gavin said, "I was wrong, Cameron. First time ever. If I had a woman like that, I wouldn't hesitate to make her mine."

The horrible notion slipped into Faith's brain that they had an outsider in the vehicle who had to be changed. "What are we going to do about Gavin?"

"I'm not biting him," Cameron said. "He'll just have to live with us and pretend everything's the way it was."

Gavin shook his head. "Faith can bite me, as long as she's gentle."

Cameron pressed his hand on Faith's thigh. "She wouldn't do any such thing."

Gavin folded his arms across his chest. "I guess I'll just have to keep the secret then."

He sounded a shade disappointed. Faith figured either Leidolf or one of his people would turn him, but it was probably better if they were all the same kind of wolf in case they tried to do what Kintail had done in Maine—pretend the wolves were his pets, one big happy family.

"Leidolf won't like it," Faith warned. "When he learns none of us ever turned Gavin, he'll probably do it."

"Then Gavin will stay home when we visit your father."

That seemed to be the end of the matter, but Faith suspected it wouldn't be. "What if there's already a pack in Seattle?"

"I thought of that. We'll just have to open a business in Tacoma or somewhere else. Maybe move to the coast of Oregon. I always liked the beaches down there when I visited. Leidolf said it was a nice place and might be just our kind of area to relocate. We'll just have to see what happens."

"And hope that we don't run into major problems," a deep male voice that she didn't recognize said from the back seat.

Faith glanced in her rearview mirror. David had shifted. The blond, bearded man with vivid blue eyes reminded her of a Norseman as Gavin quickly pulled off his parka and gave it to him.

Yep, their little band of werewolves was going to have fun with this shape-shifting business. She could see it now—all five of them vying to get into the washrooms on a plane home when they all had an uncontrollable urge to shift. Good thing they were driving.

———

Kintail woke to find himself naked in bed with a nude Lila curled up against him, sound asleep. He brushed his hand through her golden hair, breathed in her special fragrance, and assumed that she was ready to deal with whatever trauma she had experienced in the past. He'd take it slow and easy with her in any event.

"Kintail," she whispered to him, her eyes still tired.

"Sleep the drug off, Lila. We'll talk later when you're more awake."

"I'm sorry," she murmured, her hand on his chest, and he could have sworn her touch was possessive, but the tranquilizer kept her from having the force she might have used. Her eyes drifted closed. "You're mine." Even though her voice had a sleepy, drugged quality, her announcement pleased him.

He leaned her back and kissed her forehead. She lifted her lips as if asking for a kiss there. Chuckling darkly, he pressed his lips against hers, but she wasn't awake enough to respond. "Later," he promised, then slipped off the mattress, pulled on a pair of black denims, and headed downstairs to the great room where he heard Trevor talking to Whitson and Adams.

"Evening," Kintail said as he reached the bottom step.

His men nodded in greeting, but no one said anything. Probably trying to figure out if they had an alpha female pack leader now.

Both Whitson and Adams's bruises had faded to mere shadows of what they'd been. Hilson was chowing down at the kitchen table, having a midnight snack, so he seemed to be feeling better too.

"What's happening with the investigation?" Kintail asked, stalking into the sitting area, while a fire roared in the fireplace and the wind stirred the snow in little eddies outside.

Adams spoke first. "Matt's in custody and will be charged with first-degree murder in the cases of Sutter and Larson. The blond dude we chased in the ATV survived the accident and he's up on charges too. Apparently"— Adams smiled a little as he spoke—"the group was heavily into drugs. Anyway, there's tons of evidence to prove they were, and now it's their word against ours that they were tripping out when they spied the werewolves. A woman, Mary McNichol, never believed in werewolves, according to Sarge. I questioned her, but she seems sincere, so for now, she's off the hook. But we'll keep a close eye on her. Sarge is staying with Leidolf until he turns into a red wolf. So far, Leidolf hasn't seen any evidence of a change. It's probably too soon. Leidolf said he'll take him into his pack. Although if he gets out of hand, Leidolf said he'll either take care of the matter personally or hand him over to you for disposition."

Kintail gave a small smile. "He didn't mean it."

"No. He was trying to emphasize the importance of the guy obeying him while he spoke to me in front of him. He might kill him, that much was evident. But he wouldn't turn the responsibility of the job over to you."

"Leidolf's too much of an alpha for that," Kintail said. "What about Gavin?"

"Leidolf said he'd be turned."

"All right. And Kenneth O'Malley?"

"Already changed, so no more problems with him giving lectures on werewolves, unless he uses old mythologies in his talks."

"Good. Chris's body will have to disappear."

"Done. By the time the spring thaw comes, he'll be nothing but worm food. Matt didn't see what had happened to him. We cleaned up all the evidence that anyone had been killed in the house. We'll be sure to concoct a good story about how Chris went out on one of his crazy werewolf hunts without his partners, got lost, froze to death, and the animals in the wild found his body a delicious smorgasbord of sorts. Sarge will go along with it, since he was one of his best friends. Believe me, about now, the guy is willing to say or do anything to keep on breathing."

"Any other loose ends?"

"Leidolf's making sure there aren't any, and we've got a couple of men with him to help watch his back. Other than that…"

A silky feminine voice called from upstairs. "Kintail."

Everyone turned their attention to the stairs.

Maybe Lila didn't need any more time to get over her past. "Good job, men," Kintail said. "Keep me informed." The way he said it, he was certain his people got his meaning. Don't disturb him unless the building was on fire.

Then he headed for the stairs, ready to take a mate.

For the first time in years, he felt lighthearted and ready to conquer the world.

Thankfully, Cameron, Faith, and Gavin were able to sneak David into Leidolf's room at the lodge without anyone seeing him half naked, only wearing Gavin's parka, his legs and feet bare, while Elizabeth ran beside David in her wolf form. And Cameron carried a still-knocked-out Owen, in wolf form, inside.

"If you have any trouble, you know our room number," Cameron said to David and Gavin.

"I can see now why Lila was pissed that Kintail was interested in Faith." David smiled at Faith in a congenial way, sitting down on the bed, still looking a bit wiped out. Although even so, he'd managed to take down Matt just fine.

Elizabeth was sitting next to him, still in her wolf form while he stroked her back.

"I'll get Elizabeth a change of clothes in a minute. I don't think Kintail was too happy with me once I shot him with a tranquilizer dart." Faith smiled and wrapped her arm around Cameron. "There's only one wolfish guy for me."

"You should see what she did to Cameron's snowmobile. The rental people weren't too happy about it," Gavin said, "but Cameron, being the big sport he is, said it was his fault when he was trying to stop the guys who stole the machines."

Faith chuckled. "Yeah, Cameron was just afraid what the clerk would think if they knew he had such a violent girlfriend."

Cameron headed for the door with his arm around her waist. "Which is just the way I like you. I get into a fix again, you can rescue me."

David and Gavin laughed. "And us," Gavin added. "Wouldn't hurt my feelings none to have you save my butt."

"I'd say she's been approved as one of the partners." Cameron opened the door. "When Owen wakes, let him know."

"He'll be agreeable," David said. "We're just glad to be kicking for another adventure." He glanced at Gavin. "What are we supposed to do about you?"

"He won't talk," Cameron said.

Gavin shrugged. "I told Faith she could bite me, but she didn't want the job."

David laughed. "The lady's got selective taste." He rose from the bed. "I'll go with the two of you so you don't have to make another trip down here with clothes for Elizabeth."

"Night all," Cameron said to the others, then closed the door. The situation with Gavin could be resolved another day or left the way it was. All he cared about was being alone with Faith and getting on with the really important business that awaited them.

As soon as Cameron, David, and Faith headed down the stairs, Cameron said, "You know the rules about mating for life, right, David?"

"You're talking about Elizabeth and me?" David shook his head. "We've hardly gotten to know each other. We'll take our time." He raised his brows at Faith as if intimating that Cameron might want to do the same with her.

"It's a done deal where we're concerned," he said, although officially it wouldn't be until Cameron got rid of David. Not wanting to delay the inevitable a moment longer, Cameron hurried Faith to their room.

Their room. Not his or hers any longer, but *theirs*.

Inside the room, Faith fished through her bag until she pulled out a pair of jeans and a sweater. "Will these fit Elizabeth all right?"

"She's about your size," David said. "It should be fine. Welcome to the team."

"Thanks. I look forward to helping you guys out. I guess I need to give notice in Portland. Tell Elizabeth I'm thrilled she's with us. She can teach us what we need to know."

Cameron hadn't considered that, but he agreed the woman could be a real asset to the group.

David said his good-nights, and with the door bolted, Cameron eyed Faith. She smiled at him knowingly. Ever since he'd seen the angel who had ended up in his room while he was taking his shower after he'd first arrived in Millinocket, he'd known what he wanted to do. Now, he was ready to actually act on that urge. He shoved the cart of cold salmon out in the hall, too late to order anything else.

"I'm going to take a shower, Faith." He wanted to wash the night's activities out of his mind and get a fresh start. Although he hoped Faith might join him.

She nodded and stared out the window at the northern lights, their spectacular display still lighting up the sky. He thought about what Charles had said about the magical wolves coming down from the streams of lights. Charles was right. They were magical, and despite being newly turned and not able to keep the shifting perfectly under control, he felt as though he'd always been this way, and he wouldn't give it up for anything.

He took his shower, longer than usual, hoping Faith would walk into the steamy room any minute, but she never did. Finally, he shut off the water, towel-dried his body, then began working on his hair and stepped out of the bathroom.

Just hanging up the phone, Faith had removed her boots and coat and turned to smile at him. "I called my father while you were in the shower. He's fine." He noted she'd been lying on the bed, the covers pulled aside, an open invitation to join her there. She motioned to the ice bucket filled to the rim, a couple of sodas, and two packages of chips. "Dinner. No room service interruptions this time," she said, her gaze taking in every bit of his body, and she looked hungry. He definitely was hungry, and for a hell of a lot more than paltry snacks from a vending machine.

She stood against the windows where she'd left the curtains open, the aurora borealis still providing a brilliant blending of lights as a backdrop, their room dark otherwise, although he could see with his nocturnal vision as if the lights were on in the room. "Beautiful, isn't it?" she said.

"Beautiful." But he wasn't talking about the lights. He stalked toward Faith just as if he was a wolf on the prowl. Except she wasn't some meek little prey. She was every bit the predator he was: just as clever, just as undaunted in her craving to come out on top. And she was all his.

Her eyes and lips smiled, but before he could pull her sweater off, she was jerking it over her head. He slid his hands around her back, lower to her sweet ass, but didn't feel any panty lines underneath the skintight ski pants. He raised his brows and smiled a little. Worked for him.

He slipped his hands under the elastic waistband—no zippers or belts or buttons to thwart him—and cupped her bare buttocks in his hands. Her sweet flesh was soft and malleable in his greedy grasp. Already, he was hard with need from just the smell of her, the willingness, the way she touched him in return, her fingers tracing his hard back, her body pressed against his. He pulled his hands free and slipped her shirt over her head, revealing a lacy peach bra, her nipples hardened to stiff peaks. Moving a little as if to tease him with her sexy body, she brushed her lace-covered nipples against his bare chest, her belly gently rubbing his arousal.

She was his, not Kintail's or Hilson's or anyone else's who'd ever had the notion to be with the vision. And she *was* a vision—from her sparkling green eyes clouded with lust to her peach skin soft and sensuous to touch, her golden curls sweeping her shoulders, and the sweet fragrance of her desire for him soliciting his further attention.

He lowered his mouth to hers as she ran her fingers over his back, her head tilted up, her lips readied for his kiss. She kissed him back just as rabidly, and licked, and softly bit, then speared him with her tongue like he wanted to do with his cock between her legs. His hands molded to her lace-covered breasts, his fingers tweaking her nipples, her breath coming faster, her heart beating harder, and his own at virtually the same frantic rhythm. Her hands slipped down his back. Lower, until she was squeezing his ass, and when she did, he unfastened her bra, dragged the straps down her arms and covered her nipple with his mouth. God in heaven, she was perfect.

As soon as his lips tugged at her nipple, she groaned and arched against him. He released her and pulled her ski pants down to her knees, slipped his hand between her legs, and felt her drenched curls, every bit of her eager for him.

"Ready," he said as he reached down to pull her pants off the rest of the way, not willing to let another second go by without getting her to the bed. Then he lifted her under her buttocks, her legs wrapped around him, hugging him tight, her mouth opened to his. He kissed her again, his tongue spearing her mouth this time, and she moaned with pleasure. Her eyes closed and her hands gripped his back as if she was afraid he'd let her go.

But he didn't. Not even when he had her on her back on the mattress. He was between her legs now, her knees raised, her hands stretching out to him as her eyes watched him in anticipation. Her pink feminine lips had flushed to red, her center moist and swollen with need. He knew she was ready.

Faith was all that mattered now. The feel of her satiny skin beneath him. The fragrance that was hers and only hers. The way she hmmed and stroked his needs and cared about him and no one else as he lathed his tongue over one extended nipple and then the other, her breasts swollen with arousal.

She spread her legs farther, inviting him in. He obliged, filled her wet heat with his thickened shaft, stretched her and pushed and thrust as she gasped and moaned and stroked his back.

He kissed her mouth, felt her smile slightly beneath his lips as he paused to thrust deep inside her again. Then she shifted a bit, raised her legs over his back, dug her bare heels into his ass, and welcomed him deeper.

Her face was flushed with pleasure as he dove deeper, her heart beating out of control. He shifted a bit to help her climax, inserted his fingers in her wetness and stroked her swollen nub. He wanted the bliss to last forever, but she suddenly gripped his shoulders and stifled a cry, her pelvic muscles throbbing. He watched her sigh and smile, and then entered her again. With wild abandon, he thrust deep inside her, nearing his own climax until he couldn't hold back any longer. He spilled his seed, once again without a condom. A tinge of panic sneaked up on him—what would happen if Faith got pregnant?

Gavin's comment about wolf pups came to mind.

He groaned as her own muscles contracted around his arousal, milking him for every bit of him, but Faith seemed perfectly content. Still connected, he rolled off her and pulled her onto his stomach, then stroked her back. He wasn't willing to join an established pack. He did think maybe, just maybe, he ought to learn a little bit more from someone like Leidolf, who would give him one of those smirks. Yeah, the newbie *lupus garous* were clueless again. Then again, perhaps Elizabeth could be their resident adviser in all things werewolf.

Cameron held Faith close and stroked her back, feeling himself harden again as she licked his nipple and spread her legs wider over his, inviting his touch. "You know," he said, his voice still raspy, his hands sweeping lower to the tip of her spine, "we can live a very long time."

She rested her chin on his chest and looked at him with those luminous eyes of hers that said she was ready to eat him all up all over again. "Is that a promise or a threat?"

He laughed. "A promise. This is only the beginning, Faith, honey. Just the beginning."

Faith knew she'd done the right thing to come here to rescue her father's research from Hilson, even if nothing worked out as planned. She just didn't know that the man she'd wished were part of the amenities in the hotel room when she first found him would truly end up hers after all.

She licked his other nipple, and his hands drifted lower down her backside, his lips and eyes smiling. Yeah, he knew she didn't plan on letting him get any rest tonight. Maybe not for several nights. Maybe not for years. There was something that had changed about her. She still wanted to get up early, but now…she loved the night…

She wondered how it would be running with Cameron through the woods as wolves, playing and cavorting as they explored them together.

"Good," he said as if reading her mind. "It'll be good."

"Better than good." She cupped his face in her hands as if he was the most precious person alive, and he was. She kissed his mouth, emphasizing how much she wanted him all over again. "Much better than good," she repeated, her voice taking on a silky quality. "It will be magical."

EPILOGUE

CAMERON'S WOLF PACK WAS OFF TO A BAD START. NOT that he expected everything to go smoothly, but hell, he'd hoped some things wouldn't be a pain right away.

He glanced at Faith as she slept in the front passenger's seat of the Suburban, his sleeping bag draped over her body, her parka an impromptu pillow against her window as he drove the long drive back to Seattle. His mate was the only one who hadn't given him any trouble. He smiled, unless keeping him up all night was a bad thing. He yawned.

Yeah, he wouldn't be able to last at this much longer. But damn, he thought someone else could take a turn driving. Owen and David were willing, but both had complained of feeling the shift coming on. Faith couldn't keep her eyes open, and *she* was the morning person!

On top of that, Gavin had shifted twice in the four hours they'd been driving. Twice! They made him stay in the farthest-back seat he was so restless, pacing back and forth as a wolf, then occasionally he'd fall asleep, and then shift again. Cameron glowered again at David who grinned like an idiot.

David shrugged as he snuggled with Elizabeth, who slept soundly in his arms. "You know Gavin would have been hell to live with if we ran off in the woods together and left him home alone."

"You could have waited to bite him when we got home. If you had to do the deed at all."

"Owen bit Gavin, not me. And it was all because Owen was sleeping so long and Gavin got worried. He touched his chest to feel his heartbeat, and, well, you know the rest. From what Faith said, she went to tend to your wound and you bit her. So it seems the two of them were in the same boat. What's done is done, in any case."

Same old David. Perfectly laid-back. Never any problems. Especially now that he might have found his mate.

Owen scratched his head. "Are you sure we got all the Dark Angels? Are you sure that woman who was Chris's aunt wasn't guilty of complicity?"

"Kintail's men will watch her. Leidolf said Sarge turned during the night, and he wished he had let me change the guy instead—then we could have had him in our little pack." Cameron smiled at the notion, glad they didn't have to deal with someone like Sarge. But that was the call Leidolf had made to Cameron last night. Leidolf should have known Cameron would be too busy to answer the damned phone. That time or the other three times he'd called. What difference did it make that Cameron know anyway? Leidolf was the one who would be responsible for the guy.

"What about the others? What if they say Sarge helped you to locate us because Leidolf bit him?" Owen asked.

"Nah. One of Kintail's wolves bit him when they thought he was going to hurt Lila. That's the story. Lila and the pack will be creditable enough witnesses. With all of them involved in illegal drug use, Chris and Matt will have a tough time proving they're not lying." Cameron saw hotel signs at the next exit and pulled off.

Owen perked up. "Are we getting something to eat?"

"I don't know about the rest of you guys, but I've got

to get some sleep." Cameron looked at Faith. She was now smiling at him with one of those I-need-some-more-loving kind of looks, and he was sure sleeping wasn't what she had in mind.

"Hell," Owen grouched, "I've got to get me a mate."

David chuckled. "You thought you had a rough time finding the right girl before, mainly because you were too damned choosy. Now look at what it's going to have to take."

Cameron smiled. No matter how much trouble running a pack of *lupus garous* was going to be, he couldn't do without his partners in crime fighting. And Faith was the reason to make everything all right again. He pulled into the Mountain View Hotel and figured they could drive later tonight instead.

Unless Faith changed his mind.

The smile on her face said she might just do that.

At this rate, they'd never reach Seattle.

The End

WHITE WOLF
TO THE
RESCUE

A Legend of the White Wolf Novella

CHAPTER 1

HAUNTED BY HIS LAST MISSION, FBI AGENT ANDREW White stalked through Michigan's Porcupine Mountains Wilderness State Park on Lake Superior as an Arctic wolf, keeping an eye on Nettleton, one of the men he would arrest at the hotel in Ontonagon as soon as Nettleton's coconspirator Rizzo showed up and Andrew had the search and arrest warrants in hand for both men. At this point, Andrew figured the best way to keep an eye on Nettleton was to run as a wolf in the forest, sight unseen.

The park boasted sixty thousand acres of lakes, waterfalls, and hiking trails, half of the acreage in old-growth forest, a haven for wolves—both for his kind and those that were all wolf. A light snow was falling, adding to the two feet of snow already accumulated on the ground. With the chilly wind blowing his white fur and the adrenaline running through his blood, Andrew was glad for the chance to run as a wolf after the flight from Alaska, his home base.

Andrew's FBI partner, Garcia Ramirez, hadn't arrived yet, but he was human, so Andrew couldn't have run as a wolf after Nettleton if his partner had already joined him.

In the snowy woods, Nettleton was hiking quickly along the path as if he was planning to meet some other scum out here who needed clean money. A multimillion-dollar money launderer hiking in the woods wasn't something Andrew had envisioned.

Then he saw a group of Arctic wolves, four males and

a female, standing in the woods half-hidden in the snow, their white fur blending in like his did. Their ears perked up to see him, but when they saw Nettleton, they lay down behind the snowbank so the human wouldn't see them. Andrew wondered if these wolves belonged to a *lupus garou* pack here. He hoped they weren't territorial, but he didn't think they could be regular wolves. Not when they were Arctic wolves. Only gray wolves lived in the area.

Further along the trail, Andrew saw another wolf, a female gray, racing through the woods. Was she part of a mixed pack of gray and Arctic *lupus garous*? It wouldn't be that far-fetched if they were *lupus garous*. Arctic wolves actually were a subspecies of the gray wolf.

He had the strongest urge to take chase, an instinctive need instilled in his kind from birth. A she-wolf, perhaps unattached, and she wasn't with the other wolves. As an unattached male, that intrigued him to no end, making his heart pound harder. It didn't matter whether they suited each other as humans, not in that moment. He just naturally wanted to chase after her.

Nettleton had headed back to the parking lot so Andrew ran after the she-wolf. What if she was all wolf and not a shifter? They did exist here—at least for now, though wolf hunting had been approved by the current administration. If she was all wolf, that would be a bummer.

She was fast and wily, realizing right away that she had a male wolf on her tail, and she was doing everything she could to avoid meeting up with him. Which made the chase all the more exhilarating and caused him to believe she was one of his kind.

When Andrew reached a river, he lost her scent. He

glanced both ways, up- and downriver, looking for any sign of the wolf. He didn't see her anywhere. Across the river, he considered the pristine snow. No wolf prints over there either. She had bested him. He smiled, his tongue hanging out, panting from the exertion. He'd needed the run. But she'd made it even better. He just wished he'd caught her, met her, greeted her, and learned who she was. Still, she was a mystery and would remain so, which fascinated him.

He loped back to the parking area, sticking to the woods and not on the trails until he reached the place where he'd hidden his clothes. He shifted, the warmth filling his muscles with the change as the brisk, chilled air moved about him. Dressed in his jeans, hiking boots, sweater, and parka, he headed back to the parking area, determined to arrest the perps later tonight and return to Alaska for his next assignment. Though tonight, he would dream about chasing the she-wolf and catching up to her.

He just prayed this time when he arrested the perps, no one came after them to free them. Or *kill* them. The FBI never learned which was the reason for the catastrophe that had turned his life upside down. The memory of the accident that took the two men's lives and nearly cost him his own would haunt him forever.

When money launderer Mark Nettleton drove to Porcupine Mountains Wilderness State Park to take a hike, Stacey Grayson, special agent for the U.S. Fish and Wildlife Service, also known as the USFWS or FWS, followed him. At the park, she stripped out of her cold-weather gear and shifted to take a run on the wild side, assuming there wouldn't be any problems with hunters or other hikers seeing her in the snowy cold. She hadn't expected him to go to the state park and had been worried he'd gotten wind of the FWS's plan to arrest him and was going to run.

She'd also worried he'd learned they were after him and planned to take his own life, like the last criminal she'd apprehended. Intellectually, she knew there would be a slim chance that another of her perps would try to commit suicide, but still, she couldn't shake the concern that it would happen again. After seeing the man who'd sold $4.5 million dollars in elephant tusks slit his throat to avoid going to trial, she didn't think she'd ever get the horrifying vision out of her mind.

When Nettleton arrived at the park, she'd wondered if he was meeting up with Tommy Rizzo here instead of at the hotel. Sick bastard had ordered the killing of rhinos for their horns and intended to turn the money from the sale of the ivory over to Nettleton for laundering.

Stacey's partner, Kimberly Wayfair, was sick at the hotel, suffering from either stomach flu or food poisoning, which was why Stacey had decided to run as a wolf to follow Nettleton. He wouldn't have a clue that a gray wolf had him under surveillance if he chanced to see her.

A light snow had begun to fall as Nettleton finally headed for the parking area. Stacey had started to run that way, too, but then she caught sight of a large male Arctic wolf chasing after her! Where in the world had *he* come from? Though she'd gotten a kick out of it, as persistent as he'd been in trying to catch up to her. He'd never succeeded, not after she reached the river and swam down it a way. It had been as much a game for her to ensure he didn't catch her as it had been for him to chase after her. She knew he had to be a *lupus garou*. There weren't any Arctic wolves living here, she didn't believe.

Once she lost him, she returned to where she'd left her clothes in the woods, partly buried under snow and far enough off the trail for no one to see. Then she shifted, dressed, and drove back to the hotel where Nettleton's BMW was parked near the lobby. As special agents for the FWS, she and Kim took criminals into custody who were involved in the illegal trafficking, sale, and disposition of wildlife, though in his case, he was the launderer for the money from the sale of the wildlife. She was eager to arrest him and his cohort, Rizzo, who actually dealt in illegal wildlife trafficking.

She got on the phone and called Kim. "I'm returning to my room."

"Nettleton is here, right?"

"Yeah, driving a BMW. He went to a state park for a hike. Go figure. But first things first. I'll put a GPS tracker on his BMW."

"Good. Make sure he can't find it."

"Yeah, not like the second-to-last case we had, eh? But that guy was really paranoid." Hoping this guy wasn't just as paranoid, Stacey put the tracker on the BMW where Nettleton wouldn't see it. His room was next to hers, and like them, he had a poolside view, so she knew he couldn't see her from his room. "How are you doing? Do you feel like this is subsiding at all?"

"I've been out of the bathroom for fifteen minutes and then back in again."

"Ugh. I'm so sorry, Kim. I was going to go for a swim and

then get something to eat. I'll check on you afterward and see if you can eat by then too."

"Thanks. I'll be here—or in the bathroom."

"Okay, I'll call you in a little bit." Stacey climbed the stairs to the second floor of the hotel and finally reached her room down the hall.

She worried she was going to have to take these men into custody by herself, and she was really afraid this could go sideways without her partner assisting in the arrest. She was so hoping Kim would get better soon, not just for that reason though. They were taking these guys into custody tonight as soon as the wildlife trafficker showed up. In any case, she wished her friend wasn't so sick.

Stacey stripped off her clothes and put on her shimmery pink bikini. She pulled a hot-pink, tie-dyed cotton boho cover-up over her head and slipped on her flip-flops, then went downstairs to the pool.

She would swim laps and look up at the balcony periodically to see if Nettleton was sitting out there. The swimming pool area was hot and humid and empty, perfect for swimming some laps.

Andrew was sitting at a table in the café overlooking the swimming pool, drinking a beer while observing a pretty brunette swim across the indoor pool, though his mission at the hotel was to watch for Nettleton, money launderer extraordinaire, who had turned millions of dollars of bad money into good. Nettleton had retired to his room, but he had a balcony that overlooked the swimming pool, so

Andrew had perched himself in the café to keep watch over the room while his partner was out front, having a smoke and keeping an eye on the lobby in case Nettleton ran out to his BMW for something.

The perks for Andrew? Observing the brunette wearing a hot-pink bikini and swimming laps back and forth, back and forth. He could watch her all day.

Garcia preferred hanging around out in the cold and taking a smoke break to sitting in the heat and humidity of the café with a view of the pool. He hadn't seen the woman swimming in the pool, but he had a wife and a son, so he probably wasn't as interested as Andrew was. Not that anything would come of it, other than observing her. He didn't want to have a dalliance with a human female.

Andrew ordered a plate of tacos and sat back to continue to observe the woman, glancing around at the other balconies and the patrons in the poolside café from time to time. Suddenly, the scent of five different Arctic wolves wafted in the air, four males and a female, mixed with the aroma of grilled beef in the café and the slight odor of chlorine from the pool.

Andrew turned to get a look at them. *Naturally.* Wolves were curious about other wolves in any event, but they were also territorial, and he hoped these weren't part of a pack living here and not liking that he was here.

Not that he could help that. He had a job to do, and he was doing it. Were they the same Arctic wolves he'd seen at the state park? The park was only a couple of miles from here, so it was reasonable to assume they had gone running too. If they were staying at the hotel and not just eating here, they were probably also out-of-towners. He hadn't smelled the wolves' scent in the woods, so he couldn't know for sure if it was them, but because there had been four men and a woman, he assumed it was them.

The Arctic wolves all glanced in his direction about the same time, and he realized they'd picked up his scent too. He inclined his head slightly in greeting. They did likewise, and he turned to watch the object of his fascination—the woman in the pink bikini. How many laps had she swum? It wasn't an Olympic-size pool, but still, she had swum maybe ten laps already.

Nettleton came out on the balcony with a drink in hand and looked down at the pool. Andrew felt an uncontrollable urge to slap the guy in handcuffs and take him in just for looking at the woman swimming. His kind of scum had no business around decent people. Though Andrew didn't know a thing about the woman. She could be just as involved in crime as Nettleton. The perp sat down on one of the chairs on his balcony and watched the woman swim.

Andrew and Garcia were still waiting for Rizzo to arrive and on the warrants to arrest the two men. Andrew hoped the FBI would get on the ball and send word soon so they could finish this and start a new case.

The woman in pink swam to the stairs and climbed out of the pool. Man, oh, man. Toned, lightly tanned, nicely curved in a modest way, she was one looker. She caught his eye and he smiled. She returned the smile, her pretty hazel eyes reflecting the warmth from her expression. Yeah, hell, caught in the act. He was a wolf and a man, after all. But then he smelled her scent. Miracle of miracles, she was the gray wolf he'd chased in the forest. *Hot damn!* He couldn't believe he'd finally caught up with her!

Not that anything could come of it. He was on a job. Yet for an instant, he wished he was just here vacationing. He had to admit that changed the way he viewed her—not just as an attractive, physically fit human female, but as a she-wolf he'd played with in the woods.

She smiled at him in a way that said she wasn't annoyed that he'd been observing her. How could he not look? He wondered if she knew he'd been the wolf following her in the forest when she'd made her escape.

Then she glanced at another table, and he checked it out. Hell, the wolves all were watching her too, their tongues practically hanging out. If they'd been wearing their wolf coats, their tails would have been whipping up the air in a frenzy. All except the guy with the she-wolf. He was smiling, but more in amusement, Andrew thought. He frowned at the bachelor males. He'd seen her first!

—∼∼∼—

What was this? An Arctic wolf convention? Stacey Grayson had rarely seen Arctic *lupus garous* in person, but to witness five of them at one table and another lone wolf at another in one establishment? That was a first. They must have been with a pack. But the lone wolf puzzled her. He didn't like the others? Or he didn't know them? What amazed her was that the lone wolf was the one who had chased her at the park. She felt a little smug about being the victor.

The group of four men and the woman were wearing sweaters and jeans, looking casual and like they were on vacation. The lone wolf was wearing a blue dress shirt and dark-gray dress slacks, not casual at all. At least he wasn't wearing a suit coat, jacket, or blazer. He was a blue-eyed blond and had a wolfish smile.

She smiled back at him, assuming he knew she was the wolf that had escaped his attentions in the park.

Buddying up with any of them—she figured the way the guys were watching her, at least four of the men were bachelor males and very much interested—wasn't going to happen. Not that she wasn't interested in the lone wolf. Sandy-blond hair with sun-tinted highlights and a kissable mouth that turned up as his clear-blue eyes studied her—and the fact he had chased after her in the woods—made him appealing, and she wanted to learn more about him. Just for curiosity's sake. Did he always chase after lone she-wolves he'd never met before on forest runs? Or was there something unique about her that had fascinated him?

She loved her job with the USFWS, arresting the scumbags who made money off killing wildlife or selling exotic animals to the highest bidder. Of course, if people wouldn't buy them, there wouldn't be a market, so she was just as upset with them as she was with the money launderers, hunters, traffickers, and anyone else who was involved in this horrid business. She hadn't really had the time or the inclination to get involved with a male wolf who might sidetrack her from her work.

She pulled her cover-up out of a bag featuring wolves, then slipped the cotton fabric over her head and slid her feet into her sparkly flip-flops. She left the pool area and headed up the stairs to the second floor.

As soon as she entered her room, she checked her phone for messages. No search and arrest warrants yet. *Great.*

She pulled off her cover-up, removed her wet bathing

suit, showered, and dressed in jeans, sneakers, and a soft blue sweater. Lifting the swimsuit off the vinyl chair, she took it outside to hang on the railing of the balcony overlooking the pool area. She was going to leave it out there, hoping that it would dry faster, rather than in the shower. It should be dry by the time she finished dinner.

She'd no sooner hung the bikini over the railing when the top slid off and fell into the shrubs below. In surprise, she just stared at it as if hoping that if she observed it long enough, it would hop back up onto the balcony railing. She glanced at the wolves sitting in the café, all of them watching her, and felt her face heat. Then a knock on the door sounded. After leaving her bathing-suit bottom in the bathroom, intending to retrieve her bikini top from the shrubs below and have dinner, she went to answer the door.

To her surprise, Kim was standing there, looking pale. She'd been sleeping in the room next door instead of staying with Stacey, so she could have more privacy and not disturb Stacey all night. Kim was not a wolf, just a good friend and a great partner when they teamed up on assignments.

"I was going to go with you to see if I could eat something..." Still looking a little green around the gills, Kim held her stomach and hurried off. "Forget that. See you later."

"I'm so sorry, Kim." They were both hoping it wasn't a case of stomach flu, or she'd be sick for longer.

"Don't be. I'm just glad you didn't get it." Kim stood at her door and patted her pockets. "Ohmigod, no! Damn it!"

"No room key?" Stacey asked, feeling awful for her friend. Nothing was going her way.

"Nope. The key's in the room."

"Come on back to my room. I'll get your key. Is your balcony door open?" Stacey asked.

"Yeah, I was airing out the room."

"Okay, come on. Use my bathroom."

Kim looked reluctant to do it, but Stacey insisted. Once Kim was inside, Stacey headed for her balcony.

"What are you doing?" Kim didn't wait for an answer but rushed into the bathroom and slammed the door.

Stacey was afraid if she went to the front desk, they might not give her the key to Kim's room without her friend's ID. She walked out onto her balcony and glanced at the group of wolves at the one table. They were busy talking to one another and eating steak and lobster. The lone wolf was on his phone, looking at his table. She was glad none of them were watching her, and she didn't see anyone else who was observing her either. A couple of kids were in the pool, splashing around, and a man and woman were observing them. She was thankful she'd swum her laps earlier. She considered the short distance between the balconies and the wall in between them to give the guests in each room more privacy. She figured she could make it across.

She began the climb, stretching across, hoping she didn't end up with her bikini top in the bushes down below.

Her friend suddenly hurried onto Stacey's balcony and yelled, "Stacey, don't fall!"

Giving a startled gasp, Stacey nearly had a heart attack and lost her grip.

CHAPTER 2

ANDREW HAD BEEN CALLING HIS PARTNER WHEN HE glanced in the direction of Nettleton's balcony and saw the woman who'd been swimming trying to climb across her balcony next to Nettleton's room to the room adjoining hers on the other side, looking like more cat burglar than she-wolf. His heart skipping beats, he quickly left money on the table for his meal and a tip and strode across the patio next to the pool to reach the woman's balcony, intending to catch her if she fell. Then another woman yelled out her name, "Stacey," and startled her.

Stacey lost her grip for a second but grabbed hold of the railing again, to his relief.

"Kim," Stacey said, sounding exasperated, clinging to the railing, suspended between the two balconies, her cheeks flushed. "I'm doing fine."

His heart in his throat, Andrew sprinted the rest of the way to the balcony, but Stacey managed to climb around the privacy wall and over the balcony rail and called out, "I made it, Kim."

Again, he felt relief that Stacey hadn't fallen.

"Okay, I'm returning to my room," Kim said.

"No, I don't have my room key, Kim!" Stacey cried out in a hurry. "You'll end up locking me out."

That was why the she-wolf had climbed across the balcony? Because the other woman had left her key in the room? Why didn't Stacey just go down to the front desk and ask for another one?

He saw the pink bikini top clinging to a bush and remembered Stacey leaving the pool, dripping wet and looking like a wolf goddess. He rescued the wet bikini top from the shrub. He was about to take it through the building to Stacey's room when he heard her say, "No, Kim. Don't worry about locking me out. You're sick and you didn't get much sleep last night. I'll just return to my room the same way as I climbed to yours. Is the Gatorade helping?"

"I can't keep it down. But I'm sure when I can, it will help."

"Okay, I'll check on you in a bit. I need to grab my bikini top—it fell in the shrubs below—and go to dinner."

"Ugh, got to go," Kim said.

"I'll check on you in a little bit."

Waiting to make sure Stacey made it across the balconies again, Andrew watched as she climbed back around the privacy wall. He was glad she hadn't looked down and seen him there. He might have startled her. He was impressed that she was so agile and very good at climbing balconies. She finally reached her balcony, and he smiled.

Then he headed for the stairs to go to her room and give her bikini top back. Because her room was next to Nettleton's, Andrew knew where she was staying.

He had just reached Stacey's room on the second floor when she opened the door and walked into the hallway. Her gaze immediately switched from his face to the bikini top in his hand. He smiled and handed the top to her.

She frowned. "Thank you for bringing my bathing-suit top to me." She took ahold of it and tucked it into her bag.

"I planned to retrieve it right away, but I got sidetracked. My friend locked herself out of her room. She's been sick. Stomach flu or food poisoning, we're not sure which."

"I'm sorry to hear it. Then she locked you out of your room and you were climbing across balconies again."

"You watched me?" She sounded so astonished, yet he was surprised she hadn't looked down to see him there, hands outstretched, moving along her path, ready to catch her if she had fallen.

"I was poised to catch you if you fell. Why didn't you run down to the front desk instead and ask for another key?" That was what Andrew would have done. Though the way she'd handled the emergency was infinitely more fascinating than the way he would have dealt with it.

"What would the fun be in that? Besides, I didn't have her ID."

"Someone would have sent someone up to verify that everything was legitimate." He hoped she would consider eating with him at the café. Though if she wanted to go somewhere else, that would be problematic. "Do you want to have dinner with me?"

"When I left the pool, I noticed you were having dinner already."

"Right. I'll get some dessert."

"Why didn't you already?"

"I saw you doing the high-railing act and was afraid you needed a helping hand when you were climbing between balconies."

She groaned and walked with him down the hallway. "I'd hoped nobody had seen me."

"I was going to bring your bathing suit up to you, but

I figured I needed to wait down below and make sure you made it okay."

"Thanks. I didn't have any trouble."

"Except when your friend startled you."

"There was that. Are you part of an Arctic wolf pack?" she asked as they walked down the stairs.

"No. I'm a lone wolf. You?"

"On my own. What about the others who were eating in the café?"

"I don't know them, but they seem to be good friends with one another. I overheard them talking about returning to Seattle."

———

So none of the wolves were from here. On most jobs she worked, Stacey didn't run across other wolves, so this was a new one for her. She glanced in the direction of the table where the other wolves were still eating, enjoying an assortment of desserts from strawberry shortcake to chocolate crème pie. The male and female wolf who appeared to be a couple were talking to each other. The bachelor males were watching her and Andrew.

"They're a long way from home. I'm from Houston, Texas. What about you?" Stacey asked Andrew.

"Anchorage, Alaska."

"Arctic wolf. Figures." She couldn't imagine Arctic wolves getting by with running in the wilderness if the state didn't have a significant amount of snow for part of the year so they could blend in better with their surroundings. And Arctic wolves that were all wolf did live in Alaska, so they had a good cover story that way. She wondered how Arctic wolves would fare in Seattle.

He smiled. "I'm Andrew White, by the way."

"Stacey Grayson." she said.

They walked into the café and found a table overlooking the pool. She hadn't expected to have company, especially with her friend on this mission now sick. Certainly not a male wolf's company, but it was nice for a change.

"You lost me at the river." Andrew sounded amused.

"Neat trick, eh?"

He chuckled.

They sat down, and the waitress brought them menus.

"I'll have decaf coffee and one of those seven-layer chocolate cakes," he told the waitress.

Stacey smiled and looked at that menu. It sounded good, but she'd have to swim another fifty laps to make up for it. "What did you have for dinner?" she asked Andrew.

"Tacos, and they were great."

Stacey handed her menu to the waitress. "I'll have those and water."

"All right," the waitress said. "I'll bring them right out."

"What do you work at?" she asked Andrew.

"Bringing criminals to justice."

"Oh, that's great." She smiled. "I do too. I'm with the Fish and Wildlife Service."

"Ah, a special agent who goes after criminals who secure endangered species for profit, for one." He sounded impressed.

"Exactly." She waited for him to say who he worked for, but when he wasn't forthcoming, she assumed he worked undercover for some agency. Then she frowned. He couldn't be after *her* bad guys. Wouldn't her agency have known about it?

———

Andrew was glad she hadn't asked who he worked for because he really couldn't say, not that he suspected she was in cahoots with the bad guys, especially if she worked for a law enforcement agency, but it was against policy on a case like this.

"Are you just passing through?" she asked, but then the waitress arrived with a tray of tacos and dessert before he could come up with an answer.

The waitress set the plates on the table. "Would you like anything else?"

"I'm good, thanks," Stacey said.

"I'm fine," Andrew said.

When the waitress left, Andrew told Stacey, "Yeah, I'm just passing through. You?"

"Same with me." She looked like she wanted to ask him more, but she began eating her tacos.

He caught sight of Nettleton headed for the café. He looked like he was going to sit at a table next to them, and Andrew thought this was perfect. He could watch the money launderer while his delightful dinner companion would help alleviate any suspicions that he was FBI.

Stacey glanced in Nettleton's direction, then continued to eat her tacos. "These are good. I like the spicy beef. Thanks for recommending them."

"You're welcome. I'm glad you like them."

"What about the cake?"

He smiled. "Delicious. Now you know my addiction."

"Chocolate?"

He chuckled. "Yeah. It's all my mother's fault. Once she made a chocolate cake instead of her usual carrot cake, I was hooked."

"You appear to wear it well. But you'd have to dress down a bit so I could tell for sure."

"You mean like going swimming?"

"Yeah. I bet you don't even have a swimsuit with you, as dressed up as you are."

"Sure I do."

"But?"

"No buts about it. Tonight then. After the kiddies go to bed. I'll meet you down here around nine before they close up the pool and we can go swimming. Then you can tell me if I'm allowed to eat any more chocolate. As long as you're up to it." He just hoped he didn't get the arrest warrants right as he was swimming with the she-wolf in the pool.

"Deal. I'll race you."

That made him think of capturing the woman in pink in the pool, her in his arms, laughing... Hell, he had a job to do, and that wasn't part of the mission!

CHAPTER 3

THOUGH SHE COULDN'T BELIEVE SHE WAS GOING TO swim again, Stacey figured she might as well have a little more fun while she was waiting for the arrest warrants to come for Nettleton and Rizzo. Rizzo wasn't due in until after midnight, according to their intel. She still wanted to learn why Andrew was really here. She needed to check on her partner too.

Once she had eaten the rest of her tacos, Stacey said to Andrew, "Excuse me for a minute. I'm giving my friend a call to see if I can pick something up for her to eat from the restaurant."

"Yeah, sure, go ahead." He asked the waitress for more decaf coffee.

Stacey declined getting a refill for her water, pulled out her phone, and called Kim's number. "Hey, how are you doing?"

"Sleeping. *Was* sleeping. I'm so sorry that I'm not helping with the case."

"Don't be ridiculous. It could have been me who got sick. Nothing's happening anyway. If you are feeling better, I could bring you something to eat. Like chicken and rice soup? Or just plain rice?"

Kim groaned.

"Okay, not that. Does anything appeal?"

"As weird as it might sound, I feel like having an orange Popsicle."

"I'll run to the store and get some."

"If it's not too much trouble. What about Nettleton?"

"Eating at the café."

"Are you sure about not watching him?"

"Yeah. It'll only take me a little bit. A grocery store is located right near the hotel."

"Okay, thanks. I'm so sorry."

"Don't be. You couldn't help it. See you soon." Stacey ended the call and tucked her phone into her purse.

"She's still not feeling well?" Andrew asked.

"She wants something sweet and icy. I'm going to get her some Popsicles."

"Then I'll see you later to go swimming."

She smiled. "You're on." She brought out her charge card to pay her bill.

"I'll get it."

"Are you sure?" Stacey hadn't meant for him to pay for her meal.

"I invited you. Yes, I'm sure."

"Thanks. I'll see you later." She really appreciated that he'd offered.

"See you then."

Stacey still wondered if Andrew being here at the hotel had anything to do with taking her perp into custody. She sure hoped not. She really liked the wolf.

She hurried out of the café and through the lobby. When she reached her car, she drove to the grocery store, hoping the stupid arrest warrants would arrive soon!

—w—

After Stacey left, Andrew texted his partner: Our target is in the café for now.

Garcia texted back: *Okay. I'm coming in out of the cold. I'll be in the lobby watching a football game. If he leaves, I'll tail him.*

All right. I'll be swimming this evening for a little bit.

Swimming?

Andrew smiled and texted: Yeah, for exercise.

Whatever floats your boat.

The she-wolf certainly did. Andrew remained seated at the café, getting another cup of coffee while he waited for Nettleton to leave the café. The guy didn't seem to be in any hurry, reading a book while eating crab cakes, broccoli, and a baked potato and making some phone calls.

About an hour later, Andrew saw Stacey on her balcony, and he smiled. She waved at him. He raised his cup of coffee to her. Then she disappeared into her room. Before long, she was sitting on her balcony, and then her friend joined her, both of them eating Popsicles. He was glad her friend seemed to be feeling better.

Nettleton finally packed it up and left the café.

Andrew called his partner. "Hey, are you ready to get something to eat? I'll switch places with you."

"You just want to see the game."

Andrew chuckled. "I'm afraid everyone will wonder why I'm still in the café for hours. Besides, you need to eat. He's left the café."

"Yeah, he went up to his room. I'm on my way to your location."

"I'll meet you on the way." Andrew paid the bill and walked to the lobby, nodding a greeting to Garcia in passing, and took a seat by the fireplace. From here, he could watch for Nettleton if he used the elevator or stairs to return. The word was Nettleton had come here to meet with one of the men he laundered money for.

Their source had said the other man would arrive around midnight and Nettleton would take care of the transaction right there in his hotel room. Andrew had envisioned breaking into the room, guns drawn, and handcuffing the two men, then hauling them back to Alaska to stand trial. Nettleton might not be armed, but Andrew couldn't be sure of that. Rizzo would be carrying.

Andrew watched everyone who was coming and going through the lobby, looking for anyone who might be Nettleton's cohort. No sign of Rizzo yet, just families with kids, older couples, some younger couples, no one who looked like the man in question. Not that Andrew thought he would be coming this early, but he was still watchful in case the guy did show up ahead of schedule.

Andrew was looking for someone who fit Rizzo's description: a man with short, black, curly hair, his eyes nearly black. He was around five-seven and had a reputation for being tough and surly, yet from outward appearances, he looked friendly and innocuous. Nettleton was blond, muscled, blue eyes, around six feet in height. He was friendly but wary. Andrew suspected Nettleton was more of an outdoorsman than they'd thought after seeing him power hiking through the woods. Rizzo tended to frequent the bars and was always on the lookout for a new girlfriend, according to their sources.

Andrew was so busy watching all the activity in the lobby that time got away from him. When he saw Stacey coming down the stairs wearing flip-flops and the cover-up, her phone in hand, he rose from his seat. She raised her brows at him in question.

He waved at her and quickly called Garcia. "Hey, I'm going swimming if you want to swap places."

"Yeah, sure. Be there in a few minutes."

Andrew joined Stacey and said, "Sorry. I wasn't paying attention to the time."

"I thought maybe you changed your mind."

"No way."

"Were you just people watching or observing the game?"

He smiled. "People watching. A habit of mine. I'll run up and change clothes and meet you out by the pool."

"Okay, see you out there."

Once she left, Andrew still had to wait for Garcia to arrive in the lobby before he could run up to the room. When Garcia walked into the lobby, he wore a big, toothy grin. "Don't tell me the brunette headed for the pool is the reason you're going swimming. We've got a job to do."

"I'll be watching the balcony. You watch the lobby for a while."

Garcia chuckled. "I've never seen you interested in a woman while we're on a case."

"Well, this one's different." As in she was a she-wolf, interesting, and fun to be with.

"All right, but if your phone's ringing, you answer it, because we might just have the word to move on this guy in the event the other one doesn't show up."

"Right. I'll be there with you on this one. Don't worry." Andrew raced up the stairs to their room, hurried to strip off his clothes, and changed into a pair of board shorts and a T-shirt. They were always packed in his bag, and he was glad for that this time around especially. Towel and phone in hand and wearing sandals, he walked back down the stairs, waved at Garcia, who was smiling and shaking his head at him, then headed out to the swimming pool.

A few people were having late dinners, drinks, or desserts, and the lights had been lowered for more of a nighttime ambience. The lighting in the pool made it seem magical as Andrew set his towel on a lounger, his phone on a table, and his sandals beneath the lounger. Then he pulled off his T-shirt and placed it next to his towel. Stacey was sitting on the chair next to his, reading texts, then glancing up at him.

"Sorry about that," he said, hating to be late on a "date."

"No problem. That's the neat thing about cell phones. If a date is late, we can just look at texts and emails, play games, and not even miss the date."

He chuckled. "Yeah, well, I'm usually very punctual."

"The way you were dressed earlier made me believe you were. Are you sure you weren't watching the game? An old boyfriend of mine would be so entranced that a tornado could blow his house away, and as long as the game was still on, he'd be glued to it."

"Nah." He figured it was better to be truthful about that in case she'd been watching the game up in her room. He wouldn't be able to lie his way through it. Sticking to his story of people watching was the only way to go. Since it was the truth anyway. "And I'm not obsessed about anything on TV."

She removed her cover-up, her flip-flops already sitting beside her lounger, her phone on the table. "Good to know. Are you ready to get in?"

"Yeah, sure."

She looked over his abs and legs and smiled. "Well, the chocolate you're eating must be good for your muscles and bones."

He laughed.

They both dove into the water. Then they swam across the pool together, making laps. He didn't chase her because he didn't feel the pool was big enough. They enjoyed each other's company until a family of four, including a boy and a girl of about eight and ten, entered the pool. And then Andrew and Stacey moved to the deep end.

"It was nice while it lasted," she said.

"Maybe we can swim again in the morning when the pool is open and before the families hit the water."

"Sounds good to me."

<center>~~~</center>

Unless Stacey was apprehending her suspects. She just hoped Kim would be well enough when that happened.

Then Andrew's phone rang, and so did hers. They both left the pool, answered their phones, and began drying off.

"Yeah, Kim?" Stacey said.

"Rizzo's here. The man who has the money from selling the ivory. Other FWS special agents managed to confiscate the ivory and the men responsible for killing elephants, but Rizzo is in Nettleton's room now," Kim said. "We have our search warrants. I managed to make it down to the front desk to get a key to the room."

"Ohmigod, okay. He wasn't supposed to be here until after midnight."

"I know."

"I'm on my way up to the room." Stacey couldn't arrest anyone wearing a pink bikini. She threw her cover-up on.

Andrew was saying to his caller, "Hey, yeah, I'm on my way, Garcia."

"I've got to run," Stacey told Andrew and hurried off. She hoped he didn't think she was being rude, though he might think Kim was sicker and she had to hurry off to take care of her.

Andrew was right behind her. "Me too. Did you want to have breakfast together after we swim in the morning?"

She smiled back at him. "Okay." She'd have to decline if she managed to arrest her perps and was taking them back to Texas.

She ran up the stairs to the second floor, and he raced up after her. "Your room is on the second floor too?" She was kind of surprised.

"Yeah, a few doors down from yours. In that direction." He motioned to where his room was. "Is Kim all right?"

"Yeah. Thanks for asking. I'll see you in the morning."

"See you then."

He hurried down the hall, and she sprinted for her room. Once inside, she yanked off her cover-up and stripped out of her bathing suit. Then she was pulling on her clothes as fast as she could.

Once she was dressed, holstered gun ready, Kim called her. "Hey, I'm in my room with the arrest warrants and key to their room, if you want to come get them and we'll devise a plan."

"Okay! How are you feeling?"

"Like crap, but I can manage this."

"All right." As soon as Stacey left the room, she couldn't

believe Andrew and some other guy were headed in their direction too. She wondered now if Andrew was working with some law-enforcement agency that was going after her and Kim's perps!

She frowned at him and motioned to Nettleton's door and whispered, "You're not after them, are you?"

"Yeah," he said, frowning at her, his voice hushed while he showed her his FBI agent badge.

Garcia did too.

Frowning, Stacey pulled out her badge. Even though she'd already told him who she was, she figured he'd want to see proof. "They're *our* perps." But she knew it was better to have more muscle if they needed it. "Come on. We need to make vacation plans."

She texted Kim: Bringing reinforcements.

What?

Stacey texted: Two FBI agents. We're coming in to strategize.

Okay.

They'd been after these guys and building a case for months. This was the first chance they had to take them in, and Stacey didn't want to give them up to the FBI.

Kim let them into her room and shut the door. She was a green-eyed blond and looked awfully pale. Stacey didn't think she could help with taking the suspects in, so she was glad that Andrew and his partner were here to aid her.

Stacey said to Andrew, "I can't believe you're FBI."

"I don't advertise it when I'm on a case."

Kim held her stomach. "Since the FBI agents are here, make them work for their pay. I'm going to be sick." She hurried into the bathroom.

"We have arrest warrants for both Nettleton and Rizzo," Stacey said.

"So do we," Andrew said.

"How are we going to do this? We've got a key to his room." Stacey showed the key.

Garcia showed his copy.

"All right, so two of us go to the door, and one of us stays down below the balcony in case someone decides to flee that way?" Stacey asked.

"Okay, sounds good to me," Andrew said, Garcia agreeing.

"I can go down below," Stacey said, figuring as soon as they opened the door to Nettleton's room, at least one of the men would try to escape from the balcony and she'd at least capture him.

"Okay," both men agreed.

"All right. I'll text when I'm in place. Let's do this." Stacey led them out of the room and hurried down the stairs.

When she reached the swimming pool, she moved back away from the balcony so she could see the patio. The door was wide open, and there was no sign of either of the men. She watched the balcony and listened for any sign of movement. She heard Andrew call out, "FBI! Get your hands up! No, Rizzo, damn it!"

Immediately thereafter, Rizzo poked his head over the balcony and gave her a snarly smile. She whipped her gun out. "FWS special agent! You're under arrest!"

Rizzo swung over the balcony railing, gun in hand, and landed in the shrubs to break his fall. She raced forward to take him into custody, but he ignored her and ran off toward the opposite entrance to the lobby, and she gave chase.

What she didn't expect was that when she moved to grab his arm and make the arrest, he swung around and struck her in the head with his gun. She heard a loud whack to her skull, felt the crashing pain, saw a streak of light, and then darkness filled her vision. She crumpled to the ground, all thoughts of going after the men vanishing in an instant.

CHAPTER 4

ADRENALINE RUNNING THROUGH HIS BLOOD, ANDREW saw Rizzo straddling the railing to jump off the balcony. Knowing he couldn't reach Rizzo in time, Andrew bolted for the railing, hoping Stacey could apprehend the suspect without getting herself hurt.

Rizzo jumped and Andrew hoped he broke both his damn legs.

Garcia was checking out the rest of the room for Nettleton, making sure he wasn't hiding in the closet, under the bed, or in the bathroom.

"Nettleton's gone," Garcia said as Andrew ran onto the patio and saw Rizzo land in the shrubs.

Stacey tried to grab Rizzo, and he swung around, slamming his gun against her head and knocking her out.

"Shit!" Andrew said. "Rizzo's knocked Stacey out. I'm going to help her," he said, running back through the room.

"Nettleton must have flown the coop before Rizzo made it over the balcony," Garcia said, racing after Andrew as the two men sprinted down the hallway to the stairs.

They reached the lobby and Andrew said, "You have a tracker on Rizzo's Porsche, right? Go after him, and I'll see to Stacey and hightail it out of here after Nettleton."

"Will do." Garcia ran outside to the parking lot.

Andrew raced out to the swimming-pool area, his thoughts more on saving Stacey's life than on capturing Rizzo at this point. Stacey was sitting on the ground beside a shrub, holding her head, a bloodied area on her forehead. Two of the male Arctic wolves he'd seen earlier were running to help her.

Andrew quickly crouched down next to her. "What's your name?" he asked, taking ahold of her hand and hoping she was cognizant of who she was and of her surroundings.

She gave him a withering look.

"Address?"

"Just help me up. He's getting away. What about the other one?" she asked, holding her hand out for assistance.

Andrew was worried that she was injured enough that she couldn't stand on her own.

The two Arctic wolves finally reached them, the one saying, "We saw what happened from our balcony. Do you need our assistance?"

"FBI," Andrew said, pulling out his badge, then helped Stacey to her feet.

"FWS special agent," Stacey said, but she didn't pull out her badge this time. "Thanks for offering, but we've got this."

"This is a case you're on?" the one man said. "I'm David Davis, and this is Owen Nottingham. We're private investigators with an agency out of Seattle." David handed them his card with his cell number on it. "We'll be leaving first thing in the morning, but if you could use our aid, we'll hang around a little longer."

"Thanks, but we're okay," Stacey said, holding her head.

Andrew took the card and pocketed it. "Thanks for the offer, but we're going to take it from here. We have arrest warrants on these men." He started moving Stacey toward the lobby. "Nettleton most likely took off in his BMW."

She walked unsteadily toward the lobby. "Fine. We're tracking him."

"Tracking him? So are we." Andrew frowned at her. "Are you sure you're all right?"

"Yeah. I'm fine. Really. I need to go after him. He needs to be arrested."

"Together. You shouldn't drive, and your partner's indisposed. Garcia is pursuing Rizzo."

"They're *our* perps."

She took another step and swayed. Concerned that she was so unsteady on her feet, Andrew wrapped his arm around her waist. He was thinking she needed to see a doctor and that he needed to take her, even though he had a job to do. Though if he was thinking as an agent and not as a besotted wolf, he could let the other wolves take her to a hospital while he helped catch the perps. "Do I need to carry you?"

"Do I look like I need to be carried?"

Yes and *no*. Her skin was pale, except for the bloodied spot on her head, and she seemed unsteady on her feet. Yet she had such determination that he figured she'd will her injury away and nothing would stop her from getting her man.

"Come on." Taking her word for it, he grabbed her hand and ran. "If you start to faint, tell me before you pass out, and I'll carry you. Are you sure you're going to be all right?"

She gave him a scornful look. "Just hurry."

"If you've suffered a concussion—"

"I'll deal with it later. He's getting away. And you're not leaving without me. Besides, I have the tracker on my cell." She pulled out her phone and called her partner. "Kim, I'm leaving with FBI agent Andrew White. We're following Nettleton's BMW... Yeah, Rizzo got away too. Andrew's partner is going after him... I know we wanted to get both men. We will. Okay, just get well... Sure, if you feel well enough... Good show. I'll be back when I can return." Stacey ended the call. "Kim said she'd use the search warrant to check Nettleton's room and see what she can find. She'll give me a call when she learns anything. And she'd put a tracker on Rizzo's Porsche while we were in the pool swimming before she called me to let me know he was here."

"Good. Garcia did too."

"What would you have done without us?" she asked.

Andrew unlocked his Ford Bronco. "You could have told me you were after these scumbags."

"You could have told me that *you* were." She climbed into his vehicle and leaned back against the seat, looking wiped out.

"Put your seat belt on. Are you sure you're okay?"

She opened her eyes and frowned. "No. I'm not. My head is splitting in two, but I'll deal with it when I have time." She fastened her seat belt, then pulled her phone out and hooked it on his air-conditioning vent. "Follow that car." Then she pressed her head against the seat again and closed her eyes.

Andrew tore off down the road in hot pursuit of Nettleton. "Don't go to sleep."

"Bossy."

"If you have a head injury and fall asleep, I could have a dead FWS special agent in my car. And that means a hell of a lot of paperwork. I hate doing paperwork. So don't go to sleep." Andrew let out his breath. It would be nice if the agencies talked to each other once in a while and had told them that the USFWS was on this case too. "What do you have on these two men? We know Nettleton is laundering illegal money for drugs, prostitution—"

"And he's laundering money for the illegal hunting of rhinos for their horns."

"Hell."

"That's part of Rizzo's bailiwick. We've caught some of the American hunters who went to Africa and illegally killed the rhinos. They're awaiting trial. Rizzo sold the horns, and now he's trying to launder the money. We just have to nab him." Stacey got a call and said, "Yeah, Kim. What did you find? Wait, putting this on speaker since we're working with the FBI on a joint task force now."

Andrew chuckled. He wondered what his boss would think of that.

"We hit the jackpot. We've got Nettleton's laptop and a suitcase full of money," Kim said.

"That's better than we could have expected," Stacey said.

Andrew was glad for it.

"He didn't have time to grab the laptop. Thankfully," Kim said.

"Rizzo hit Stacey with his gun." Andrew wanted to tear into the guy for hurting Stacey. They'd have to add more charges to the ones they already had filed against the men.

"He hit you? That's striking an agent and resisting arrest," Kim said. "Are you okay?"

"Yeah, once the headache quits. Did you find anything else?" Stacey sounded aggravated that everyone kept mentioning her injury.

"A pair of ivory cuff links and a tiepin."

"Evidence. Good. Confiscate it all, and we'll turn it over to our agency."

Andrew frowned. It looked like he and Garcia were losing their grip on the case.

"We'll talk later. We're still trying to catch up to Nettleton."

"Okay, I'm heading back to my room. I'll call to have this picked up in the meantime."

"You know, this was our case too," Andrew said, glancing in Stacey's direction.

"Right," Kim said, answering instead. "Thanks for helping us to catch these guys." Then she ended the call.

"What's your cell phone number?" Stacey asked Andrew, pulling hers off his vent.

"You're asking for a date?" Andrew raised a brow, smiling a little at Stacey. He knew she wasn't, but there was just something about her that made him want to tease her a bit.

"In case we get separated."

"We better not. I'm still concerned you might have a concussion." If he had anything to do with it, they wouldn't be separated until he returned her safely to the hotel. He pulled his phone from his pocket and handed it to her. "Add your contact number in there for me, will you?" Then he gave her his phone number, and she added it to her contact list.

"And Garcia's number?"

"Hell, here I thought you wanted mine to keep in touch, for more than just a job."

"In case I lose you, I can call him and tell him so."

"He's in my contacts under Garcia Ramirez. I'm not losing you, and you're not losing me."

"That's always great to think positively, but it's also great to be prepared." She set her phone back up on his air vent so they could watch Nettleton's flight. "He's turning off on the main highway."

"Yeah, he's not going to get away." At least Andrew hoped not.

"What triggered the FBI to go after these two?" she asked.

"With Nettleton, we knew he was laundering money for drugs and prostitution. And Rizzo was selling drugs and dealing in prostitution. The money from the sale of rhino horns must be something new."

"It is. We took down the other guy who was laundering money from the operation. So they found Nettleton, their new guy, who was willing to take over the business of giving them clean money. Four and a half million dollars' worth. If they keep this up, there won't be any rhinos or elephants alive that are living free. But they don't care anything about that."

"And for what? Trophies?" Andrew asked, wondering how she could deal with being upset over seeing the murdered animals. He didn't think he could work her kind of job.

"They claim the snake-oil medicine they make out of some of the animals' parts will cure any ailment. I can't understand how naive people can be to believe that crap. All foolishness, but enough crazy people believe it works that they're willing to pay for it, which means hunters are out there killing the animals to make all that money. Our organization is really shorthanded, but luckily Border Patrol is alerting us if they see packages crossing the border that look suspicious: tons of tape used, lots of stains on the packages, suspicious addresses.

"We're not the only ones dealing with this though. I just learned they had Asiatic bears' stomach bile and tiger bone from a rare species being shipped through one of the airlines at Heathrow. They even discovered snakeskin boots with the snake's head attached to the front of one of the boots as if the wearer has to prove it's the real deal and not some imitation. I can't imagine someone wearing something like that. It's just an awful racket."

"It is. I don't know how you have the stomach for it."

"I love animals. I can't imagine people illegally killing or selling the animals, but then again, greed and power account for all of it. Someone has to be the advocate for the animals."

"I admire you for your work. At least it's good news that Border Patrol is helping you out. Now you have the FBI assisting you with a case."

She smiled. "We sure do. So how were you involved in this when you're from Alaska?"

"That's where Rizzo was dealing the drugs and had a house of prostitution set up. Nettleton met up there to handle some of the money from illegal gains."

"Okay, and Nettleton is from Houston. Rizzo had been meeting him there too. It looks like Nettleton loves to move around so no one catches on to what he's up to."

"I agree. At least we have been aware of what he's up to."

They'd been driving an hour already, and Andrew still hadn't caught up to Nettleton. They'd closed the gap some but not enough. He sure hoped they didn't lose him.

"He's stopped," Stacey said, pointing at the phone.

"Maybe he's filling up his gas tank. When we apprehend him—"

"We're taking him back to Houston," Stacey said.

She definitely was territorial when it came to her prey. Andrew knew how she felt. Which one of them wanted him worse was the question. If Garcia apprehended Rizzo, he could take the perp to Alaska, but Andrew still didn't want to give up Nettleton to Stacey and let her turn him in.

"Have you got a good case against Nettleton?" He didn't want her arresting him only for her organization to lose him at trial, and then the guy would take off and be running his operation again.

"Yeah. Airtight. What about you?"

"The same. If you take him in, let me know when he goes to trial, and if he walks, we'll arrest him and take him to stand charges in Alaska."

Stacey finally smiled. "You have a deal. So he's been laundering money up there too?"

"He travels a lot. I imagine he's had dealings in a number of states, any of which might want to prosecute him too."

"We got lucky and learned about it though."

"Right. And it's a federal case because of the millions of dollars he's handled." Andrew considered the direction Nettleton had been headed. "You don't think he's driving to Texas, do you?"

They were getting closer to his location. Andrew hoped Nettleton would stay put long enough that they could catch up to him.

"He's got lots of family and friends and cohorts in Texas, any number of them willing to hide him to keep him out of jail. He could even be heading for Mexico. If he goes to trial, a lot of nervous criminals who have paid him to make their money legitimate might want to put him out of commission. If they learn that we're after him, they might be after him too."

That was what Andrew was worried about, even up here. What if some of Nettleton's cohorts or other contacts came after him to silence him or free him, just like what had happened to the two men who killed a gang leader that Andrew arrested last month?

"Well, you play with fire…" Andrew looked at the GPS signal. "He's on the move again. I hope he didn't find the tracker and transfer it to another vehicle." That could put a real crimp on them catching him. "Then again, you have one on his vehicle too. I'd hoped he would stay put for a little longer." Andrew glanced at Stacey, still concerned about her head injury. The area surrounding the cut on her forehead was turning black and blue. "How are you feeling?"

"The headache's going away. Thanks for asking. It helps to be a wolf with our faster healing genetics."

"At least Rizzo didn't shoot you. But the guy is violent and dangerous."

"I figured he didn't shoot me because everyone would hear it, start taking videos, and call the local police."

"They would have." Andrew could envision it on the nightly news.

"I was surprised to see the two wolves come to help us."

Andrew snorted. "They came to help *you*, not *us*." He observed the night sky, the moon nearly full, a smattering of stars sprinkled against the darkness. The light snow flurries they'd had earlier in the woods had quit, and the sky only had a few scattered clouds. He looked up at the moon again and wondered if she was a royal wolf or not. "Do you have any trouble with shifting during the full moon?" He was thinking if she was a more newly turned wolf, she might have to shift at some point. He did have the notion that he might be the one collaring the guy. Then again, he'd feel somewhat guilty about it when he was promising her that she'd be able to take Nettleton in.

"I'm a royal wolf," she said. "I'm not going to shift because of the full moon unless I want to. Forget claiming the perp for your own." Then she frowned. "You're not going to shift, are you?"

He shook his head. "I'm a royal too."

"Okay, good, because I was going to take over the driving otherwise."

"There's no need to. You know those other Arctic wolves were newly turned."

Stacey looked skeptically at Andrew.

"They were. I overheard them talking about the full moon and having trouble with shifting, and then one of them said, 'Speak of the devil,' then hurried off. I suspected he had to shift."

"All of them? They couldn't have *all* been newly turned. Maybe just one of them, and he's now part of their pack."

"All of them. They were talking softly, but with our enhanced hearing, I could make out what they were saying. They were concerned that they would have trouble running their business in Seattle during the full moon. I guess that's their PI business. One of them had mentioned Elizabeth, a wolf who had aided them in escaping another pack, having to return to the pack because of a family emergency. Which was a shame because she'd been born as one of our kind. So I figured the others hadn't been or that they didn't have enough wolf roots to keep them from shifting during the full moon. Anyway, naturally, I was curious about how that had all come about, but I had business to attend to, and being nosy about theirs wasn't in the plans."

"You were watching me swim."

Andrew chuckled. "Yeah, and I was watching Nettleton's balcony. He had come out and sat there several times. But he stayed put when you showed up to swim."

"I can't believe all those Arctic wolves were newly turned. Someone would need to show them the ropes. And cover for them when they can't help but shift. It's a good thing we didn't take them up on their offer of help."

"I agree." He glanced down at the tracker on Stacey's phone. "As to Nettleton, we couldn't learn if he's carrying or not. No registered weapons. Do you have any intel on that?"

"No, but he could have illegal weapons. I mean, if I were him and had all the money he has to handle, I'd certainly be carrying," Stacey said.

That was what Andrew figured too. "Right. He's never been charged with any crime before either."

"That's probably why so many crooks trust him with their money. He seems legitimate, and he's gotten away with this for so long. We only caught up with him because he began meeting with Rizzo, and we had learned Rizzo was trafficking wildlife. Then we learned Rizzo wasn't the only one using Nettleton's services. We took a hard look at where he was getting his income from and what his role was in meeting up with so many criminals. The guy's got a lucrative job funneling money into offshore accounts, and he has a print shop in Houston as his cover. But he likes to travel to different places to pick up the money. He takes trips to the islands, and we're sure it's for offshore banking."

Andrew agreed with that. "We had him on surveillance

at a hotel on Grand Cayman Island a couple of weeks ago. He was carrying a briefcase chained to his wrist while he was checking into the hotel."

"You went there?"

"Yep. It's a great vacation spot, if you have the opportunity to just vacation there. When Garcia and I went that time, it was off-season, which meant it was hot and muggy, but we still enjoyed it as much as we could take time to do so. They have a forest there, and sometimes I ran as a wolf in the woods. Sometimes I wish Garcia was a wolf, too, and he could enjoy what I do. I've been fortunate that he's not into taking walks at night with me."

"Man, I need to become an FBI agent if you get to go to Grand Cayman Island."

"You could just go with me on a trip there sometime."

She smiled at him. "Are you paying?"

"Sure."

She chuckled.

He couldn't believe he'd offer to pay her way to Grand Cayman Island when he barely knew her! But as a wolf, he felt a real affinity for her. "We'll get a cabana, no balconies for you to climb across."

"A cabana with separate bedrooms?"

"Sure."

"I'll take you up on it. When are we going?"

He laughed. He didn't think she was serious, but if she was, he was all for it.

CHAPTER 5

ANDREW AND STACEY WERE STILL FOLLOWING Nettleton's GPS signal when Garcia called Andrew on his Bluetooth. "Hey, partner, Rizzo's stopped for gas. I'm about to apprehend him, but I've called the local police for backup."

"Oh, good show. We haven't gotten close to Nettleton yet. Let us know what happens."

"Will do. Out here."

"I wish I could be with him. I hate not watching his back," Andrew told Stacey.

"I agree. I know Kim feels the same about me. Hopefully, the police will be there to help your partner when he goes to make the arrest." Then they got a break. "Nettleton has stopped again," she said, pointing at her cell phone on the vent.

"Good. We're going to catch up to him this time."

She wished they would and that Nettleton wouldn't put up a fight. At least her head didn't hurt any longer.

They finally reached another hotel where they saw Nettleton's BMW parked out front. "He's staying here for the rest of the night?" Stacey was excited and hoped that they'd be able to grab him this time.

"Most likely. We just need to find where he's staying."

It was now midnight, and Stacey wished they'd gotten the two men at the other hotel. She called Kim. "Hey, we've found Nettleton. He stopped at another hotel."

"Oh, good. What are you going to do?"

"Find where he's staying and arrest him. How are you doing?"

"Better. Did Garcia get Rizzo?"

"We've haven't heard from him. He was about to make an arrest." Stacey hoped he was okay. "Get better."

"Thanks. Let me know what happens."

"I will."

"Let's go," Andrew said.

"What about Garcia?"

Andrew got on his phone as soon as they left the vehicle. "No answer. He could be in the middle of an arrest," he told Stacey.

She sure hoped so.

They headed into the hotel lobby and saw Nettleton getting a room. The hotel clerk handed him a key. Andrew pulled Stacey into his arms and kissed her.

She wanted to laugh at his action, but she was a professional and knew what he was doing—trying to pretend like they were a couple coming to get a room, waiting for the clerk to be free. She kissed him back and was thinking that if they really did go to Grand Cayman Island together, she was going to enjoy the trip with the wolf. She figured they'd end up in one room, but she had to be sure that if things didn't work out between them, they had two rooms and could still have fun on the island.

As soon as Nettleton went up in the elevator, Stacey and Andrew strode to the check-in counter and showed their badges.

"We have an arrest warrant for Mark Nettleton," Stacey said.

The clerk called the night manager, and he gave them a key to his room.

"Second time's the charm, right?" Stacey said to Andrew as they took the elevator to the fourth floor.

"Yeah. No balconies in this place, and he's not going to be able to scale the building out the window. I doubt they even open."

"Good. Then we'll have the door covered."

They hurried down the hall toward Nettleton's room and finally reached the door. Stacey took a deep breath and let it out. Andrew had his gun out and so did she. He nodded to her, giving her the go-ahead to do this. She appreciated that he didn't mind her taking the lead.

She knocked on the door and called out, "FBI and FWS agents here, Nettleton. Open up! You're under arrest." She really didn't like talking to the door, but she was afraid Nettleton wouldn't open up no matter what if she tried housekeeping or room service or any other ploy.

Of course Nettleton didn't open the door. Stacey swiped the key card and the light turned green, but when she tried to shove it open, she found he'd bolted the door.

"We need to go in through an adjoining door if there's a connecting room to his," Stacey said.

"I'm on it." Andrew called down to the front desk and got ahold of the manager and told him the situation. To Stacey, he said, "The manager is calling the people in the connecting room next to his. He needs to get them out of there in case there's any shooting when we go in through that way."

"Good idea."

Stacey fought pacing in front of Nettleton's room, she was so anxious to get him. The manager soon met them up at the room, rolling a luggage cart, and knocked on the door of one of the rooms next to Nettleton's. A man answered, frowning at him and at the agents. "Thanks for the heads-up. We're packed already."

Stacey didn't blame him for looking growly. They'd woken him in the middle of the night, but it was better to move them out to keep them safe.

"Come on, honey, kids." The man ushered them out of the room.

The manager and the guest loaded the cart with their bags. The manager gave a key to Andrew and then hurried off to the elevator with the family to help them get settled and to stay out of the line of fire.

This time, Stacey let Andrew do the honors. He opened the door between the rooms first, then went to unlock the one to Nettleton's room. As soon as he unlocked it, he readied his gun. She was right behind him, ready to burst into the room as soon as he said it was time. He shoved the door open and shouted, "Mark Nettleton, we have two warrants for your arrest."

Andrew's cell phone rang, but he couldn't answer it now. She hoped it was Garcia calling and he had good news concerning Rizzo.

Andrew peered into the room and said, "Put down the gun. Now." He moved into the room and Stacey joined him, both telling Nettleton to put his gun down.

Nettleton still had his gun aimed at them, but she didn't think he wanted to add murder to his list of crimes. At least she hoped she was right in her assumption.

"The more criminal stuff you do, the deeper in you're going to get," Andrew said.

"Give it up. We already have Rizzo, and he's spilling his guts about what you've done for him," Stacey said. "Like Agent White said, you're getting yourself deeper into trouble if you resist arrest."

Andrew's phone rang again, but he kept all his concentration on Nettleton, just as Stacey was doing.

Nettleton pointed the gun at his own head, and Stacey felt sick to her stomach. "You'll get time, but you have so much more time to set your life right and live it to the fullest. You don't want to do this. Really. Believe me. I died once myself." Not that she remembered anything about what had happened, but she would never forget her parents making such a horrible fuss over her in the hospital when she'd come out of the coma that she didn't think they'd ever let her go anywhere by herself again. But she did remember in vivid detail when the perp she was trying to arrest blew his brains out.

Andrew was staring at her, and she wanted to tell him to watch Nettleton and not her. But Nettleton seemed to reconsider killing himself. She couldn't watch another perp do that in front of her.

"What happened?" Nettleton asked, pulling the gun away from his head.

"Drunken driver ran up on the sidewalk where I was roller skating. I was pronounced dead on arrival at the hospital, but my guardian angel was watching over me. I knew then, once I was myself again, I had to live every day to the fullest, enjoying what life has to offer us."

Frowning, Nettleton nodded. "Yeah, hell, you're right." Then he made a dash for the door, but he had forgotten he'd barred it, and that stopped him from making his escape. He struggled to unbar it, but Andrew grabbed him and slammed him against the door while Stacey seized Nettleton's gun. Andrew yanked Nettleton's hands behind his back while Stacey holstered her gun and got out a plastic tie. She handed the tie to Andrew, who secured Nettleton's wrists behind his back, then read him his rights.

She couldn't help but be amused that Nettleton had said she was right about not killing himself and then thought he could make a last attempt at fleeing.

Stacey served Nettleton her search warrant and then began to look for any evidence in his hotel room that they could use in the case against him. She opened up his suitcase and found stacks of hundred-dollar bills. "A suitcase full of money." She went through the bureau drawers, but Nettleton hadn't unpacked anything. She checked the closet, under the beds, and in the bathroom while Andrew made Nettleton sit on the bed and watched him.

Then Stacey and Andrew switched places so he could give the room another look to ensure she didn't miss anything.

"We'll take everything with us because it can't be left in the hotel room," she said. "Let's get him out of here."

Relieved they finally had Nettleton in custody, Stacey hoped Garcia was all right, and she was damn glad Nettleton hadn't shot and killed himself during the standoff. Or gotten away again.

CHAPTER 6

ANDREW HADN'T BEEN SURE IF THEY WERE GOING TO have a shoot-out or not, the way Nettleton wouldn't back down. He was surprised when Nettleton aimed the gun at himself. Andrew was proud of the way Stacey had talked him down, but now he wanted to know the whole story about the coma she'd been in, unless she had just fabricated it to talk Nettleton out of shooting himself. Andrew was glad they were able to take him into custody without a shot being fired.

He got on his phone and called Garcia back. "Hey, we got Nettleton. What's going on with Rizzo?"

"He got away. That guy is one slippery bastard."

"We'll get him," Andrew assured him. "No one was hurt?"

"No, he just slipped away. I'm glad you got the other one. We're turning him over to our organization, right?"

They put all the luggage into Andrew's vehicle and secured Nettleton inside, then Stacey checked over the BMW and found a gun in the glove compartment.

"No. This one goes to the FWS. We'll get the other one."

"Rizzo got away?" Nettleton said. "Hell, you said they caught him and that he was spilling his guts."

"He was," Andrew told Nettleton. "Except after all was said and done, he escaped. But we have plenty to implicate you anyway."

"Our snitch says that Rizzo's fleeing to Grand Cayman Island," Stacey said.

Andrew glanced in Stacey's direction. He reminded himself Rizzo was theirs to arrest. Still, he had offered to take Stacey with him to the island. It wouldn't be a vacation, not until they took Rizzo into custody, but they could still have fun afterward.

Stacey was on her phone, giving the hotel name and address to someone. "I'll leave the keys to the car at the front desk. Okay, thanks." She turned to speak with Andrew. "I'll be right back. I'm going to drop off the car keys so that FWS agents can pick up the car and go over it with a fine-tooth comb. Is Garcia all right?"

"Yeah, he's glad we caught this one."

"I sure am too. Be right back." She hurried into the hotel.

"You know, a lot of people are going to want you dead," Andrew told Nettleton. "You might be better off if you tell us everything you know and then they'll put you in the witness protection program."

"If you're trying to intimidate me..."

"I don't need to. It's your neck. You don't have any family to speak of. No girlfriend. So wanting to see family who aren't in the program wouldn't be an issue. You just couldn't return to Houston."

Nettleton didn't say anything, but Andrew hoped he was thinking it over, and he hoped Nettleton would give them everything he had on the criminals he was working with. Andrew hated to let Nettleton off the hook, but if they could put away the drug lords and others that needed the illegal money laundered, they'd have a winning streak.

He saw Stacey leave the hotel and return to Andrew's vehicle. "FWS will take care of his vehicle. We've got his guns and more money so we're good to go. We just need to return to the other hotel. I called Kim, and she's feeling much better. Though she's upset about the situation with Rizzo."

"At least we got the moneyman," Andrew said, glad they had Nettleton, though he was sure someone else would soon fill the money launderer's shoes. Andrew drove off to the hotel they'd been staying at, wanting to get this over with so they could all get some sleep and go after Rizzo. "I guess you have to take him back to Houston to stand trial."

"We do. But we still need to arrest Rizzo."

"Since he's fled to Grand Cayman Island, I was thinking you could go with us." He sure hoped she'd want to join them.

She sighed. "I thought when you paid for my way out there it was supposed to be a vacation."

"It will be, after we capture Rizzo. Or you could join me afterward."

"Are you kidding? Rizzo's our collar." She looked dead serious too.

He chuckled. So they were back to that.

Stacey pulled out her phone. "I'm calling my boss."

He needed to do that, too, but explaining how an FWS agent took custody of their perp was another story.

"This is Special Agent Grayson, sir. Rizzo got away, but we have it on good authority that he's going to Grand Cayman Island... No, I know. We'd have to get the local police involved. We have an extradition treaty with the islands, so no problem there. The FBI has two agents going there... Yes, they helped us with the case. We're working on this together. Nettleton's ours, but it wouldn't matter as long as one of us charges him with the crimes and he's incarcerated." She glanced at Andrew. "Yes, they still want to charge him for the crimes he committed in Alaska. Hold on, let me ask." She turned to Andrew. "When are you leaving for Grand Cayman?"

"As soon as we can pack and get a flight out of here."

"We still need to be on this case," Stacey told her boss. "All right, the FBI is paying my way." She smiled at Andrew. "No, I'm not working for them," she said to her boss. "Okay, one of the FBI agents is paying my way, and once we have Rizzo, I need a vacation... Yes, on Grand Cayman Island." She settled back against the seat, looking lots less tense. "Thanks."

She ended the call. "My boss said he's paying for Kim's and my flight and accommodations to Grand Cayman Island and that we need to get the local authorities involved."

"Garcia is already working on it." Andrew was grateful that Garcia was just as determined to get these guys and put them behind bars. His partner never had to ask what he had to do next. He was always on top of things.

"Good. We make a great team."

"I wholeheartedly agree. What are we going to do about Nettleton?"

"FWS agents are going to meet us at the hotel to take him into custody. If he chooses to talk and he wants witness protection, the U.S. Marshals will get involved." Stacey yawned, then looked at her phone. "Before we catch a flight out and on the flight, I guess we can get some sleep. Okay, there are two flights: one at six in the morning and one at eight at night."

"We would never make the morning flight. We'll go with the evening one." Andrew was thinking how he could enjoy

the time before they had to head to the airport—another
run through the state park, more swimming in the pool,
meals together. He hoped she was agreeable, but he knew
they had to sleep after they got in and handed Nettleton
over to the other FWS agents.

"We'll have three stops and get in at eleven thirty the
next morning." She looked up something on her phone
and said, "The Cayman Brac Parrot Reserve maintains 280
acres of old-growth forest. The FWS gave them a grant to
do it to help protect the parrots. They're an endangered
species, native only to the islands, and some of the birds
are being illegally captured and sold in the black-market
pet trade. They often don't survive before they're even sold.
The locals are building up the islands so much and cutting
down the trees where these rare animals live, and it's so sad.
But we could go there for a hike."

"That's wonderful that the FWS gave them a grant. And
yeah, I'd like that."

"We do what we can."

Andrew glanced in his rearview mirror, seeing the
headlights of another vehicle some distance back, and his
skin prickled with concern. "We might have a tail."

She glanced over the back of her seat and watched the
headlights of the vehicle some distance behind them. "It's
a pickup truck."

"Yeah." Like the one that had struck his car when he was
transporting his suspects to jail a month ago, the experience
that still gave him nightmares. "I've tried speeding up and
slowing way down, but they're maintaining their distance
from us no matter what speed I'm going."

"The driver could be tired, like we are, and not watching

his speed, just mesmerized while following your taillights and keeping the same distance so that he's not driving on top of you or having to pass you in the dark. We've been traveling through farmland, no main roads intersecting this one, and the few farmhouses I've seen through the trees surrounding their homes had no lights on. Everyone's probably in bed sleeping. If he's up to anything sinister, I would expect him to do it now while we're out in the boonies."

"I'm sure you're right." Andrew glanced back at Nettleton. He was leaning against the seat, head tilted to the side, eyes closed, appearing to be sound asleep.

Hopefully, they would continue on their way like this, no problems, just a quiet drive back to their hotel.

"Can you get some sleep?" Andrew asked her.

"I want to, but I need to lie down. I can't sleep on planes either."

"You can put your head in my lap and sleep on the plane trip to Grand Cayman Island."

She chuckled. "What about Kim?"

"I can have only one head rest on my lap at a time."

She chuckled. "You know what I mean. I should be sitting together with her on the plane, and you and Garcia can be together."

"Us wolves need to stick together."

She glanced back at Nettleton.

"He's asleep." It didn't matter anyway if they mentioned the wolf equation. If Nettleton were pretending to be asleep and overheard Andrew, the human wouldn't have a clue what he was talking about.

Andrew kept an eye on the truck behind him and swore

it was creeping closer. Stacey kept glancing at her sideview mirror too. "The truck's driving closer," she said, confirming what he was afraid of. "Still there could be nothing to it. He's just inching up. Not rushing up on us."

"Right." Then he saw a truck driving toward him. The vehicle might be nothing to worry about, but he hadn't seen any other traffic on this road all night long, and it seemed like too much of a coincidence that two trucks were now meeting on the road at the same time. "Here comes another truck."

"Going the other way."

He hoped she didn't think he sounded too paranoid. But then the truck behind them closed the distance between them—fast. "The one behind us has nearly reached us."

She pulled out her gun and placed two clips in the cup holder on the console between them. He pulled his gun out and set it on the console.

"There's a road going off to the right up there. We can get to it before either of the trucks reaches us. Can you turn off on it without losing control of your vehicle?" she asked.

"Yeah." Andrew hoped so anyway. He eased his foot off the gas and took the hard turn to the right. His Bronco wobbled a bit on the road, but he soon had it back under control.

She was watching the action in the side mirror. "Ohmigod, you were right about the men."

He glanced at his rearview mirror. Both trucks reached the road and tried to make the turn, the one just a little ahead of the other, but the one truck's front end smacked into the other guy's tail end. Both trucks spun out of control and flew into the ditches on either side of the road in opposite directions. Thank God for that. It would give Andrew and her a little more time to evade the trucks.

Andrew kicked his Bronco into high gear and called Garcia on the Bluetooth. "We're coming in hot. Two pickup trucks are on our tail." Or would be once the trucks got back on the road. Andrew still needed to head north, and this road was taking them east.

"Turn left up there." Stacey was on her cell phone, looking up directions for the hotel. She set her phone on his AC vent so he could follow along while he changed direction and the GPS rerouted them.

As soon as he made the turn, she said, "Turn right at the next road coming up."

"That's going out of our way." But he figured she had a plan.

"Correct, but they haven't come to the turnoff yet for this road. Hopefully, we can make a left up ahead before they know we turned off on this next road."

He took the next right and then the next left.

"I'm on my way," Garcia said over the Bluetooth. "I'm following your signal."

"You've got a tracking device on Andrew's car?" Stacey asked, sounding surprised.

"Yeah, in case we lose track of each other. He's got one on my truck too." Garcia paused. "At the rate I'm going and the rate you're going, we should make contact in about twenty minutes."

Andrew handed her his phone. "You can track Garcia's truck on the tracker on my phone."

Stacey checked his phone and then smiled. "Good, he's close. I wish we knew where the other guys are. The trees between the properties and along the shoulders of the road will help to keep them from seeing us as we make the turns. I'm glad it's not just farm fields where they didn't leave trees around or among the crops for a windbreak." She looked at her phone again. "Keep going straight and then up ahead, take a right again. So far, so good as far as them not finding us yet." She watched her sideview mirror again.

"Good thing *they* don't have a GPS tracker on *my* vehicle."

"Correct. They probably split up, looking for us. They have to be some of this guy's cohorts."

"Men hired to assassinate him, maybe. Us, for sure." Andrew couldn't believe this was happening again. He just prayed they had a better outcome this time. That was when he saw the lights of the truck that had been following them the first time. *Ah, hell.*

Stacey saw the truck at the same time he did. "He's back!"

"And he'll call the other one and tell him where we're at," Andrew warned.

"A few minutes to your location. Hell, I think I just spotted the other pickup truck," Garcia said.

"Watch your back, bro," Andrew told his partner.

"Yeah. Hopefully, he won't realize I'm coming to aid you. Shit, he probably figures no one else would be traveling these back roads but someone who's coming to back you up."

Over the Bluetooth, they heard a loud crash of metal and Garcia swearing up a storm.

The guy behind them was speeding up to slam into them.

"Are you okay?" Andrew asked Garcia, getting ready to brace for impact.

"Yeah, off in the ditch. The other guy's coming for you, but I'm getting back on the road in a sec. I'll help take him out."

"Okay, good show." Andrew hoped Garcia could manage it with a damaged vehicle. He turned to Stacey. "We're about to be hit. Get ready."

She unbuckled her seat belt, rolled down her window, and leaned way out the window. That sure as hell wasn't what he had in mind when he wanted her to be safely buckled into her seat and bracing in crash mode.

"Move the Bronco to the left side of the road," she said.

"Hell, Stacey! If they hit us, I could lose you." He couldn't believe how vulnerable she was making herself. Not that they weren't in a lot of trouble, and he could use her help, but not by risking her life this way.

Stacey began firing rounds at the truck behind them.

Nettleton woke up, saying, "What the hell's going on?"

Both of them ignoring Nettleton, Andrew was trying to speed up to prevent the aggressor truck from ramming his vehicle while Stacey was so exposed. She kept firing at the truck behind them. Glass shattered in its windshield, one of the headlights was knocked out, and the truck suddenly took a swan dive off the road, into the ditch, and hit the trees.

Andrew was glad Stacey's plan had worked, but they were still faced with the truck barreling down the road, coming at them head-on.

Nettleton dropped to the floor of the back seat and cowered down there.

It looked like the black pickup truck was playing chicken as he headed straight for them.

Stacey said, "Move over to the right of the road."

Andrew knew she couldn't shoot at the truck when he pulled over into the right lane. "Put on your seat belt."

But she didn't. She put a new clip in her gun. "Okay, he's moved over to our side of the road, and he's still planning a head-on collision or daring us to swerve off the road to avoid it. Pull over to the left side of the road."

Wondering what in the world she was up to, Andrew did as he was told. Before the truck could switch lanes and move back into position to ram him head-on, she began firing at the truck's windshield. She hit their tires and fired at the windshield again. The truck suddenly veered off into the ditch on the opposite side of the road and slammed into the trees.

Hell, he wanted her on his team permanently! Andrew pulled the Bronco to a stop.

"We have to go back and patch them up, if they need patching up, and arrest them," she said. "You can arrest these men. Unless they have been involved with illegal wildlife trade, they're all yours. And Garcia's."

He was amused she would tell him he could apprehend these men. "They could be ready to gun us down." He called the local police and told them what had happened.

"What the hell's going on?" Nettleton asked.

"Looks like someone sent some hit men after you. Don't worry. We saved your ass, this time," Andrew said.

Garcia managed to reach them, and they looked back in the direction of the two trucks, their headlights illuminating the area around them, the snow, trees, and road. There was no sign of movement in the vehicles. Garcia's front bumper was crumpled, but he seemed to be able to drive the vehicle without any trouble.

"Let's go," Andrew said, backing up his Bronco toward the first of the disabled trucks. When they were close enough to it, they watched again for any sign of movement. The driver was at the wheel, another man in the passenger seat, groaning.

Garcia was driving his truck toward them, and when Andrew parked his vehicle, Garcia got out to help him arrest the men. "Sorry I didn't take the other truck out and you had to deal with both of them."

"No problem. As long as we're all fine and we stopped them, it doesn't matter who did it," Andrew said.

Stacey frowned at them. "*Sure*, it matters."

Both men smiled at her. Andrew could see Stacey had a real competitive edge. He didn't blame her though.

"The driver's been shot in the shoulder," Garcia said, yanking the truck door open and pulling the driver out of the truck. A gun slid onto the floor of the vehicle.

The other man had bashed his head against the windshield. Andrew helped him out of the truck, then they laid both men on the road. Garcia holstered his gun and went back to his truck.

"Watch them, will you?" Andrew asked Stacey. "I'll get my first aid kit and patch these guys up before the police get here."

"Okay. We need to go back and get the other men too," Stacey said.

"We will, once we stabilize these men and make sure they're not going anywhere." Andrew hurried back to his truck and checked on Nettleton.

He was peering out the back window, visibly shaken, his eyes wide, and he was shivering.

"Are you okay?" Andrew asked, grabbing his first aid kit from under the driver's seat.

"Yeah, better than those two." Nettleton motioned with his head toward the injured men.

"Lucky for you. Stay put." Then Andrew hurried back to where Stacey and the wounded men were.

"Hey," she asked the man she'd shot, "Is that all of you? This guy and you?"

He nodded and groaned with the effort. She began looking over their driver's licenses and calling the news in to her boss as Andrew returned with his first aid kit.

Garcia headed back to the injured men with a first aid kit in hand too and was on his cell phone, updating the police with what had happened. "We'll need paramedics and a couple of ambulances."

Once Stacey and Andrew had bandaged up the one man's head and Garcia had taken care of the other man's shoulder, they cuffed them, just in case, and left them on the road for now, covered up in a couple of emergency blankets.

Garcia joined Stacey and Andrew in Andrew's Bronco, and he backed it up all the way to where the other truck had crashed. Andrew parked the car, and then they all had their guns out, ready for anyone who might be aiming to shoot them.

One of the men was on the ground, his neck broken, but there were no bullet holes in his body. He'd been ejected from the truck, the passenger door thrown open on impact. He was very much dead. The other man had a head injury and was moaning about his wife and kids. He shouldn't have been in the line of work he was in if he had a family to worry about.

"Is that all of you?" Stacey asked the injured man as Garcia and Andrew hauled him to the road and Stacey began bandaging his head.

"Yeah," the guy slurred.

The truck suddenly burst into flames, and Andrew was glad they'd moved the injured driver to safety first, even though moving people with significant injuries could cause more issues. Andrew found the ID on the dead man, and Garcia was looking at this man's ID. They heard sirens in the distance and saw lights way up ahead on the road.

Andrew was glad the police were on their way and could get these men to the hospital, the morgue for the one. Then he and the others could get back to the hotel to turn Nettleton over to more FWS agents. He was ready to call it a night and glad they had at least kept the men from killing their perp or the agents working to protect him.

Once the men were loaded in the ambulances and the agents had told the police all that had happened, the ambulances and police cars took off in the direction Andrew and his partner had to drive. They figured this worked out well in case anyone else tried to take Nettleton out before they could hand him off to other agents.

"I was afraid that the men might have called whoever sent them to tell them they had been thwarted, and he'd send replacements. But these men could be on their boss's hit list themselves now for fouling up the mission and getting caught." At least Andrew hoped they would be, four more menaces taken off the street that way.

"I agree and I'm impressed that your instinct told you the other truck was in collusion with the first one. You were right about the truck behind us and the one in front of us both aiming for us," Stacey said. "It was a good thing that Garcia showed up when he did to help us deal with the fallout."

"He's a good partner. When I need him to watch my back, he's there."

Nettleton grunted. "You could have warned *me* that we were in imminent danger."

"What would you have done if you'd known?" Andrew asked.

"Braced myself for impact."

"You were better off sleeping through it," Stacey said.

"As if I could have slept through all that shooting!"

"At least she wasn't shooting at *you*," Andrew said.

Stacey smiled at Andrew.

He was beginning to think Stacey made a damn good partner too. He was just glad the other truck hadn't hit him and killed her. He wanted to talk to her about taking dangerous risks like that, but he figured she had her way of doing things, just as he had his way, and he suspected she wouldn't be open to criticism or suggestion.

"Good work back there," Andrew finally told Stacey.

"Uh, right. We had to do something or we were all toast."

"If the truck coming at us had hit me—"

"If we had ended up smashing into the trees, what do you think would have happened? We would have been injured, possibly as bad as they were, and they would have finished the job, not patched us up and called the paramedics."

Stacey could have been dead if she'd flown out of the car upon impact. But he had to agree that if the others had taken advantage of the situation, the men wouldn't have hesitated to kill them all, Nettleton included.

CHAPTER 7

THEY WERE ALL QUIET ON THE WAY BACK TO THE hotel, exhausted, and Stacey couldn't wait to take a shower and hit the sack. Nettleton had fallen asleep in the back seat again.

She was certain Andrew hadn't approved of the way she had handled the drivers in the two trucks, but she'd had to do something drastic. She couldn't leave it to fate that she and Andrew and their charge would make it back to the hotel in one piece. Not as determined as the men had been to stop Andrew and Stacey from turning Nettleton over to the other special agents.

She wasn't going to ask Andrew what he would have done in her place. Probably nothing as wild as she'd done.

When they arrived at their destination, he parked as close to the hotel as he could get. She saw three Arctic wolves getting into a vehicle. What the hell? The woman and man who appeared to be a couple waved at them in greeting. Then Stacey recalled what Andrew had told her about the group of Arctic wolves staying at the hotel. They were all newly turned. She really felt for them and wondered how it could have happened. They needed someone who had control over their shifting to aid them.

If she hadn't had a case to work, she would have done it.

"Hell," Andrew said, seeing the wolves sitting in the two back seats of the SUV. "I told you they were newly turned. All of them."

"Yeah. I wish we could help them, like they wanted to aid us earlier."

"I wish so too. But we've got this mission to complete. My boss wouldn't understand if I suddenly had to 'escort' a group of people to Seattle."

"Mine either. And neither would our partners understand what was up."

That was the thing about being wolves. In a way, they belonged to a secret society, and everything they did as wolves had to be done in secret.

Garcia had parked nearby, and Kim was waiting in the lobby for them with the other FWS agents.

"Those sure looked like Arctic wolves climbing into that SUV," Garcia said as they entered the lobby with Nettleton in hand.

"Yeah. White German shepherds. Beautiful dogs," Andrew said, "but they do look similar to Arctic wolves. None around here though, you know. And trained to just climb into an SUV, no leashes or anything?"

Garcia was still frowning. "I didn't think they allowed pets at the hotel."

"Not sure about that," Andrew said.

Stacey was glad Andrew came up with a quick story as she dragged a half-asleep Nettleton into the hotel. "Come on, Nettleton. You already got some sleep."

"Your shooting messed up my REM sleep."

They quickly turned Nettleton over to the other FWS special agents, who took custody of him, telling Stacey and Kim they did a great job and praising the FBI agents for helping out. Then they hauled Nettleton off.

"Are you sure you're all right?" Kim asked Stacey. "You've

got an ugly gash and bruises on your forehead. Do you need stitches from where Rizzo hit you?"

"No, I'm fine. You know bruises don't last long on me. The cut will heal up quickly. And you're finally okay?" She was hoping Kim wouldn't have any further stomach trouble on the plane later that night.

"Yeah. Garcia was nice enough to pick up a roasted chicken for me to nibble on from the grocery store since the restaurant was closed. The boss said you strong-armed him into consenting to send us to Grand Cayman Island after Rizzo."

Stacey smiled. "Yep, but we're going with Garcia and Andrew."

"I can't believe you talked him into it. You are my favorite partner for all time. Garcia also told me you went in with gun blazing, shooting at the guys who would have killed all of you if they'd had half a chance."

"Yeah, you know me. I don't like to give up my suspects to unknown assailants." Stacey sighed. "Let's get some sleep."

"Do you want to have brunch with us tomorrow?" Andrew asked, as if he was worried she was mad at him over her putting her life at risk.

"Yeah, sure," both Stacey and Kim said.

Before they went to their rooms and to bed, they settled in the lobby, pulled out their phones, and each made their plane reservations for Grand Cayman Island, their heads together as they considered the seating arrangement on the plane, trying to get seats as close together as they could. There were only two seats right next to each other at this late date.

Kim immediately said, "Why don't you and Andrew sit with each other, Stacey, so you can strategize about how we're going to take Rizzo into custody, since we're working on this case as a joint operation. Garcia and I can take the other seats that are close by." She glanced at Garcia, who was smiling, and nodded.

Stacey so appreciated Kim for making the offer and Garcia for going along with the plan. She wouldn't have suggested it herself, but she suspected her friend and Garcia recognized she and Andrew were enjoying spending the time together in more of a dating way.

"Okay, we're all set," Kim said, finalizing her plane reservation as everyone else did the same. "Let's get some sleep."

This time, they went together up in the elevator to the second floor since they were all staying on the same floor. But Andrew walked Stacey to her room as if he was taking her home from a date, and Kim smiled and said good night and continued on the way to her room.

Garcia had already headed for his and Andrew's room in the opposite direction.

"Listen," Andrew said, taking a deep breath and letting it out. He ran his hands over Stacey's arms in a comforting caress. "I... Thanks... You saved our bacon."

She knew that he really felt something for her and that she'd scared the shit out of him when she'd leaned out the window and begun shooting at the pickup truck in pursuit of them. It wasn't just that he didn't approve of how she'd handled the situation, and she appreciated that he was coming around enough to thank her for her actions.

She pulled him into her arms and kissed him, having wanted to do that since she'd swum with him in the pool earlier, but not with an audience. He wrapped his arms around her in a tight hug, indicating he wanted the intimacy as much as she did.

"You're one hell of a special agent," he said, "and I know it would be difficult for us to…see each other further after we apprehend Rizzo, but I'd sure like to explore options."

"Even after I blasted away at the other drivers and put myself at risk?"

He smiled. "Yeah, I will have nightmares about it tonight though. Between you clinging to balconies and then hanging out the vehicle window and shooting at the bad guys, I'm sure I'll have trouble sleeping."

"Do you need me to scare away the nightmares?" She didn't wait for an answer and pulled him into the room and shut the door.

"You sure you want to do this?"

She raised a brow and folded her arms. "Don't make me beg."

He chuckled. "Good. I'm just calling Garcia so he doesn't worry something bad has happened to me."

"After what we've been through, that's an excellent idea. We don't need any more work-related excitement tonight." She ditched her coat on the chair, and he pulled his off too.

"No, just this." He cupped her face in his hands and kissed her cheeks and then her mouth, tenderly, passionately, deepening the kiss, his tongue and hers stroking each other, tantalizing.

She pressed her lips against his, rubbing them gently, then sucked on his lower lip. Her blood heated with desire at the contact. She loved the feel of his lips pressed against hers, his hands caressing her arms.

"Uh, hold on just for a second, before we get too carried away and Garcia starts calling me." Andrew called Garcia and said, "Hey, I'm staying at Stacey's room. Yeah, see you in the morning."

Andrew was glad Garcia hadn't made a wiseass comment about him staying the night with Stacey. Maybe he was afraid she might end up being Andrew's wife, so he put a lid on it.

Andrew pulled off her sweater, and she sat down on the bed to remove her boots.

"I can't believe a mission to take down bad guys has a silver lining," she said.

He removed his boots and socks, then pulled off her socks. He leaned down and kissed her cheek. "I still can't believe that you were the she-wolf I chased at the park, the bikini-clad woman in the pool, and a hotshot special agent all in one."

She was still wearing jeans and a pink lace bra, looking sweet and sexy, not like she was the kind of woman who would climb across balconies to get into her room and her friend's or hang out a car window, trying to stop the bad guys from slamming their trucks into his Bronco, bullets blazing the whole time. He had expected her to wear something more like black lace, cat burglar Rambo-style, after seeing her in action.

He just knew she was the one for him. She made him think of possibilities he'd never considered before. Of being mated, enjoying each other after work was done and every time in between when they could spend the time together, being wolves together—and that was something he really missed.

He looked into her eyes and saw the desire for him, as much as he craved being with her. She kissed his lips as if she wanted to eat him all up, and he was willing for her to do so.

Then she was in his arms again. He was kissing her, pressing his aroused cock against her, letting her know just how much she'd already turned him on. She rubbed against him, telling him she was eager for this too. He pushed her back against the mattress, and then he was kissing her again, rubbing his cock against her mound, nibbling her lips and caressing her cheek and feeling the raw passion filling his blood. Their pheromones were all over this—howling that they were meant to be together.

She ran her hands over his ass and practically purred when he kissed her neck, then throat and jawline, then moved to her mouth again. He groaned as she continued to caress his backside, her touch making his cock stand at attention. Then he slipped off her bra and cupped her breasts. "Beautiful." Her nipples were a dusty rose, her breasts ivory, the rest of her skin lightly tanned, showing the outline of her bikini. He unfastened her jeans and pulled them off to find she was wearing matching pink lace panties. He smiled.

He kissed each of her breasts, loving the warm, velvety feel of her skin. His tongue lathed one sensitive nipple and then the other one, both peaking to his touch. She moaned with enjoyment, pleasing him that he was pleasing her.

He swept his hand down her abdomen until he found her mons and began to work his magic on her. Groaning, she moved against his questing fingers. He began stroking her faster and she arched her back, her legs parting further, her hands clinging to the bed.

He thought she was about to come, and he moved to cover her mouth with his, kissing her deeply so she wouldn't cry out, and she groaned. They just kissed, but then she sighed and reached down to stroke his raging hard-on. Her warm hand on his erection, she moved up and down with the right pressure and speed, and he rolled over on his back. She climbed onto his legs and sat there, stroking him, smiling, her face still flushed from her own orgasm. She looked perfectly pleased, a woman after his own heart. This was the stuff of fantasy and yet the real deal, and he couldn't have been more ecstatic to have met up with the she-wolf he'd chased in the woods, to learn she was the kind of woman for him.

Every stroke brought him closer to heaven on earth. The strain of needing to release and wanting to hold off was killing him. He ran his hands over her thighs, thinking how much he'd love to center his cock between her legs and thrust. Just the visual of him penetrating her brought him to climax.

She smiled. "Penny for your thoughts."

"You beneath me, around me, enjoying this." Then he pulled her into his arms and kissed her forehead. "We need to sleep, but afterward?"

"Hmm, just my thought too." Then she snuggled with him, and he hoped in the morning she wouldn't regret having gone even this far with him and that she'd see this as only the beginning for them.

CHAPTER 8

EVERYONE SLEPT IN LATE THE NEXT DAY SINCE THEY didn't have a flight until that evening, and when Kim came out of her room, she saw that Andrew was coming out of Stacey's. She gave them both a big smile.

He hoped she hadn't heard them making love a couple of times during the night.

They met with Garcia in the café at the pool to have brunch. Andrew was still dying to learn more about Stacey's near-death experience because of the one he'd had when men had wrecked his vehicle and his perps were killed. But he was afraid she wouldn't like him bringing it up during the meal if Kim didn't know about it and she didn't want anyone else to hear of it.

"After the meal, did you want to..." Andrew hesitated to finish his question. He wanted to run with her in the woods as wolves, but he didn't want Kim and Garcia to come along or that would be the end of that plan.

"Go to the state park?" Stacey asked. "Yes, I'd love to."

"Not me," Kim said. "I'm just feeling well enough to eat light foods, but hiking for even a short distance in the snowy outdoors doesn't appeal. I'm going back to my room to watch something on TV and get some more rest. Hopefully, by the time we get to Grand Cayman Island, I'll be feeling one hundred percent, and if we catch the bastard, we can spend some time snorkeling."

"What about you?" Andrew asked Garcia.

He gave Andrew a small smile. "I'm going to the lobby and watch the game on the big screen."

Pleased that this was working out so well for him and Stacey, Andrew was ready to enjoy the time with her.

They each paid for their own meal and then everyone split up. Garcia went to the lobby, Kim to her room, and Andrew and Stacey had to retrieve their coats and gloves and hiking boots for the first part of their trek from her room.

"I know it's light out, but with as much wilderness as there is, I thought we'd run as wolves," he said.

"I was thinking the same thing. But remember, you hide better in the snow with your beautiful white fur. Still, I thoroughly enjoyed the park yesterday, so sure, running as wolves will be great."

They walked out to his vehicle, and Andrew told her about the nightmare he still had over his last case. "Was the story you were telling Nettleton about dying true?"

"Yeah. It was. I had hoped it would change his mind about killing himself."

"I had a near-death experience too, but I never thought about mentioning it in that context. Though I might have scared him instead, and it might have had the opposite effect on him."

"Oh?"

"My last case turned out bad. I was transporting two men who had murdered a drug lord, and on the return trip to Anchorage to turn them in, I saw a truck following us and realized they were hit men."

"Oh, that's why you were anxious about the pickup truck following us on the return to the hotel. I don't blame you, and your instincts saved us. If that had happened to me, I would have believed the same thing. And you were right. So what happened?"

"They totaled my vehicle and managed to kill the men I had in custody. I was dead when the paramedics arrived, but they revived me. I died again on the way to the hospital. But I wasn't in a coma like you. I didn't remember what had happened to me or the others for a while, having suffered short-term memory loss. Once I remembered what had occurred, I learned the hit men had vanished. They might have just planned to stop me, kill me, and free the arrested men.

"What do you think?"

"I've gone over that scenario so many times in my mind, and I'm still not sure what to think. The one guy fired shots at me. I swerved my vehicle to avoid being hit. Their truck hit my car so hard, it flipped several times. The car stopped rolling, and we were turned upside down when I heard the truck's brakes squeal to a stop. I knew I was in trouble. I couldn't hear my charges' heartbeats, so I was afraid they had died.

"Then I heard the men running down into the ditch. I couldn't get my gun out. I remember desperately wanting to pull it from my holster, but I couldn't get it out before the men reached me and killed me. That's the last I recall. I think I'd died by then, and I think that's why they didn't shoot me full of holes, so I considered myself extremely lucky."

"Did you have trouble with being in the hospital and healing so fast?"

"Yeah. I had a girlfriend at the time, and she tried to get me released from the hospital as quickly as she could. She was afraid I wouldn't have control over my shifting while I was so out of it. I was healing so fast, they let her take me out of the hospital and she dumped me off at Garcia's house."

"Why? If she was your girlfriend, she should have watched over you. I would have."

He smiled. "Thanks. She was so angry I was nearly killed that she decided she didn't want to be mated to an FBI man. Garcia had to put up with me while I healed up."

"So you and your girlfriend had been living together."

"No, but I needed someone to look after me until I healed. Garcia's wife watched over me while I colored pictures with their three-year-old son."

She smiled. "I can see you doing that."

"His pictures looked better than mine, I have to admit."

She laughed.

Andrew parked at the state park, but neither of them made a move to open the vehicle's doors.

"But your girlfriend really dropped you for good? You died and came back to life twice, and she left you?"

"Yeah. I was full of self-recrimination at the time, knowing I should have done anything I could have to keep those men alive for the trial."

"You couldn't help it."

"You're right, but I still felt it was my fault, irrational as it was. I should have had backup, but we were shorthanded, and I had to apprehend them. Garcia had taken his wife and child to the hospital when the little boy had a high fever."

"So it wasn't your fault. Let's go running. And when we return, I'll tell you my story."

———

Andrew loved that they were running through the park together this time and that he was not chasing a mystery wolf but someone he could relate to and who had made a great partner during a dangerous mission that helped to keep them alive and take down the bad guys. He couldn't have asked for more.

He hadn't expected her to start snuggling up next to him, which was a wolf's way of saying she was damned interested in him. Wolf bonds definitely rivaled human marital bonds, and the wolves showed affection throughout the courtship and through their mated years, which for wolves were forever. For them, this was just like humans holding hands or arms wrapped around waists or shoulders as they walked together, their bodies snug. After his former girlfriend had dumped his butt, Andrew hadn't been close to another she-wolf like this, not before or since. Not like this.

Then again, after last night, this was like an extension of the human aspect of courtship, and he was thrilled to enjoy the walk with her. This time, it was just the two of them, no other wolves, no one to keep under surveillance, but they were wary of running into humans, in case anyone was out in the snow hiking off-trail.

She licked his cheek and he licked hers back. He didn't know where they were going with this. As much as he wanted to see more of her, they worked for different agencies and lived in different parts of the country. Yet when a wolf found a potential mate, he or she would do whatever it took to be with the other. The innate draw was so strong between them, their pheromones firing up as they continued to make wolfish contact, that it wasn't conceivable that they would just go their separate ways and forget about each other.

She bit at his cheek in fun and he nibbled on her ear. Then she ran off toward the river and he took up the chase. They ran for about an hour and then chased each other back and forth, finally heading to the parking lot to return to the hotel where he wanted to swim with Stacey in the pool again.

They finally reached their clothes, quickly shifted, dressed, and followed the hiking trail back to the parking lot.

"Do you want to go swimming when we get back?" he asked her as they got into his vehicle.

"I'd love it."

"So tell me your story about defying death," he said.

"I was seven and roller-skating on the sidewalk in front of my house. We lived at the end of the road that branched out like a T. You either had to turn left or right when you reached the end of the street. The pickup didn't stop but barreled through me, then the shrubs. He was going so fast, he drove straight through our big living-room window and ran over our sofa into the wall several feet behind it. My dad was working on power lines for the electric company, and my mother ran out of the house, calling 911. My mom and dad really thought they'd lost me for good."

"You are an only child?" Andrew asked.

"Yeah. It's unusual for us not to have at least a twin, but that's the way it is."

"It's the same with me."

"Really. My parents were like your ex-girlfriend and wanting to get me out of the hospital as soon as they could after I came out of the coma, for the same reason your girlfriend—"

"Ex."

"Uh, yes, ex, got you out of the hospital. I didn't remember what had happened. My parents had to show me pictures of the truck sitting in their living room. The drunken driver went to jail for ten years."

"You're a royal but you're young, relative to how long we live," he said. She had to be if her mother was calling on a phone when they were outside the house.

She asked, "Are you an old wolf or young?"

"Young."

She smiled. "Good. Me too. It's hard mating, um, seeing a wolf who is a lot older than you yet can look the same age. He'll have experienced so much more than a young wolf."

"I agree. You said your folks wouldn't let you out of the house after you were injured."

"They took me to a skating rink and finally ended up putting a sidewalk all over our three acres in the backyard so they wouldn't have to constantly take me to the skating rink. They built a short wall in front of the house to try to prevent anyone from running into their house again. They even put in a large tree, though it would still take years to grow before it could really protect the house. They wanted to build a taller wall, but building restrictions permitted only a three-foot wall out front."

"Did they have any more trouble?"

"No. Between the wall and the city putting up warning markers that glowed at night when headlights reflected off them, they never had any more problems."

"Did you see a light when you died? Or ghosts or anything?"

"I saw a light, but when I finally came to, I thought it was from some of the lights in the ER operating room."

"Same with me. I didn't feel as though I had an out-of-body experience. Then again, maybe it was like a dream that slips away from your memories upon waking."

"Huh, now that's an interesting notion. Maybe."

That afternoon, they swam in the pool, but Kim joined them after a while.

"Would you ladies like something to drink?" Andrew asked, getting out of the pool.

"A Coke," Kim said. "Bad habit, I know. I should be more like Stacey and drink tons more water."

"Stacey?"

She smiled at Kim. "Water, thanks, Andrew."

"Thanks, Andrew," Kim said.

"You're both welcome." He winked at them, then pulled his towel around himself, slipped his sandals on, then headed for the drink bar, wanting to give the ladies some time to visit after all that had happened.

"Ohmigod, I can't believe you slept with him last night," Kim said to Stacey.

Stacey knew as soon as Kim thought Andrew was out of earshot, she'd bring that up. She also knew Andrew could still hear them with his enhanced wolf hearing until he'd put more distance between them. "It was the least I could do after I scared him to pieces, trying to stop the bad guys from taking us down."

"What did you do? Oh, no, not your John Wayne cowboy impersonation as you're riding the horse and shooting back at the bad guys."

"John Wayne?"

"Or Rambo. I don't know. Or another one of those cool guys who don't take any guff off the bad guys. Don't tell me you were hanging out the window, shooting at the perps."

"Someone had to do it. Andrew was too busy keeping the car steady so I wouldn't fall out the window on my head."

Kim shook her head and smiled as she saw Andrew coming with a tray of drinks. "Now I can understand why you would have given him a near heart attack. Just like you did with me last year. This isn't just a fling, is it?"

"No. I told you when I met the right guy, I'd know it."

"I just didn't believe you really meant it. I guess I've lost my job at trying to get you set up with my brother."

"How many times do I have to remind you he has a steady girlfriend?"

"Yeah, but he's going to dump her any day now."

"You've been saying that for three years."

"I like you way better than I like her. You like me better than she likes me too."

"He's much more into a preschool teacher than a woman who hangs out a window and shoots at bad guys, believe me."

"Who?" Andrew asked, setting the tray on a table.

The ladies got out of the pool and wrapped towels around themselves.

"Kim's brother," Stacey said, taking a drink from the bottle of water.

Kim opened her bottle of Coke. "Thanks! Well, he's a doctor, and if you needed bandaging, he could do it."

"You're saying I have some competition?" Andrew said.

"No," Stacey said, taking a seat on one of the chairs at the patio table.

"Yes," Kim said, taking another of the seats. "You know, Stacey, it's always better to let on the guy's got to work for it."

"He's not interested in me," Stacey said for the hundredth-and-first time.

"That's because she's always with him!"

Stacey chuckled, lifting her water bottle in salute. "I rest my case."

Kim turned to Andrew, who was sitting next to Stacey, drinking a beer. "So she told me she nearly scared the tar out of you with her wild window shooting."

"Yeah. But she made up for it last night."

Stacey gave him a cross look, and she could have socked him. Not that Kim didn't already know what was going on, but she hadn't expected him to mention it in front of her.

Kim laughed. "Now you're going to have to make it up to Stacey tonight. Speaking of which, I guess the place that Garcia booked has enough rooms for all of us? But I snore, so Stacey will have to sleep elsewhere if she wants to get any sleep before we head back home."

Kim did not snore! Stacey couldn't believe she'd say that, but she realized her friend was trying to ensure that Stacey could stay with Andrew. She supposed she should have told her that already.

"Stacey and I are getting our own place so we can stay a little longer after we're finished with this mission," Andrew said.

"Aww." Kim smiled. "I'm so glad the two of you are going to have some fun after this is all over with. I'm staying with Garcia then?"

"If that's all right with you," Andrew said. "He's already talked to his wife and she's fine with it, as long as I've got a new girlfriend. She's been trying to set me up with a friend of hers forever, before and after my girlfriend and I split."

Kim frowned. "This isn't a case of rebound, is it? If you hurt Stacey, I'll be all over your ass."

Andrew laughed. "No. That was a year ago, and this is definitely not a case of rebound."

Kim sighed. "Okay, good. I'll tell my brother he lost out."

"Don't you dare," Stacey said. "He cares about his girlfriend."

"Not enough to marry her."

Stacey smiled. "Hey, it's about time for dinner, and then we'll need to go to the airport. But we need to change into our clothes first."

They all went up to their rooms, dressed, packed their bags, and took them down to their vehicles. Then they ate at the café for dinner. Afterward, they drove to the airport, eager to find Rizzo and take him into custody so after that, Andrew and Stacey could start their real get-to-know-each-other time.

CHAPTER 9

ON THE FLIGHT TO GRAND CAYMAN, ANDREW AND Stacey sat together, while Garcia and Kim took their seats. Stacey's eyes were half-closed, and Andrew offered his travel pillow to her, but she declined his offer. "Do you want to put your head on my lap so you can sleep? I don't offer my lap to just anyone, you know."

"I thought you'd never ask." She smiled. "What about you?"

"I can lean against the window and sleep just fine."

"That's why you wanted the window seat."

"It's the only way that I can sleep." But he wanted her nice and rested so they could catch up to Rizzo and take him into custody.

"Thanks. This is great." She resettled herself so she could lie on her side, her head resting against his lap.

He felt like they were a couple already, homey and comfortable with each other, and he hoped the way he was feeling toward Stacey was shared by the she-wolf. She moved a couple of times, trying to get comfortable, and then she finally fell asleep. Before they knew it, they were landing and catching another flight, all four of them running to make their connection, Garcia carrying Kim's bag, and Andrew hoped it didn't mean she was feeling bad again. He offered to take Stacey's carry-on bag, but she just shook her head, practically out of breath. The flight was already boarding the last couple of people when they arrived at the gate, and they hurried to get their seats, glad they still had them.

"That's the way to get the adrenaline going," Stacey said after they took off and she could lift her armrest and cuddle next to him.

"Yeah, and some exercise in."

"But we're still getting our exercise in when we reach the island."

He chuckled. "Yeah, whatever your heart desires."

"Good. As soon as Rizzo is history, I have a huge list of things I want to do."

They napped again but then were landing and had to put their armrests back in place and bring their seat backs upright. They landed again, but this time, the gate was closer and they had some time to make a pit stop and then board the next plane.

Kim was practically sleepwalking to the restroom while Stacey kept her from entering the men's room, to Andrew and Garcia's amusement. Then they caught the last flight to Grand Cayman and were glad they wouldn't be making any more stops.

The sound of the air rushing past the plane and the engines' roar blocked out conversation between passengers sitting near them, all but a baby's shrill cry that could be heard over anything.

And then they were landing in paradise, the time now nearly noon, and they could see the clear, aqua waters below and the white sand beaches growing closer.

"Beautiful," Stacey said, leaning over Andrew to get a good look.

"Yeah," he said, but he didn't mean the island or the

water. Stacey's sweet scent tantalized him, her fingers skating over his arm, heating his blood, her pheromones teasing his.

She turned to smile at him. "You are one hot wolf." She kissed his nose, then sat back in her seat.

"Did you want to change places?"

"No way. I get off the plane quicker this way."

He laughed. "I would be a gentleman and move out of your way so you could go ahead of me."

She smiled and rested her head against his shoulder. "Did we agree that we would take Rizzo into custody?"

"You mean the FWS agents?"

She smiled. "Yeah."

"Uh, I think we agreed on the FBI agents getting credit for this one."

"Are you sure?"

"Is this a trick question?" He suspected if he told her he'd let her have Rizzo, that would give him more brownie points with her. Unless she thought less of him for being too easy. Garcia would tell him he had fallen hard for the woman if Andrew told him they had to give Rizzo up to the other agents.

She just smiled again. And then they were landing, and he was glad they were finally here and eager to learn where Rizzo was now.

—m—

When they arrived at the airport in Grand Cayman, Stacey and Kim were in awe. It was warm and the sky was a brilliant blue, a smattering of white, fluffy clouds drifting across the sky. No snow here, and Stacey and Kim were delighted.

They rented two separate cars so that Garcia and Kim could use one to look for Rizzo and Stacey and Andrew would use the other. Their cabanas were right next to each other. Garcia and Kim didn't plan to stay at the resort beyond capturing Rizzo and taking him back to the States. Stacey and Andrew wanted to go to the grocery store to set up housekeeping for the week.

They gathered in the living room of Stacey and Andrew's cabana, all done in white and blues, with pictures of rose hibiscus on the walls and large windows that looked out on the sugar-white beaches, palm trees swaying in the breeze, and the aqua-blue waters.

Garcia called the local police to see if they had located Rizzo yet. They'd hoped the police hadn't alerted Rizzo that they were on to him, but they needed their help in extraditing him.

When Garcia got off the phone, he shook his head. "The local police haven't seen him. The island's small though. Twenty-two miles long, about four miles wide, totaling seventy-six square miles. The police checked to see if he'd left for the sister islands, Cayman Brac and Little Cayman, but they don't believe he's left this island."

"But they know he's here for sure?" Stacey asked.

"Yeah. A man fitting his description arrived here. They were too late in arresting him, but when they talked to the staff at the airport, several had witnessed him. He was carrying a briefcase, chained to his wrist, no other luggage, and that's what everyone noticed," Garcia said.

"I can't go with you to the grocery store," Stacey said to Andrew with great regret. "He's seen me. Even if he doesn't recognize me, like if I wore a big, floppy hat and sunglasses, we can't risk it." She hated not being able to go with Andrew and to be stuck in the cabana for the time being, but she couldn't jeopardize the mission. "Once we have the groceries, we can make sandwiches here." She gave Andrew a hastily scrawled grocery list. "By the way, did he see any of the rest of you when we tried to apprehend him? Garcia? You tried to chase him down."

"No. Just my vehicle, and we have different ones here."

"He didn't see me either," Kim said. "I was indisposed."

"He didn't see me," Andrew said. "I'm going to run to the grocery store and pick up the food. Sliced ham, turkey, roast beef, and corned beef, cheese, lettuce, mayonnaise, mustard, anything else?"

"How about bread? Oh, and Coke and chips," Kim said. "Um, and chocolate chip cookies. Got to have my chocolate with my meal."

"I'll second that," Andrew said, smiling.

"Do you want me to go with you?" Kim asked.

"Sure, why don't you come along."

"Great. I've been so cooped up after being sick that I just want to get out and see things, especially since I won't be here long. That is, if we can catch this guy soon."

Stacey gave Kim a look that told her not to question what was going on with her and Andrew, but Kim only smiled back at her. Stacey knew Kim would ignore her warning look.

Then the two of them took off, and Garcia went out to the back patio and looked at the clear, shallow, reef-protected lagoon. "Beautiful. When my son gets older, I plan to bring the family here. Maria would love it."

"Andrew said you have a three-year-old son."

"I do." Garcia turned to look at her as she leaned over

the railing on the patio, watching the seabirds in flight. "He got really sick a month ago, and I wasn't able to be Andrew's backup. Did Andrew tell you he died?"

"Yeah, during the mission where he was transporting his charges to jail. We have that we died in common." She explained what had happened to her.

"Damn. Sounds like a cosmic connection sort of thing between the two of you. Am I going to lose my partner?"

"Who says anything is going to come of this?"

"My wife always says I don't ever notice what's going on with people and relationships, even when it's happening right in front of my face, but even I know that he's not giving you up for anything."

She smiled. "I might just feel the same way about him."

"Then I'm losing a partner." Garcia looked down at her, frowning.

"Only if I move to Alaska and he decides to join FWS." She wasn't sure what a rigamarole it would be to join the FBI, but she really loved her job and wanted to continue to try to do what she could for wildlife. She didn't even know if she could find a position in Anchorage. But she'd check into it.

"Hot damn. Well, not the part about him leaving the FBI to join your organization, but moving to Anchorage? That sounds great."

"It's pure speculation. Nothing may come of it." She spied a couple jogging on the beach and wanted to do that with Andrew as a wolf while they were here.

"No way. He's not giving you up. You and his ex-girlfriend are the difference between stormy weather and clear skies."

"Oh?"

Garcia smiled. "Yeah. I was glad he didn't marry her.

She wanted him to quit the FBI. Go fishing like her father, and she was volatile about it. I think he kept hoping that she'd reconsider, but when he was injured, that was the last straw for her. Andrew's good at what he does, and he worked too hard to get where he's at. I'd hate to see him give it up. Not to mention he's the best partner I've had. He has a natural instinct for knowing when danger's near. Like a sixth sense. He's gotten us out of more binds by warning me when we've got trouble. The first couple of times, I didn't believe him, but it soon made a believer out of me."

That was the wolf equation working for him, she'd bet. Smelling the scent of the perp—anger, fear, intense dislike—could clue him in when outward signs didn't give an inkling of what the guy was up to.

"I'm not going to try to convince him to leave the FBI. That's totally his choice. You know, we haven't even talked about any of this."

"You will."

She smiled at Garcia. She liked him, but she would hate having to give up her job in Houston and she'd miss Kim if she left. Then again, what if her pre-honeymoon on the island turned out to be a disaster? She would be considering a move and there wouldn't be any need.

~~~

"I've never seen Stacey fall for a guy that fast. You'd better not be toying with her heart," Kim told Andrew as they picked up groceries.

"We're enjoying each other's company," Andrew said.

Of course it was more than that, but not that a human could understand.

"I think you're good for her. She never likes any of the guys I try to match her up with. She's really picky. But you seem to have just what she needs in her life." Kim threw a package of chips into the basket. "Will you move to Houston if you can get a position with the FBI there?"

"It's something to consider."

"That sounds suspiciously like that's something you *don't* want to consider." Kim sounded distrustful of him as she put a supersize bag of chocolates in the cart. "That's for both you and me," she said when she saw him looking at the size of the package.

He laughed.

When they arrived back at the cabana, they made sandwiches and plans of what to do next.

Garcia smeared mustard and mayonnaise on his bread and then added lettuce, roast beef, cheese, and tomato. "Man-size," he said when he saw everyone watching him stack up his fixings.

They smiled at him.

"Okay, so Garcia and Kim are going together in their rental car to search for Rizzo?" Andrew asked, making a ham and cheese sandwich.

"I'm thinking I might just walk along the beach, sand in my toes, sandals with me so I can slip into the hotels and check them out." Kim prepared a corned beef sandwich. "I suspect he won't be lounging around a lobby, but what if he is? Or eating at one of the cafés. If he doesn't suspect we know where he is, he won't be hiding in a room, most likely."

"That sounds like a terrific idea. I wish I could go with

you." Stacey added tomato slices to her roast beef sandwich, and they all took seats at the dining table.

"I'll drive around the opposite end of the island, maybe check out the bars," Andrew said.

"I'll sure be glad when Rizzo's in custody," Stacey said.

Andrew reached over and squeezed her hand. "We'll let you know when we find him."

She smiled. "Yeah, I want to be part of taking him down, but really, I'm looking forward to just enjoying the time here with you."

"Yeah, but if this goes where I'm thinking it will, where will you end up? In Alaska? Houston? Or somewhere else?" Kim asked.

"Alaska," Stacey said before Andrew had a chance to say anything. "I think it would be the perfect place for us—from everything Andrew has told me about it."

He hadn't said a thing to her about Alaska. He suspected she felt he would be safer as an Arctic wolf in Alaska rather than in the Houston area. He appreciated her concern.

"I knew it!" Kim said.

"This isn't a done deal," Stacey said.

Kim scoffed. "I know you. You're totally hooked on Andrew. I can see why though. Will you be staying with FWS?"

"Yes," Stacey said. "We might be able to work some cases together, but it probably wouldn't happen. I'd have to apply for a job with FWS in Anchorage. They might not have anything available, or they might not even want to hire me."

"With your great arrest and conviction record, they'd hire you in a heartbeat." Kim pointed to Andrew with half of her sandwich. "He's awfully quiet. Maybe he's not ready for the ball and chain yet?"

Andrew smiled at her. "If it means being with Stacey, yeah, I'm ready." It all had to do with being wolves. He was certain if he was just human, he'd want to wait a bit to really get to know her. But wolves had a sixth sense about which wolf was the one for them. They could deny it all they wanted, but the need and want wouldn't go away. And he knew if he returned to Alaska without confirming this was what they wanted, he wouldn't be able to stop thinking of her and wanting to be with her—forever, as mated wolves. It wasn't something humans could understand. They might lust after a person, win them over, then grow tired of them after a short time, or even years, and leave to find someone else. It just wasn't in the wolf's nature.

"Not to change the subject, but while you all are looking for this guy, what am I supposed to do?"

"Just relax." Andrew suspected that wasn't part of Stacey's work ethic when she still had a job to do. "You can't really do anything for the time being. We'll all check in with each other to let you and everyone else know how we're faring."

"All right. I'll be the guard of the cabanas, watching for anyone who might be suspect snooping around the places."

"Exactly." Andrew knew she didn't feel that would happen, but he was glad she was playing along with it and not all morose about it.

"I'll clean up everything when you go," she offered.

"Okay, thanks. Andrew and I picked up some snapper and rum cake for dinner, so we can enjoy that later," Kim said. "Besides, after your wild shoot-out, you deserve to take some time off."

"I'd rather help capture this guy—"

"So you can get on with playing with Andrew in the sun and sand," Kim said. "I totally understand it. We'll get Rizzo as soon as we can."

"Absolutely." Stacey smiled at Andrew.

He wasn't waiting to have fun with Stacey, however.

Once they were done with lunch, Kim and Garcia went to their cabana next door to take off in his car, and Andrew kissed Stacey goodbye. She gave him a hug and a kiss.

"Be safe," she said. "I worry that when we catch up to him this time, he'll be shooting to kill instead of just using his gun as a bat."

"You stay safely inside. No going out to sunbathe or stroll along the beach."

She smiled at him. "I think you know me better than that. Not until after we nail him." She gave him another kiss.

Before he left, he asked, "You really are considering moving to Alaska to be with me?" He was thrilled, but he didn't want to get his hopes up if she hadn't really intended to do that.

"You'd be safer as an Arctic wolf there."

"Thanks for worrying about me as a wolf. We're known as Alaskan tundra wolves, or barren-ground wolves. Alaska has one of the largest gray wolf populations in the United States, and you would be known as an interior Alaskan wolf if anyone caught sight of you. Their pelts are anywhere from black to white to every shade of tan and gray in between so you'd fit right in. You wouldn't miss the warmer temperatures in Houston? All those hot, green days? We have long white days and long dark nights and long daylight periods. Some can't get used to it. What if you came up there and tried it out for a year first to see if you could live with it?"

"I suspect you can make those long dark nights just as memorable as the long sunny days. If I can't live with it, we can talk about it then."

"If you can't, I'll move anywhere you want to go. Hell, even Seattle, where that Arctic wolf pack is going, might work."

"That's not a good idea. I could see us constantly having to take care of them when they can't go out during the full moon. Not that I don't like helping people out, but we both have jobs and have to have time for us."

"All right. Let me go do this, and hopefully, we'll find this guy quickly. How hard can it be on an island this size?"

CHAPTER 10

THREE DAYS LATER, THEY STILL HADN'T FOUND RIZZO, and neither the FBI agents nor the special agents for the FWS could hide their disappointment. Stacey and Andrew had continued to make love to each other—unconsummated, though they were about ready to make the commitment for life.

"He must be holed up somewhere, afraid to show his face," Kim said as they gathered together in the living room of Stacey and Andrew's cabana.

It had become the gathering spot for making plans, eating meals, and just letting their hair down.

"Or he's left the island, or he never arrived and the word we had from informants wasn't correct, or he got spooked, fearing we knew where he was headed and made other plans." Stacey was tired of this and ready to finish the job. It wouldn't have been so bad if she could have helped to locate him, being an active member of the team, but sitting in the cabana, unable to leave it day after day, was really wearing on her nerves. Especially when she wanted to get out-of-doors during the day and at least enjoy the scenery.

"We can't stay here forever," Garcia said. "Our boss is already saying Rizzo has probably slipped through our net again and we've lost him. He's ready for us to return home."

Stacey knew that was coming next. The whole idea was that they would arrest Rizzo, and she and Andrew could have some vacation time for the rest of the week. If they had to chase after him somewhere else that he might have gone, that would be the end of having any fun in paradise. She wanted to pull her hair out, she was so irritated. Though she had been working on getting a job with the FWS in Alaska in the meantime. Because of her background, she already had their attention. She had to tell her boss she was making the move whether she got the job up there right away or not so he could fill her vacancy.

He'd tried to convince her that the FBI agent whom she'd fallen for should take up residency in Houston. She couldn't tell her boss that she needed to be somewhere that an Arctic wolf could live. Not to mention it would make it easier for her to be seen in the wild up there too. Luckily, the few times she'd been seen in state parks in the Houston area, they only believed she was a dog running loose. Not that she wanted to be referred to as a dog or have animal control trying to pick her up, but it was safer than if someone thought she was a wolf. Still, they'd found red wolf-coyote mixes near Galveston, so what if they found a rare gray wolf in the area? She could just imagine being tagged and monitored!

She took a deep breath, thinking about the situation here again.

Sure, she and Andrew had run as wolves along the beach late at night when nobody was out and about, but she wanted to do some fun things with him during the day too. Even just looking for Rizzo while she was with Andrew made it more fun!

"Do you think he's on to us, if he's here and hiding away?" Stacey asked.

"Could be. Even the police might have tipped him off accidentally, and he left already," Garcia said. "But while we're here, this is what Kim and I are going to do today. We're going to pose as a couple. We'll dress like tourists and hit the beaches, though I'm sure he won't be lying around on the sand, nor will he be strolling along the water's edge. But we'll do like she did earlier—duck into the restaurants and check out hotel lobbies."

"I'll wait for word from all of you. As usual," Stacey said, unable to hide how glum she was feeling. She really had believed they'd find him quickly, but if he was hiding in a room, like she was at the cabana, who knew when they'd find him? It could take forever. With the kind of money he was making from all his illegal operations, he could probably stay here for a long time. They had to get back to their jobs and new missions. But she didn't want to leave the island unless she knew for sure that he had flown the coop.

"What if I go out and you can follow me, or one of you can, and the others can watch to see if he shows himself, like to leave or to come after me. I imagine that it would be more than likely he'd leave to avoid apprehension," Stacey said.

"No," Garcia said, everyone else agreeing with him. "It's too iffy that we'd catch up to him in time."

"I'll bring you your favorite strawberry ice cream when I return for lunch," Andrew said, giving her a kiss.

She knew he didn't think that would make up for her being stuck here, but she was glad he offered. She let out her breath on a heavy sigh. "Thank you. I'm okay. I just wish we could catch the bastard."

"We all do." Andrew gave her a hug and a kiss. And then he left with the others.

She moved her chair over to the window to people watch like she'd been doing, seeing the couples and individuals running or walking along the beach, kids creating sandcastles, and a few people wading in the surf. She might not be able to leave the cabana in search of Rizzo, but at least she could feel like she was looking for him. She really didn't expect to see him walking along the beach.

After an hour, she stopped to get a glass of iced tea, then sat down to observe the people coming and going again.

That was when she thought she saw Rizzo. Or at least she thought it was him. She jumped up from her chair. He was walking along the beach with a blond babe hanging off his arm. Someone he picked up here? Or someone he was with already? If it was Rizzo. He was wearing colorful board shorts and a tank top. She was wearing a bikini and a sarong, and they were both carrying their sandals.

Stacey couldn't lose sight of the man, just in case it was him. She grabbed her big, floppy hat and a pair of sunglasses and her phone, then headed outside. Even though she didn't want to jeopardize the mission by showing herself to him, she knew if she lost him now, they might never learn if he was their man or not.

She locked the place up, then texted Andrew: It might not be Rizzo, but there's a guy walking along the beach with a blond, and it sure looks like him. I'm following him to see where he goes, and you can check it out.

Andrew texted back: *I'll let everyone know. Don't let him see you. I don't want you hurt.*

She was glad he didn't tell her to return to the cabana because she might blow their case, that he was more concerned about her safety. Not that she would have listened to him. If this was Rizzo, they needed to know it pronto.

She texted: I'm sufficiently disguised.

She didn't believe Rizzo would recognize her or figure she was out here following him if he was clueless that she was here.

Andrew texted: *I'll park the car at our cabana and meet up with you on the beach.*

She texted: They're headed south.

Then she took some pictures of the couple and sent them to Andrew and the others.

She texted: I wasn't able to get a shot of them from the front, but it looks like his build, swarthy, tanned skin, and dark, curly hair. When I first saw him, I thought it was his distinctive profile.

Yeah, that looks like him from the back side. Okay, parking at the cabana now. Garcia said he and Kim would head in the direction that would mean they'd approach Rizzo and they can see for sure if it's him. I'm on the beach now, jogging to catch up to you. I see you wearing your white shorts and pink halter top.

She turned to look and smiled to see Andrew sprinting to catch up to her. He was wearing board shorts and sandals and had his T-shirt in hand—sexy and all wolf. She continued to walk at a fast pace, not about to slow down and then have to jog after Rizzo, if it was him. Andrew didn't take long to catch up to her, and to her surprise, he grabbed her up and swung her around, like he was totally thrilled to see her, and she nearly lost her hat. But she was laughing and glad he wasn't upset with her for leaving the cabana.

Maybe he was glad they might have some resolution in the case. Then he set her down on the sand and kissed her.

"Good job," he said for her ears only as the seagulls called out to one another, the breeze tossed her hair about, and the waves crashed on the beach.

Then Rizzo stopped and talked to the blond.

Stacey and Andrew were a long way from the suspect, but still, should they keep walking, pause and look at the ocean, or wade into the water? She figured it would look less suspicious if they just kept walking.

Then the guy nodded to the woman, and he and she started walking again. Stacey took a breath of relief. "We're mating tonight," she told Andrew. She'd decided she didn't want to wait. She knew in her heart that he was the right one for her. They needed to get their affairs in order, including her getting a new job and moving her things to Alaska to join him.

"Hot damn! You sure you want to wait until tonight?"

She chuckled and grabbed his hand and hurried him along the beach. "We have a mission first."

"Somehow I knew you'd say that."

"Do you think it's him?" she asked.

"It's a good possibility."

They saw Garcia and Kim coming from the opposite direction, playing in the water as they walked, dodging waves as they broke onto shore, and laughing like a newlywed couple. Stacey hadn't realized her friend could be such a consummate actress.

Suddenly, the man they thought was Rizzo and his companion turned and headed toward a hotel. Now they had to be careful so that Rizzo wouldn't realize they were following them, but they couldn't lose the couple either.

Garcia and Kim played in the surf right where they

were, not moving from the spot, but they were watching Rizzo.

"Want to get a drink at the café?" Andrew asked Stacey, not waiting for her answer but hurrying her toward the beachside café of the hotel.

"Yeah. I'll sit outside, and you can run inside and get us drinks." She didn't really mean it. The part about her sitting outside, yes, since she needed to keep her hat and sunglasses on. But Andrew getting her a drink, no. She knew Andrew didn't mean it either, that he was going to head in after Rizzo and see where he went.

When Andrew came back outside with two bottles of water and a couple of menus, she was surprised. He leaned down and kissed her. "I need to run to the restroom, honey. They're inside, ordering lunch. I thought we could too."

"Okay, sure." She began looking over the menu. "What do you want? I can order while you run back inside."

"Grilled salmon."

"Okay, I'll have the shrimp salad."

"Thanks." Then he went back inside, she figured to see what was going on with their suspects.

Garcia and Kim passed her table, not bothering to look at her, and went inside.

Stacey took a relieved breath. She and Andrew couldn't watch Rizzo inside the restaurant, if that was who it was, but Garcia and Kim could.

Then everything went to hell.

With her enhanced hearing, she heard Garcia and Andrew say, "Rizzo...you're under arrest for trafficking and prostitution."

Rizzo made a break for it, and Stacey was there to stop

him. He had a gun out and was about to fire a shot at her, but she swung her big hat in his face and knocked his gun aside. Before he could aim again, Andrew came to her rescue and jumped on the guy's back, taking him down to the sand, jerking an arm behind his back as Kim brought out a plastic tie for him.

Garcia had ahold of the blond and was on the phone to the police. "Yes, you might want to question the woman too."

"I told you I didn't want to walk with you along the beach!" Rizzo told the woman, outraged. "I shouldn't have listened to you!"

So the woman had insisted he take her for a walk? Good one on him.

The woman smiled at Rizzo and brought out a badge. "I don't know who these other people are, but I've had you under surveillance for a long time."

Stacey and the other agents stared at her. "Kim and I are from the U.S. Fish and Wildlife Service in Houston. Andrew and Garcia are with the FBI out of Anchorage. Who are you?"

"FBI in Michigan. We've been trying to capture him for years. I'm Amy Southwater."

They each introduced themselves to her, but they weren't giving up Rizzo to the agent. What if she wasn't really an agent? And she was working with Rizzo?

The local police showed up and took both Rizzo and the woman into custody to verify she was who she said she was. The extradition papers were signed, and Garcia and Kim packed their bags to take Rizzo back to the States. It turned out that the woman was legit, but they had claims to Rizzo already and had okayed it with the local police before she had. Miffed, she ended up booking on the same flight as they were taking home.

"How did you think you were going to arrest him and transport him out of here if you didn't work with the local police to get the extradition paperwork?" Stacey asked Amy.

"Oh, I wasn't going to do that."

"You were going to try to kidnap him and sneak him out of here?" Kim asked, her eyes wide.

"Of course not. He was going to take me home with him, and once we were on U.S. soil, I would have arrested him."

Stacey smiled. "That would have worked."

"You don't have a partner on this assignment?" Garcia asked Amy.

"Not for a job like this." Amy frowned. "My boss is going to have a conniption that I let Rizzo get away."

"He didn't get away," Andrew said. "He'll face charges in Alaska."

"And Texas," Stacey said.

"All right, and Michigan," Amy added.

"And Michigan," Stacey and the others agreed.

CHAPTER 11

WHEN THEY WERE READY TO GO TO THE AIRPORT, AMY hitched a ride with Garcia and Kim and Rizzo, and Andrew and Stacey followed them to see them off. After that, they could enjoy the rest of their stay on Grand Cayman.

"I guess we'll be seeing you in Alaska soon," Garcia said, giving Stacey a hug. "See you soon, man," he told Andrew.

"We will," Andrew said.

"And I'll be missing you, but I'd love to come and visit," Kim said.

Stacey gave her a hug. "We'd love to have you come visit."

"You can visit us anytime," Andrew told Kim.

Amy said goodbye to them, too, not too miffed they'd taken the man she planned to arrest into their own custody.

Stacey was superexcited about getting settled with Andrew in Anchorage. She'd told her parents late last night what was going on so it wouldn't be so much of a shock when she and Andrew were mated. Andrew had called his parents, too, and they were ecstatic, mentioning grandkids a dozen times during the brief talk they'd had.

Then Amy, Garcia, their prisoner, and Kim went through security, and Stacey and Andrew returned to their cabana to start their vacation.

"You were serious about a mating, right?" Andrew asked, glad they were done with the mission and could have some real fun.

"Tonight. We didn't have lunch, and I want to go swimming, take a cruise, go snorkeling, run through the forest, feed the manta rays, take a sunset dinner cruise, walk the plank of the pirate ship—"

"And we will. But a mating first."

She smiled and put her arms around Andrew's neck. "Now I know you have your priorities straight. Not that you're getting out of doing all the rest of the stuff, but for now?"

He swept her up in his arms and took her into the bedroom. "A mating."

That was one good thing about mating in paradise. Lots fewer clothes. He slipped off his sandals and jerked his T-shirt over his head. She pulled off her halter top and kicked off her flip-flops.

He began kissing her, deeply and hungrily. He ran his hand over her breasts, feeling the soft mounds, the nipples hardening to tight points against his palms. Their tongues did a mating dance as their breathing grew shallow. His cock stood at attention and poked at her belly. Smiling, she rubbed her body against his erection, making him hot all over.

He knew he was the luckiest wolf ever. He couldn't believe what had started out as him trying to catch her and losing her ended up with him catching her for real. Or was it that she had caught *him*?

He eased her onto the bed, wanting to mate with her in the worst way to make her his. She spread her legs, beckoning him to join her, her hand rubbing her belly in invitation.

"I didn't think I'd ever get this lucky to find the love of

my life while trying to arrest my suspects," he said, kissing her shoulders with reverence, her skin soft and wearing the fragrance of lavender.

"I love you, too, and I'm glad we found each other like we did." She touched his arms.

Before he really got into the mating, he paused. "Did you want to wait on babies or..."

"We're wolves, and having our offspring is all part of the successful continuation of our species and will bring even more joy into our lives. But we both work and love our jobs, so what do you think?"

"I think we should let nature take its course." He was ready for the whole tamale. That was the thing about wolves that made them so special. They adored their kids and others of the pack did, too, all helping to teach them what it meant to be one of their kind.

Then he kissed her belly and she ran her fingers through his hair. "I agree."

He leaned over her and kissed her mouth, loving the softness of her lips pressing against his. Luscious, eager to join with him. Then she parted her lips, letting him in. Their tongues connected, caressed, and stroked, delving deeply. Her heart was pounding like his, and their blood was rushing through their veins at hyperspeed, the adrenaline preparing them for loving. Pheromones were doing a tango together, and he couldn't imagine not being a wolf and being able to tap into those special feelings.

"Hmm," she murmured and kissed his mouth again. She licked his lips and ran her fingers over his waist.

He began kissing her again, her eyes, her nose, her cheeks.

She smiled. "I love your dimples when you smile."

"I love yours."

He smiled and ran his hands over her shoulders, kissing her throat, and she moaned a little. He licked and suckled her right breast, then moved over to do the same with her other breast, loving how smooth and soft and warm they were to his touch, how her nipples responded, reaching out to him.

She took his hand and guided him to stroke her clit, and he was eager to do so. He began stroking her, stopping to swirl a finger inside her and then massaging her sensitive nub. Moving her hips, she pushed against his questing finger, and he rubbed harder, letting her guide him. She began thrusting her pelvis, and he rubbed faster and harder.

"Ohmigod, yes! Oh. I. Love. You," she said breathlessly and pulled him down for a kiss and a hug. "I want you inside me now."

He didn't wait for her to tell him again and buried his cock between her legs, feeling the ripples of her climax gripping him as he entered her. He pushed deep and moved in and out with an unhurried rhythm, loving the feel of her heated flesh surrounding him and the way she was meeting his thrusts. And then he was speeding up, hard, fast thrusts, claiming her for his very own, her legs wrapping around his hips.

"Oh yeah," she groaned, and he felt the same way, loving this, loving her, loving the way her body wrapped around his in a heated embrace.

The pace became frenzied as he felt as though he was reaching the highest mountain peak. His body tensed and he quickened the pace again, ready to climax. And then he was coming and exploding inside her, feeling elated, satiated, and on top of the world. He let out a long, low growl with release. "Oh, baby, you are mine."

She chuckled as he collapsed on top of her. She wrapped her arms around him and kissed him, and he kissed her back. "*You* are all *mine.*"

"What kind of a place do you have in Anchorage?" Stacey figured she should have already asked Andrew about the living arrangements as they snuggled together on the bed after sleeping. She'd never been moved like she had when she and Andrew made love. He was divine, and though she wanted to do all the things she'd told him she wanted to do, she was eager to make love to him the whole time too.

"I have a studio loft apartment. Since I travel so much, I didn't want anything more than that," he said, caressing her arm.

"I have a two-bedroom apartment."

"We'll get a house. With you there, I'll want to spend a lot more time at home."

She smiled. "I've given my boss two weeks' notice, and I have an interview scheduled for a week from today in Anchorage."

"Already? That's great news."

"Yeah. I knew where we were headed the moment you chased me in the woods as a wolf."

He laughed. "A woman's wiles."

"I'd love to stay with you like this all day and night, but let's get out and see the island and do some fun things."

He rolled over to reach his phone on the side table, and

then they snuggled together and began to plan the days they had left there: feeding the rays while snorkeling with them, a run through the forest, and a hike as humans there too on another day. Lunches out, dinners in, which meant lots more loving. A pirate cruise for one afternoon, and a sunset catamaran cruise one night. Yeah, they were all set.

She slid out of bed and grabbed her pink bikini out of her drawer. "Snorkeling with the manta rays first. The rest of our life afterward."

He grabbed his board shorts and pulled them on. "You read my mind." Before she had her bikini top fastened, he swept her hair aside and fastened it for her, kissing her neck afterward. And then with rented snorkel equipment in hand, they left in their rental car to start their dream vacation as mated wolves. "Celebratory dinner and special rum drinks of the island tonight?"

"You're on!"

EPILOGUE

EXPECTING ANDREW TO GO BACK TO ALASKA WHEN Stacey returned to Houston after their time in paradise, she was surprised he insisted on going home with her.

"No territorial issues, right?" she asked as they boarded the flight to Houston.

He cocked a brow. "What if you decided Alaska was too cold for your blood?"

Loving him, she smiled at him. "You just wanted to offer your lap to me so I could sleep on the plane."

"That's it."

What she couldn't believe was that Kim and her boss had set up a farewell party for her at the home office in Houston and everyone was there to wish her well. They had wanted to see the FBI agent who had stolen her away and had secretly invited him to attend. She was grateful to them for including him since he was such an important part of her life.

Even her parents came and were delighted that Andrew was part of the family now.

"I have a feeling I'll be looking into doing some work up in Alaska before too long," her dad said. "I hear the fishing's good and wolves do well up there."

She gave him a big hug, tears filling her eyes. She was thrilled her parents would consider moving to Alaska. She hadn't thought they would.

"We can do it," her mother said, hugging her next. "If we

take a lot of trips to a place where I can enjoy flowers. But more than anything, we want to be close by when the little ones come."

"They have a lot of flowers in Alaska, just for a briefer time," Andrew said.

"I'm so glad you want to live there too." Stacey hoped her mother would enjoy living there and not feel the need to escape the cold, snowy weather all the time!

Stacey's dad put his arm around her mother. "She will love it, because I'm taking lots of time off so we can enjoy it together. We're not getting any younger, you know."

"My parents will take you to all the places you'd like to see and more," Andrew promised them.

Her parents were thrilled that his parents would do that. They didn't live in a pack, but the two families would be more than enough to become a pack of their own.

"That'll be great." Stacey was glad to hear his parents would help to make them feel welcome. Everything had happened so fast that they hadn't had time to do much getting acquainted. She knew her dad would do everything in his power to make sure her mother was happy in her new home, just like her mother wanted for her dad.

She thought the world of Kim and her boss for giving her such a nice send-off.

In a month, Stacey was working at her new job, Nettleton was in jail awaiting trial, and Andrew and Stacey were living in their new home. Her parents had moved there and were already taking trips with his parents to places all over Alaska before the snows arrived later in the year. She couldn't have been any happier in her new job and with her mate, his parents, and hers all living in the same area. Most of all, she adored Andrew, who couldn't tell all his agent friends enough about her exploits and all of whom wanted her to be their partner!

Andrew was one lucky wolf to have found a mate who loved Alaska as much as he did. He hadn't expected to gain a couple more parents, but they loved him as if he were their own son. And he thought the world of them too. They fretted as much as his parents about his and Stacey's missions, but he treasured them for being concerned for them. Coming home to see Stacey at night, when they both weren't taking down criminals away from home, was the best thing ever—a dream come true, and he loved her with all his heart.

He had arrested a couple of drug dealers and confiscated fifty thousand dollars' worth of weapons and five million dollars' worth of drugs and had returned home to get some sleep. He pulled into the two-car garage and was surprised to see Stacey's car there. Concerned she was sick, since she was supposed to be on an assignment in Juneau, he rushed through the house looking for her.

He found her sound asleep in bed, naked, her shoulders bare. He leaned over and kissed her shoulder, and her eyes slowly opened. She gave him a tired smile and closed her eyes. "Tired."

"You've been gone for three days. Did you get your men?"

"Hmm."

He hurried to strip off his clothes. "I know you wouldn't

be here if you didn't." Then he was joining her in bed. He figured she was exhausted, so he wasn't going to make hot love to her unless it was something she couldn't live without, even though he desperately wanted to.

As soon as they were in bed together, she ran her hands over his chest and began kissing his mouth. "I need to sleep, but I need this more."

"I know what you mean." He began kissing her. "I love you and couldn't be any happier than I am that you joined me here. And that you love it here too."

"I do. I can't wait to see what you do when the days are superlong. I love how you handle supershort days."

Loving and more loving, day or night, worked well for him.

He'd never chased an unknown she-wolf through the woods before. There had been just something about her that had willed him to get to know her better right from the start. And they were here in mated bliss, loving each other, wolves who'd found their special, forever mate.

**Read on for a sneak peek at
the next book in Terry Spear's
Billionaire Wolf series**

NIGHT OF THE
Billionaire
WOLF

**Coming soon from
Sourcebooks Casablanca**

CHAPTER 1

"ACCORDING TO MY WEATHER APP, THE DELUGE OF RAIN starts again in two hours," Lexi Summerfield warned her personal assistant, Kate Hanover, while looking at the app on her cell phone. They only had three days to locate the message, or it would no longer be relevant. The text she had received made it clear she had only one shot at this, and then it could be too late. They had to locate the message before the men who were hired to kill her father got wind of it.

As a gray wolf, Lexi hated that she couldn't be close to her father like she'd always been. Not now that he was in the Witness Protection Program with a different identity, location, and job. None of which she knew. In fact, she didn't want to know about any of it, or she could put his life in jeopardy, should the reason he was in witness protection—Joe Tremaine—send more of his thugs to try to learn from her where her father was. She didn't know what her father had to tell her, but it was important enough he'd contacted her surreptitiously, putting both their lives at risk.

As she and Kate packed their backpacks for the hike, tension and stress filled Lexi with dread that she might not be able to find the message in time. She paused to take another drink of water, her mouth dry and her darn hands sweaty. She was fighting the urge to clench her teeth.

It wasn't just that she missed her dad and wanted to keep him safe. A year ago, she'd lost her mother when a ferry crashed into a bridge in Brazil, sending her mother's car and another plunging into the water, and none of the bodies had ever been found. Her mom had helped Lexi with her business, encouraging her all the way. She was the reason Lexi had stuck with it during the highs and lows of starting her cosmetics company.

So many things reminded Lexi of her mother, whose hobby was growing flowers from seeds and cross-pollinating them to create new varieties. She'd even named one, a purple daylily, Lexi Love because purple flowers were Lexi's favorite. The fragrance of her mother's roses, gardenia, jasmine, and honeysuckle scenting the air was one of Lexi's fondest memories, and when she had a chance, she was re-creating her mother's garden in her own yard as a memorial. Her mother had been a pediatrician and loved taking care of sick kids and making them feel better, which was why she'd been in Brazil—taking care of Mexican wolf shifter kids in a pack for two months before she died. Lexi missed her, and so did her patients.

Lexi packed away her camera, determined to take pictures as good as her mother's, to use all the tips her mother had taught her—how to make the lights and shadows and colors pop. How to compose the pictures for the most appealing result. Photography had been another of her mother's hobbies, and she had taken the pictures of Lexi's cosmetics to use for her website and product promotions. Lexi could hire someone else to do them now, but she felt connected to her mother when she took the photos herself, now that she was gone.

She regretted every day her mother wasn't here. Just as Lexi missed seeing her dad whenever he wasn't busy working in his family practice clinic doctoring patients. She wondered what her father was even working at, now that he couldn't work as a doctor. She hoped he was doing well and that he was happy. But she suspected he missed her and her mom as much as she missed them both.

"Do you have your noisemaker in case we run into any black bears?" Lexi asked Kate, getting her mind back on the business at hand.

"The horn is in my backpack. Relaxing and communing with nature as wolves is just what you need, even if this is a high-priority mission." Kate brought out their protein bars and filled her own travel mug with water. "You have a full schedule of appearances next week, and the tea and dinner engagement with the Denalis. You really have to take a break every once in a while."

Not that this was a real break. Well, sure, Lexi was enjoying Redwood National Park as a wolf, trying to relax when she wasn't looking for the message. As far as she knew, she was the only one of her kind who had made over a billion dollars in the cosmetic industry. Work would always be waiting for her, and sometimes a body just needed to have some fun for a change. Not that her work was all work. She enjoyed what she did, but always being on a schedule could be exhausting.

She still had to locate the message her dad had sent her, buried like treasure in the redwoods. He'd Facebook-messaged her with a cryptic note that only she'd know how to decipher—Wolf at Red Fish Falls—and included a simple, hand-drawn map that indicated where he'd buried the message. They'd vacationed here some years ago, she and her family, and her father had fondly referred to the area where they'd seen several fish in the creek below one of the waterfalls as Red Fish Falls.

Kate slipped her 9mm into her holster and pulled her lightweight backpack over her shoulders. "Ready to go?"

"Yep." Even though Lexi didn't feel she really needed a bodyguard all the time, she felt having Kate serve as *both* her personal assistant and her bodyguard worked well. She hadn't thought she could get used to living with someone she didn't know, but she was thoroughly enjoying Kate's company, as if she'd found a sister.

With a double black belt in a couple of different martial arts forms, all her combat arms training, and a degree in marketing, not to mention being a she-wolf, Kate was perfect for the job. Several male wolves had applied for the position, but Lexi felt it was easier not having to fend off a potential suitor's advances, if one became attached to the idea that he might mate her and enjoy her wealth too. The money could be a real draw for roguish types.

"It's fun being with you because your presence is so sought after," Kate said, her short black hair in a bob, her blue eyes sparkling. "Sure, all the attention is on you, but it's exciting to bask in your limelight. I know you like your solitude, so I'm glad you enjoy my company when we're on our own."

"You're great at coming up with fun activities. I always feel comfortable around you, not needing to have a public face for show all the time."

"Not at first though," Kate said, smiling. "We had to have ice cream cones dripping all over us in the heat last summer, and we laughed so hard that we lost the rest on the sandy beach. That was my second day on the job, and our relationship was totally transformed."

Lexi smiled. "I had never considered eating ice cream

on the beach. Now I know why. The heat and ocean breeze were too much for the soft, top-heavy swirl of ice cream to manage. We couldn't lick it fast enough."

"Yeah. I don't think I've ever been that much of a sticky mess before at the ocean, even when I was a kid. That was definitely an icebreaker."

"I agree." Lexi sighed. She had never been popular around males or females, mostly because she'd been shy. Some attributed her "aloofness" to being a snob because she was the daughter of physicians, but it wasn't like that. She just wasn't all that outgoing, and when she finished her public appearances to promote her business, she loved retreating to the solitude of her ocean-view estate.

The tabloids often mentioned that Lexi was one of the most sought-after eligible bachelorettes, and that didn't help either. Numerous human males had tried to meet her and told her she was beautiful, intelligent, sweet, desirable, and anything else they could come up with to try to convince her they were really interested in her and not her wealth. If they only knew she had a real growly side to her personality and no human mate would do!

After several disastrous dates with wolves who had an agenda, she'd made a new rule for herself. Three dates was all she'd allow herself with a wolf. If he didn't have what it took to be in a relationship with her for longer than that, she was calling it quits. Kate thought it might take longer than that, but Lexi was afraid if she dated a guy more than three times and wasn't serious about mating him, it wouldn't be fair to him.

She looked over the hand-drawn map of where they were supposed to search for the message again. Waterfall. North of the cabins. Rocks.

No matter what, she couldn't have reporters learning her dad was very much alive. As far as everyone knew, he was dead. Her mom had died before her father witnessed the district attorney's murder in San Antonio and testified against the drug lord. He hadn't had any choice. Joe Tremaine had seen her father witness the murder. If the drug lord had been a wolf, her father could have just killed him himself, if he'd had the chance. As it was, her father had to be taken into the Witness Protection Program and then officially declared dead. Lexi wasn't supposed to ever have any contact with him. She loved him for having asked her first whether he should testify against Joe Tremaine.

Despite having to cut ties with her father, Lexi knew it was the only thing he could do. He was a marked man anyway. She knew in her heart that he had to put the drug lord behind bars and pretend he was dead while Tremaine was locked away. Hopefully, her father would remain alive.

The U.S. Marshals would kick her father out of the Witness Protection Program if they learned he'd met with her though. Her father's mention of Wolf at Red Fish Falls had to mean he wanted to meet her as a wolf, if she could locate the message he'd buried out here for her to find and learn where the meeting would take place.

"We need to do some more martial arts training," Kate told her, bringing Lexi's attention back to her friend.

Kate had taught Lexi some of her black-belt jujitsu moves, which Lexi hadn't expected when she hired Kate. But she loved it.

"I thought we were on a break," Lexi cheerfully reminded her. Except for trying to find her father's message.

"Right, but think of how much fun it would be to get a workout at the cabin. Fresh air—"

"Rain's coming."

"Well, we can practice inside the cabin then. We can move some furniture out of the way."

"Okay, sure."

Dressed in jean shorts, hiking boots, and T-shirts, and both wearing lightweight backpacks carrying their water, bug spray, protein bars, satellite phones, cameras, ponchos, a couple of garden trowels, and first aid kits, they headed down the trail from the cabin. Lexi also had a Glock tucked into her backpack, figuring she really wouldn't need to use it. But she was aware Joe Tremaine's men could still be searching for her father if they weren't convinced he had died in the car crash. And they could be watching her, too, to see if she and her father met up with each other.

While Lexi and Kate hiked along the rugged stretch of northern California's coastline, they talked about different marketing options for Lexi's Clair de Lune Cosmetics, the French name meaning "light of the moon." Their voices would help scare off any bears that might be in the area. Lexi loved taking pictures of the redwoods in all their glory, battling the winds and the salty sea air as she and Kate hiked toward the location where they believed the message was buried. She was soaking up the scents of the redwoods, and the squirrels and rabbits that lived here.

"You know you have your pet rehoming party coming up. When are you going to bring home your own little cutie pie?" Kate asked. "I know you lost your Misty some years ago, but don't you think it's time to give another needy pet a home?"

"My problem is I want to take all of them home: fluffy and shorthaired, large and small, any breed, any mix. If I can't give them all a home, I feel it's not fair to the others. They look at me with their sad eyes and just beg me to love them. All of them. Not only that, but the last two parties I sponsored, the dogs I fell in love with went to families who will give them tons of loving and attention. Maybe the next pet party." Lexi glanced at Kate. "Don't tell me *you* want a dog."

"Me? No, I'd just take care of him or her when you didn't have time. I mean, just call it an additional duty."

Lexi smiled at her. "You *do* want a dog."

"I love dogs. I haven't had one since I was a kid, but in my line of work, I can't possibly have one of my own."

"Okay, now you can."

"But what about you?"

"We'll need two, you know. So they can play with each other. The problem is that not all dogs like us if we haven't raised them from puppies, so we need to find two that are not afraid of our wolf scent and who are okay when we shift. I'd hate to have to rehome my own rehomed pet."

"Agreed." Kate was smiling.

"You know you could have asked me."

"I just kept thinking you'd get one, and with this party coming up, I thought I'd mention it."

"They'll have venders at the party, so we can pick up whatever we need for the dogs right there. Plus, a percentage of the proceeds go to the Fur Babies Rescue Center."

"Oh, that's good," Kate said.

They'd walked for about an hour at a good brisk pace in the heavily damp air, except when they'd paused to take pictures of the towering redwoods and more birds—Steller's jays, a golden-crowned kinglet, and a pileated woodpecker. The ancient and majestic trees gathered moisture from the dense coastal fog, making Lexi feel as though she was in a magical fairy garden. The redwoods were so tall and wide that they seemed part of a mythical, primeval landscape.

"I hear the waterfall nearby." Kate slipped a little on the muddier part of a trail. "He said it was near the waterfall, right?"

"According to this map, yes. Unless it's a different waterfall." Lexi sure hoped not.

They finally reached the falls, the rush of water flowing over the cliff and running into the stream below.

They both looked at the simply sketched map.

"Maybe we just have to move rocks over there," Kate said. "Instead of digging for it. This looks like the drawing of rocks on the map."

"Over there? By the big one?" Lexi pointed at the area that looked similar.

"Yeah."

They headed for the larger rock, and at the base, they began moving the rounded river rocks away from the big one, but after several minutes, they reached soil.

"Do we dig now?" Kate asked.

"Yeah, let's try that." Lexi pulled out her trowel, and Kate did the same with hers.

Both of them began to dig, but after several minutes, they hadn't found anything. They filled the hole back up, then moved the rocks back to where they'd been and started working at another spot. Two more times they moved rocks, dug in the dirt, then replaced the disturbed materials. Lexi paused to take a picture of the waterfall.

"I'm wondering if it's located at a different waterfall." Disappointed, Lexi had really believed she would find the message at the first place she looked. She shouldn't have been so optimistic. "It's hard to tell from this simple map. There aren't any features that would indicate this place over any others."

"Except his map indicated that the site was northwest of the cabins, and this is the first set of waterfalls located in that direction," Kate said.

Lexi hadn't told Kate what the secret message was about or who it was from. She'd let it slip that the person who had buried it was a he, so she'd left it at that. She'd hoped she'd smell her father's scent when she looked for the message, but she didn't smell any sign of him anywhere. She'd only received the text message from him this morning, and then she and Kate had needed to pack and travel here in a rush to begin to look for it.

They'd seen several waterfalls, and all the creeks had fish swimming in them, so that didn't help in narrowing things down to a particular waterfall. Her family been to several on their vacation here, and her father had said the same thing about all of them.

Lexi had informed Kate that she couldn't tell her any more about the message or its sender or she'd have to kill her. Kate had laughed, but the truth was that Lexi worried about someone else killing Kate *and* her, if they knew Lexi's father was still alive. Since Kate wouldn't let Lexi search for the message on her own, Lexi had taken her into her confidence—at least as far as searching for the message.

"How long do we have to find it?" Kate asked.

"Three days. After that, the location of the message will be irrelevant."

"So we keep searching. You know, I was thinking more about our marketing. We always do kind of a high-fashion setup for the promo videos. I was thinking we could do some out here. More for the outdoorsy girl—like us—with an outdoor-woodsy theme, a getting-back-to-nature concept. The idea would be that no matter whether you're in the city or roughing it in the woods, your makeup will last and protect you from the elements and enhance your natural beauty."

"Now see, that's why I hired you! You're perfect for this job. We could do some of that now while we're staying at the cabin."

"That's what I was thinking. I figure we could slip in some promo, and we'd both have fun doing it in between trying to locate the message." Kate glanced at the rocks they'd replaced. "We'll find it."

Lexi hoped. She pulled out the park map. "There's another set of falls over here. Still northwest of the cabins, just a little farther north." Her phone rang, and she struggled to free it from a zippered pocket on her backpack. She recognized the phone number on her caller ID and scoffed. "It's suitor hopeful number three." She answered the call and said in her most professional business voice, "Lexi Summerfield, how may I help you?" The breeze blowing the branches and birds singing in the background would be a sure giveaway that she wasn't at home and on the job.

"It's Randy Wolfman. I want to take you out for dinner on Monday night at six."

"Randy, you're a nice guy, but you and I don't really have

what it takes to be a couple. I'm sorry, but it was nice that we had a couple of dates anyway." Three, but who was counting? Once she'd decided on her new rule, she'd become determined to stick to her plan: give the guy three chances to change her mind and then move on. She truly was a romantic at heart, and she worried that Mr. Right Wolf—who really was the one for her and not seeing her just because she was sitting on a load of money—would show up, and here she'd be dating Mr. Wrong Wolf. She was afraid she'd lose her only chance at having the wolf of her dreams.

"Aww, come on, Lexi. We'll have a great time," Randy said.

She thought he liked going out with her because they each paid for their own meals, since she didn't want the wolf to feel he had paid his way into her life. "Sorry, it wouldn't work out between us. I hope you find the right wolf for you."

"But—"

She ended the call and blocked his phone number.

Kate was smiling at her. "He would never take no for an answer."

"You're right. And I have a hard time rejecting people. I just need to start telling them I'm not interested."

"Are you afraid you might dismiss the wrong guy?"

"No. If one of them was the right wolf, I'd smell his interest and our pheromones would go through the roof when we got close. I danced with all five wolves who have asked me out on separate occasions, and not one of them did that for me. Sure, they wanted to have sex, that much was obvious from their full-blown erections, although that would mean mating for life. But our pheromones were a fizzle, no interest at all."

"Which begs the question: Can we find more than one wolf who can do that for us?" Kate asked quite seriously.

"I think so. I don't believe only one wolf in the whole wide world would be the one for each of us. We might never find that wolf. I'm sure it has something to do with genetic predisposition, what physical qualities a potential mate has that suit our physical needs in order to create the best offspring. That's all on the pheromonal side of us. Then there's the human equation, the needs and wants and desires. The social and emotional compatibility. It's complicated. But I can tell you right now that these guys were more interested in money than me. They were trying way too hard to prove they really were into me, and it wasn't working."

"You're easy to like."

"Friendship is fine. Mating for life is a whole other story." Lexi had never checked into their backgrounds, something she would definitely have done if one of the wolves had really moved her.

"I agree with you there."

The rain-saturated breeze switched, and Lexi smelled the scent of a male wolf and a black bear that had passed through there recently.

"The wolf has to be a *lupus garou* like us," Kate said, "since no one has reported any sightings of wolves in the area. Maybe the wolf was the one who left the message?"

"I don't believe so." Lexi didn't think her father would ask another wolf to get involved in this. The fewer people who knew about it, the better. "And there's a female black bear, by the smell of her, roaming the area. Keep your eyes peeled and continue to make noise. We need to head on back before the rain starts anyway. We can check the other location later. It will take us about an hour to reach the cabin."

Kate laughed. "How often does the weatherman get it right?"

Lexi saw a fairy ring of mushrooms and took another picture. "Yeah, I know. But you know me. I always try to give him the benefit of the doubt."

Light rain began to fall, and then the drops grew bigger. Lexi hurried to put away her camera, and both laughing, they pulled out their ponchos. They were already soaked by the time they got the ponchos on. Still, they'd be protected somewhat from the continuing rainfall.

A couple of young bear cubs cried out somewhere in the distance, and Lexi's adrenaline surged. "Do you hear that?"

"Yeah, they're close by. It sounds like danger to me."

"They're crying for their mother. They have to be in trouble. I'll see if the park rangers can rescue them." Lexi hurried to get her phone out and called the ranger service. "Hi, my friend and I were hiking, and we heard the distress calls of a couple of bear cubs."

"We've got our hands full with a family of hikers who have lost their way, including one who's badly injured. And a search party is looking for another missing hiker. We can look into the cubs' situation after we've taken care of the hikers in distress."

"Thanks." Lexi ended the call.

"You didn't tell them where the bear cubs are."

"The park rangers are too busy with human distress calls. You're my bodyguard. You can protect me." Lexi left the designated trail, which she wouldn't normally do as a human because she didn't want to trample the vegetation.

The bear cubs' cries guiding her, she raced through the forest as best she could, trying not to stumble over tree branches and fall into the ferns filling the understory.

Kate trailed close behind her. "This is a dangerous idea. Where there are cubs, there's a mother bear nearby. The female bear we smelled, I betcha."

"Unless something has happened to her. And then we need to rescue them."

"What do you propose we do? Take them home with you?"

Lexi was sure Kate wasn't being serious. Wolves raising bear cubs at her oceanside home? No way.

"Once we rescue them, I'll call the park rangers to pick up the cubs and take care of them if the mother doesn't come for them. The rangers can find a home for them. As young as the cubs' cries sounded, they wouldn't be able to make it on their own."

Lexi and Kate continued to move quickly through the underbrush in the direction of the cliffs. Lexi's skin prickled with unease, her stomach twisting in knots. From the sound of the cubs' cries, they were way down below the cliffs, and the only way to reach them quickly would be climbing down there. That terrified her. Worse, her fearful scent would clue Kate in.

No way had Lexi wanted anyone to know what had happened to make her fear cliffs. She prided herself on keeping her secret. But even now, she suffered a flashback: gasping as a wolf as the soil and rocks at the edge of the cliff gave way, free-falling toward the rocky ground, praying some of the tree branches would help to break her fall. They did, scraping and bruising her, but she still landed badly on the rocks below and broke her left hind leg. Just from the memory, she felt a shock of phantom pain shoot up her left leg. That would be the last time she'd fight with a boyfriend and take off on her own without telling anyone where she'd be.

It had been a stupid thing to do, something she had seen others do in videos on *I Shouldn't Be Alive*—in other words, going alone, not telling anyone where she'd be, not having a satellite phone in remote areas, and not having water with her—though as a wolf, that was understandable. She'd sworn she'd never do anything that dumb herself. Worse, she'd been in her wolf form and couldn't climb to safety with a broken leg, so she'd had to shift into her human *naked* form before help arrived.

She and Kate finally reached a steep cliff and Lexi hesitated, not wanting to get near the edge that, according to forest ranger reports on the area, were known to crumble. Chills raced down her bare arms and legs. She had to force herself to move toward the cliff's edge. Slowly, so she wouldn't end up falling and breaking a leg like she'd done before.

"Are you okay?" Kate asked.

"Yeah, sure. The cliff face is unstable. I'm just being careful." But it was a lot more than that.

"Okay, yeah, you're smart to do that. I guess I can't talk you out of taking this dangerous route and looking for a safer way to get down there instead."

"I don't want to risk delaying the rescue." Lexi finally reached the edge. She observed the rocky cliff, looking for the best way to climb down, terrified she would fall. The mewling cries were coming from the base of the cliff near a couple of trees.

"This is not what I had in mind when I signed up to... Holy shit," Kate said, peering over the edge of the cliff.

Lexi looked down at the swollen creek rushing along the banks of the cliff. "The creek's risen because of all the rain. The cubs are crying in a den down below. They could drown. We have to save them." Lexi started down the cliff, grabbing whatever she could—rocks, tree roots, vines—to keep from falling to her death or breaking a leg or more. She grabbed what looked like a stable rock, but as soon as she tried to hold it and move her right foot to another rock, the one in her left hand pulled free. She fell and cried out, grabbing for anything that could stop her fall. She grasped a tree root and hung on for dear life, her breath coming out in harried puffs.

"Oh God, hang on, Lexi. I *really* didn't sign up for this." Kate waited to descend so she didn't cause an avalanche of rocks and dirt to collapse on Lexi.

"You don't have to do it."

"Are you kidding? Then you'd be able to take all the glory!"

Lexi smiled, then frowned. If the mother bear attacked them, there wouldn't be much glory in that.

CHAPTER 2

RYDER GALLAGHER, FORMERLY GOING BY HIS FIRST name, Ted, had changed it due to issues he was having with a man of the same name that credit companies were after, and of course, all Ryder's friends were having trouble with the transition. He was taking another hike, killing time before his friend Mike Stallings arrived at the cabin campgrounds. Ryder thought he heard women's voices every once in a while and took a trail headed in their direction. He wasn't the kind of guy who liked solitude. Though this was better than just sitting in the cabin waiting for Mike to turn up. Not that Ryder planned to hike with the ladies.

One of the women squealed and then both laughed. He smiled. He didn't want to intrude too much. He wasn't interested in befriending a couple of human women, but he was drawn to check them out.

Their good humor lightened his mood, which had been somewhat dampened by the sudden change in plans. Mike had needed to stop and see his parents on his way to the cabin. They were gray wolves, so family was important, but Mike's parents' anniversary had slipped his mind. Ryder and Mike didn't want to lose their cabin rental reservation for the rest of the week, so Ryder had shown up alone until Mike could join him. Their jobs as bodyguards were stressful, and they needed all the vacation time they could get.

Ryder reached the place on the trail where he thought he'd run into the two women, but there was no sign of them, and he didn't smell their scents in the area. He heard their voices again, farther away. What trail had they taken? He had been sure this one would intersect with theirs.

Then from a different direction, he heard bear cubs crying out in distress. The women forgotten, Ryder immediately went into rescue mode. He ran through the ferns in the direction he thought the cubs were, but knew he'd find them faster if he ran as a wolf. Already well off the trail, he pulled off his backpack and began to strip out of his shorts, socks, hiking boots, boxer briefs, and T-shirt. He shoved his clothes into his backpack, then hid it in the ferns.

Off and running, he headed for the cliff where he'd heard the bears crying, wishing Mike was here to help him. At least he was glad he had detoured to the other trail in an attempt to run into the ladies, which had made it possible for him to hear the bears' cries much more distinctly and reach them faster. Now he just had to get to them before it was too late.

Her heart hammering, Lexi was still trying to make her way down the cliff, her fingers clinging precariously to the loose rocks, dirt, and mud, the water rising steadily down below, the poncho hampering her efforts. If she hadn't been so concerned about reaching the cubs as quickly as possible, she would have thought to shove her poncho in her backpack. "Remove your poncho before you climb down. Mine's getting in the way while I try to find footholds."

The earth crumbled more, and she knew she was going to be cut and scraped up, just like Kate would be. Hopefully, that would be the worst of it. If she could only extract the bear cubs without getting into a confrontation with the mother bear!

The rain was still coming down, making it worse. Her hands were wet and so were the rocks she was trying to hold on to, which meant everything was slippery. Suddenly, the rocks supporting her gave way. Her heart beating hard, Lexi cried out as she tumbled down the last ten feet. She landed in the rising water with a splash.

"Lexi! Ohmigod!"

"I'm okay. I'm at the base of the cliff. I'm okay." Short of breath, her heart beating way too fast, Lexi scrambled to her feet.

"Are you sure?"

Lexi knew Kate would do anything to help rescue the cubs too.

"Yeah, just don't fall like I did." As if Lexi could have prevented it. "Just scraped and bruised, sore muscles, but no broken bones."

"Okay. God, you scared me." Kate removed her poncho and shoved it into her bag, then pulled her backpack back over her shoulders and began her climb down.

The water was swirling around Lexi's shins and she was edgy, waiting to catch Kate if she fell. "You would have done this on your own if I hadn't made the decision to aid them and gone down first."

Rocks skittered down the cliff below. Lexi's stomach clenched, her body tense, ready to spring into action if Kate lost her hold on the rocks. Lexi wasn't sure if it was harder watching Kate trying to make her way down safely or doing it herself.

The rock Kate was holding on to came loose and she cursed, sliding down a few feet, grabbing for something to stop her fall. Lexi's heart caught in her throat, and she lunged forward in rescue mode, arms outstretched.

Acknowledgments

I want to thank my family for always being there for me while I dive into my adventures, helping me brainstorm when I need them to, and encouraging me always. To my fans who continue to write heartfelt letters about how much they love the worlds and the characters I create. To my editor, who loved the tag I'd created for *Legend of the White Wolf* from the very outset and is a dream to work with. To my publicist, who helps me market my books to the nth degree and, no matter how harried she probably is, never lets on. To the art department that makes the most beautiful covers, art any author would be proud of. And to my Rebel Romance Writers who are always there for me through all the worst dilemmas! Thank you!

About the Author

USA Today bestselling author Terry Spear has written over sixty paranormal and medieval Highland romances. In 2008, *Heart of the Wolf* was named a *Publishers Weekly* Best Book of the Year. She has received a PNR Top Pick, a Best Book of the Month nomination by *Long and Short Reviews,* numerous *Night Owl Romance* Top Picks, and two Paranormal Excellence Awards for Romantic Literature (Finalist & Honorable Mention). In 2016, *Billionaire in Wolf's Clothing* was an *RT Book Reviews* top pick. A retired officer of the U.S. Army Reserves, Terry also creates award-winning teddy bears that have found homes all over the world, helps out with her grandbaby, and is raising two Havanese puppies. She lives in Spring, Texas.

THE LEGEND OF
ALL WOLVES

For three days out of thirty, when the moon is full and her law is iron, the Great North Pack must be wild...

The Last Wolf

Silver Nilsdottir is at the bottom of her Pack's social order, with little chance for a decent mate and a better life. Until the day she meets a stranger and decides to risk everything...

A Wolf Apart

Only Thea Villalobos can see that Elijah Sorensson is Alpha of his generation of the Great North Pack, and that the wolf inside him will no longer be restrained...

Forever Wolf

With old and new enemies threatening the Great North, Varya knows that she must keep Eyulf hidden away from the superstitious wolves who would doom them both...

"Wonderfully unique and imaginative. I was enthralled!"
—**Jeaniene Frost**, *New York Times* **bestseller**

For more info about Sourcebooks's books and authors, visit:

sourcebooks.com

Also by Terry Spear

Wolff Brothers
You Had Me at Wolf

SEAL Wolf
A SEAL in Wolf's Clothing
A SEAL Wolf Christmas
SEAL Wolf Hunting
SEAL Wolf in Too Deep
SEAL Wolf Undercover
SEAL Wolf Surrender

Heart of the Shifter
You Had Me at Jaguar

Billionaire Wolf
Billionaire in Wolf's Clothing
A Billionaire Wolf for Christmas

Silver Town Wolf
Destiny of the Wolf
Wolf Fever
Dreaming of the Wolf
Silence of the Wolf
A Silver Wolf Christmas
Alpha Wolf Need Not Apply
Between a Wolf and a Hard Place
All's Fair in Love and Wolf

Silver Town Wolf: Home for the Holidays

Heart of the Jaguar
Savage Hunter
Jaguar Fever
Jaguar Hunt
Jaguar Pride
A Very Jaguar Christmas

Highland Wolf
Heart of the Highland Wolf
A Howl for a Highlander
A Highland Werewolf Wedding
Hero of a Highland Wolf
A Highland Wolf Christmas

White Wolf
Dreaming of a White Wolf Christmas
Flight of the White Wolf

Heart of the Wolf
Heart of the Wolf
To Tempt the Wolf
Legend of the White Wolf
Seduced by the Wolf